Praise for *The Church of Dead Girls*

"If ever there was a tale for a moonless night, a high wind, and a creaking floor, this is it. . . . I don't expect to read a more frightening novel this year. Very rich, very scary, very satisfying."
—Stephen King

"A complex parable of social disintegration . . . Dobyns's sad and disquieting novel carries a contemporary moral, true in even the smallest American towns."
—*The New York Times Book Review*

"A chilling evocation of small-town life turned upside down. Dobyns delivers the goods."
—*San Francisco Chronicle*

"Edgy tension and considerable suspense. . . . This could be any small town, and that truth is perhaps the most frightening thought of all."
—*The Washington Post Book World*

"The creepiness mounts with Hitchcockian intensity; the bloody conclusion is worth the wait."
—*The Chicago Tribune*

"Tantalizingly sinister . . . Dobyns hooks us from the very first sentence."
—*People*

"Dobyns delivers all the satisfactions of a good thriller writer . . . but he also captures something beyond the reach of most genre novelists: a sense of life on the page. . . . Every summer, readers look for a novel that will keep them turning the pages without insulting their intelligence. It's unlikely there will be a better novel this season than *The Church of Dead Girls*."
—*New York Daily News*

"In its Gothic evocation of small-town life and mob hysteria, it often suggests the influence of Sherwood Anderson and Shirley Jackson, and Dobyns knows his upstate New York setting as well as Frederick Busch and Joyce Carol Oates."
—*The Atlanta Journal-Constitution*

blue
rider
press

The
Church of
Dead Girls

Also by Stephen Dobyns

BLUE RIDER PRESS

New York

The
Church of
Dead Girls

A NOVEL

Stephen Dobyns

blue
rider
press

An imprint of Penguin Random House LLC
375 Hudson Street
New York, New York 10014

First trade paperback edition 1998
Copyright © 1997 by Stephen Dobyns
Penguin supports copyright. Copyright fuels creativity, encourages diverse voices,
promotes free speech, and creates a vibrant culture. Thank you for buying an authorized
edition of this book and for complying with copyright laws by not reproducing, scanning,
or distributing any part of it in any form without permission. You are supporting
writers and allowing Penguin to continue to publish books for every reader.

Blue Rider Press is a registered trademark and its colophon
is a trademark of Penguin Random House LLC

Library of Congress Cataloging-in-Publication Data

Dobyns, Stephen, date.
The church of dead girls : a novel / Stephen Dobyns.
p.   cm.
ISBN 978-0-14-310782-8
1. Missing persons—Fiction.   2. New York (State)—Fiction.   3. Psychological fiction.   I. Title.
PS3554.O2C48   2015   2015017173
813'.54—dc23

Printed in the United States of America
1   3   5   7   9   10   8   6   4   2

Book design by Gretchen Achilles

For Toby and Catherine Wolff

The
Church of
Dead Girls

Prologue

This is how they looked: three dead girls propped up in three straight chairs. The fourteen-year-old sat in the middle. She was taller than the others by half a head. The two thirteen-year-olds sat on either side of her. Across the chest of each girl was an X of rope leading over her shoulders, down around her waist, and fastened in the back. All three girls were barefoot and their ankles were tied to the legs of their chairs. Even so, the ropes were loose, as if to hold their bodies erect rather than to keep their living selves prisoner: meaning they had been tied after they were dead.

I didn't witness this. I only looked at the photographs my cousin showed me. There were many photographs. And he said the police had a videotape of the entire attic, but I never saw it.

Perhaps the chairs were two feet from one another. Because of the dryness of the attic, the girls looked old. They didn't look like teenagers anymore. They were gaunt and bony and resembled women in their seventies. A large air conditioner and dehumidifier had been kept running all day long, day after day, and the moisture had been sucked from their bodies. They were dried out and their skin looked like dark wrinkled paper. But they were not equally dried out because they had been killed at different times, so the girl killed most recently looked youngest. The girls' heads were tilted back or to the side. The one in the middle had blond hair. Long strands hung across her face. The others had brown hair. All three had hair down to the middle of their backs and perhaps this meant something. It gave them a virginal appearance. Although now, looking so old, they appeared nunlike, spinsterish. And by the time the photographs were taken their hair had become dusty. And they were emaciated, at least two of them were, as if they hadn't been fed. But perhaps this was an effect of the dryness. All the vibrancy had been leached from their skin. The hollows of their cheeks were startling indentations. Their gums had receded from their teeth.

What were they wearing? Not their original clothes. Those had been taken from them. They wore handmade gowns cut from thick velvet. The middle girl's was dark green, with long sleeves and a hem that nearly reached her ankles. The girl on the right wore a gown of dark red, the one on the left a gown of blue. But to speak of the colors is to say nothing. Sewn to the dresses, pinned to them, even glued to them, were stars and moons and suns cut from white or yellow sparkling cloth. But also animals, or rather their silhouettes: dogs and bears, horses and fish, hawks and doves. And there were numbers that seemed random—5s, 7s, 4s—the glittery numbers one buys at the hardware store to stick on mailboxes. There seemed no pattern to them. And pieces of jewelry, cheap costume jewelry, were pinned to the velvet and were draped over the numbers and stars and animals: bracelets and necklaces and earrings. It took a moment to see the actual color of the dresses because they were so covered with numbers and jewelry and patches of fabric.

Did I mention the words? Some of the patches had words written on them, but not words that made sense, "CK" and "NT" and "TCH" and "FIL." Fragments of words, the beginnings and ends of words. What could they have meant to anyone? Also attached to the cloth were brass bells and little mirrors, pieces of metal and multicolored glass balls.

Presumably this clutter of patches and jewelry, words and numbers had been affixed to the dresses after the girls were wearing them and once they were tied to their chairs, because there were none behind their backs or under their bony buttocks. One understood that the girls had been placed in the chairs and decorated after they were dead. And such a labor must have taken days because nothing was helter-skelter.

What of the chairs themselves? They were straight-backed, but they hadn't been bought anyplace. They were amateurishly made, knocked together from two-by-fours, and they leaned crookedly. But one didn't notice they had been built from two-by-fours right away because nearly every inch of their surfaces was covered with the shiny tops of tin cans or round red reflectors or the bottoms of glass bottles, green and yellow and clear and brown. Most were nailed down but the circles of glass were held in place by bent nails tacked around their edges.

The chairs shone and glittered and—how shall I say this?—they seemed to stare back at the viewer. They were not stationary. Their color and shininess made them active, even aggressive. The legs of the chairs were wrapped in tinfoil and the metal circles and glass and reflectors were stuck on top of the foil. But again one realized it had been done after the girls were already seated, because where they were leaning or where they touched the seats the wood was bare.

And the attic? It was a large room with a pitched ceiling. At its highest it was perhaps twelve feet, but it sloped down to two feet on either side. The room was about thirty-five by fifty feet, with a curtained window at either end. The air conditioner had been fixed into a skylight in the middle and near the peak of the roof. But I never saw the whole thing; I only saw it from different angles by combining the photographs. Between the studs were strips of insulation with shiny foil backing, so the whole room sparkled and must have seemed absolutely alive in the light from the candles. Hundreds of strips of tinsel also hung from the ceiling. Perhaps they moved slightly in the drafts from the air conditioner. And how they must have sparkled.

Because that was the other thing: the candles. Many were stubs but the stubs had been replaced and replaced again, so that whoever lit them had come to the attic and lit them many times. In the photographs the candles were not burning. One had to imagine them, to imagine their reflections in the insulation's tinfoil backing, their flickering in the glass and red reflectors and metal discs adorning the chairs, their twinkling in the cheap costume jewelry pinned to the girls' dresses. How busy the attic must have been in the light of these candles and each candle reflected hundreds of times. The walls, chairs, clothing: a conversation of light, an ecclesiastical shimmering. And how the faces of the three girls must have glittered. The combination of light and shadow must have made their faces quicken, as if the girls weren't dead, as if they had never been dead.

But all this must be imagined. I know for a fact that the authorities never lit the candles. They simply took their photographs, removed the bodies, and dismantled the whole spectacle. I don't know if it is being stored someplace or if it was destroyed. One can imagine the unscrupulous trying to steal it, planning to put those flashing chairs on display for others to pay money to see. Perhaps they would put mannequins in the chairs and dress them as the girls had been dressed. The Church of Dead Girls it might be called, or the Monster's Den.

Because surely the person who killed the girls was a monster. But hadn't this person lived among us? Our town is not large. This person came and went, conducted business, had acquaintances, even close friends. Nobody looked at this person and thought, Monster. Perhaps this was the most disturbing aspect of the business: that the person, on the surface at least, never seemed extraordinary, or none of us had the wit to identify the signs. What would those signs have been? Wouldn't evil or monstrosity call attention to itself? And yet this person had a place within the community. How do you think it made us feel about one another, even afterward, when the discoveries were made? If one of us who had such an awful secret seemed innocent, then what about the others? What were their secrets? And were they looking at me as well? Of course they were.

Three dead girls in three straight chairs, collapsed against the ropes, heads tilted, their skin papery, their bare feet on the wood floor looking more like paws than feet, brown and bony. Their mouths were slightly open and their lips pulled back. One could see their small teeth, imagine the dark dryness of their tongues, the darkness of their silent throats. How their teeth must have glittered in the candlelight. And their eyes, half open as if the girls were drowsing, they too must have shone.

But there is something else. Their left hands were missing. Each girl had her left hand severed at the wrist. One could see their wrist bones. And those stubs, they must have glittered as well. In the photographs, there was a startling milkiness to these wrist bones. The skin and flesh had receded, shrunk back, letting the wrist bones jut from the stumps. Their whiteness and roundness made me think of eyes, blind eyes, because, of course, how could these white bones ever see?

And the missing hands? They weren't in the attic, nor were they in the house.

Part One

One

Afterward everyone said it began with the disappearance of the first girl, but it began earlier than that. There are always incidents that precede an outrage and that seem unconnected or otherwise innocent, a whole web of incidents, each imperceptibly connected to the next. Take the case of a man who cuts his throat. Isn't it a fact that the medical examiner finds several practice nicks, as if the deceased were trying to discover how much it might hurt? And in the case of our town, even before the first girl's disappearance, there were undoubtedly several events comparable to two or three nicks on the skin above the jugular.

For example, on a Tuesday morning in early September, just after school began, a bomb was found on a window ledge outside a seventh grade classroom of the Albert Knox Consolidated School. It appeared to be three sticks of dynamite wrapped together with silver tape. Two green wires descended from the dynamite to a paper bag resting on the grass. A student pointed it out to the English teacher, Mrs. Hicks, and she rang the alarm. We get bomb scares sometimes; all schools do. They are malicious pranks and no bomb is ever found. Mostly when school is closed during the day because of a bomb scare there is a party atmosphere. No one believes in the threat and you can hear the students laughing and chatting as they hurry from the building.

But on this day in early September news of an actual bomb spread quickly. Students were frightened. Sarah Phelps, an eighth grader, was knocked down on the stairs as she ran from the building. Other students were bruised as well. There was no orderliness in our departure. The officious teachers like Lou Hendricks and Sandra Petoski stood at the head of their students and kept control. But others weren't as capable and in some classrooms—Mrs. Hicks's, for example—there was panic. Mrs. Hicks is a nervous, excitable woman and she must have felt that she had at last found something to be sincerely excited about.

The building was closed and everyone hurried out to the parking lot. I guided a few of my own biology students, tenth graders, but most of my charges had disappeared. Harry Martini, our principal, had gone to see the bomb and came running back. He wore a white short-sleeved shirt with large half-moon sweat marks discoloring the fabric beneath his armpits. Harry is rather stout and running takes effort. He made us move to the far end of the parking lot and onto the playing fields, where the ground was muddy. We have six hundred students and we made quite a crowd. Luckily it wasn't raining.

Ryan Tavich, who had recently been made lieutenant, was the first of the town police to arrive, quickly followed by three squad cars. Ryan took charge. He was in plainclothes—a gray suit, as I remember—with a tweed cap balanced on the back of his head. The police set up a barrier. Then we settled down to wait for the state police bomb squad to arrive from the barracks in Potterville. The students milled around. When it became obvious that school would be closed for the day, some students with cars drove off and a few others went with them. But most chose to remain, to see if there would truly be an explosion.

That morning I watched events through my own good-humored ignorance. No girls had disappeared. The town had a certain wholeness and the mayor could speak of a sense of community. Now I look at that same scene through the filter of other events and I see fragility where I had imagined resilience, the fleeting where I'd seen permanence. It was a warm morning and only a few maples had begun to turn. Crows called from the oaks beyond the baseball diamond. The sky was that deep blue one gets in the early fall with two or three small clouds scudding across it. The school was situated at the northern edge of town, and over the trees I could see the steeple of Saint Mary's and part of the red roof of the four-story Weber Building, our biggest building. A golden retriever had appeared from one of the nearby houses and it rushed from one group of students to another, pausing only long enough to have its ears scratched or to be thumped on the back.

I see them standing together. Meg Shiller with her long brown hair talking to shy Bobby Lucas, whom I had recruited for the chess club. Bonnie McBride with her usual stack of books, Hillary Debois carrying her violin case. Sharon Malloy running her fingers through her blond hair again and again. There must have been students whose names I didn't know, but it felt like I knew them all. In some cases, I had been a classmate of their parents. A few boys began tossing a football. Two others had a Frisbee. Teachers looked at them impatiently, as if to say that we weren't there to have fun.

The students are better dressed in September: new clothes, new shoes, new haircuts. In September, even the teachers feel hopeful. Harry Martini paced back and forth between the students and the town police, forming his own barrier. I'm afraid I have never liked him, and he walked splayfooted like an old mother goose, heaving his stout belly after the movement of his legs. The teachers themselves reminded me of mother hens. It was not the first time that such comparisons occurred to me.

It took thirty minutes for the state police bomb squad to arrive and by then the school buses had come to take most of the students home. Many wanted to stay but Harry Martini wouldn't allow it. The thing on the window ledge looked quite formidable and there was no telling how much damage it might cause. The school was a two-story building of yellow brick, built in the mid-1950s, and one imagined the bricks flying through the air like shrapnel. And of course Harry was terrified of doing something that would get him in trouble with the school board.

I myself decided to stay to see what would happen, though Harry gave me a look. From where I stood at the edge of the police line, the bomb was a silver shape against the window. About twenty other teachers remained as well and some people had driven out from town. Franklin Moore had come from the *Independent* and he interviewed Ryan Tavich. The two were close friends, played basketball on Thursday evenings in the high school gym, and often were together on weekends. Both looked very serious. Ryan kept taking off his cap and pushing back his short black hair. Franklin was tall, thin, and in his midthirties. He also interviewed Mrs. Hicks, who kept saying, "We're lucky we weren't killed." She said it with a different emphasis a dozen times, as if practicing to get it right.

Franklin's daughter, Sadie, had been a student in my seventh grade science class, a pretty brown-haired, long-legged girl who carried herself like a dancer. By the time her father arrived, she had gone home on the bus. Her mother died of breast cancer two years ago and I assume Sadie went home to an empty house, as did many of the students with working parents. Within a month, children wouldn't be allowed to be home by themselves.

From the way the state police captain behaved, I expected the bomb to explode momentarily. The police moved their barriers even farther across the parking lot, pushing all of us onto the playing fields. Though Ryan Tavich was nominally in charge, the state police captain took over immediately. I didn't hear what they said, but the captain's facial expression was severe, as if Ryan had done something wrong, which of course he hadn't.

Cars were driven around to the rear of the school so they wouldn't be damaged in an explosion. Two of the bomb squad men wore padded suits with silver helmets that made them look like spacemen. With binoculars they studied the bomb and paper bag for quite some

time, then they approached with infinite care, carrying what looked
to be a large white garbage can.

We held our breaths. Really, most of us expected to see those
white-suited men blown to smithereens. One of the men moved forward, slowly craning his head to peer inside the bag. He paused,
looked down, then waved impatiently to his partner, who hurried
over and looked in the bag as well. Even dressed as they were, I could
sense their relief. Inside was a brick with the wires wrapped around it.
It could never have exploded. Still, the men took great care in putting
the dynamite, or what appeared to be dynamite, inside the white garbage can. Then they put the garbage can in a white panel truck and
drove away.

The police began to dismantle their barriers. Franklin Moore interviewed the state police captain. Later we learned that although the
bomb contained dynamite it lacked a detonator. It had only been put
on the window ledge to scare people. That same afternoon, Phil
Schmidt, our police chief, admitted it was the second bomb to be
found. One had been placed a few days earlier at Pickering Elementary School. This was a disturbing discovery and it brought our town
a certain attention. TV crews visited from Syracuse and Utica. Everyone wondered where the next bomb would turn up. The state police
kept an extra trooper in town twenty-four hours a day and the police
department took on another patrolman.

There was much speculation as to who had placed the bombs.
Had it been a single person or a group? Was it a prank or had there
been a more complicated idea behind it? For instance, members of
the Ebenezer Baptist Church had been quite vocal about reestablish-
ment of prayer in the schools. I heard people wonder out loud whether
someone in the church's congregation had finally gone around the
bend and issued a warning, as it were. One heard many such theories.
An angry parent? A teacher or staff member who had been fired?
Such theories were more harmful than the bombs themselves. They

created a finger of suspicion that could be directed at anyone, depending on events. And that was no small thing, considering what events would soon occur.

Our village, Aurelius, has a population of seven thousand, down from nine thousand at the turn of the century. The town was incorporated in 1798 with land granted to soldiers after the Revolutionary War. The county seat, Potterville, is ten miles to the south. Utica, forty miles to the northwest, is the nearest big city. Before the Erie Canal was built, Aurelius was just south of the main highway going west, and until the Greek Revival period it was known as Loomis Corners. Then the new name was adopted in 1843. We still have many good examples of Greek Revival architecture, large white houses with white columns. But once traffic began on the canal, Aurelius never got any bigger, while the towns along the canal grew and grew. Some people saw that as a bad thing, some as a good thing.

Afterward the changes were small. A Civil War monument was erected in front of City Hall: a tall column with a bronze soldier holding a musket. A train station was built, lasted a hundred years, went through a decline, and was reborn as a pizza parlor. The elms were cut down, leaving Main Street rather bare. Aurelius College, which began as a girls' finishing school, became a girls' junior college in the 1920s, a girls' four-year college in the 1950s, then went coed in the 1970s. It has five hundred students. There's a good equestrian program and a few graduates go directly to the veterinary school at Cornell.

A strip mall was built at the edge of town with an Ames, a Wegmans supermarket, a Napa auto supply store, and a Fays Drugs. Perhaps a hundred people work in Utica and commute. Others work in Potterville or for the pharmaceutical company in Norwich. There's a rope factory at the edge of town and a small electrical company be-

longing to General Electric. Many farmers grow cabbage for sauerkraut, which is processed in Potterville. A Sauerkraut Queen is chosen
each fall. We have a small hospital and a movie theater called the
Strand. We now have three video stores.

The library is adequate and can get books from the larger library
in Potterville or even farther away. We have two car dealerships: Jack
Morris Ford and Central Valley Chevy. The Ford dealership also sells
VWs. The Chevy dealership also sells Toyotas. And both sell trucks,
of course. For years it's been true that more people seem to move
away than move to Aurelius. I always notice houses for sale. The
Readers' Club still meets once a month at the library just as when I
was a young man. The Terriers, the high school football team, were
district champions last fall but lost the state finals to Baldwinsville.
Everyone was hopeful for a while. The college football team, the Ro-
mans, placed third in their league, with Hamilton placing first. The
train service between Utica and Binghamton ended forty years ago.
The bus service ended eight years ago. The opera house hasn't had a
show since *Li'l Abner* in 1958. One often hears about plans for reno-
vation, but they never come to anything. We have two motels—
Gillian's and the Aurelius. The big hotel in the center of town burned
when I was away at college in Buffalo in the 1960s. Now there is a
small Key Bank on the location. We have two Italian restaurants,
plus a McDonald's, a Dunkin' Donuts, and a Pizza Hut. The book-
store, Dunratty's, has gradually become a gift and stationery shop,
but they will still order books for you. The Trustworthy Hardware is
going strong, as is Weaver's Bakery. We have two bed and breakfasts,
which often have guests in fall to see the foliage, as well as parents
visiting the college. We have six churches. Saint Luke's Episcopal
used to be the largest, with Saint Mary's next, but now both have
been left behind by the Good Fellowship Evangelical Church, which
meets in the old A & P. Besides Phil Schmidt, the chief of police, we
have ten full-time policemen and four to six part-time, depending on

the time of year. We have four police cruisers. The fire department is mostly staffed by volunteers, although the fire chief, Henry Mosley, draws a salary.

The downtown is made up of two- and three-story red brick buildings. The top halves—the cornices, pilasters, and simple friezes depicting Progress and Liberty—have some charm. The Weber Building, on the corner of Main and State, displays pedimental windows with round gables on the top floor. Every so often an effort is made to have it named a national landmark. The bottom floors of the building, however, have been modernized with Formica, plastic, and aluminum, show windows and metal doors. That was done in the 1950s. Now the big stores responsible for the renovations—Western Auto, Monty Ward, Rexall—have departed and the buildings look run-down.

City Hall stands across the street from the Weber Building and is more Gothic than classical, with its turrets and red brick. Twenty white marble steps climb to the big double doors. The woodwork is dark and the windows dusty. The mixture of the stately and the shoddy gives our downtown an ambivalent quality and there are always empty buildings for sale.

There must be hundreds of towns like ours in the East. Sleepy, they're called. Sometimes one or another has a star football team or basketball team. The countryside around Aurelius is hilly, with long ridges running north to south and narrow valleys with small rivers or lakes between them. The prosperous farms are in the valleys, the poorer farms are on the hills. Apple orchards lie to the west toward the Finger Lakes. Loomis River runs through Aurelius and there is trout fishing in the spring. Quite a few people have camps on the lakes where they go in the summers or for ice fishing in the winters.

Before that fall when everything went wrong my colleagues at the high school spoke of having a comfortable life. Sometimes a couple or a family went down to New York City for a visit or to see a play, but most stayed in Aurelius. I won't say they felt smug, but they didn't quite see the point of other places. The college had a lecture series and once in a while a string quartet visited from Syracuse, though few townspeople went. Occasionally someone organized a bus trip to a Syracuse football or basketball game. A lot of men hunted in the fall and one heard gunshots from the hills. People tended to vote Republican but they might vote for a Democrat if an exciting prospect came along.

Really, the most excitement our town had seen in years was stirred up by the *Independent* and that was owing to its editor, Franklin Moore. Some people thought Franklin should have taken a job at a paper in Utica or Syracuse after his wife died, which would have allowed many in the town to continue to sleep soundly, though the fact that his newspaper reported certain events hardly made him liable for the consequences of those events. Others thought he should have remarried, meaning he should have done something to occupy his time more fully and left us in peace.

Two

Franklin Moore wasn't originally from Aurelius. That is not to give him any special charge for what happened, though a few argued that if Franklin had been from town he would have been more circumspect. Perhaps there is something about being an outsider that leads one to act without that sense of investment which might be found in someone with closer ties to the community. People said that Franklin had nothing to lose; he wasn't wedded to Aurelius; he could move if he wished; he had no real ties. But that wasn't true. He had his daughter.

Franklin came here from Rochester five years ago with his wife, Michelle, and Sadie, who was eight at the time. In Rochester he had been a reporter for the *Chronicle*. Before that he had been in journalism school at Cornell and earlier, as an undergraduate, he had written for the *Sun* and become one of its editors. Originally he was from the New York City area.

Franklin was named associate editor of the *Independent* with the understanding that he would be editor within two years. But within a year of moving to Aurelius, his wife developed breast cancer. She was not yet thirty. I believe she worked as a photographer in Rochester and she did freelance work for the *Independent*. Her illness put an end to that. Its progression was sadly familiar: a mastectomy, chemo and radiation therapy, metastasis, further operations and therapies, and then death. By that time they had lived in Aurelius for three years. As happens in a small town, we got involved in her story and watched her get progressively worse. Michelle was buried in Homeland Cemetery and her family came from Bronxville for the funeral.

During the two years of his wife's illness Franklin had indeed become editor of the paper and he worked hard even though his attention and much of his time were focused on his wife. She was a strikingly beautiful dark-haired woman who had to undergo not only sickness but all the humiliations that went with it—the mastectomy, the sallow skin, the loss of her hair. These she faced with a strength that impressed everyone who knew her.

I met her when her daughter, Sadie, was in my seventh grade science class and she and her mother came to school for a parent-teacher conference. Was Sadie working well? Was she attentive in class? The mother assured me I shouldn't worry about giving Sadie too much work, that she was a hard worker. Michelle Moore was very thin at that time and wore a wig, though an attractive one. Yet the simulated health radiated by the wig and the heavy makeup made her seem already like death's creature, even though she was dressed up, disguised as a living, vibrant woman.

She sat by my desk in my classroom, urging me to be tough on her daughter, not out of meanness but to make Sadie a better student. She was clearly a woman who didn't have much time left, yet she made no reference to her illness and almost defied me to notice it. She had great pride, a trait noticeable in Sadie, too, and she spoke of her daughter as eventually going to medical school or veterinary school. In a town where many youngsters drop out of high school and only half the graduates go to college, her ambitions for Sadie were noteworthy. Michelle Moore sat very straight in her chair, talking quietly, sometimes touching a long finger to her chin, sometimes straightening her scarf, and keeping her dark eyes on me the entire time. If she was in pain, she gave no sign of it.

Three weeks later, at the end of October, I heard she was dead.

Sadie was out of school for a week and then returned. I searched her face for signs of grief and saw the pallor, the deep seriousness, but she never mentioned her mother or what she had seen. Her mother died at home, having collapsed in the kitchen. Franklin called the doctor but it was too late. People said they were fortunate that it happened so quickly, but what do people know? In such remarks, aren't they always talking about their own deaths? Who knows whether one way is better than another.

Six months after the death of Franklin's wife, people began to see a change in the *Independent*. It became more aggressive, more socially conscious in its editorials. There were more interviews with local residents. People spoke of Franklin's undergoing a great change after his wife's death, but I think mostly that he had more time and he wanted to distract himself from his grief. Simply put, he had several more stories in the paper each week, along with his editorials and columns. Other than Franklin, the paper employed one full-time reporter, a sports reporter, a photographer, and a woman who acted as receptionist, office manager, and copy editor. Without getting any bigger, the paper became more packed somehow; there was less filler.

But perhaps it was more than being energetic and needing to be distracted. "People need to be woken up," Franklin would tell me. He even seemed to drive faster. He had a blue Ford Taurus and one always saw it whipping around corners. Franklin was thirty-four by then. He was an inch or two over six feet, quite thin, with light brown, almost reddish hair, which he wore long and swept back from his forehead. When he walked, he leaned forward so that the top part of his body, the part jammed with intention, would arrive sooner than the lower half. He spoke quickly and a little loudly, and if you were slow in answering a question, he would offer up several alternatives and let you choose. He had a few freckles on his thin face that made him look boyish. And he had a sort of innocence, if that's what you call it when you think others share your passion for the world.

Many people found him pushy but Aurelius is a rather pokey town and its natural pace is no faster than a dawdle. Franklin seemed to move swiftly but perhaps this was the normal speed at which the world moved. He was energetic and caring. He came to every single parent-teacher conference and talked passionately about his daughter. The only peculiarity—and perhaps I'm wrong to find it peculiar—was that he made no mention of his wife. I attributed this to his struggle to move beyond his grief. But in talking about his daughter and her childhood, Franklin would give the impression—accidentally, I am sure—that he had always been a single parent, that Michelle never existed.

Another change was that Franklin sold the ranch house he had owned at the edge of Aurelius and moved downtown to Van Buren Street. In fact, he bought a house one house away from my own, a white Victorian that seemed too large for just him and Sadie. All the houses on Van Buren date from just after the Civil War, except for the Sutter house, which was the original farmhouse in this area. The house where I live by myself was the house my mother was born in and the one she returned to after the death of her husband, my father, in the war—the Korean War, that is. People said Franklin wanted to be nearer the paper but it also seemed that he wanted to escape the reminders of his dead wife. He even sold his Taurus and bought a white Subaru station wagon.

I would see him outside painting or mowing or raking the leaves. He did everything quickly, almost impatiently. Sadie had a mountain bike, purple with yellow streaks like lightning, and I would watch her riding by. If she saw me, she would wave. She was very thin and her brown hair streamed behind her.

I have heard it said that after his wife's death Franklin lost all civic sense in how he managed the newspaper's connection with the town. Indeed, people claimed the paper's relationship to Aurelius was getting increasingly adversarial. For instance, in his editorials Franklin began to argue that the city council needed to adopt a five-year capital-improvement plan, that the paving and repaving of streets was done unsystematically and the city's sewer system was in bad repair. He argued that if the city council adopted a specific plan, voters would have an exact idea what needed to be done and the city would establish a clear method of channeling its resources instead of being propelled from one minor calamity to another.

Franklin also took issue with the school board for rejecting a proposal to give administrators and teachers a 7 percent pay increase plus dental coverage. The main problem was the dental coverage. Given that nearly half the county lacked health insurance, the board didn't see why the administrators and teachers should have both health insurance and dental insurance.

Franklin argued that the school should set a standard of excellence both in the classroom and in its faculty, that Aurelius could only hope to attract first-rate teachers by offering a decent pay and benefits package. In these editorials Franklin was able to suggest not only that the city council and the school board were in some way backward but also that the schools' teachers and administrators were not of the highest caliber.

Perhaps understandably, many people were content with life as they lived it. We knew the members of the city council and the school board. They weren't bad people. They served their terms, then were reelected or replaced. Franklin's articles, editorials, and columns never caused outrage, but it was like someone sprinkling sand in your bed. When people saw him coming, they ducked. I expect if he hadn't been handsome, if he hadn't been a recent widower with a young daughter, he would have been even more unpopular. He was affable and treated people with respect. But for those who were the subject of his writings, he became a cross they had to bear. They didn't wish him harm but they wished he would go away. Because people began to pay attention. They noticed things they hadn't noticed before.

Even if they disagreed with Franklin, they perhaps began to think that Aurelius was less perfect than they had supposed.

Franklin's weekly interviews were even more vexatious than his editorials. He had a way of getting people to say things about themselves that others didn't wish to hear. One of the first was with Herb Wilcox, a local realtor and insurance broker who had been on the city council for twenty years. Everyone knew Herb. They knew his wife, Betty. They watched his three kids grow up. Two went off to college and young Bobby took a job in his dad's office. In the interview Herb made it clear that everything about Aurelius was just right.

"I've been to other towns, I like other towns, but none match up with what we've got here. We got first-rate schools, a good hospital. I can't imagine why people move away. Take my kids Bruce and Mary Lou. Both had scholarships to Aurelius College, but Bruce went to Albany and Mary Lou went to Cortland State. Now Bruce is up in Cohoes. What kind of place is that?"

It continued like this and readers understood that Herb wasn't talking about the perfections or imperfections of Aurelius but the departure of his two older children, his love for them, and his disappointment. Franklin had revealed an area of Herb's vulnerability. Somehow it made Herb smaller, if that is what happens when a person suddenly becomes more human.

The next week Franklin had an interview with Will Fowler, the city manager. We have both a mayor and a city manager. The mayor is elected but he doesn't receive a salary, though he has a secretary, an expense account, and a small discretionary fund. Usually he is a man in the community who likes to shake hands. The city manager is different. He is hired by the city council and often comes from outside the community. Our present mayor, Bernie Kowalski, refers to Fowler as his whip. "I got a whip and the whip gets things done," Bernie often says.

Franklin asked Will Fowler about Aurelius. "It's a pleasant town full of pleasant people." Did he find it perfect? "I find it less than perfect," he said. What about the city council? "I find them less than perfect as well." Did Fowler have any specific complaints about the council? "Perhaps some of them have served for too long." What did Fowler feel about the need to adopt a five-year capital-improvement plan? "Potterville has one. Any town our size usually has one. The trouble is that such a plan makes the city council publicly accountable. Maybe they don't want that." And one last question. You moved here six years ago from Albany. Do you ever miss Albany? "Certainly. It's a bigger city."

Those who had read the interview with Herb Wilcox the previous week felt that Herb had been made to look foolish. By being such a booster he was hurting Aurelius, while his claim of the town's perfection was an excuse not to work harder. As for Will Fowler, he seemed not to appreciate Aurelius at all. He would rather be in Albany. "He thinks we're hicks," one of my fellow teachers said.

And perhaps we were hicks, but we didn't care to think about it. As with Herb Wilcox, we felt we knew more about Will Fowler than we cared to know. "Who does he think he is?" I heard a teacher complain. Fowler was the man hired to operate the town. People wanted him to feel fortunate that he lived in such a nice place. Now they knew otherwise.

Of course, most of Franklin's weekly interviews didn't have such strong repercussions. Still, we learned about one another. It turned out that Tom Henderson, who managed the Trustworthy Hardware, built ships in bottles. Margaret Debois, a nurse at the hospital, played jazz piano at Tiny's in Utica. Lou Fletcher of Fletcher's Feeds was a Baker Street Irregular and was saving his nickels to take a Sherlock Holmes tour of London. A few people refused to be interviewed, such as the fire chief, Henry Mosley, and the pharmacist, Donald Malloy. And I myself refused.

"But why?" Franklin asked me. It was over a year ago and I was raking my front yard. He had seen me and wandered over.

"I don't find myself interesting."

"You worked in New York as a scientist and then came back to Aurelius. That's interesting."

"I was a technician. And whether it is interesting or not, I don't choose to be interviewed about it."

I didn't mean to be rude, but after I said I didn't want to be interviewed, he should have accepted it. It wasn't that he found me interesting. He knew nothing about me except what he might have heard from his daughter. Most likely he was thinking about next week's interview and saw me raking my yard. And many of the people he interviewed weren't interesting—car mechanics, baggers at Wegmans, a plumber. But I must say that in most he found something colorful, which perhaps was why I refused to be interviewed. I didn't want people to look at me and think, "Aha, I know something about you." As it was, I believed that Franklin respected me for turning him down. We began to see each other more often. Not as friends but as friendly acquaintances. Occasionally he would drop by and I would give him a cup of tea or I might stop by his house and he would offer me a beer. As I say, only a single house separated us.

Surprisingly, the interview that had the most impact was not with an ordinary townsperson but with a history teacher who had been hired at the last minute by Aurelius College for the second semester. The hiring was done quickly. I say this because if there had been a conventional search this fellow wouldn't have gotten the job. Not that he was incompetent or stupid. Far from it. But he was a Marxist and an Algerian. He was also outspoken. Before the interview we knew nothing about him except that he drove a little red Citroën that he brought down from Kingston, Ontario, where he had been living. First we saw his car, the red Citroën. Then we learned his name: Houari Chihani.

Three

Franklin interviewed Chihani in his office at Aurelius College. The main campus, dating from the 1870s, is made up of red brick buildings arranged around a quadrangle of maples and oaks. The buildings have white trim and ivy, white pillars and broad granite steps. Unfortunately, owing to budget constraints, the buildings have become rather shabby, with peeling paint and bricks that need pointing. And the lawns are somewhat ragged, the shrubbery uneven. As for the students, they tend to be a mixed lot. While some programs, such as the equestrian program, draw good students, the SAT scores of the remainder are inconsiderable.

There are many schools in central New York and Aurelius College was rarely a first choice. So the college had special programs for students with learning disabilities, programs for the dyslexic, programs in English as a second language. Some students were bright young men and women from less-than-adequate backgrounds, but many were at Aurelius because no other college accepted them, for one reason or another. And if they did moderately well, they tended to transfer after their sophomore year.

One could say that the students had been exposed to little but what they might glean from MTV and *People* magazine. They did not contemplate the past, nor did they speculate on the future. For most this didn't matter. They would never be thinkers and all the fuss about learning disabilities and the mentally challenged was only so much hubbub to disguise the fact that they were not very bright. But a few students were intelligent and were only waiting for the right person to come along: like a dry sponge waiting for a drop of water. It could have been anyone. Unfortunately, it was Houari Chihani.

He was a man in his fifties, fifty-five to be exact, who was raised in Algiers, then went to Paris as a teenager during Algeria's war of liberation against France. His father was a doctor, his mother a teacher. Possibly they felt closer to their French rulers than to their fellow Moslems. And during that war the rebels attacked the moderate Moslems as ferociously as they did the French. For a few years Houari Chihani studied at the Sorbonne, then he left France for Montreal, where he entered the university. It was at the Sorbonne around 1960 that he became a Marxist. It seems ironic that so many Marxist intellectuals came from the privileged classes. Having been brought up in comfort, they sought to deny that comfort to others, while still living comfortably themselves. Although perhaps this wasn't entirely true in Chihani's case for he seemed to have an ascetic nature.

Chihani remained in Montreal for three years, then he was accepted for graduate work at the University of Chicago, where he got his PhD in history. There was never any doubt about his brilliance. Despite his accent, he was a superb and persuasive teacher. The difficulty was that he wasn't simply a teacher, he was a proselytizer of almost religious zeal. Consequently, wherever he taught, he was instrumental in either beginning or taking over the college's Marxist club or reading group. Perhaps it would have been wiser to have gotten tenure before making himself so obvious on campus; on the other hand, his imprudence only testified to his integrity. He made it perfectly clear where he stood. And it should be said that many believed the controversy he brought to a department was healthy controversy. But the result was still that, after two or three years at a college, he always moved on. Michigan State, Carnegie-Mellon, the University of Windsor, Cleveland State, Lafayette College, Olivet College—till at last he was teaching history at a small college in Kingston, Ontario. And he had lost that job, or rather he had not been rehired for the following fall. He had just one semester left to teach.

In December, however, Max Schnell, a popular history teacher at Aurelius College, was killed in a car accident. The college needed an immediate replacement and Roger Fielding, the history chair, was authorized to begin a search.

Fielding advertised for someone specializing in modern European history and Houari Chihani applied. He looked very good on paper: the PhD from Chicago, the many publications, the praise of his students. Even his recommendations from the colleges where he had taught were good. Often such recommendations are less than candid, especially if they are written for someone whom the college wishes to move elsewhere. The dean of college X wanted Chihani gone and so he wrote him a glowing report. And it should be admitted that Roger Fielding and Priscilla Guerthen, the academic dean, had certain ambitions for Aurelius. Their eyes were perhaps bigger than their stomachs and they saw in Chihani someone who might bring prestige to their little community. After all, wouldn't his books and his many other publications mention that he taught at Aurelius College? And so Chihani was offered a job.

Chihani had no qualms about quitting Kingston College before the end of the year. They had said they didn't want him back, and if he could do a small disservice in return, then he would. He packed his books, shipped them to Aurelius, drove down in his red Citroën, and was in residence by the beginning of January. He had three classes: Western Civilization, Nineteenth-Century European Political Movements, and Capitalism and Labor. By the beginning of February he had started a small reading group, less than half a dozen students, which he called Inquiries into the Right (or IIR), a sufficiently vague title. This was when Franklin Moore interviewed him.

Chihani's office was in Douglas Hall, the humanities building, just to the side of the administration building. It was a third-story room with a skylight and Franklin said there weren't enough shelves for Chihani's books, so that cardboard boxes were stacked against the wall. Franklin described Chihani as a tall, handsome man whose face suggested some bird of prey. Indeed, I remember his nose as quite long and thin with a distinct bend in the middle. High cheekbones, a jutting chin, and thick black curly hair. His skin reminded me of the oak finish of a table or desk. He had long, thin hands, a basketball player's hands, though he took not the slightest interest in sports. He always wore a dark suit, a white shirt and a tie, and sometimes a beret.

A detail that Franklin didn't mention was that Chihani's left leg was longer than his right, so that his right shoe had an extra-thick sole, at least three inches, and Chihani limped when he walked, swinging his right foot, which then struck the ground with a clumping noise. Often he used a cane. I would sometimes hear him in the Carnegie Library in town, prowling back in the stacks, and I would know it was Chihani by the sound of his one heavy shoe striking the wooden floor.

During the interview, Chihani sat behind his desk, which was bare except for a white pad of paper, an expensive gold pen, and the telephone. Franklin sat across from him. He asked Chihani if he minded if he taped their conversation but Chihani preferred that he didn't. So Franklin took notes. At first he assumed that Chihani was glad to be at Aurelius College. Within seconds, however, he understood that Chihani felt that the college was fortunate to have him. Chihani was not a man with a sense of humor about himself. He admired himself as a brain and as a man with a message. And perhaps his only reason for agreeing to see Franklin for fifteen minutes was to impart some of this message.

Franklin began by asking Chihani how he liked Aurelius, a trivial question to which he expected a trivial reply. He was feeling his way into the interview. Chihani said, "It is a small town like many others: quaint, picturesque, and ignorant."

Franklin asked him what created that ignorance.

"No knowledge of the world, no sense of the past, no sense of the future."

Chihani sat in his shirtsleeves with his elbows resting on his desk and the fingers of his right hand pressed against the fingers of his left, making a sort of tent.

Does one need a knowledge of the world, asked Franklin, to have a happy life?

"Not necessarily, but if one wants to raise oneself above the cows and sheep, one needs knowledge. You will argue that cows and sheep have contented lives. I would argue that their ignorance leads to their slaughter. Actions have consequences. Ignorance about the nature of those actions does not free a person from responsibility for the consequences."

Franklin realized he was on unsteady ground. Interviewing Chihani would be unlike interviewing a local dentist or baker. So Franklin asked Chihani about his past: his youth in Algiers, school in Paris, the universities of Montreal and Chicago. Chihani was divorced and without children. He had no siblings. His parents were dead. He said that he had no idea how long he would be in Aurelius but that as long as he had his books it didn't matter where he lived. He had rented a house in town. He didn't expect to buy a house, because he didn't believe in ownership of the land.

Franklin said that Chihani spoke slowly but without pause or hesitation. He was not a man short of ideas. Nor did he blunt his message with diplomacy.

Franklin said it was too bad that the position at the college should become available as the result of a tragedy.

"It was not a tragedy," said Chihani. "A shame, perhaps, even a great pity. But the accidental death of a human being engaged in his daily responsibilities is never tragic."

He left a wife and two small children, said Franklin.

"Then it is an even greater pity, but it is not tragic."

Franklin asked what Chihani thought about his students at Aurelius.

"Youth is expected to be ignorant. That is a definition of youth: it is unknowing. One assumes the young are capable of being taught. Here the students are not only ignorant, they are apathetic. However, in any situation one finds a few willing students, and that very willingness creates intelligence, or a readiness that passes for intelligence. And those few students can enlist others. Wherever there are a few ounces of chaff, one finds a few grains of wheat. Here there is much chaff."

And Mr. Chihani's colleagues at Aurelius?

"They are like the students in their ignorance, but their minds have calcified. At best they may impart information which conventional wisdom deems useful. The degree to which the students digest this wisdom depends on the degree to which it is made pleasurable. But true knowledge does not depend on charm. The reasoning faculties of the listener are all that are required to convince him of its truth."

And why did Houari Chihani teach?

"I teach to help young people take responsibility for the world and responsibility for one another. There has to be a consequence for education. Mostly that consequence is seen as increased earning power. That is a chimera attached to another chimera: limitless growth. I feel the consequence of education must be responsibility and change."

By change did Chihani mean revolution?

"That is a melodramatic word. I mean responsibility for the world. Historically, we see a fraction of the population taking advantage of the majority, making them ignorant consumers. They work hard at pointless jobs in order to buy the clothes, cars, and toys which they believe will make them happy. They fall into debt, become a version of wage slaves, and seek distraction in violence and sporting events. Education is minimized, the arts are discredited. The alternative is a society which values its members equally, a society which takes responsibility for its people and which acts out of that sense of responsibility, a society which works to decrease the greed, ignorance, and baser natures of its participants, instead of encouraging them."

Do you call that Marxism? asked Franklin.

"One finds many of these ideas in Marx, but just as the theories of evolution have gone beyond Darwin, so have the theories of economics gone beyond Marx."

But don't you teach Marx?

"His ideas were a beginning. You can argue that these ideas also exist in the New Testament. Our job is to prepare young people for the twenty-first century—that is a more complicated task than simply teaching Marxism."

And what did Mr. Chihani think of the people of Aurelius?

"They are asleep. This is the condition they prefer. They are afraid of the world and sleep is a way of dealing with their fear. Someday they will wake. Perhaps something frightful will happen. Indeed, there is no better invitation to the frightful than ignorance—that is, sleep."

Four

Franklin's interview with Chihani made no one happy. Roger Fielding and Priscilla Guerthen were seen as having made an error in hiring Chihani, which led people to recall errors they had made in the past. When the paper came out on Thursday, the third Thursday in February, the president of Aurelius College, Harvey Shavers, called Roger and Priscilla into his office and read them the interview out loud. People passing in the hall spoke of hearing Shavers's voice. He was a big man and he had a big voice to go with it, a voice well-practiced in public speaking. Shavers was primarily a fund-raiser and he knew how difficult it would be to raise money within the community if someone at the college went on record to call members of that community stupid. For Shavers, what was important was the appearance of quality rather than quality itself. As he had discovered, the brilliant rarely conceal their gifts, meaning they talk too much and create unfortunate publicity. Far easier to have silent mediocrity posing as quality than to have the real thing.

And in the faculty senate there was talk of demanding an explanation. Hadn't the teachers' credibility been disputed? Robinson Smart, chair of the English department, said he would have difficulty facing his students unless Chihani made a public apology to the entire college. These ideas were argued back and forth until it was decided it would be a mistake to give Chihani a soapbox from which to make additional remarks. Instead, the faculty senate agreed to vote on the possibility of censure should Chihani ever again insult their competence as teachers.

The student senate went further and sent a delegation of three students to Chihani to demand an explanation.

"Do you deny that you are ignorant?" asked Chihani.

There followed a certain discussion of the word *ignorance:* how it cast no aspersion on ability, potential, or intelligence. For instance, Chihani confessed himself ignorant of Japanese.

"You should welcome your ignorance," said Chihani, "because it enables you to learn."

They were sitting in his office. That February was very snowy, with only two days entirely free of bad weather. More than three feet of snow covered the ground. It seemed that every time I glanced outside I saw snow blowing past the window.

"What I object to," said Sharon McGregor, who was vice president of the student body, "is that you think I need to know Russian history in order to be a veterinarian."

"Absolument pas," said Chihani, "only to be a *good* veterinarian."

The reaction outside the college was not as strong but it was bitter. There has always been a division between the farming community—the cabbage growers and dairy farmers—and the town itself. The farmers tend to feel a certain scorn for the town and even more scorn for the college. That Chihani was making rude remarks only confirmed their beliefs. The college was made up of idiots and here was a specific idiot to prove the point. The fact that he was a foreigner, a non-Christian, and a Marxist made it worse. To those few farmers who cared, Chihani wasn't quite human. His little red car, his beret, and his oaken skin were too eccentric. He was discussed briefly in the few bars where farmers assembled, then dismissed. Manure smelled, and Chihani had only shown proof of his smell.

Among townspeople the reaction was fiercer. Many thought Aurelius a fine place and here was this Marxist claiming it was less cultured than the North Pole. In taverns the complaints against Chihani tended toward violence: somebody should kick his ass. In politer circles there was talk of Chihani's ignorance of community values. The doctors, lawyers, and businessmen spoke of the warp and woof of friendships and relationships that kept any town running smoothly. Even at Albert Knox Consolidated School there was talk among the faculty of sending Chihani a letter of censure, though nothing was done about it.

If Houari Chihani realized his unpopularity, he gave no sign of it. He taught as ever, arguing his positions in his dry, passionless voice. He was observed downtown and at the shopping mall. Chihani was one of those people who never seemed to take their eyes off their destination, who didn't let their eyes wander curiously over other people or things. He stared straight ahead, as if surrounded by empty space. Often his red Citroën could be seen driving through the snow to his house, then back to campus, then around town on various errands: to Wegmans supermarket, the Trustworthy Hardware. It would have been better if he had driven a more conventional car because his little Citroën was like salt in civic wounds. And indeed, five days after the interview appeared in the *Independent*, Chihani emerged from Wegmans one afternoon to find his windshield smashed and a large stone sitting in the front seat. He put his shopping bags in the trunk, returned to the store, and telephoned the police. Chuck Hawley, a cousin of mine, responded to the call. There was no sign of the culprit and it was clear that Chihani had called the police only for insurance purposes.

"He wasn't even angry," said Chuck. "Snow was blowing into the car but this guy didn't even notice. He made his statement, signed the form, and that was it. I asked if he'd seen anyone or if he had enemies. I'd read the interview, of course. He said there was no reason for him to have any enemies. Then he got into his car and drove off with the snow blowing in his face. He must have been freezing."

The day after Chihani's windshield was smashed, Franklin stopped by my house in the evening with Sadie, and I gave them each a cup of tea. On a bookshelf in the parlor I keep the books my mother read as a young girl, and Sadie settled down to read *Understood Betsy.* She sat with her feet tucked under her in the old wing chair. Her brown hair fell forward to frame her face. She was the image of her father, long and bony. I also set out a plate of sugar cookies. Sadie would take one and break off small pieces to put in her mouth. Other than saying hello, thank you, and good night, I don't believe she spoke.

Franklin was restless and didn't care to sit. Though he felt guilty about having run the interview, his very guilt angered him, as if feeling guilty indicated that he wasn't as good a newspaperman as he should be.

"I neither changed what he said nor exaggerated," he explained. "If anything, I played down what he told me. I didn't want to make him seem like a fanatic."

Franklin wore an old sheepskin coat that reached his knees. Around his neck was one of those British university scarves, blue with two red stripes. He held an Irish fisherman's hat in his hand and kept hitting it against his leg, knocking off drops of water. Franklin must have been hot but he gave no sign of it. He wore boots with Vibram soles and as he paced back and forth he deposited little wedge-shaped chunks of snow on my grandmother Francine's Turkish carpet. I'm sure he wanted a cigarette, though I don't let anyone smoke in my house. Now and then Sadie would smile at him fondly and go back to her book.

"All kinds of people live in a town," Franklin said. "If everyone acts the same, what's the point in that? Just the fact this sort of debate exists shows the town isn't sleepy."

But it seemed there wasn't any debate, just anger and resentment. Most of the resentment was aimed at Chihani, but people also knew who had been the medium for Chihani's views. If Franklin hadn't conducted the interview, no one would have been any the wiser about this Marxist in our midst.

Franklin flung his scarf on the couch. It seemed a considered gesture, not quite studied, not quite spontaneous—the gesture of a man who isn't sure who he is and so assumes a borrowed gesture, one that he thinks correct for the occasion.

"My job as a journalist is to make people think. I can write nice stuff they won't pay attention to, but that means I won't be doing my job."

I asked what he was going to do about the smashed windshield.

"I'm going to write an editorial about it."

And that's what Franklin did. When the paper came out on the first Thursday of March, it contained an editorial by Franklin attacking whoever had smashed Chihani's windshield, as well as those people who felt that vandalism was deserved. "If we have any richness as a town," he wrote, "it must be in our diversity. We are different from one another—not only is this our wealth, it should be our pride. . . . The person who smashed the windshield of Houari Chihani's car was attacking that very wealth. . . . We must see Chihani's presence as a virtue. He helps us see ourselves, and to see ourselves is to improve ourselves."

I doubt that editorial smoothed any wrinkled brows. As I heard one man say in the faculty room, "Franklin's shaking his finger at us again." It would have been better to drop the matter and let people forget Chihani, but Franklin took the opposite tack. Since he was afraid of being thought cowardly or, as he might have said, unprofessional, Franklin began to ask Chihani his opinion on various events both in town and in the world at large. He didn't do this regularly, but every so often there would be an article that included an opinion of Chihani's. Mostly these were innocent. For instance, during a debate about health-care reform, Chihani was quoted as saying that any country that pretended to be civilized had to care for its people. But in some cases, Chihani's remarks were disturbing and eventually they became more disturbing than anything he had said in his original interview.

It would be incorrect to suggest that Chihani's remarks were received with universal scorn. One tiny group applauded them. That was Chihani's reading group. At that point, Inquiries into the Right had five members. Perhaps we can all recall such fringe groups in college. Seeing its members together, one would be aware more of psychology than of intellectual belief. The shy, the pimpled, the resentful—one felt they had joined in order to be against something rather than for something.

For instance, there were two brothers, Jesse and Shannon Levine, a sophomore and a junior respectively, skateboard nihilists whose boom boxes broadcast a music in which static played an integral part. They had blond goatees and were as skinny as whippets, which made their knees and elbows look huge. And they had homemade jail tattoos on their hands and arms: small messages of love and hate, anarchy and discontent. Invariably they wore jeans, T-shirts, and large basketball shoes with the laces undone. Their father taught psychology at the state university in Cortland. Before taking a class with Chihani, they had been on academic probation. Chihani focused them sufficiently to allow them to achieve a C average. He also focused their resentment. Instead of just feeling angry, they now had an intellectual argument to validate their feelings. This made their rebellion a rational act, a sensible course to follow.

I would see Jesse and Shannon downtown. Their new beliefs gave them a cloak that freed them from their defensiveness and let them assume a sort of superiority. They developed Chihani's manner of keeping their eyes trained straight ahead, of looking as if they were always alone. They put aside their skateboards for the books Chihani explained to them. They saw the rest of us as deluded, culpable, greedy. Their language came to display a jargon that formed a barrier between them and the unenlightened. They believed Chihani's interview to be an attack against the complacent and they looked forward to future battles. They saw themselves as soldiers and began to dress in dark jeans and jerseys that had a vaguely paramilitary air. They even tied their shoes.

Another member of the IIR was Leon Stahl, an overweight young man who slept during the day and read and argued all night. He seemed never without a family-size bottle of Coca-Cola. He had a round pimply face and a little black moustache. He wore white shirts, gray around the collar, with discolored splotches on the back where pimples had burst. He celebrated his ugliness as a blow against convention, though if he had lost a hundred pounds he would have been handsome enough. Leon panted dreadfully and had a key for the elevators that were reserved for faculty and the handicapped. Before he met Chihani, his favorite book had been *The Golden Bough*. Now he read Chihani's books and articles and could quote whole passages. He was a passionate arguer and known for never giving up. Once he engaged two other students in an argument on the evils of private property that lasted twenty-six hours. As a freshman he had joined the debating club, as a sophomore he had been elected president, and as a junior he was barred from membership. He wore thick glasses in flesh-colored frames and the lenses always had large, fat thumbmarks across their surfaces. He came from Dunkirk, south of Buffalo, where his parents were high school teachers.

A fourth member was Jason Irving, a tall, thin young man who I had assumed was gay, but later he claimed to have no sex at all. He chain-smoked and drank endless cups of coffee. He played chess with a clock. Jason was vain about his long hair and combed it constantly. He liked to sit in McDonald's and read *Das Kapital*. He was exceedingly polite with his *pleases* and *thank yous,* but beyond that he never seemed to talk. He wore inexpensive rings on all his fingers, even his thumbs. Jason was a good student and wanted to go to graduate school in history. Before joining the IIR he had memorized the sentence "The small black rabbit has stolen the fat hunchback's yellow bicycle" in twenty-six languages, including Farsi. That had been the extent of an intellectual ambition that he later exchanged for Marxism.

The fifth member was a young woman, Harriet Malcomb. She was a junior from Binghamton with long dark hair that hung loose, and she was considered quite beautiful. She was thin to the point of seeming anorexic and she never smiled. Her face had a pallor accentuated by chalky makeup so she resembled a character from the Addams Family. People said she had been sexually abused by a cousin as a young child. When I asked how they knew such a thing, I was told that Harriet herself told the story. Although a radical feminist, she dressed revealingly, showing off her legs and breasts. She often flirted with young men and then, when they responded, she would find fault with them. Perhaps *flirt* is too strong a word. She would appear available, and when the young man tried to approach her, she would show herself unavailable. And she would criticize the young man for approaching her, as if it indicated his sexism, even his bestiality. One had the sense that not only did she think badly of men but she manipulated events to make them seem worse. She was close friends with Jason Irving and they often wore the same clothes, red silk shirts and baggy khakis. Leon Stahl believed that he loved her, and he would follow her around, panting. She would be kind to him, more often than not, and send him on endless errands to buy cigarettes and chewing gum, which was probably the only exercise the poor fellow got. The two brothers, Jesse and Shannon, seemed immune to her charms.

These five students constituted the reading group. Each week they met at Houari Chihani's small house on Maple Street to discuss what Chihani had assigned them: basic Marxist texts, for the most part. When the interview was published, Chihani had been on campus for about seven weeks and it was impressive that he already had a following, though a small one.

The IIR was jubilant about the interview. These were youngsters whose facial expressions ranged from the critical to the sneer. Now they looked happy. The public would understand they were a force to be reckoned with. And when Chihani's Citroën was vandalized, they were all set to picket City Hall until Chihani persuaded them not to.

In the week after the appearance of the interview five new members joined the IIR. Four were from the college: Barry Sanders, a biology student, who had grown up in Aurelius; Bob Jenks and Joany Rustoff, theater majors who had been dating since high school in Utica; and Oscar Herbst, a history student from Troy. He was a sophomore and said Marxism was terribly underrated. These four were young, uncertain, and average, with a vague disaffection that made them latch on eagerly to Chihani's group. The fifth new member was a different sort altogether. First of all, he wasn't part of the college. Though born and raised in Aurelius, he had gone to college in Buffalo. Secondly, he was older, about twenty-three, and he had returned to Aurelius after having been gone over a year. His name was Aaron McNeal, and his father, Patrick, had taught with me at the high school.

Five

When Aaron McNeal came back to Aurelius, I was aware of a collective sigh of disappointment. We had followed his tangled story for most of his life. We knew his parents' depressing narrative and his mother's awful end. To see Aaron was to bring these stories back to us.

Aaron's mother, Janice, had left her husband when Aaron was six. Instead of moving from Aurelius, she bought a house two blocks away on Hamilton Street in order to be near her son, or so she said. Patrick was able to retain custody of Aaron because of his wife's sexual liaisons, of which she made no secret and which involved some of Aurelius's most eminent citizens, including Judge Marshall, who disqualified himself from the custody hearing in Potterville. There was even a question of Aaron's paternity, it being a popular joke that Patrick McNeal was probably the one man in Aurelius with whom Janice didn't have sexual relations.

Janice was Patrick's second wife. He was older than she and had been married to a woman in Utica by the name of Rachel or Roberta, I can't remember which. In any case, they had had a daughter, Paula, who, from what I can gather, was often the one to take care of Aaron. Some people argued that it was Janice's jealousy of Patrick's former wife and her resentment of Paula that caused her to act badly, but I'm not sure that Janice needed an excuse. She had a lot of energy and she found her husband dull, though she may have liked him in a sisterly sort of way.

Once Janice was separated from her husband she continued to

have many men friends. She worked as a technician for the drug company in Norwich and, fortunately, many of her lovers came from there, meaning they were beyond the limit of our gossip. Aaron spent his time in both houses, though Patrick was legally in charge of him. Paula herself spent no time with her stepmother, which seemed to confirm the arguments of those who said that Janice resented her. I saw Patrick often at school and I felt sorry for him. The students knew of Janice's indiscretions and they made his life a misery. It was even claimed that three seniors had visited Janice one night and she had given them their pleasure. At least that was what they boasted. In a small town like ours, something that has happened and something that has not happened but is gossiped about are equivalent. Possibly these youngsters had never been with Janice, but considering the talk, it made no difference.

One would think, given the attention, that Janice was a great beauty; that wasn't the case. She was short, a trifle overweight, and her mouth was large. When she laughed, one saw all her teeth. She had curious eyes, tipped up at the corners and of a greenish color. Her nose was slightly puggy, her chin slightly square. She had short dark hair that curled beneath her jawbone. Perhaps I am a poor judge of female beauty, but I was surprised that men found her attractive. She dressed well, carried herself well, and clearly had a sense of dignity, but when all is said and done I found her somewhat dumpy.

If Patrick had been able to forget his ex-wife, his life would have been smoother, but he clearly adored her and any talk about Janice tormented him. My policeman cousin, Chuck Hawley, once found Patrick outside Janice's house at two in the morning. He offered to give Patrick a ride home but Patrick refused. Chuck said that Patrick was crying. He joked about that. I asked him if Patrick had been drinking but he said no. "He was as sober as a judge," he said.

People expected either Patrick or Janice to leave Aurelius, but neither did. One felt that even though they were divorced, their main relationship was with each other, as if she enjoyed torturing him and he had a need to be tortured, though I am sure they would have denied this.

If Aaron was damaged by his parents' relationship, he gave no sign of it. At least at first. Perhaps this was due in part to his half sister, Paula, who seemed very loving. Aaron was a friendly little boy who would politely greet everybody on the street by name. And he dressed well and seemed very clean, with his blond hair brushed and his freckled face shiny and smiling. While still in grade school, he began delivering the Utica and Syracuse papers, riding his bike with his springer spaniel, Jefferson, running behind him. He seemed to have few friends but he also seemed not to require them. This was untrue, of course, because everybody needs friends, but he seemed content by himself or with only the companionship of his dog and so no one worried, or if they did they soon forgot about it. It was only later, when people recalled his solitude, that they tried to make something of it, offering it up as a kind of proof.

Clearly, Aaron knew about his mother because she was very open about her boyfriends, and other children taunted him about having a mother whose morals were questionable. I had Aaron in two classes: eighth grade science and tenth grade biology. He was very bright, the sort of eager youngster who always raised his hand and volunteered to do extra work. I had the sense that I would get to know him well, but I never knew him any better than I did on the first day of class.

At sixteen Aaron had reached his full height of five foot ten. His blond hair had become light brown. He was thin without appearing delicate; rather, he had the body of a gymnast, though he took no interest in sports except for riding his bike. He would have been handsome if his eyes weren't so close together, which gave him a slightly fishlike expression. He also had a small L-shaped scar on his left cheek where his dog had bitten him. Aaron had been delivering papers when Lou Hendricks's malamute had gotten loose and attacked Aaron's dog. Aaron had flung himself into the battle and his dog had become so panicked that he bit Aaron, who was thirteen at the time. Even though Aaron received stitches, the scar remained obvious, especially when he got angry. Then, while the rest of his face grew pale, the L-shaped scar would redden.

Once, when Aaron was in eighth grade, his mother came in for a conference. I won't say she flirted but she made me quite uneasy. She stared at me with her slanted eyes and wouldn't look away, till I myself was forced to. Of course I knew Janice's reputation. It was one of those school events when parents go around meeting their children's teachers, spending a few minutes with each. Janice seemed mildly interested in Aaron's schoolwork, but after I established that he was doing well she asked me instead about living in New York City. Someone had told her I once lived there. "But why would you move back to Aurelius?" she kept asking. I was quite relieved when her time was up and the next parent arrived. During tenth grade parent-teacher conferences, Janice never appeared. Of course I often saw Patrick and he knew that his son was doing well.

Adolescence is a dreadful period. We tend to notice those youngsters who misbehave and call attention to themselves, but there are others, equally miserable, who receive no help simply because they are silent. I expect Aaron was as miserable as any, but it wasn't until his senior year we had any sign of what some people saw as his dark side. Perhaps we wouldn't have seen it even then if it hadn't been for another boy, Hark Powers, who had long been one of Aaron's tormentors.

Hark Powers was one of those youths who excelled at sports and little else unless it was bullying. Perhaps Hark envied Aaron's scholastic ability. Perhaps his sensibilities were truly offended by the behavior of Aaron's mother. In any case, by tenth grade, Hark had begun to taunt Aaron. Both were in my biology class and I had to seat them as far apart as possible. Aaron received an A, Hark a D. He would have flunked if Coach Pendergast hadn't convinced me to let him pass so that he could play football.

Hark Powers outweighed Aaron by fifty pounds. He came from a farming family, the youngest of five brothers who had wound their way through the school system without distinction. Hark wore jeans and jean jackets, kept his dirty brown hair long, and clunked around in black motorcycle boots with a chain across the instep. He seemed to find the behavior of Aaron's mother the funniest thing imaginable. The fact that Aaron's father was a teacher only egged him on. Even in my tenth grade biology class I had to chastise him for singing "I wonder who's poking her now" which he rendered to the tune of "Back in the Saddle Again."

There were many small incidents between Hark and Aaron. Once Hark dropped a lit cigarette butt in the cuff of Aaron's khakis and set them on fire. Several times he dumped food on him in the lunchroom. I'm sure there was an incident every week: taunts or winks, passing notes around the class about somebody being a whore. I could give many examples that were sordid and typical of this kind of bullying. Aaron even had to stop riding his bike to school because Hark would damage it.

Aaron never responded. He wiped the food from his shirt, poured water on his burning cuff, and ignored the taunts as if they never touched him. And the fact that Aaron didn't respond led a few other boys to taunt him as well, though most left him alone, not from kindness but because Aaron was too peculiar in his silence. This bullying went on for several years, never violent enough to attract the attention of the authorities, never sufficiently negligible to be forgotten.

There is a lunch counter in Aurelius—Junior's—where students go after school to play video games and have a snack, usually pretzel rods and a cherry Coke. And there is a magazine rack and a jukebox. Some days there might be thirty kids in Junior's. Hark was in Junior's nearly every afternoon, but Aaron never went there, not even to buy a magazine.

One afternoon in May of his senior year, Aaron entered Junior's around four o'clock. There had been another incident that day in the lunchroom in which Hark had poured his drink, some orange mixture, onto Aaron's plate of macaroni and cheese. That seems trivial and Hark had done worse, but this behavior had been going on for a long time. Later I heard people say that they would have thought Aaron had gotten used to it, as if being a victim were something one got used to.

When he saw Aaron, Hark called out, "Hey, whore boy." He sat at a table with his girlfriend, Cindy Loomis, and two other young men, all of whom looked forward to being entertained.

Aaron wore a white shirt and khakis, which was important, considering what happened. Cindy told me later that Aaron was smiling, not a particularly friendly smile but certainly harmless-looking.

"Tell us how your mother does it with sailors." Hark laughed. He was smoking and flicked his ashes on the floor.

Aaron approached in a relaxed manner and Cindy said they expected him to say something, maybe make a joke of his own. When he reached the table, Aaron winked at Hark, then bent over to speak to him in private. Hark was surprised but he leaned forward so that Aaron could say something in his ear. Aaron had never spoken to him. Otherwise, most likely, Hark wouldn't have leaned forward like that.

Instead of speaking, Aaron grabbed Hark's ear with his teeth and bit down. Hark yelled. He kicked out at the table, knocking the glasses onto the floor. Hark grabbed Aaron's shirt but the pain must have been excruciating. Aaron backed up, dragging Hark out of his chair. He had most of Hark's ear in his mouth. Hark kept trying to hit Aaron, but he was stumbling and kept yelling. Junior hurried out from behind the counter. Aaron dragged Hark backward as he bit down. Then he clamped his teeth shut and gave Hark a shove. Hark staggered across the restaurant, holding his hands to his bloody ear. Aaron stood by the door, then he reached in his mouth and removed something. It was Hark's ear, three-fourths of it, at least.

Junior shouted at Aaron, "Give it back!" Presumably he thought that the ear could be sewn back on. Of course everyone else was shouting as well.

Aaron put the ear back in his mouth and began to chew it. His white shirt was covered with Hark's blood. Hark himself was lying on the floor with his knees drawn up, screaming. Cindy was with him but most of the kids just watched Aaron chew up Hark's ear. Then Aaron spat it out and the ear plopped down on the white marble floor. One of the boys described it as looking like those chewable wax Halloween lips: a pink formless blob, lying on the white marble and half across a green plastic straw that someone had dropped.

Aaron ran his tongue around the inside of his mouth and glanced around him with perfect calm. Junior called the police.

Aaron spent several hours in jail before being bailed out by his father. During his last years of high school he seemed to despise his father. They were never together and in school Aaron would pass him without even a nod. And Chuck Hawley told me that when Patrick picked up his son at the police station, Aaron refused to look at him.

Although Aaron was charged with assault, the matter never came to trial. Many people said how Hark had tormented Aaron. It must have been clear that Aaron wouldn't be convicted. Instead, it was decided that he should seek psychological counseling. He didn't return to school but studied at home and took special tests. He was an A student and had already been accepted at Buffalo. The point was to keep him out of school because he was certain to cause a disruption.

Hark stayed out of school as well. There was no question of the ear's being replaced. Aaron had chewed it to a lump. The ear was put in formaldehyde and kept as evidence. Chuck Hawley told me it was quite an item at the police station. Deputies from other towns and even state troopers showed up to look at it.

Aaron went off to college. Patrick continued to teach. Janice worked in Norwich and had her boyfriends. Once during the summer I saw Hark on the street. He had a bandage over the place where his ear had been. Later it healed to a pink scar. Hark let his hair grow over it. I don't know if plastic surgery could have given him another ear or if he chose not to do it. Patrick certainly would have paid for it.

Aaron was gone for three years. I suppose he might not have come back if it hadn't been for the death of his mother. It isn't new to say that a town is like a family. Even strangers share your experiences. You drive down the same streets, shop at the same stores. Nobody could be more of an outsider than I am, but Janice's death was a rude invasion into my life as well. It affected how I saw the world, how I saw my neighbors. If it did that for me, others must have been affected more drastically. And of course it wasn't just a death, it was a murder.

Six

Janice's body was discovered by Megan Kelly, who came to Janice's house every Wednesday morning at ten to clean. It was mid-October and the furnace was on. The house was hot. Janice's three cats, two black ones and a calico, were frantic. They had eaten their food and were starving. People were surprised the neighbors hadn't known something was wrong just from the sounds of the cats, their yowls. But neighbors said they were used to loud noises coming from Janice's house.

Mrs. Kelly was a solidly built woman in her sixties. She claimed she knew something was wrong the moment she opened the door. Certainly the cats were carrying on, but Mrs. Kelly said there was also a smell, the faint sweet smell of early corruption. One of the cats escaped the house immediately, the other two wound themselves round Mrs. Kelly's legs so she nearly fell. Mrs. Kelly hung her coat in the hall closet and got the vacuum cleaner. First she vacuumed the hall. The cats stayed nearby, which surprised her since they hated the noise. Janice was one of those women who felt that rooms should be "bright" and the walls had a pink and yellow wallpaper hung with reproductions of French paintings with lots of flowers and light: Matisse and Bonnard, especially Bonnard. She had heavy furniture with pale flowery covers and a carpet with purple and yellow triangular patterns.

When Mrs. Kelly pushed the vacuum cleaner into the living room, she saw the body. Janice lay on her back between the couch and the fireplace wearing a blue terry cloth robe that must have belonged to one of her larger male friends. The robe was open, so Mrs. Kelly could see bare skin underneath. Janice's face was a bluish color. Her slanted eyes were open and bulging, rolled up as if trying to look back at something on the mantel. She had been strangled but that wasn't the worst thing. The worst thing, according to Mrs. Kelly, was that Janice's left hand had been severed at the wrist and her bone stuck out "just like a white stick in a pool of blood." Mrs. Kelly first thought that the cats had eaten the hand but that turned out not to be the case.

Mrs. Kelly ran next door to the Washburns' to call the police. Within ten minutes three patrol cars arrived, creating more excitement than Hamilton Street had seen in decades. The officer in charge was Ryan Tavich. He was in his midforties and generally well-liked. The trouble was that he, too, not long before, had been one of Janice's lovers.

And this became a problem: Janice's lovers. Because once the case had begun and no murderer was found within twenty-four hours, attention turned to these men. Some had families and had been seeing Janice secretly. Now their lives were turned upside down. They were suspects, or potential suspects. And not all of them were known, so that men whom no one thought were involved with Janice might indeed have been involved. There was much speculation about this and much exaggeration.

Chief Schmidt called the sheriff in Potterville. Then the state police were called. Ryan, in his own mind at least, was treated quite shoddily. He was a thick, rectangular man, a weight lifter whose shoulders, chest, hips, and thighs all seemed the same distance across. And he had a broad face with a square jaw, short black hair, and dark, almost sullen eyes. The kind of eyes that suggested disappointment. He began the investigation and conducted the first interviews, mainly with neighbors and Janice's ex-husband, Patrick. Then Phil Schmidt talked to the mayor, who talked with the city manager, and it was thought best to remove Ryan from the case.

We had reporters coming down from Utica and Syracuse, even Albany. And the wire services sent the story all over. The fact that Janice's left hand was missing gave special notoriety to the whole business. For a few days one saw camera crews hurrying into City Hall. And so Ryan's affair with Janice, even though she had broken it off the summer before, was considered a problem by everyone except Ryan himself. He had never made a secret of dating Janice. He was single, divorced actually, and they had been seen together, going either to dinner or to the movies. His involvement with Janice made Ryan eager to catch whoever had killed her. To the others, it made him a suspect. And unfortunately the sheriff's department and the state police often treated small-town policemen with disrespect, if only because town police were paid less. They knew Ryan and perhaps liked him, but in their eyes he wasn't quite professional.

Ryan talked to Franklin about this. It was shortly before Michelle died, though everyone thought she would last longer. Sadie was eleven at the time. Ryan went over to Franklin's house, not the one near me, but the ranch house on Jackson Street. Michelle had a bed in the den. The house had a medicinal smell and was kept warm, about eighty degrees. Toward the end Michelle always felt chilled and kept asking her daughter to turn up the heat.

The two men had a couple of beers in the kitchen. When healthy, Michelle had been an energetic housewife despite her job as a photographer, but now that she was sick the house was somewhat shabby. Not that Franklin was lazy or didn't know how to vacuum—he was simply stunned by his wife's illness and had trouble doing anything other than his newspaper work.

Ryan hadn't come to see Franklin because of Janice's murder but because they were friends and because of his sympathy about Michelle's illness. Such understandings have few words attached. So their talk mostly concerned the trivial: how well the high school football team was doing and the chances for the Buffalo Bills in some upcoming game. But Franklin understood that Ryan also grieved. Janice had been dead less than a week.

"Did you love her?" asked Franklin.

Ryan shifted in his chair. "There was a way she could fill your mind."

"Who broke up with who?"

"She thought I was getting too attached to her."

Franklin waited for Ryan to say more but Ryan was digging at the label on his Budweiser bottle with his thumb.

"Did it make you angry when she broke off with you?"

"Sure, but I knew she was right. Are you talking to me as a reporter?" Ryan made an attempt at a grin.

"I just wanted to know how you were feeling."

"I'd think about her all day long. And when I got to her house in the evening, I hardly said hello. I'd just start touching and kissing her. She'd bite my lip. It was painful. Even a week after she broke off with me, I could feel it. And I didn't want the feeling to go away."

"How long did you see each other?"

"Three months. And she was seeing someone else as well. I didn't care. She might have been seeing a couple of guys for all I know. More power to her."

"Do they have any idea who killed her?"

"In the autopsy, they figured she'd recently had sex with someone. Then they'd have the DNA unless he'd used a condom. But there was no trace of anything. So maybe it was a woman who killed her. A jealous wife or something."

"What about the hand?" asked Franklin.

"There's no way to explain it. Crazy, that's all."

"And you've been taken off the case completely?"

"The state police are conducting the investigation. They think it looks bad if I'm connected with the case. They had to look hard to find guys who *weren't* involved with her. She'd even been into the sheriff's department. Of course the state cops won't admit anything."

"She had a healthy appetite."

Ryan kept his eyes on the floor. "You could call it that."

"Was it just the sex that, you know, kept you seeing her?"

"If it was just that, I'd have already forgotten her. She was a wonderful woman: funny, energetic. Hell, I'd have been happy to hang around her even without the sex."

"But you'll stay out of it?"

"I can't get her out of my mind. She had a cranberry mark right below her navel. I see it all the time. I'm not going to get Schmidt mad at me, but I'll keep my mind on it. If she was killed by someone in Aurelius, I'll find out."

"And what will you do about it?"

"I've got to let my feelings settle. When I went into her house that morning, I hadn't been there for months. I recognized the smells and on top of those smells was this other smell, her death smell. She was on the floor, her face all blue and her eyes rolled up. I used to kiss that face. I don't know if you can imagine seeing the face of the woman you love like that. The awfulness of her dead face." Then Ryan remembered Michelle in the next room and he felt abashed and became silent.

Aaron came back from Buffalo for the funeral. He was a senior in college, majoring in mathematics. He didn't stay at his father's house, but at Gillian's Motel. People were struck by this. If he had wanted, he could have stayed with many people, but he chose to stay at the motel. And he was obvious about it, not that he should hide it, but he mentioned it to people, as if staying at Gillian's made a kind of statement.

Paula had come back as well and stayed with her father. I hadn't seen her for some years and she had grown quite beautiful. She certainly had not been unattractive before, but she had exchanged her teenage prettiness for a womanliness. She was tall and thin, with wavy black hair that hung past her shoulders. And she wore glasses with large round lenses. She had finished her master's degree at Binghamton and was working for IBM.

The funeral was held at Saint Luke's Episcopal Church. Patrick sat in front with Paula. Aaron sat across the aisle and a few rows behind with a cousin who had come from Scarsdale. The church was crowded. Of course there were Janice's colleagues from the pharmaceutical company in Norwich, as well as some relatives, even several neighbors. But many people went out of curiosity. Along with Ryan Tavich, who sat with Franklin, there were a number of men in the church, some alone, and it was impossible not to speculate that these men had been involved with Janice.

Janice had been cremated, and on a stand at the front of the church rested a white cardboard box about the right size for a corsage. It was amazing to think its contents had been powerful enough to turn the hearts of so many men topsy-turvy. Around the stand were asters, lilies, and roses, hundreds of roses. McHugh's Flower Shop on Jefferson Street was quite sold out and flowers were sent from as far away as Utica. Even this was amazing, in that the volume of flowers exceeded the volume of the little white box by about a thousand to one. And it was hard not to imagine that the box contained not her ashes but her heart.

Father John conducted the service and Eunice Duncan played the organ. Bach, I think. Father John spoke of Janice's career as a scientist, of her being a woman active on the frontiers of medicine, though, as I say, she was no more than a technician. He spoke of the tragedy that Janice had been taken from our community so violently. He spoke of her energy and good humor. He spoke of her warm and loving nature. In truth, that was the only remark which, by the farthest stretch of the imagination, might have referred to her men friends.

A certain tension arose from the suspicion that Janice's murderer was in the church at that moment. Ryan kept looking around and there were plainclothesmen in evidence, including one in the organ loft with Eunice Duncan. Did they expect the killer suddenly to betray him- or herself when confronted with that sad little cardboard box and the doleful words of Father John? I suspect many people thought something theatrical would happen, which was partly why they came. But in fact, nothing happened.

The service came to an end and people wound their way to Homeland Cemetery, a procession of cars with their lights on led by the Cadillac hearse from Belmont's Funeral Home. It was raining, the leaves had turned, and the peak of color had passed. Perhaps half the people in the church went to the cemetery, Ryan Tavich and Franklin among them, as well as several plainclothesmen. Father John spoke to the people grouped by the grave and there were many umbrellas.

Homeland is a pretty place, with large oaks and quite a few stones from the Victorian period, weeping dryads and angels. People formed a semicircle and Aaron stood across the grave from his father and his half sister. It was a little grave for a little box and was dwarfed by the flowers, especially the roses, which had been brought from the church. The grave would soon have a very large stone, paid for by Patrick. Someone said the stone was so big that it could have included a drawer in which to put the box of ashes. Others felt that the purchase of such a stone, at least six feet high, was an act of defiance on Patrick's part. Still others found it in bad taste, as if Janice shouldn't have a stone, as if her ashes should have been sprinkled somewhere along the Loomis River.

Nothing out of the ordinary happened. The service ended and

people departed, leaving a muddy trail through the wet grass. Before the end of the month some of these same people joined together again for the funeral of Michelle Moore, and this time Franklin and little Sadie would be the chief mourners. It was a much smaller funeral with far fewer flowers but with a full-sized casket. No policemen came, except for Ryan Tavich.

Seven

I would hear about the murder investigation from several sources, including my cousin. The investigation was hampered by too many leads—all of Janice's lovers—and none: no one had seen anything. Many of Janice's lovers were identified. Their alibis were questioned. A certain scandal accompanied this, since some were married, involved with other women, or well-known within the community, like Judge Marshall in Potterville. And there was the likelihood of more lovers who hadn't yet been identified. There was also the chance that the murderer was a woman. And of course it was possible that the murder was unconnected to Janice's love life.

It was hard not to brood about Janice's missing left hand. Presumably it existed somewhere. In volume it must have equaled the contents of the white cardboard box. Why had it been taken in the first place? To kill Janice in a jealous rage was perhaps understandable; to cut off her hand was an act of madness.

Several times I heard from my cousin that the police were about to make an arrest, but nothing happened. Some of the men involved with Janice had no alibis, or very poor ones, but that fact by itself didn't establish guilt. Patrick McNeal was interrogated and the police in Buffalo were asked to establish where Aaron had been at the time of the murder. Even Paula's movements were scrutinized.

As more days passed, we increasingly realized that answers would be slow in coming. One began to hear more often that the murderer was somebody from out of town, somebody unknown to us. The murderer must have come from Utica or Syracuse, even Norwich.

The state police had taken over the case altogether, though the sheriff's department still had a deputy involved. But the state police had resources that the county didn't. As for our own policemen, Ryan Tavich alone remained busy, but only in off-hours and mostly with discretion. After all, he was a suspect himself.

It was determined that Janice had been killed late Sunday night or early Monday morning. Her neighbors said she had been out all evening and must have returned after they had gone to bed. There was no clue to where she had been, though about eleven she had stopped for gas at the Cumberland Farms on the north side of town. But no one came forward to say that he or she had been with Janice. In the afternoon she had raked leaves on her front lawn. The questions were: Where had she spent the evening, when had she come home, and had she come home alone? After two weeks went by without any answers, interest began to wane.

In any case, soon after the funeral, interest in Janice's murder was partly eclipsed by the behavior of her son, Aaron. He presumably meant to return to college, but instead of leaving after the burial, he remained in town. He was just twenty-one and he was observed in several of our local bars.

There was a waitress, Sheila Murphy, who worked at Bud's Tavern, a red-haired woman a year or so older than Aaron. I had had her in science class—a good-natured but thoroughly mediocre student. Sheila had waited tables at Bud's since high school graduation. Her father worked for the city road crew. The mother, I believe, did little but play Bingo.

No one realized that Aaron was seeing Sheila and perhaps he hadn't been seeing her, in the normal meaning of the term, except in the tavern, till one night about two weeks after his mother's funeral. They appeared to have no history, or rather their history began in medias res.

What happened was this. Around two-thirty in the morning a

dozen people in Gillian's Motel were suddenly roused by screams of pain and rage. At least that is what witnesses told Franklin. These were people passing through town—salesmen, business people—and perhaps there were a few local men and women engaged in secret assignations, though usually they go to Potterville for that, or farther afield.

Several men ran into the hall, pulling up their trousers or straightening their pajamas. Just then Aaron's door flew open and Sheila Murphy came rushing out. She was wearing jeans and nothing else. There was a large amount of blood on her breasts. I say "large amount" because the witnesses disagreed as to how much, but even a small amount would have been terrible and of course she was screaming. She had large breasts and it became clear that the left one was bleeding. Blood dripped on the carpet and even got on the walls. One of the men took her into his bathroom. Another called the police. Aaron appeared at the doorway. He was said to be smiling, not a happy smile but somewhat boastful. He was shirtless and his long hair was out of its ponytail. Several men mentioned the L-shaped scar on Aaron's left cheek, how it was red while the rest of his cheek was pale.

It turned out that Aaron had bit Sheila, nearly taking a piece out of her left breast. He bit her to the extent that she needed stitches. My cousin answered the call. Aaron refused to talk. In fact, Chuck had to protect him from several of the men in the motel who felt that Aaron should be punished right there.

By this time Sheila had stopped screaming and stood in the hall with a blood-stained white towel pressed to her breasts, calling Aaron an animal and a pervert. Of course everyone in that part of the motel was wide-awake and the owners, Jimmy and Kate Gillian, were terribly upset. People assumed Aaron was drunk. Chuck took him away, trotted him in handcuffs down to the police station. An ambulance arrived to take Sheila to the hospital, though she claimed that she didn't need one, that she could drive herself, but in the end she rode in the ambulance. Someone gathered up the rest of her clothes. The Gillians tried to calm their guests and eventually everyone returned to their rooms.

The fact that three years earlier Aaron had bitten off Hark Powers's ear was lost on no one. People called Aaron The Vampire. His actions were horrible, but they also had a comic quality, although not for the people concerned. Aaron and Sheila had been drinking and had returned to Gillian's after Bud's closed. Sheila said Aaron wanted her to remove her jeans and she refused. They argued, then began to wrestle. Sheila was a big girl and her years of tavern work had accustomed her to the worst of male behavior. Anyway, she fought back. It was then that Aaron bit her and wouldn't let go until Sheila struck him with her knee in the groin area. By then Aaron had done his damage.

Aaron claimed to have been drunk, but that excuse was insufficient. Charges were filed and a court date was set. Once again Patrick bailed his son out of jail and bail was accepted on condition that Aaron live in his father's house. Ryan Tavich talked to Sheila and to the judge. Much was made of the fact that Aaron's mother had been buried two weeks before. Although Sheila was furious, she had a kind heart. The upshot was that Aaron paid her medical bills. He received a suspended sentence and one year's probation. He also had to enter therapy, which he chose to do in Buffalo, with the result that by the beginning of the second semester he was back in college.

People were surprised that Aaron had got off so easily and some, like Hark Powers, went so far as to suggest a conspiracy in Aaron's favor, but there was little evidence of that. We all realized that Aaron had been fortunate. And we were pleased when he left town. It seemed the last page of an unpleasant story.

As the months passed, people stopped thinking about Aaron. Hark Powers took a job as a mechanic at Jack Morris's Ford dealership. Whenever I saw him, which was not often, I would think of what Aaron had done to him, because even though Hark wore his hair long we all knew he was missing an ear. And he hadn't changed. He was still loud. He was still a bully. If Aaron's attack was meant to teach him a lesson, it hadn't, though perhaps he was more careful about whom he abused. For a short time he dated Sheila Murphy, which seemed appropriate since they both bore Aaron's tooth marks, but it didn't last. Sheila said Hark slapped her, and people said she was one of those women destined to be abused by men. But once I went into Bud's Tavern just to have a look at her and she seemed perfectly pleasant, though she was loud and smoked too much.

No one saw Aaron for more than a year. He got his degree and did a semester of graduate study in computer science. Presumably he communicated with his father and half sister, but even that was unknown to us. Because we taught together, I saw Patrick often, but he had become more withdrawn and wouldn't socialize. People said he was looking for a job in another town. And the fall after Janice's murder, he moved to Utica. Coincidentally it was at that time that his daughter returned to take a job as a guidance counselor in the dean of students' office at the college. Even people who felt that Aurelius was the best town in the world didn't see why she had returned. In fact, she moved into her father's house.

I don't think anybody realized Aaron was back in town, too, but his sister must have known and others as well, though Aaron avoided the bars and didn't seem to go out much. He had moved back in December, rented an apartment in a brick apartment complex near City Hall, and was employed as an analyst for a database company in New York City, meaning he worked at home with a computer. This fact struck me as the strangest of all. Aaron had a job that enabled him to live anywhere, but he chose to live in Aurelius. But hadn't his sister moved back as well, as if both needed to be near Janice's ashes? Though perhaps that is too melodramatic.

As for Janice's murder, the police were no further along than on the day of her death. Often in these cases there is knowledge even when there is no concrete evidence for a grand jury. The police have suspicions, even certainties, which get talked about. But in this case there was nothing. It was assumed that Janice met someone passing through town, or perhaps someone had visited her from out of town. Of course all the people staying at the motels, even motels fifty miles away, had been investigated.

The dominant theories were those easiest to believe: the killer was someone from far away. If anyone suggested that the killer might be a person we saw regularly—a teacher at one of the schools or someone who worked in a shop—that suggestion was met with scorn. In our minds, the case was closed. There was even a sanctimoniousness about Janice's death: that the nature of her life, its sexual untidiness, had brought about her demise.

But we'd thought the case of Aaron McNeal had been closed as well and here he was again.

Eight

Besides Aaron, I happened to know another member of Inquiries into the Right, Barry Sanders. I had taught him in three classes—general science, biology, and advanced biology. Now he was a biology major at Aurelius College. I had tried to get him to go to one of the better state colleges, but he chose to remain here in order to be near his mother, who claimed to be sick, though I believe her illness was greatly exaggerated. Barry had been one of my best students and if he were fortunate enough to have a career in biology much of the credit would be mine.

What made it possible that Barry might not have a career in biology wasn't his intelligence but his own uncertain nature. Even getting him to take my advanced biology, a class reserved for very few and taught in my own free time, had required much persuasion.

One thinks of the course that people cut through life. For some it seems simple. They don't hesitate. They are handsome and intelligent and life opens up to them as the Red Sea opened before Moses. But even into the lives of these people a shadow might come. For instance, Franklin was a person whose progress seemed charmed, but who could have anticipated the death of Michelle? I would hear people say it wasn't fair, but what does fairness have to do with anything? Yet some people appear to make it all the way through without mishap. They lead happy lives and leave behind them happy children.

Others have a constant struggle. They are shy or peculiar-looking. They stutter. They have no ability at athletics. They never lose their self-consciousness. They stumble and have a foolish snicker. They talk when they shouldn't and remain silent when they should talk. When they hear laughter, they assume it is directed at them. Though smart, they feel stupid. Though creative, they feel dull. Their path through life resembles that of a person wading through deep mud. And many appear born this way. It almost makes me believe in reincarnation, how some people's lives seem a punishment. And what could it be a punishment for if not for some previous sin?

Barry Sanders was albino: white hair, white skin, and pink rabbity eyes that he squinted and blinked constantly behind the dark lenses of his glasses. He was also overweight, not fat but a victim of the many treats—cookies, brownies, fudge—that his mother made for him, which was her way of apologizing for the fact that he was different from other children. And Barry was short. He was short all through school, and when he attained his full height he was five foot six. And he was shy, which was a particular curse in someone so noticeable.

In grade school Barry was known as Little Pink. Though an average student, he was quite bright. It was only anxiety that kept interfering and hurting his grades, for Barry never forgot himself. It was as if he were always outside himself, seeing himself in the classroom or standing at the edge of the playground, seeing his peculiarity in relation to others.

He lived alone with his mother, Mabel Sanders, on Birch Street. The father had disappeared when Barry was two. Mabel was office manager at State Farm Insurance. She felt that Barry was frail— although I think that untrue—and treated him as if he might break at any time. On spring days when other children removed their jackets, Barry was still bundled up. He wasn't allowed to go trick or treating on Halloween. He couldn't participate in sports.

Barry was the best student in my eighth grade science class and he didn't say a word the entire year. He sat to the side about halfway back and kept his head down. He was so shy that I myself was shy about calling attention to him. I talked to him occasionally after class but he found even that a torment, especially when I was praising him for something he had done well. The boys who called him Little Pink, I made them stop.

In tenth grade biology he was better, but he still wouldn't talk in class. A few times, however, we spoke after class, and by the end of the year he might even initiate the conversation. Of course our conversations dealt with science. I knew nothing about his life out of school, though I knew who his mother was and where they lived. I took to lending him copies of *Scientific American* when I was done with them, and he came to expect this and received pleasure from it.

In the spring of Barry's senior year I realized he was gay. He was taking my advanced biology class and doing well. The class met at the end of the day and he would often stay after, at least once a week. It took several months to reach the subject of Barry's homosexuality, but at last he admitted he had had a brief affair with a man in town, though he wouldn't say who. When I tried to quiz him, he withdrew almost entirely. His fear seemed directed not at me but toward the man with whom he had been involved. The only further piece of information was that Barry called this person "a professional man," as if to indicate that he wouldn't go out with riffraff. Then it turned out that this was how the man had referred to himself. Though I knew of a few openly gay men, I didn't think it was any of them. This became for me another of Aurelius's small mysteries. The subject also made me mildly uncomfortable. Not the subject of gayness but perhaps Barry's interest in me as a single man. We never reached the point where I had to say I was unavailable, but I suppose Barry sensed it. When Barry started college, I felt quite relieved. At least I wouldn't be seeing him every day.

For the first year he lived at home. Relations between Barry and his mother, however, became strained. It wasn't that Barry was rebellious, but he was sullen and, I think, resentful, as if his mother were at fault for his condition. She surrounded him like an old blanket, making him take pills when he wasn't sick and fussing about drafts. She wouldn't even let him mow the lawn, saying the outdoors was bad for him. She hired a neighborhood boy to mow it. A few times Barry described to me how he'd sit at the front window watching Sammy McClatchy mow the lawn and wish that he could be the one doing it. Really, it was a pathetic story.

But at Aurelius College Barry began to make friends. Not many, just two or three, but they gave him a world to set against the world of his mother. He would still visit me at school, ostensibly to borrow my *Scientific Americans*, and he would tell me about young men who seemed utterly dull except for an interest in chess, science fiction, or Dungeons and Dragons. But by the second semester of his freshman year Barry entered into a relationship with one of them, a piano student from Wilkes-Barre. It didn't last, and the result was to make Barry even angrier, not at his gayness or his mother or about being an albino but at life's whole dreary setup, the fact that one is born, slogs along, and is dragged out against one's will, usually screaming.

Well, there was nothing unusual about this. Barry was tired of being a freak and he sought people and systems to blame. That was why he moved into the dorm during his sophomore year, though it meant he had to work in the school cafeteria fifteen hours a week. It's odd with people who are shy: they never quite learn how to speak, to feel at home with words in their mouths. Barry enunciated each word as briefly as possible and the result was to give his speech a jerky quality. Mostly he talked about school, his mother, and how he was doing, fairly general talk. At the end of the first semester of his sophomore year, he was still seeking something that would free him of this terrible self-consciousness. That was when Houari Chihani arrived at Aurelius College.

Barry didn't have Chihani as a teacher that spring, though he knew of him. How could he not? But he also knew of the reading group because he was friends, or at least acquaintances, with Jason Irving, since both belonged to the chess club. And, like others, Barry might have assumed that Jason was gay, though, as I said earlier, Jason appeared to repudiate both sexes. Barry wouldn't have joined the IIR at the beginning. He hated to call attention to himself. But after Franklin published his interview with Chihani, Barry grew curious. Then, when the theater majors Bob Jenks and Joany Rustoff joined, Jason began to pressure Barry to join too.

I don't know if Jason would have persuaded Barry if Aaron Mc-Neal hadn't also joined right then. Barry was three years younger and didn't know Aaron personally. But he knew his story as it had gradually become exaggerated. Certainly it had been dramatic for Aaron to have bitten off Hark Powers's ear, but by the time Barry heard the story it had been raised to the level of high opera. Even Aaron's attack on Sheila Murphy was turned into a tale that reflected credit on Aaron, though mostly among those luckless young men for whom Sheila was out of reach.

Barry joined Inquiries into the Right around the end of March. He was proud of his decision. He was striking a blow for something important, though he was never able to articulate the exact nature of that important thing. But he talked to me about it. Every couple of weeks he stopped by the high school and once or twice he visited my house, though I often discourage such visits from students or former students. After all, people gossip.

At the beginning the IIR met Monday evenings in a seminar room in Webster Hall. Chihani discussed the rise of the middle class after the French Revolution, the nature of imperialism, and the exploitation of labor. The group read and discussed Marx, but also Veblen and novels like *The Grapes of Wrath,* for Chihani's aim was not only to teach his charges but to make them indignant. And of course Chihani controlled the discussion with his dry, passionless voice—the voice of reason, he would have said. These youngsters knew nothing of history and so even tales about the government's involvement in Latin America upset them. In high school, American history had been a happy story; now Chihani told them the sad one.

If the IIR had been confined to these Monday meetings, it would have remained a relatively innocent endeavor, but soon Chihani began inviting the group to his house on Fridays. These were social occasions, though for Chihani no occasion was purely social. For instance, if he played music, he might play Paul Robeson and tell his students the story of that frustrated man. Or they might see a video, like Woody Guthrie's story, *Bound for Glory*. Chihani was always teaching, even when he seemed to be orchestrating a social event. And much of what he said was accurate. He didn't need to invent stories about the villainies of capitalism. Many true stories were available.

As others began to join the IIR, the meetings leaned more toward discussion than lecture. The members discussed their reading, discussed Marx, and they discussed what was wrong with Aurelius. We were the IIR's sample community. We were an illustration of what could go wrong. The youngsters who had been members longest— Jesse and Shannon Levine, Leon Stahl, Jason Irving, and Harriet Malcomb—became, as it were, noncommissioned officers. They felt proprietorial toward Chihani and argued with the new members. The difficulty was that Aaron was older and had read more. He became the leader of the new members. While he did not argue with Chihani, he argued with Harriet and fat Leon Stahl over interpretation. Both old and new members competed for Chihani's favor. Chihani saw this and encouraged it. After all, he wanted converts rather than friends.

We would see them other times as well. Whenever it snowed, two or three IIR members would shovel Chihani's walk and driveway. When the weather improved, they would all sit in Chihani's backyard on Friday evenings and argue over endless pitchers of ice tea. This was obvious to the neighbors, and even the most tolerant felt suspicious. Sometimes voices were raised and sometimes there was laughter.

By April the five new members met every Thursday in Aaron's apartment downtown. I don't believe they saw themselves as opposed to the others but Aaron went over what they were to discuss for the following week, coaching them, so they could hold their own against Leon and Harriet. Barry was excited about these meetings and he came to have a crush on Aaron, running little errands for him and following him around. Aaron had no sexual interest in Barry but he was flattered by the attention. Or even if he wasn't exactly flattered, Aaron liked to exercise his power, what little power he had. He enjoyed sending Barry on errands. He even began calling Barry Little Pink, though, I think, affectionately. At least Aaron wouldn't let anyone else call Barry by that name.

At the Monday meetings the main competition was between Aaron and Harriet. Even though Leon Stahl was well-read, he appeared, in his fatness, rather comical. He sat on the floor and needed help to get to his feet. Jesse and Shannon would drag him up, while the others laughed. For Chihani, too, there was something corrupt about being so fat. It indicated a lack of discipline, and though Chihani didn't mock Leon, he talked to him about losing weight. I believe that Leon did cut back on his Coca-Colas or at least switch, temporarily, to Diet Coke. Leon was the most intelligent of the students, but his obesity and the various comic elements that surrounded it, such as his passion for Harriet Malcomb, kept him from being an intellectual leader. That left Harriet and Aaron.

According to Barry, the two despised each other, but it wasn't so simple, nor perhaps was it true. In her way, Harriet was quite vicious. Her beauty, her shiny black hair, her pallor, her tiny waist and large breasts—these were her weapons. At school she wore short skirts and sweaters, away from school she wore jeans and T-shirts, both very tight. Aaron seemed indifferent to how she looked. In meetings, he spoke to her courteously but condescendingly, and always briefly, as if eager to turn his attention to someone else. She spoke to him sarcastically and he listened without apparent emotion, except perhaps with a slight smile.

Around the middle of May, Aaron mentioned to Barry that he was going to "get" Harriet Malcomb. Barry assumed he was going to make a fool of Harriet among the group, which was incorrect. They were having lunch at Junior's, Aaron had a hamburger. Barry, having decided he was a vegetarian, ordered a salad. They sat at the counter. Aaron's hair was receding a bit, which gave him a slight widow's peak and made him look rather distinguished. He still wore his hair in a ponytail.

Barry asked what Aaron meant by saying that he was going to "get" Harriet Malcomb.

"I want to make her my soldier." Aaron cocked an eyebrow at Barry as if to suggest that Barry understood his meaning.

"How can you do that?"

"By making her my whore."

Barry disliked talking about sex and he had come to think such conversations intrinsically wrong. Of course he knew that Harriet was beautiful but he prided himself on being immune to her charms. He began to stutter.

"Wha . . . what do you plan to do?"

"I want you to take her a letter." And Aaron withdrew an envelope from his canvas book bag.

It was then that Barry understood that the day, the lunch, the time had all been chosen with the idea of delivering this letter. After all, the letter was already written. It was Thursday and Harriet had no classes on Thursday. Indeed, she made it clear that she reserved Thursdays for her IIR reading.

"What does the letter say?"

Aaron handed it to him, then grasped Barry semi-affectionately by the back of his neck. Barry wasn't sure if Aaron meant to stroke him or to lift him like a kitten.

"It invites her to talk. It flatters her mind."

Nine

Barry delivered the letter. It was two o'clock on a Thursday afternoon in May, a blustery spring day with the sky clear one moment and full of dark clouds the next. Dust blew from the sand spread on the streets during the winter. A few retired people raked dead leaves from under their rhododendrons. Barry drove a rusty Ford Fairlane that had been his mother's, a car with broken springs and collapsed shock absorbers that swayed like a ship on the ocean. From the rearview mirror hung a deodorant dispenser in the shape of a pine tree.

Harriet Malcomb lived in the attic apartment of a house on Adams Street, two blocks from campus. Barry parked in front and went upstairs. Despite Janice McNeal's murder, houses in our town are never locked, though Harriet had a lock on her apartment door. She didn't look pleased to see him, seemed exasperated and scornful, but I am sure that was to some extent his own anxiety. Harriet was wearing shorts and a Colgate sweatshirt. Barry gave her the letter and she began to shut the door, "in my face," Barry said.

Barry put his hand on the door. "I'm supposed to wait for an answer."

"Then wait," she said, shutting the door.

Barry stood in the hall. He wished he had something to read, not really to read it but to seem occupied when Harriet reappeared, to show he wasn't simply waiting but was reading as well, that he had forgotten about the waiting. The window in the hall faced the campus and he could see the white cupola and bell on top of the administration building. A dog barked downstairs. In the distance, he heard a motorcycle rushing through its gears, whining to the top of each.

Ten minutes later Harriet opened the door. She still wore shorts but had replaced the sweatshirt with a white blouse. Barry didn't like the blouse because it made her look demure and he didn't trust that. Her black hair was gathered behind her head in a loose braid held by a thick red elastic. She also wore a necklace of blue beads.

"I'm ready," she said.

Since Barry didn't know what was in the letter, he wasn't sure what she meant but he hated to seem confused. "My car's outside," he told her.

They walked downstairs. Barry held neither door for her, not the front door nor the door of the Ford Fairlane. All the way over to the brick apartment complex by City Hall, he tried to think of something to say. Harriet stared straight ahead and Barry thought she did this in imitation of Houari Chihani.

Aaron's apartment complex was called Belvedere Apartments. His particular building contained four apartments with a hall in the middle rising to the ceiling of the second floor, from which hung an ornate but cheap-looking chandelier. Aaron's apartment was on the second floor. Harriet followed Barry upstairs and Barry knocked, twice, then once, which was his private signal, not that Aaron demanded a signal.

When Aaron opened the door, he seemed in no way surprised to see Harriet. "Come on in," he said. The apartment had a large living room facing State Street, a bedroom, and a small kitchen. Aaron's work space and computer were in the bedroom. On the walls in the living room were posters of Zapata and Pancho Villa over the word "*Huelga!*" There was a bookcase jammed with books, a stereo, several armchairs, and a modernistic blond couch, long and low to the floor. There was also a braided rug.

Aaron turned to Barry and said, "Why don't you go into the bedroom and wait."

Barry understood they were engaged in a sort of adult game. "Sure," he said. He went into the bedroom, shutting the door.

There was no keyhole and this disappointed him. Over the single bed was the Vermeer portrait of the woman with the yellow scarf. The life in her eyes, her zest for living, contrasted with the ascetic nature of the room. White walls, white floor, a desk made from a white door, a Compac computer, telephone, and fax machine, a Hewlett-Packard printer. The only decoration on the desk was a framed photograph of a young woman with turned-up eyes and a large mouth, a face Barry found slightly froglike. He picked up the picture and after a moment he realized it was Janice McNeal, Aaron's mother. Perhaps he would have guessed this earlier if the woman in the photograph hadn't been so young, not much older than Aaron himself.

Barry walked to the door. He heard Aaron talking but he couldn't make out the words. The tone was insistent. Barry assumed they were talking about their Chihani discussions, then he heard Harriet say "No" quite loudly and he heard Aaron laugh. A chair was knocked over. Barry stood with his hand on the knob. He thought of Harriet's willingness to come with him and what that might mean.

Barry grew increasingly unhappy. He walked to the phone and wanted to call someone but he didn't know whom. He felt apprehensive and didn't know what was happening. Now Aaron's voice was louder and insistent. Barry approached the door again and heard a slap, then a second one and a cry from Harriet. Again Barry put his hand on the knob. After a moment, he heard Aaron pronounce the word "Asshole," almost affectionately.

Barry hurried to the window. He was nineteen and many things frightened him, especially things he didn't understand, which was a lot. He blinked into the sunlight. He saw Houari Chihani's red

Citroën turning the corner onto Monroe Street. He recognized many of the people he saw, even if he didn't know their names.

After a while he heard Aaron calling.

"Little Pink, Little Pink!"

Barry hurried back to the door.

"Little Pink, come in here!"

Barry opened the door. Harriet was lying on the braided rug. Her shorts were off and the skin of her hips was very white. Aaron was on top of her with his khaki pants around his ankles. Harriet was staring at the ceiling, then, slowly, she looked at Barry. He thought there was something wrong with her eyes. She looked at Barry and said, "Little Pink," very quietly. Aaron was propped up with his hands on the floor next to Harriet's shoulders. He wasn't smiling; rather he seemed to be glaring at Barry, who jumped back and shut the bedroom door. Turning his back to it, Barry pressed his hands against his ears and slid down until he was sitting on the floor. He stayed there. He looked at how his sneakers were double-knotted. He removed his hands from his ears and heard a cry. Quickly he pressed his hands to his ears again. He felt lonely. He watched the shadows move across the floor and up onto Aaron's single bed. He looked at the window and imagined throwing himself out but he knew he would only hurt himself. Soon, however, he needed to go to the bathroom, which was in the other room. He kept his hands to his ears. Soon the shadows completely covered Aaron's bed.

Then the door abruptly pushed against his shoulders and stopped, then a fist hit it three times. Barry scrambled to his feet. Aaron stood in the doorway, Harriet a few feet behind him. Both were dressed.

"We're going out for pizza," said Aaron. "Want to come?"

Barry started to say he wasn't hungry, then he didn't say anything. He nodded. But he still had to go to the bathroom. He went in and locked the door. As he was washing his hands he saw a piece of paper on the floor. It was the note he had delivered to Harriet. Barry put it in his pocket.

After Barry got home that evening, he took out the note and read it. "We have much to give each other. I need your help. Come with Little Pink." He didn't see why the note had convinced Harriet to come to Aaron's or what Aaron meant by "help." He felt betrayed that Aaron had referred to him as Little Pink.

Barry didn't go to the IIR meeting the next week, nor did he go to the discussion at Aaron's house on Thursday, nor did he go to the meeting on the following Monday, the last Monday in May. On Tuesday, Aaron called him.

"Be at my house Thursday night," he said. Then he hung up.

Barry kept having sexual fantasies about Aaron. He imagined himself on the floor where Harriet had been, with Aaron on top of him and thrusting himself into him. At first Barry tried to stop these fantasies, then he gave himself up to them and masturbated. As for Harriet, he hated her. And he imagined, quite foolishly, that if it hadn't been for Harriet, Aaron would have paid more attention to him, sexual attention, that is. He kept reading the note that Aaron had sent. "We have much to give each other."

When Barry went to Aaron's apartment on Thursday, he found all the members of the IIR. Aaron sat on the couch and Harriet sat with him. Although touching, they weren't caressing or showing affection for each other.

From that time forward Aaron was the unofficial leader of the Inquiries into the Right. As for Chihani, he was the group's mentor. He didn't direct the IIR; rather, the members came to him for guidance. And it was Aaron who took them to Chihani, or that was the impression. At the Thursday night discussions at Aaron's apartment, they went over the assigned reading and Aaron made sure they understood it. Friday evenings, many of them went to Chihani's house for discussion and coffee, but Aaron often didn't attend. He was friendly with Chihani but also cool. He didn't fawn like some of the others, especially Jason Irving, who followed Chihani around like a dog. Aaron kept his distance, though intellectually he always deferred to Chihani. And when Chihani asked a favor, to get something or fix something, Aaron did it efficiently. But he never hung out at Chihani's house.

Aaron and Harriet were often together. She would spend the night at Aaron's and it was hard not to imagine them in Aaron's narrow bed. This was torment to Barry. In public Aaron and Harriet were rarely demonstrative. Sometimes they held hands but even that seemed cold, as if something had accidentally entangled their fingers: the wind or circumstance. But in private they were passionate, even loud, because a teacher at the high school, Martin Tyson, had an apartment in Aaron's building and he said he had heard glass breaking and furniture being overturned. Once he knocked on Aaron's door to see if everything was all right.

People remembered Sheila Murphy and they looked carefully at Harriet, searching for a bruise or some unhappiness. But her skin was as clear and pale as ever. If Aaron left marks, he left none that showed. Probably there were no marks. But given Aaron's history, people almost hoped to see marks, see an outward manifestation that his peculiar history was continuing as they had known it would. Sheila Murphy still worked in Bud's Tavern and she was skeptical. "You wait," she kept saying.

Ten

It is perhaps unique to a small town that the narratives of people's lives continually cross one another. Someone is part of your daily existence for a while, then drifts away, then comes back again. You see the same people on the streets and in the stores. You have brief conversations and receive news about your neighbors. Even I, who lead a secluded life, can't go shopping at Wegmans on Saturday afternoon without talking to four or five people. I discover that Mrs. Dunratty has had the flu, that Tom Henderson's daughter Midge is graduating from Cortland State, or that old Mrs. Howster hit a deer with her Dodge Caravan. I look forward to these talks. And I make a point of buying my *Independent* and *Syracuse Post Standard* at Malloy's Pharmacy, instead of having them delivered, because of the brief conversations such visits afford me.

Vicariously, my life is quite extensive. And of course the result is that I feel more involved than I really am. I worry about Mrs. Howster and feel glad for Tom Henderson, though some might argue this sort of contact allows me to feel involved yet celebrate my isolation at the same time.

For a year or so after his wife's death, Franklin Moore remained very private. He looked after Sadie. He maintained his friendship with Ryan Tavich. He worked hard at the newspaper. But he was in his midthirties. It stood to reason he would develop interest in other women. And given the size of our town and the small number of available women, it was probably inevitable that he would turn his eyes toward Aaron's half sister, Paula.

Paula was thirty and single. People spoke of her as having lived with a man in Binghamton for four years but he drank and it ended badly. Indeed, it was said she had to get a restraining order against him, and people claimed this was one of the reasons she had moved back to Aurelius. Perhaps another reason was the availability of her father's house, which was standing empty. I expect Patrick meant to sell it since he was determined to teach in Utica and was clearly finished with our town. But when Paula returned to Aurelius, Patrick rented his daughter the house for a small sum. That was typical of Patrick. He couldn't let her use the house for free. He had to impose a restriction that put distance between him and his own child, though I never heard that Paula complained about the arrangement. But Patrick always felt more comfortable if there were paperwork and lawyers, which was something for which his late wife had mocked him, that he used lawyers as other men used condoms. Coincidentally, Henry Swazey, Patrick's lawyer, had been one of Janice's lovers.

Paula had been back in Aurelius for several weeks before I knew she was here. She kept to herself and rarely went out. Although one might ask where there was to go in Aurelius if one didn't bowl, play bingo, or belong to a church or fraternal organization. Several times she attended cultural events at the college—a speaker or a chamber group. I'm sure most people had no idea that Paula had returned, though if they paid attention they might have seen her walking her dog, Fletcher, in the evening, a tall tan and black mongrel, part Lab and part shepherd.

But Franklin's position as editor of the *Independent* gave him access to whatever was happening. So it was inevitable that he would visit the dean of students' office and it was inevitable that he would see Paula.

She had cut her wavy black hair so it reached no further than her jawline and it had become quite curly. Patrick's first wife, Rachel or

Roberta, had been Jewish and the mixture of Jew and Scot gave Paula an exotic appeal. Her eyes, for instance, were light blue. On the other hand, she was slightly old-fashioned in her clothes and mannerisms, which is more common of people in small towns. And her glasses gave her an apparent seriousness that seemed in keeping with her position at the college.

Paula and Franklin made a handsome couple. Franklin with his khakis and tweed jackets, Paula with her plaid skirts and white blouses. People wished them well. Their unfortunate histories—Franklin's first wife dead of cancer, Paula's stepmother murdered—probably saved them from the touch of malice found in most gossip. Not that Franklin and Paula carried on a great public romance. They were too discreet for that. But they would be seen together at the movies or a restaurant and sometimes Franklin's white Subaru station wagon would be parked in front of Patrick McNeal's house late at night.

Ryan Tavich might have dated Paula as well if he hadn't been involved with her stepmother. Ryan was squeamish about such connections. But because Ryan and Franklin were friends, the two men and Paula occasionally drank together at Bud's Tavern or went cross-country skiing in the forest preserve that bordered Lincoln Park. Ryan was dating as well, but he never settled on one woman. People said he was still stuck on Janice. Occasionally he went out with Patty McClosky, who was Chief Schmidt's secretary, and sometimes Ronnie Glivens, an O.R. nurse at the hospital.

The person who didn't like Paula was Sadie, though perhaps that isn't accurate. She would have liked Paula if Paula hadn't been involved with her father. Thirteen-year-olds have complicated but, in some ways, rudimentary minds. After the death of her mother, Sadie was very close with Franklin. They went everywhere together. When Franklin became involved with Paula, it meant he couldn't spend as much time with his daughter. Often Franklin and Paula would take

Sadie along to the movies or for walks in the state park, but while Sadie wasn't rude, she was silent and unhappy.

Sometimes Franklin would talk about this when he came over. "She thinks I'm letting down her mother's memory," he said.

"She's jealous of your time," I would tell him.

It was she herself, rather than the memory of her mother, that Sadie felt was being betrayed. She felt she'd been replaced, which was silly, but, again, she was only thirteen. And Sadie had heard the stories, terribly exaggerated, about Janice and her murder, and she imagined that the same wickedness—meaning promiscuity—must exist in Paula, even though the two women weren't related. The irony was that when Paula's father, Patrick, had begun dating Janice twenty-five years before, Paula had felt the same jealousy toward Janice, though in that case perhaps Patrick should have heeded the warning.

Sadie began to punish her father, though she didn't see it as that. She began doing poorly in school and leaving the house without telling Franklin where she was going. This upset him considerably. Sadie had always been responsible, and as a single parent Franklin relied on her responsibility, in that she was sometimes left by herself. Franklin had a cleaning woman, Megan Kelly, the same woman who had found Janice McNeal's body, and Monday, Tuesday, and Wednesday nights Mrs. Kelly would cook for Franklin, or rather for Sadie, because Franklin's duties at the *Independent* usually kept him away on those nights.

Often when Sadie left the house without saying where she was going, she visited me, and of course Franklin knew this, because I told him, though I never told Sadie that I was tattling on her. Ever since she was eleven I have amused Sadie by showing her the specimens I keep in jars of formaldehyde. Pickled punks, I call them. There are several frogs, a rat, a rattlesnake, a human fetus with its eyes closed that I inherited from an earlier biology teacher, ten eyeballs originally belonging to cows, and a fetal pig. I've collected these over the years to use in science classes. The formaldehyde has turned them all the same dark color and the rat's hair has mostly fallen out. The cows' eyes display a gloomy intelligence and the fetal pig looks sad. Sadie was always fascinated with the human fetus, wondering who its parents were, what it might have been like had it had the chance to grow up. It made her quite philosophical.

But other times Sadie would go off by herself on long walks or bike rides and it could be worrisome, especially if Franklin wanted to take her someplace else or just wanted to know where she was. Sadie had several good friends her own age, including poor Sharon Malloy, and she was often at Sharon's house. But Sharon's parents weren't all that attentive and didn't always let Franklin know when his daughter was visiting them.

At times Paula tried to take Sadie out by herself but either Sadie would refuse or, if she went, she would be silent. This went on for about six months and I was impressed by Paula's persistence. But Sadie disliked Paula's company, or perhaps it was just stubbornness. As a result Franklin began to spend more time with Paula apart from Sadie, which made the situation worse.

Franklin hoped the problem would go away. After all, Paula was kind, told funny stories, and bought Sadie nice things—Franklin couldn't imagine that Sadie wouldn't come to like her. But Paula's qualities made Sadie suspicious.

"Why does she bring me presents?" Sadie asked. "She brought me a sweater on Sunday, a blue crewneck."

"She wants you to like her," I said.

"I don't want to like her."

"What did you do with the sweater?"

"I gave it to Sharon. Don't you think Paula smiles too much?"

In an adult such behavior is neurotic, but an adolescent can combine neurosis with normalcy in the same package. I helped Sadie with her schoolwork and her grades improved, but her sudden disappearances continued and by late spring Franklin spoke of taking her to a counselor in Hamilton. Paula must have suggested that, since counseling was her field. Of course Ryan Tavich alerted the other members of the police department that Sadie was wandering off, and several times one of the officers brought her home, an event that set the neighbors to buzzing.

I would have been more worried about Sadie's behavior if I hadn't benefited from it. Though I don't miss having a family, there was a sweetness to Sadie's presence. I myself would feel foolish and adolescent and scold myself after she'd gone, although these occasions were perfectly innocent. Still, I would have hated it known at school that I had spent an evening making chocolate chip cookies with Sadie Moore. It wasn't that we made cookies every day, perhaps only once a month, but I looked forward to it. Though I knew I should try to convince Sadie of Paula's good intentions, I didn't want to pester Sadie or make her distrust me. And this was my fault, that her visits were more important to me than how she got along with Paula.

Ryan Tavich also took an interest in Sadie and, I imagine, tried to get her to accept Paula. He and Sadie went skiing together in winter and trout fishing in the spring. Ryan was not much of a conversationalist but he would talk about the various trees and wildflowers, how trout live and what they do at various times of the day. He was a practical man without much imagination, and he gave Sadie information about the world.

So Sadie and I made chocolate chip cookies and looked at dead things in jars, and Ryan Tavich took her fishing—nothing had happened yet to make the sight of an older man with a young girl seem remarkable in any way. But there was another man in Sadie's life who caused more concern: Aaron McNeal. Even Franklin worried about

Sadie's friendship with him, given his history. Sadie, I suspect, knew of her father's ambivalence and was to some degree—quite innocently, of course—manipulating it. Franklin spent time with Paula and so Sadie spent time with Paula's half brother. It must have struck Sadie as fair.

Paula's own relationship with her brother was complicated. She had helped raise him and was often responsible for him when he was little. But Paula had not liked her stepmother and Aaron resembled her. They had the same slightly up-turned eyes. He even had some of her mannerisms—the way Janice shrugged one shoulder or covered her mouth when she laughed.

And what were Aaron's feelings toward his sister? After Patrick and Janice were divorced, Paula not only took the place of Aaron's mother but stood in Janice's way. Paula nurtured him and isolated him. It was Paula who gave Aaron books and took him to the town library. She had even tried to protect him from Hark Powers when Hark came to the house to taunt Aaron. And perhaps she encouraged Aaron to fight back, though of course she wouldn't have urged him to bite off Hark's ear. Family relationships are almost impossible to sort out: like lies on top of dislike, love on top of selfishness. And envy, resentment, anger—the whole porridge can be a problem. I feel myself lucky to have had no siblings and only one parent, but there is no way I can clearly unravel my relationship with my mother, especially in those last years before her death.

When Franklin began to date Paula, Aaron hadn't yet returned to town. Then around three months later, in December, he arrived and they had Christmas together, which must have been a nightmare. Sadie found fault with Paula's presents: this sweater was the wrong color, that blouse too small. And Aaron was cool with Franklin, though Franklin was perfectly polite to him, even kind. One would have thought that Aaron might sympathize with Franklin because of the death of Michelle, but he was so caught up with his own story that other people's grief wasn't credible to him. And perhaps he resented Franklin's ease with the world. Franklin had a stable life. He wasn't casting about for a direction. And, of course, Paula loved him, which was a thing that Aaron might resent, if only because he wanted Paula's attention himself.

In that way Aaron and Sadie were alike, and during that Christmas they played Monopoly and threw snowballs, mostly at Franklin. But it was after Franklin's interview with Houari Chihani and after Aaron had joined the IIR that he and Sadie began to spend time together, which made Franklin fear that something else might be involved. Aaron would give Sadie small gifts—inexpensive jewelry and sometimes a book. Franklin didn't trust Aaron, though he wanted to. But Paula, Aaron's own half sister, didn't trust him either.

"You don't know what Aaron's going to do next," Franklin told me. "Mostly he's like anybody else, then he'll do something almost perverse, like giving Paula's dog rum punch or hiding my keys for the fun of it. You know how with most people you're really having two conversations? There's the hidden one under the one you're having? You see someone's fear or pride or vanity, which is like a second subject matter. With Aaron I never see that hidden conversation." Franklin laughed. "It's too hidden. And without it I never have the sense of what he's going to do next or why he does what he does. I can't see how his sense of cause and effect operates. It's like the surface of a pond. Something's stirring underneath, but I don't know what."

It wasn't that Sadie spent a great deal of time with Aaron, but sometimes she would be seen in his car or she would call her father from Aaron's apartment and ask to be picked up, though Aaron lived only about eight blocks away. Sometimes they would be seen together in Junior's eating an ice cream. They seemed to like each other but Aaron was twenty-three and Sadie was thirteen, and we all knew Aaron's history.

Sadie also knew Aaron's history, but she romanticized him. She saw him as a victim. And she knew that her friendship with Aaron distressed her father and somewhere in her adolescent soul that gave her pleasure. Once she took a red pencil and made an L-shaped mark on her left cheek just like Aaron's scar. When Franklin saw it, he wanted to make Sadie wash it off, but he said nothing.

Eleven

It is significant that none of the ten members of Inquiries into the Right left Aurelius that spring when classes ended at the college. Most found summer jobs in town. Harriet Malcomb worked as a hostess at the Pine Cone Inn. Leon Stahl was a clerk at Ames. Jesse and Shannon Levine got jobs on the grounds crew at the college. Oscar Herbst had a job at Aurelius Lumber. I'm not sure about the others. But the group continued to meet two or three times a week. They read the books that Chihani assigned and met at Aaron's apartment to discuss them and to define the jargon, though they never called it that. Sacred nomenclature, was more like it. On Friday nights, a few were to be found at Chihani's house for further discussion on a more social level. Jesse and Shannon mowed Chihani's lawn along with the college lawns. Joany Rustoff did Chihani's housework, vacuuming and washing up, though Chihani paid her for this.

The members of the IIR had become believers, some more than others. In Barry's case there existed the great desire to believe in *something*. Then Chihani came along. And that seemed true of them all except Aaron: the desire to believe preceded the object of faith. Each of the ten members of the IIR felt a lack, which was eventually filled by the IIR itself, but who is to say it couldn't have been filled by classic ballroom dancing or joining Greenpeace or buying a dog? Had I suggested this to Barry he would have been insulted. Each member believed that his lack had a specific size and shape and only the IIR could fill it.

The exception was Aaron. I doubt that he was a believer; rather, he was a reluctant nihilist in search of alternatives to nihilism. But he had a peculiar sense of humor—one hesitates to call it humor—that showed itself in a spirit of contrariness. This made him more problematic than the others, because when there were divisions between the members of the IIR, Aaron was amused by the contrariness of that as well. Indeed, he might encourage such divisions. But I was mistaken to think that Aaron was directed by whim. He had a single passion that surely directed his actions—but I get ahead of myself.

It was too bad that Aaron often missed the Friday evenings at Chihani's, because they became self-criticism sessions. I was touched by how Barry would tell the group his feelings about being an albino and short. He even admitted that he hated to be called Little Pink. These were fairly typical and thick-headed young people and through Chihani's prodding they came to see a few of their flaws: their envy, their sloth. Leon Stahl was forced to confront his gluttony. Jason Irving talked about his fear of sex. Bob Jenks and Joany Rustoff admitted how they used their relationship to push away the rest of the world. I can't believe that Jesse and Shannon Levine ever saw themselves as anything but superior, but under Chihani's tutelage they came to see how they privileged their own point of view over that of others. And if nothing was wrong with Chihani's creating a sense of awareness on the part of his followers, perhaps it was a mistake to replace their weaknesses with his own particular brand of Marxism.

Like Aaron, Harriet Malcomb seemed to have no interest in self-criticism. She said she had to work at the Pine Cone Inn on those nights but maybe Aaron didn't want her to attend Chihani's sessions. Maybe he feared they would lessen his influence over her. It was difficult to gauge how much control Aaron had over Harriet, especially after she started going out with Ryan Tavich. Ryan had seen her at the Pine Cone Inn, where he had taken Ronnie Glivens for dinner. Then Harriet had called him.

"Sure I'm going out with her," said Ryan, when Franklin asked him one Thursday night after basketball. "A beautiful woman wants to see me, I'd be crazy not to go out with her."

"You're more than twenty years older," said Franklin.

"I can count okay," said Ryan. "If it doesn't bother her, why should I worry about it?"

Harriet was taller than Ryan, but he was muscular from his weight-lifting regimen and not bad-looking. It seemed odd that they would go out together, but we had not yet reached the point where oddity immediately caused suspicion.

"What do you talk about?" asked Franklin.

"Cop stuff. She likes my war stories."

The meetings at Chihani's house were kept under his strict control. And when Aaron did attend, he was a different person, studious and deferential.

At a Monday meeting at Chihani's in July the IIR members were to have read C. Wright Mills's *The Power Elite.* Chihani's living room was quite spartan: two platforms with futons for couches, several straight chairs. The only decoration was a red and blue Algerian rug on the wall; on the floor was another rug of different shades of brown and tans. No books, music, or photographs. Though Chihani had many books, they were upstairs. Chihani served mint tea without sugar and sugarless wheat crackers from Canada.

He sat in a chair; the others were scattered around the room.

"And what do you call fairness?" Chihani asked. "Any of you may answer."

"What's good for the greatest number?" asked Leon. He sat on the floor with his legs crossed, but his legs were too fat to cross easily and he had to hold on to his shins to keep them from pushing outward.

"Then what is good?" asked Chihani. He had a dry voice and he clipped his words so that each syllable seemed exactly the same length.

"What's good is what is equitable," said Harriet. She sat on a futon with Aaron, who was leafing through a French magazine.

"'From each according to his abilities, to each according to the amount of work performed,'" said Leon, quoting Marx.

"And why is that fair?" asked Chihani. "Is this idea of fairness based on a subject's moral demand?"

"It's based on a theory of history," said Leon.

"Explain yourself," said Chihani.

"History is progressive," said Leon. "It moves toward the accomplishment of a better social order."

"Again I ask you, what is better?" said Chihani.

"The emancipation of humanity," said Shannon.

"Why is this better?" asked Chihani.

"The exploitation of man by man creates friction within the society," said Harriet. "All are not working for the betterment of humankind. Any group that is left out is an exploited group, a group which will eventually turn against those in power."

Leon raised his hand and began reading from Marx. "'When a great social revolution shall have mastered the results of the bourgeois epoch, the market of the world and the modern powers of production, and subjected them to the common control of the most advanced peoples, then only will human progress cease to resemble that hideous pagan idol, who would not drink nectar but from the skulls of the slain.'"

"I like that part about the skulls of the slain," said Oscar. Set into his lower lip was a gold stud, far to the left side. When listening, he liked to play with it with his tongue, as if tasting something sweet.

"Lenin said that what is moral is anything that helps to destroy the old exploiting society and to unite the workers into creating a new communist society," said Harriet.

"Doesn't that argue that the ends justify the means?" asked Barry. He was proud to have spoken; he rarely spoke.

"What's wrong with that?" asked Oscar.

"Evil when used for good is no longer evil," said Aaron.

"That's a questionable philosophy," said Leon.

"Sometimes yes," said Aaron, "and sometimes no."

"What about the police?" asked Leon.

"Leon's scared of the police," said Oscar. He was the sort of here-tic who desired proof and had little interest in the theoretical. He was like a garage mechanic who saw no reason to discuss a car's problems philosophically. But that isn't quite right. Oscar wasn't a fixer. It was demolitions that excited him. He wanted to dismantle.

Although winters in Aurelius were cold, snowy, and long, the sum-mers are like a gift, sunny and not too hot. That summer was partic-ularly sweet. I remember a week in July when it rained for a short time every night, but the days were clear. Briefly it seemed that na-ture had gotten it right. Even though my lawn is large, I choose to mow it myself. I like my neighbors to see me working in the yard, as if this makes me one of them. Sadie sometimes helped me and I paid her a small sum to take care of my flowers, with the result that I had geraniums, impatiens, and day lilies. And she helped paint my ga-rage, white with green trim. She wore shorts and T-shirts. To my disappointment it was clear that she wouldn't be a child much longer.

As I have said, the IIR met throughout the summer, but there was a restlessness about them and there were tensions within the group. I can't believe that Chihani encouraged this, though possibly he didn't notice. But according to Barry, Aaron encouraged it. He despised a smooth surface. For several days in July, he spent all his time with Joany Rustoff, taking her to the movies and going swimming. Per-haps he was trying to make her his soldier as well, whatever that meant. This bothered Harriet and Bob Jenks. Then Aaron stopped seeing her, which upset Joany herself. They didn't have sex, I don't think, but at first he seemed to like her, then he seemed indifferent. She was blond, pretty, and wore tight jeans and halter tops. She had a little turned-up nose like movie actresses from the fifties and she took pride in it in the way some people take pride in their brains. She rarely wore makeup but she wore it during those days when Aaron was courting her. Then it was over and Joany went back to Bob.

Tension also existed between Barry and Oscar Herbst. Oscar despised Barry. He disliked that Barry was albino and disliked that he was gay, because Barry had admitted being gay in one of Chihani's self-criticism sessions. Oscar disliked that Aaron treated Barry as his personal pet. Perhaps Oscar wanted this position himself, but it led him to try and split Barry off from Aaron.

And Jesse and Shannon displayed a recklessness, getting drunk in bars and being loud. And how else to explain Harriet's affair with Ryan but recklessness? When they were seen on the street or driving by in Ryan's Escort, she was literally hanging on him. Indeed, extravagant behavior became increasingly apparent among them all as the summer wore on.

For instance, there was the party they had in early August, which Aaron arranged. It was to be a midnight party in Homeland Cemetery at the edge of town. I'm not sure that the others, except Oscar Herbst, really wanted to go. Leon Stahl, who disliked walking, especially through a cemetery, stated several times that he wasn't "a party animal." Barry didn't want to go but neither did he want to be left at home. I expect Joany and Bob Jenks went in order to show that they were unaffected by Aaron's flirtation with Joany some weeks earlier. Harriet went and broke a date with Ryan to do so. In the end, even Leon had second thoughts and said that if he taped his knees maybe it would be all right. As it turned out, he was better off having stayed at home.

The group had a small boom box. They had paper cups, a gallon of orange juice, and a half gallon of vodka. They had several six packs and I believe they had pretzels.

"No balloons?" I asked Barry later.

"Stop it," he said.

Barry said he constantly imagined a bony hand reaching from a tomb to grab his leg or poking up from the ground to snatch at the cuff of his pants. As a result, he tried to stay in the center of the group and kept bumping and jostling the others until they grew quite annoyed. Perhaps they were all nervous. After all, they were trespassing and it was midnight. There was only a quarter moon, but Aaron had a flashlight, as did Shannon and Bob Jenks. Barry hadn't thought to bring one.

Near the center of the cemetery was a slab of granite in front of an obelisk about fifteen feet tall. This was the family plot of Hyram Peabody, a nineteenth-century Aurelius banker. The slab was eight feet by six feet and across it was written: "The Spirit of Progress Was His Constant Charge." On either side of the obelisk were smaller tombstones, belonging to Hyram Peabody, his wife, and his sons and daughters, several of whom had died as young children. The oaks in that part of the cemetery were quite old and near the obelisk stood five or six dignified marble tombs with Greek pillars. One, belonging to Cyrus Tucker, was as big as a small cottage.

When I was in high school in the late fifties and early sixties, it was said that daring couples came at night to have sex on Hyram Peabody's slab of granite, and several times fellow students claimed to have seen condoms in the grass or on the stone itself, though who knows if they told the truth.

The granite slab was Aaron's destination. They would dance on it. They would drink screwdrivers, be obscene, and discuss Marx. As they made their way between the graves, Aaron teased the others by saying, "What's that over there?" or "Did you hear that?" Then they would crowd closer together.

Shannon set the boom box at the base of the obelisk. Aaron put on the Doors. Oscar made drinks. Bob and Joany danced to the *Mahagonny* song about the moon over Alabama: "Oh, show me the way to the next whiskey bar." They danced jerkily, ironically. Jason turned his back to the others, then crossed his arms, putting his hands over his shoulders and undulating his body so that he seemed to be embracing somebody even thinner than he was.

"Give it to her," said Shannon.

"Ya-hoo," said Jesse.

Barry stood as close to Aaron as he could without touching him. He was afraid to sit; he imagined the ground's opening up and his being sucked inside. He didn't know why he had agreed to come. Wherever he looked, he saw something potentially terrifying.

"What's the difference," asked Oscar, "between epistemological dialectics, ontological dialectics, and relational dialectics? Whoever gets it rights gets a blow job from Joany."

"Shut up," said Joany indignantly.

"Then from Harriet," said Oscar.

"Leon could answer," said Barry, feeling he should stand up for the one person smart enough not to attend.

"That's why we didn't want him here," said Oscar.

"I'd hate to blow Leon," said Harriet. She laughed and Aaron laughed with her.

Barry felt a wave of terror that Joany or Harriet would want to touch his penis with their mouths. He drank his screwdriver. He couldn't taste the vodka but he knew it was there. The flashlights made zigzagging patterns of light across the ground.

"Do people die because they deserve to die?" asked Jason.

"They die because they're old and sick," said Harriet.

"They die because they're bored," said Aaron.

The moon shone through the leaves of the oaks. Harriet had set six candles on either side of the boom box. Though the night seemed windless, the candle flames flickered as if to the music.

Aaron and Bob Jenks began discussing pauperization and the difference between relative and absolute pauperization. They had both had several drinks. Bob said that pauperization was now mostly confined to peripheral third-world countries.

Oscar Herbst said, "Let's fuck a pauper!"

"Hey," said Shannon, "paupers are our people. Let's fuck a capitalist."

"A dead capitalist," said Jesse.

"I bet we can push over some of these stones," said Oscar. He pushed at the obelisk but it didn't move.

"Don't!" said Barry.

"Hey," said Oscar, "Little Pink doesn't want to upset the sleeping capitalists."

"Yow, wow, wow!" howled Jesse.

"Be quiet," said Harriet. "You want someone to call the police?"

"This stone's loose," called Shannon from five yards away.

"That's a small one," said Aaron indignantly. "Clearly that belonged to a poor person, one of the impoverished."

Oscar began pushing at a larger stone belonging to Wilhelm Bockman, who had owned a knitting mill in Aurelius. "Come on," said Oscar. Jesse and Shannon joined him. They rocked the stone back and forth. Barry covered his ears. He was sure something terrible would happen. The stone was about six feet high. Bob and Jason joined them; Joany pushed as well. The stone teetered, then fell backward with a thud.

"That fixes the fucker," said Oscar.

"Who else?" asked Shannon.

"Let's push over the obelisk," said his brother.

They began pushing it, but it wouldn't budge. Aaron helped. The obelisk soil wouldn't move.

"Come on, Little Pink," said Aaron.

"No."

"Do what I say."

"I don't want to," said Barry. He turned his back to the others but it made him feel too alone, so he turned around again.

"Fucking capitalists," said Oscar. "Let's get more stones."

In the next half hour, they pushed over ten tombstones. Barry stood by the obelisk, mostly by himself. He found some comfort from Jim Morrison's voice but the song scared him: When the music's over, turn out the light.

At one point Harriet joined him. "You're a sissy," she said. There was a hint of kindness in her voice.

"I know it. I'm sorry."

"Don't tell the police." Her face was a pale circle in the darkness.

"I'd never do that."

"You'll make a silly revolutionary, Little Pink."

"I don't want to be a revolutionary," he said.

After a while the others came back to the Peabody obelisk. Oscar threw himself on the ground and appeared to go to sleep. Shannon and Jesse drank beer. Aaron made several screwdrivers and handed them to Harriet, Jason, and Bob.

Barry reached for one.

"You don't get one," said Aaron. "You've been bad."

Oscar was lying on his stomach with his face in the grass. "Bad, bad, bad," he said.

"Cancel my subscription to the resurrection," sang Jim Morrison.

Aaron looked around, first in one direction, then another. "My mother's buried in here," he said.

"The murdered lady," said Bob Jenks.

"I think she's over there," Aaron said. He began walking to his left. Harriet went after him. The others watched. Oscar jumped to his feet and followed. Shannon and Jesse went as well.

Barry was left by himself. He looked around, then ran after Jesse. "Wait up," he called.

Janice McNeal's grave was in a recent part of Homeland; its tall rectangular stone still looked new. There were flowers on the grave and Barry wondered who had put them there. Aaron, Bob, and Shannon shone their flashlights on the stone.

"Should we knock it over?" asked Oscar.

"Don't even try," said Aaron.

"What was she like?" asked Harriet.

Aaron didn't answer at first. Then he said, "She liked to get fucked."

Nobody said anything.

"She liked to jack men off and see their jism shoot into the air."

"She told you that?" asked Harriet.

"Other men told me," said Aaron. "They thought I should know what my mother was like. I can sit in Bud's Tavern and some drunk will come up and say, 'Your mother liked to jack me off.'"

A car passed on the street.

"Fuckers," said Shannon. The beam from his flashlight danced on Janice's tombstone.

Aaron appeared to get angry. "You think there's something wrong with jacking somebody off? Maybe she liked it. She liked lots of stuff."

"What do you think about her murder?" asked Barry. He didn't quite mean it that way. He wanted to know if Aaron suspected someone of having done it.

"What the hell do you think he thinks?" asked Jason.

"It seems to me," said Oscar, "that Little Pink's been getting away with a lot tonight."

"Shame on Little Pink," said Shannon.

"He didn't help with the capitalist stones," said Jesse.

"I think," said Oscar, "that it would be honoring Janice McNeal's memory if we gave her Little Pink's pants."

Shannon laughed. "Great," he said.

"And underpants," said Oscar.

Barry stepped back but was immediately grabbed and pushed to the ground. Shannon knelt on his shoulders as Oscar and Jesse began to work on his belt buckle. The others stood back, then Bob Jenks joined them as well.

Barry struggled. "No!" he cried, and Shannon put a hand over his mouth. They pulled off Barry's sneakers, then began tugging at his pants. As he twisted back and forth, he could see Aaron and Harriet standing above him, looking down at him. Harriet had a little smile. Aaron's face showed nothing at all.

When Barry's pants and underpants had been removed, Shannon and Jesse continued to hold him down. Oscar stood up and focused his flashlight on Barry's genitals.

"No wonder they call you Little Pink," he said.

"Hey, Barry," said Shannon, "when do you think it'll start growing?"

They continued to joke about his penis.

"Maybe it needs vitamins," suggested Joany.

"Or Rapid-Gro," said Bob.

Aaron didn't say anything. He looked at Barry, then looked away. Barry squeezed his eyes shut and wanted to disappear.

Oscar draped Barry's pants over Janice's tombstone.

"Oh dear departed one," he said, "we place this tribute upon your tomb so you will know that you have our unending devotion."

They shone the flashlights on the tombstone. Hanging down, the legs of Barry's jeans made an upside-down V bracketing Janice's name.

"Let's get out of here," said Aaron. "I'm bored."

Oscar grabbed the pants and ran off toward the street. Jesse followed and Shannon ran off as well. The others hurried after them. Barry stayed on the ground with his hands over his eyes. He realized he was lying above Janice's remains. He didn't move. The dark grew darker. A night bird called. After another moment, he could hear nothing at all.

Barry kept his hands over his eyes. "Little Pink," he said out loud. "Little Pink." In the silence, it was as if he were shouting. He no longer heard the others, but then a car rushed away squealing its tires. He still expected to be dragged down among the dead, but now he wanted it to happen.

But nothing happened. Barry lay there for nearly an hour, then he got too cold. He made his way to the street. They had taken his shoes as well. By his watch he saw it was three-thirty in the morning. He stepped on gravel and hurt his bare feet.

"Little Pink," he said out loud.

Once he got to the street, he stood behind a tree. There were no cars and the houses were dark. It was a mile to where he lived. It was less to his mother's house, but he couldn't go there. Barry imagined walking across town without his pants. He was bound to be seen. He wanted to stay in the cemetery and never leave. He felt the dead were lucky.

Around four-thirty he heard a car. He hid behind the tree. The car pulled up in front of the fence and a door opened.

"Barry!"

It was Aaron.

Barry came out from behind the tree.

Aaron stood by the fence. He held Barry's pants. He looked at Barry, then tossed his pants to him.

"Get in the car," he said.

Twelve

Aaron was ten years older than Sadie, surely too much to make them contemporaries, though I have friends ten years my junior or senior and I see them as contemporaries. But Sadie was thirteen. No one approved of their friendship and Sadie was warned against it. Just the fact that Aaron was interested in Sadie was taken as evidence that something was wrong. And that was another point: Why was Aaron interested in Sadie, why did he want to spend time with her? It is one of the complications of life that nothing is done for one reason. There may be many reasons, both conscious and unconscious. My favorite chair for reading is the one in which my mother used to read to me. Yet when I moved back to this house, I didn't realize it was the same chair, even though I probably sat in it for several hours each evening. It had been reupholstered from a dark brown fabric to a light blue fabric with yellow flowers. It wasn't even the most comfortable chair in the living room; the arms were lumpy and the seat sagged. Yet something led me to pick it out as my reading chair. Psychologically, it was the chair most comfortable for me. This is an example of an unconscious reason.

Aaron may have liked Sadie because she was uncorrupted and looked at the world with wonder. That certainly was one of my reasons for liking her: her vision was not yet jaded. Beyond that she was energetic and enthusiastic, courteous and pretty. And she had a sense of humor, a delight in the slightly peculiar that I found charming, such as the stories she made up about my fetal pig or the nearly hairless rat in its jar of formaldehyde, which she named Tooslow and for which she invented adventures where nothing turned out right.

Aaron must have had some other reasons too. Given his history, he was familiar with the dark side of human life. With Sadie there was no dark side, or perhaps she was pre-dark side. Even the idealism of the IIR, as foolish as it seemed, was based on the hope that the dark side could be erased from human experience by changing human institutions, though I'm sure this insight would have surprised some of its members. That idealism, however, was one of the reasons Aaron had joined, even if he had half a dozen others. Sadie's innocence attracted us both. On the other hand, I would never have done anything to put Sadie in danger, but that didn't seem entirely true of Aaron.

Ten days after the graveyard incident Aaron took Sadie to a flooded quarry several miles east of Aurelius to go swimming. It was private property and the sheriff's department patrolled it because over the years there had been three or four drownings. There was also old machinery either under water or poking up through the surface: contortions of rusted metal so deteriorated it was impossible to guess its original function. Franklin would have been upset had he known that Aaron was taking Sadie to such a dangerous place, but he knew nothing about it until later.

I gather that Sadie had been begging Aaron to take her all summer and so perhaps he wasn't one hundred percent guilty. On the other hand, he had told her about the quarry and had probably made it sound exciting. People went swimming in the quarry when I was a boy and even then it was known as dangerous. I never went myself for fear of making my mother angry.

Aaron parked his old Toyota under some trees about a mile away and they hiked across the cornfields and through a patch of woods to the quarry's edge. Sadie had made salami sandwiches and they had a six pack of Pepsi in a small cooler. It was mid-August and hot. A blue, cloudless day. Cicadas were whining. It hadn't rained for over a week and everything was dry. They left Aurelius around ten and reached the quarry an hour later. Sadie had wanted to bring her dog, Shadow, a black cocker spaniel who hated exercise, but Aaron told her to leave it behind.

The incident at Homeland Cemetery had drawn a lot of attention but no one was charged and the vandals remained unknown. There was an article in the *Independent* and Franklin had written an editorial about how the character of the present could be judged by its respect for the past. A dozen tombstones had been tipped over and one was cracked in half. Many beer cans had been found. It was assumed that high school students were responsible. No one seemed to suspect the IIR, though some people must have. A few months later and the IIR would be suspected of everything from stealing missing dogs to throwing trash on the streets. A local Boy Scout troop volunteered to clean up the graveyard and the police patrolled more carefully.

When Sadie mentioned the graveyard to Aaron, he admitted he had been there.

"Did you tip over tombstones?" asked Sadie.

"A couple. They were heavy."

They had reached the quarry and were following a dirt path around the edge, a low bluff above the water. The pond was about a hundred and fifty yards across and had a ragged oval shape. Four boys were jumping into the water from a tree branch on the other side and a dog was barking.

"Weren't you scared of getting in trouble?"

"We didn't think about it. The dead don't care and the living weren't around."

"Why'd you do it?"

"Boredom, I expect."

They chose an open spot by the water where three logs made a triangle. A fire had once been built in the center, leaving a dark burned place. Beyond the logs a bluff rose up about twenty feet above the water. Sumac grew along the shore. Aaron and Sadie were directly across the quarry from the four boys, who were at the end of a dirt track where sheriff's deputies now and then appeared. The dog kept barking. One of the boys shied a stone at it but missed.

Aaron, who was often silent with others, was talkative with Sadie. I'm not sure he was really different with her, but he appeared less guarded, less ironic. He, too, had grown up in Aurelius and seemed a happy child. The change came in his teens. Superficially, it could be blamed on Hark Powers, but Hark simply represented the world. One could also blame Aaron's change on the arrival of puberty and an awareness of his mother's life. His father's life, too, for that matter.

Aaron would talk to Sadie about what he read—the history, philosophy, and social fiction that he had from Chihani—but also about growing up in Aurelius, delivering papers with his dog, and his own visits to the quarry when he was even younger than Sadie.

He mentioned leaving Aurelius. "Not right away. But I've been thinking I'd like to get a motorcycle and ride through southern Mexico—Chiapas and the Yucatán—where they've been trying to start that revolution."

"What revolution?" asked Sadie. They had unpacked their lunch and were eating the sandwiches. Aaron had taken off his shirt and wore a pair of black swimming trunks that came halfway down his skinny thighs. He sat on the ground leaning against a boulder. Sadie sat on a log. She wore cutoff jeans over a green tank suit. She had long legs, much longer than her torso. On her knees were the traces of roller-skating scars from years before.

"Revolutions are about a redistribution of power," said Aaron. "A guy has a stick and he uses it to whack the people around him, till someone takes it away. Then someone else has the stick for a while. And *he* whacks at the people around him. In southern Mexico it's the Indians against the landowners."

"Does there always have to be a revolution?"

"Not necessarily. You want to get the stick from the guy who's whacking you—revolution's the last thing you try."

"Could you do your work down there?"

"Wherever there's a phone line."

"What do you do as an analyst? Do people tell you their problems?"

Aaron laughed. "I only analyze data. Dead things. Right now I'm analyzing the database of a hospital in New York to help them determine whether it would pay to expand their department of obstetrics and gynecology."

Sadie wrinkled her nose. "That doesn't sound exciting."

"You'd be surprised at how peaceful it is. Every bit of information finds its little home."

"And what do you plan to do after the revolution?"

"Anyone who makes plans for after the revolution is a reactionary. At least that's what Marx said." Aaron took a can of Pepsi from the cooler, opened it, and handed it to Sadie. "If a guy has a stick, he'll use it to whack people around him unless there are laws to stop him. He did it when people lived in caves and he'll do it when people travel in rockets."

"He's a bully," said Sadie.

"Everybody's got a bully in him someplace." Aaron paused to wonder if that was true. "At least that's what I think." He poked at his bare feet. They were big feet with long toes. He could pick up pebbles with them.

"Do I have a bully in me?" Sadie asked, teasing a little.

"Maybe. You have to get a stick first."

"Did you bite Hark Powers because he was a bully?"

"I bit him because I was sick."

"What about Sheila Murphy?"

"I was angry with her but I was sick then, too."

"Were you angry with her because she wouldn't . . . you know?"

"I was angry because she wouldn't answer my questions."

"What kind of questions?"

"Just questions."

"Are you still sick?"

Aaron scratched the top of his head. "I'm not sure."

Sadie started to ask something else, stopped, then asked, "What did his ear taste like?"

Aaron took a mouthful of Pepsi and rolled it around in his mouth. "Waxy," he said, "like a waxy piece of salami. I wouldn't recommend it."

"What does it mean to be sick?"

"It means doing something and knowing you shouldn't do it but doing it anyway."

"Did you come back to Aurelius because you're sick?"

"No, I had clear reasons for coming back here."

"To learn about revolution, to join the IIR?"

"I'd decided to come back before that."

"Did you come back because of your mother?"

"Partly. I want to find out who killed her."

Sadie lowered her voice. "Do you have any ideas?"

"It was one of her boyfriends and it's someone who's good at staying hidden. Maybe a priest, maybe a doctor, maybe a cop."

"So you have people in mind?"

"Sure." Aaron stood up. "Hey, aren't we going swimming?"

"What about Harriet?" asked Sadie, not quite finished with her questions.

Aaron stood ankle-deep in the water. "What about her?"

"Do you love her?"

"She's a friend," he said. "And she's my soldier."

"Do you have other girlfriends?"

"Lots."

"Do you have sex with all of them?"

Aaron grinned, then his face grew serious. "Just about." He dove in the water and swam out about twenty-five feet, then he turned and dog-paddled as he called to her, "Are you coming in?" He flicked his head to get his hair out of his eyes.

"Are there snakes?"

"You think they'll mess with you?"

Sadie dove in as well. Aaron swam with his head out of the water. Sadie swam as she had been taught on the swim team. Aaron tried to catch her but she was faster. He rolled over on his back and kicked his way back to shore. His body was very white, as if he hadn't taken off his shirt all summer. He was thin and his ribs stuck out. Sadie swam after him.

Aaron scrambled out of the water and began climbing the dirt path to the top of the bluff.

"Are you going to jump from there?" called Sadie.

"Why not?"

The bluff wasn't a perfect ninety degrees so Aaron had to run to clear the shore. His long hair fanned out behind him. He pulled up his knees as he fell and hit the water about ten feet out. A spray of water rose around him. Aaron swam to shore. When he got to the bluff again, Sadie was looking over the edge.

"It's scary," she said. The drop seemed as high as a small house and there was the danger of not jumping out far enough.

"Only if you think about it."

"Is it deep?"

"Deep enough." Aaron moved back about twenty feet and ran. When he jumped, he spread out his arms and yelled. He hit the water and for about thirty seconds he didn't reappear. Then he popped up a few yards from where he had gone under the surface.

"Don't do it if you don't want to," he called. He swam back to shore. Sadie was again looking down from the edge.

"It's a long way," she said.

"That's what makes it fun," said Aaron. "Just make sure you jump out far enough." He climbed onto a boulder to watch.

She disappeared from sight and Aaron waited. Then she suddenly reappeared and flew into the air, white and slender. She shrieked and kept her body straight, descending feet first. She hit the water about eight feet from the shore.

When Sadie broke the surface again, Aaron saw from her face that something was wrong.

"I hit something," she cried. "It hurts."

Aaron jumped off the boulder, then waded into the water to get her. He lost his balance and went under, then spluttered to the surface. Sadie swam to shore. He grabbed her arm and they both scrambled up onto the bank. Sadie's left leg was bleeding.

"Something was down there," she said. "I scraped it." Her teeth were clenched.

Aaron bent down by her leg, trying to wipe away the blood to see the size of the cut. It kept bleeding. He cupped his hands into the water and washed her leg. The cut was a deep scrape from her knee up along her thigh.

"Can you stand up?"

"It hurts."

Aaron took his towel, soaked it in the water, then wrapped it around Sadie's thigh. "I'll get you to a doctor." He began putting on his shoes.

Half supporting her, he got Sadie across the fields to his car. She was light enough that he could have easily carried her.

Sadie didn't say anything. She was trying to concentrate on not crying. She kept pursing her lips. Aaron didn't say anything either. If he felt responsible, he didn't mention it.

Aaron meant to take her to the emergency room at the hospital, but by the time they got to town the bleeding had stopped. "I don't need to go to the hospital," said Sadie.

They discussed it. At last they decided to stop by the drugstore and take care of the leg themselves.

There were two drugstores in Aurelius: Fays Drugs in the strip mall and Malloy's Pharmacy on Main Street. Donald Malloy had moved to Aurelius from Buffalo some years before, following his brother, Allen, a doctor and the father of Sadie's friend Sharon. Donald Malloy was a heavy man in his midforties with sandy red hair and a red face. He wore a white coat with his name across the breast pocket in red lettering. He was alone in the pharmacy. A woman by the name of Mildred Porter also worked with him but she was on her lunch break.

Malloy urged Aaron to take Sadie to a doctor.

"It's stopped bleeding," said Aaron. "We can take care of it ourselves."

"Let me see it," said Malloy. He had a high, reedy voice. Sadie said his breath smelled sweet, as if he had been eating mints.

Sadie sat up on the counter by the old-fashioned chrome cash register. Malloy took the towel off her leg. The scrape was about twelve inches long.

"Nasty," he said. "You should have a tetanus shot." He cleaned the cut with alcohol, which caused Sadie to squeeze Aaron's hand. "You're a brave girl. What's your name?"

"Sadie Moore."

Malloy mentioned that he knew her father, then he nodded to Aaron. "And I'm sure I know you but I don't recall . . ."

"Aaron McNeal."

"Ahh," said Malloy. He returned to cleaning the rest of Sadie's thigh with a piece of cotton.

"Is my reputation that bad?" asked Aaron, intending a joke. "You probably knew my parents too."

"Yes," said Malloy, "I remember them both." He seemed on the brink of saying more but then changed his mind. He had large pink hands and the fingernails were perfectly manicured. Taking a tube of ointment, he dabbed it on and around the cut. Then, very precisely, he set a square of gauze on top. He paused and gestured to a ring on the middle finger of Sadie's left hand, a cheap silver ring, engraved with a dove, that Aaron had given her.

"Why do you wear that ring?" asked Donald.

"It's pretty. A friend gave it to me."

"Do you know what it means?"

"Does it have to mean something?"

"All creatures have meanings. For instance, a lion might mean courage or it might mean the great beast in the Book of Revelation."

"I suppose a dove means peace and friendship," said Sadie. "Even love." Her cheeks reddened a little.

"Those are some of its meanings," said Donald. He began to put tape around the gauze.

"What else does it mean?" asked Aaron. He stood beside Sadie, resting a hand on her shoulder.

"It could signify the divine victim, or even hope."

"What do dogs mean?" asked Sadie, with more interest.

"It depends on the breed. Most simply they signify fidelity." When Donald had finished with the tape, he patted Sadie's knee. "Don't forget the tetanus shot. My brother can do it or his nurse. Go over there right now and I'll call him."

Sadie touched the bandage, which was precisely aligned on her leg with the white tape running vertically and horizontally like a professionally drawn game of tic-tac-toe. "This is great," said Sadie. "You should have been a doctor."

"My brother got there first," said Donald. Then he smiled.

"How much do I owe you?" asked Aaron.

Malloy shook his head. "It's my good deed for the day."

The pharmacy was cluttered with displays of greeting cards, magazines, coolers with soft drinks and ice cream. Near the door was a large basket of volleyballs and basketballs. Next to it were boxes of badminton sets.

"You want anything?" Aaron asked Sadie. He felt they should buy something after Malloy's kindness.

"We were going to get a volleyball," said Sadie.

"Good idea," said Aaron. He chose one and tossed it to Sadie. Then he paid for the ball.

As Malloy handed Aaron his change, he asked, "Didn't your father move to Utica?"

"He's teaching high school there." Aaron's tone suggested that he was speaking of a distant acquaintance.

"And you have a sister, if I'm not mistaken?"

Aaron laughed. "She's Sadie's father's girlfriend. You see how incestuous it gets?"

He put his arm around Sadie's waist and helped her out of the store. Malloy watched them go.

Aaron took Sadie to the doctor's for her tetanus shot, then drove her home. That night when Franklin saw her bandaged leg, he asked what had happened. In telling him the story, Sadie didn't think to hold anything back. After all, it had been an adventure.

Thirteen

Ryan Tavich lived alone in a brick bungalow on Jackson Street, where he had been since first moving to Aurelius in the late 1970s. It had two maples in the front yard and no backyard to speak of. I knew one of his neighbors, Whitey Sherman, and Whitey said it often seemed that no one lived in Ryan's house, that the house appeared vacant. I might have suspected something bizarre, but Franklin had been in Ryan's house and he said that nothing could be plainer. The only peculiarity was that Ryan's two living room chairs had been scratched to ribbons by his cat, a large black and white animal with extremely fluffy fur named Chief.

Ryan had a collection of jazz records and in the basement he had his weights. There was nothing on the walls except over the fireplace, where he had hung a picture showing a pheasant skimming the tops of yellow cornstalks. And there was a small bookcase, though Ryan got most of his books from the library and wasn't much of a reader anyway. On top of the bookcase was a stereo and an electronic chess game. In the corner was a locked wooden cabinet where Ryan kept his hunting rifles and shotguns. He had had several dogs, setters mostly, but he didn't have one now because he didn't want to upset the cat.

When Ryan left in the morning, he'd shout, "Guard the house, Chief." And when he came home at night, he'd call out, "What's new, Chief?" In the interim Chief would tear up the furniture.

Ryan Tavich was originally from Oneonta, but he left when he was eighteen and joined the army. Although the Vietnam War was going on, he was sent to Korea, where, as he told Franklin, "I froze my ass off."

Franklin had done an interview with Ryan several years earlier. It wasn't one of his better ones, either because Ryan gave nothing away or because he had little to say about himself. After the service, he worked for a security company in Albany as a guard, went to the police academy, then worked as a patrolman in Cohoes before taking a job in Aurelius. Police are poorly paid in small towns and the jobs attract men who either can't do better or want to be in the town for a specific reason. Ryan fit neither category. He was good at his job and could work anywhere in the country. Instead, he settled in Aurelius, which was our gain, but I sympathized with how he was gossiped about, as if he had a secret in his past.

He had few friends other than Franklin, and Ralph Belmont, the undertaker, and Charlie Kirby at the YMCA, but he had great loyalty to them. Consider, for instance, the hours he spent with Sadie, taking her fishing and even hunting. I assumed he used these occasions to praise Paula McNeal or to convince Sadie that she was harmless, but Sadie said that he never mentioned Paula.

Though Ryan dated a number of women, he never dated one for long. Sometimes he broke it off and sometimes the woman broke it off, but if the woman broke it off it was because she knew there was no future in the relationship, that Ryan wouldn't settle down on someone else's terms. The exception was Janice McNeal. It was Franklin's opinion that what made Janice different was her sexuality. She was the kind of woman who completely controlled whatever man she was with and perhaps Ryan liked that.

Franklin said that Ryan still talked about her and talked about her sexuality.

"She would describe how each man's come tasted different," he had told Franklin. "How some was sweet and some tasteless and some tasted bitter. I asked about mine and she said it ranked between sweet and tasteless."

And who did Ryan think had killed her?

"I'm sure it was someone in town. Someone who came to her house on foot and left on foot."

Could it have been a woman?

"A woman wouldn't have strangled her."

Sometimes Ryan struck me as dense. I would think that he lacked all imagination, that he was someone who hadn't married or found a companion because he was perfectly happy in his own company. But I was also jealous of his relationship with Sadie and must not criticize him unjustly. At times he seemed no more than a dark block of wood, but maybe that was because he wasn't very tall and because his weight training had made him so rectangular. I should say he was someone with whom I rarely spoke.

But he gave the impression of loss, of secrets, and it was easy to imagine something's having happened in his childhood or even in the service in Korea. Franklin said that Ryan's parents were dead but he had a sister in Corning. I believe she was married to a man who worked for the glass company. More likely Ryan was like a plant that never develops. He lacked the final something that makes a person link with life, become part of the flow of life. And perhaps I wasn't entirely comfortable with him because the same thing could be said of me.

I often wish that people had little screens in their chests, small television monitors, that you could flick on and see the interior lives within. I don't mean blood pumping and lungs flexing, but what they think and worry about and love. Because otherwise it is all speculation and observing their actions, then coming up with a few possibilities that one tries to shift into the realm of probabilities.

For five weeks during July and August Ryan dated Harriet Malcomb and saw her often. I assumed what brought them together was purely sexual, because what would they have to talk about? But later I found that was not entirely the case. Then Ryan broke up with her, primarily because of her involvement in the vandalism of Homeland Cemetery. He didn't report it, even though he understood it made him an accomplice after the fact. It seems he was unsure of Harriet for other reasons too. As he told Franklin, "She asks too many questions about Janice."

Three weeks after Ryan stopped seeing Harriet, the phony bomb was found at Albert Knox Consolidated School. Right from the start, Ryan conducted his own investigation with officers on the Aurelius police force. I say that because the state police were also investigating. But ever since Janice's murder, Ryan hadn't had a good relationship with the state police. Though he worked with them on a hundred other matters, he couldn't forget how he had been removed from the McNeal case. Professionally, he knew that the state police's behavior had been correct, but personally he found it unforgivable. That was another trait of Ryan's: he had a long memory. He didn't treat the state police with anger, he simply remembered, with the result that if there was a case in which they were involved he might not tell them all he knew.

One Friday morning ten days after the bomb had been found at Knox Consolidated, Ryan left his office about nine without saying where he was going. This was not especially odd, but Patty McClosky, Chief Schmidt's secretary, said she saw him checking his pistol and putting a pair of handcuffs in his pocket. Privately, Patty called him Old Silent.

Ryan took an unmarked police car, a gray Ford Taurus, and drove over toward Aurelius College, which had been in session since the end of August. It was one of those cool sunny days that make you realize that summer is gone and something new is beginning. Kids were in school and the streets were quiet.

Ryan parked on Juniper Street near the corner of Spruce, a few blocks from the Aurelius campus. He locked the car, checked a piece of paper he took from his pocket, then walked half a block back to 335 Juniper, a white Victorian house that had been broken up into six apartments rented by students. The house needed paint, the front porch sagged, and the front lawn was a mixture of weeds and bare dirt scarred with tire tracks. Two empty Budweiser cans lay on the porch.

Ryan Tavich entered the house. Oscar Herbst rented an apartment on the second floor. Ryan checked the number on the door against the number written on the paper, then he knocked.

After a moment, Ryan heard a muffled voice. "Who is it?"

"Police," said Ryan.

He waited. Then he knocked again, louder. He paused and listened at the door. Quickly, he stepped back and kicked at the lock. The door flew open. Ryan ran into the room. He started to draw his pistol, then didn't bother.

Oscar, wearing a T-shirt and jeans but barefooted, was halfway out the window. Ryan grabbed him by his belt and yanked him into the room. Stumbling, Oscar fell to the floor. He darted a look at Ryan, then jumped to his feet and ran toward the door. Ryan grabbed him again, a little rougher this time.

"Stop it," said Ryan.

Oscar again tried running for the door.

Ryan grabbed him, slapped him, then put the handcuffs on him. Oscar was about four inches shorter than Ryan.

"We're going to the police station," said Ryan. "Do you want your shoes?"

Oscar licked at the stud in his lip. "Fuck you," he said.

Ryan took the shoes anyway.

On the street, Oscar tried to run again, but Ryan held him by the back of his neck. "You want me to carry you?" said Ryan.

He put Oscar in the backseat of the Taurus, then drove to police headquarters.

"You still fucking Harriet?" said Oscar behind him.

Ryan didn't bother to answer.

"You should be scared of me," said Oscar.

At headquarters, Ryan took Oscar into his office and shut the door.

Patty McClosky saw all this. A few minutes later when Phil Schmidt left his office to play racquetball at the Y, Patty said, "Ryan's got a college student in his office. He's got handcuffs on him."

Schmidt shifted his weight from one foot to the other. He hated to be late for his racquetball games. Just then Ryan came out of his office with Oscar.

"This kid's confessed to planting those bombs," he said.

Ryan booked Oscar and put him in a cell. He left it to Phil Schmidt to call the state police.

Though Oscar had confessed, he also claimed to have acted on his own. A man walking his dog early in the morning had seen him outside Knox Consolidated, and another witness had placed Oscar outside Pickering Elementary School the week before.

"They weren't real bombs," said Oscar. "It was a joke."

That same Friday and over the weekend, Ryan talked to the other members of Inquiries into the Right, including Houari Chihani. All claimed to know nothing of Oscar's actions.

The problem was Aaron. Ryan was positive that he knew more than he was telling, but Ryan had a complicated relationship with Aaron. After all, he was still in love with Aaron's dead mother.

"I don't know anything about those bombs," said Aaron. "Oscar must have been acting on his own."

"He never said anything about it?" asked Ryan.

"Not to me he didn't." He spoke coolly to Ryan, as if he disliked him.

Aaron kept Ryan standing in the hall outside his apartment door. Ryan wondered if Harriet was with him and he imagined her naked body in Aaron's bed. She, too, had told Ryan that she knew nothing about the bombs.

Franklin interviewed Oscar in jail. Because Oscar was arrested on Friday and the paper didn't come out until the next Thursday, everybody knew about the arrest from the Utica and Syracuse papers long before the *Independent* was printed.

Oscar told Franklin, "They're lucky they weren't real bombs." Then he said, "Why don't you write a story about a cop fucking a student half his age?" And he called Franklin "a capitalist lackey."

"What's a lackey?" Sadie asked me when the paper came out.

"A servile follower," I told her.

"Like a servant?"

"Technically, I believe it's a footman."

Oscar spent the weekend in jail. On Monday his father drove down from Troy to bail him out. After talking to the judge, Mr. Herbst withdrew his son from Aurelius College and took him home. There would be pretrial hearings and other visits to Aurelius before the trial, but otherwise Oscar would stay in Troy.

The news that Oscar had planted the bombs was surprising and in trying to explain it people heard a lot about Inquiries into the Right. Questions were raised at the college and in the city council concerning the possibility of banning the group.

There was also an attempt to remove Houari Chihani from his position at Aurelius, but Chihani was used to such tactics and retained a lawyer. He was in the second semester of a three-year contract and unless wrongdoing could be proved against him he planned to stay every minute of his time. Of course he had no hope of being rehired at the end of his contract, but by then the whole matter was irrelevant in any case.

Ryan talked to Chihani in his home. Had he perhaps encouraged Oscar and the others?

"Why would I do such a thing?" said Chihani. "I am a philosopher. I am not a revolutionary."

"Don't you preach revolution?"

"I teach people to see clearly. I preach accuracy of vision."

"Don't you feel some responsibility?"

"None."

"What if it had been a real bomb?"

"But it wasn't."

"Oscar Herbst was your student."

"He has an excitable nature. That is a matter of genetics more than education. You would do better quizzing his parents."

"Do you know what conspiracy is?" asked Ryan.

"Conspiracy is something that needs to be proved in a court of law," said Chihani.

Franklin talked to Chihani as well.

"Education," said Chihani, "provides young people with information about the world. If those young people act upon that information, we cannot blame their teachers, just as we cannot blame the newspaper for the news that it prints. I am simply the medium for a particular kind of information."

"Don't you feel responsible for Inquiries into the Right?" asked Franklin.

"They are a study group, nothing more. They read books and meet to discuss them."

"Do you think one of these books set off Oscar Herbst?"

"We go back to the nature of information. It is possible that Oscar was driven to action by something he read. He's enthusiastic. In learning about the nature of the world, he grows indignant. That's not surprising, is it? But what worries me, Mr. Moore, is that you consider punishing the book and the teacher."

"I assure you I have no such intention."

"Then I do not understand the direction of your questions."

It seemed unlikely to some people that Ryan Tavich could have deduced Oscar's involvement without there having been an informer within the IIR. There was much speculation about this. Harriet swore she had told him nothing. After all, they had stopped seeing each other weeks before the bombs were found.

On the Sunday morning after Oscar's arrest, Barry was on his way to Aaron's apartment. The weather was mild and a few maples had begun to turn, branches of orange leaves on predominantly green trees. As Barry turned onto the sidewalk in front of Aaron's unit, he heard a car pull to a stop at the curb. He turned to see Jesse and Shannon getting out of their Chevy, recognizing their blond ponytails even before he saw their faces. Since Aaron had said nobody else would be coming over, Barry felt disappointed. Then he realized that Jesse and Shannon were angry. Barry hurried toward the door of Aaron's unit.

Jesse tackled him before Barry got halfway. When Barry tried to scramble to his feet, Jesse slapped him in the face, knocking off his glasses.

"You told," said Jesse.

"Told what?" asked Barry.

"Told about Oscar," said Jesse.

"No, I didn't. I swear I didn't."

Barry sat on the ground, rubbing his face with one hand and holding his glasses with the other. The bridge had snapped and he held the two pieces in his palm. He kept blinking. Without his glasses everything was bright and wobbly.

"You're lying," said Shannon.

Barry heard the front door of the apartment unit slam open, then he heard Aaron's voice. "Leave him alone."

"He told the cops about Oscar," said Shannon.

"Little Pink didn't tell anyone about anything," said Aaron.

"I bet I can make him talk," said Shannon.

Aaron put a hand on Shannon's arm. "Did you hear what I said?"

Barry couldn't see very well and the sunlight hurt his eyes. He could just make out Shannon's and Jesse's blond goatees. The brothers looked at each other. Jesse shrugged.

"Come on," said Shannon. They walked back to their car. Protruding from their skinny backs, their shoulder blades under their T-shirts looked like incipient wings.

Barry got to his feet. He rubbed his face where it had been slapped. "I didn't tell, I really didn't."

"Don't blubber," said Aaron. He took Barry's arm and began leading him to the door. "I know you didn't tell."

Fourteen

Oscar's arrest was accompanied by a sense of completion: a crazy thing had been done and a crazy person had been found responsible. Much was made of the fact that Oscar wore a gold lip stud. What wouldn't have made sense would have been for the culprit or culprits to be so-called normal teenagers known to everyone for years, although that had been feared. The only regret was that the rest of the IIR couldn't be tied to the bombs as well. Surely all ten members were involved and Chihani had encouraged them. At least this was argued. Because it was known that Franklin was seeing Paula McNeal, it was supposed that Franklin was protecting her half brother. And everyone knew of Ryan Tavich's relationship with Aaron's mother. There was much talk about a conspiracy of silence between these men, and the person who spoke most loudly about a conspiracy was Hark Powers. He would hold forth at Bud's Tavern on how Chihani and Aaron were plainly behind the phony bombs. Of course, since Aaron had bitten off Hark's ear, Hark's credibility was suspect. But people talked among themselves and it seemed unlikely that Oscar had acted on his own.

The rumors of Franklin's and Ryan's complicity grew so common that one morning Phil Schmidt called Ryan into his office. Schmidt had been police chief for twenty-five years and had come to see Aurelius as his personal property. He was a big man with a big stomach and he liked to rest his hands on it when he talked. He wore suits rather than uniforms, but they were suits that resembled uniforms:

blue and shiny. His wife, Gladys, worked at the post office and between them it seemed they knew everything to be known in Aurelius.

"I don't want to offend you, Ryan," said Schmidt, "but I need to ask one question."

Ryan knew what was coming. "I'm not trying to protect Aaron McNeal," he said.

"D'you think he was involved with those bombs?"

"Aaron denies it and Oscar says he did it by himself."

"Do you believe them?"

"I don't work according to belief, I work according to evidence." Ryan caught hold of his growing irritation and took a breath. "I know nothing more than I put in my report. And Franklin doesn't either, for that matter."

"Are you friendly with Aaron?"

"Are you kidding? He seems to hate me."

If Phil Schmidt was satisfied, others weren't. Chihani was grilled by the college president, Harvey Shavers. His secretary described how she could hear Shavers's booming voice and Chihani's dry voice going back and forth for an hour. At last Shavers gave up, apparently having learned nothing.

The Good Conduct Committee of the college queried the members of the IIR who were students. Since they hadn't been caught in any wrongdoing, they couldn't be punished, but Barry said they were reminded of the college's fine tradition.

"Wherever you go," Dean Phipps told them, "people don't see Jason Irving or Harriet Malcomb or Bob Jenks. They see Aurelius College."

Shannon Levine made half-audible pig noises with his hand covering his mouth, though Barry said that Shannon was scared. Had it been known they had vandalized the cemetery, they would have been expelled. Every week in the *Independent* there were indignant letters about the vandalism and every week Chief Schmidt said that the investigation was continuing.

Fear of conspiracy can be an insidious fear. The fact that the IIR claimed to be innocent was meaningless. People believed they were plotting. This very belief became a kind of evidence. Very few people felt the bombs were the end of it and most waited for a new transgression. Indeed, they looked forward to it.

Then something happened that almost wiped Oscar Herbst and his phony bombs from people's memory. But it didn't wipe them out completely and that was part of the problem.

Megan Kelly lived in a small white house at the edge of Aurelius, the last on Jefferson Street before the intersection with Adams, which along that stretch has Hapwood's Tire and several town storage sheds. The first house on Adams leaving town is a farmhouse, the Bells', a quarter of a mile from town. Megan Kelly was in her midsixties. Her husband, Winfred, had worked as assistant manager at the Trustworthy Hardware but he had died of a stroke five years earlier. They had had four daughters, all of whom had moved away. To supplement her Social Security, Mrs. Kelly cleaned people's houses.

Mrs. Kelly had worked for me for several months, cleaning every Thursday, but I found her something of a busybody and I let her go. She was too curious about my habits and too ready to offer advice as to how I should live my life. I tried to accept the fact that Mrs. Kelly was probably lonely and so took a strong interest in the people for whom she worked. Never did I suspect anything malicious about her interest or that she was a gossipmonger, but her attention to my life was a pressure I didn't feel I needed. This was partly my own sensitivity.

On Monday afternoon, September 18, Mrs. Kelly was tidying up her living room. "Puffing up the cushions," as she later explained. It was a little past three and by five-thirty she had to be over at Franklin Moore's, no more than a five-minute drive away. Glancing from her living room window, Mrs. Kelly saw Sharon Malloy on her bike on Adams Street, bicycling out of town. She assumed that Sharon was on her way to the Bells', whose daughter, Joyce, was Sharon's age. Sharon was wearing jeans and a blue crewneck sweater. On her back was a red canvas book bag. Her bike was a red and blue mountain bike called a Husky. School had gotten out about fifteen minutes earlier.

Sharon Malloy was fourteen years old and in ninth grade. Her family had moved to Aurelius from Rochester in the mid-1980s. Mrs. Kelly had gone to Dr. Malloy several times about her rheumatism. Though she liked him, she preferred doctors who were actually from Aurelius. Dr. Malloy was an outsider and Mrs. Kelly felt uncomfortable when he touched her. Not that he wasn't always courteous.

Mrs. Kelly noticed Sharon Malloy, that was all. Several cars went by but the only one she recognized was Houari Chihani's red Citroën. Mrs. Kelly knew that car—everybody did—and she thought about what she'd read in the *Independent* about how a friend of Mr. Chihani's, or maybe a student, had been arrested for leaving those bombs at the elementary school and high school. For Mrs. Kelly this was evidence of the creeping corruption of the cities, evidence of decay and dissolution, which was a phrase that Mrs. Kelly liked.

After another minute or so Mrs. Kelly went into her kitchen to fix herself a cup of tea. Her kitchen window was at the back of the house and also looked out on Adams, but it faced south rather than north. In the distance she could see the silo poking up by Frank Bell's barn. She expected to see Sharon Malloy again on her bicycle, but the girl wasn't there. Mrs. Kelly looked at her watch, then looked out the window again. She opened the kitchen door and went out on the back step.

Mrs. Kelly was not a suspicious person, but ever since she had discovered Janice McNeal's body nearly two years earlier she had come to every event expecting the worst. If she hadn't found Janice's body, she probably wouldn't have thought twice about not seeing Sharon. But in Mrs. Kelly's mind the world had grown craftier since Janice's murder and more perilous. Mrs. Kelly thought how first she had seen Sharon and now she didn't. But shouldn't Sharon be there? Mrs. Kelly again looked at her watch, then raised herself up on her tiptoes on her back step to improve her view. She was sure only a few minutes had passed. She didn't see how it was possible for Sharon to have reached the Bells' already.

Mrs. Kelly went back into her kitchen and as she waited for the teakettle to boil she thought about Sharon Malloy. If the girl had already reached the Bells', then it indicated that she herself had lost all track of time, which was a possibility that worried her. She had an older cousin in Munnsville whose memory was gone and her own mother had grown forgetful toward the end. Mrs. Kelly prided herself on the sharpness of her mind and this apparent slippage caused concern. But she also thought about Janice McNeal, not in an ominous way but as an example of the unexpected. And perhaps Mrs. Kelly was also a little bored and the prospect of a puzzle enlivened the afternoon.

After the kettle had begun to whistle and Mrs. Kelly poured the water across the tea bag in her cup, she went to the phone to call the Bells. Sylvia Bell often gave her a ride to mass and Mrs. Kelly had sometimes taken care of Joyce when the girl was younger. On the window ledge above the sink were a half dozen tomatoes that Sylvia had dropped off the day before.

Joyce answered the phone.

"Did Sharon get there?" asked Mrs. Kelly, feeling foolish.

"Not yet," said Joyce, "but I'm expecting her any moment. Do you want me to have her call you?"

Mrs. Kelly experienced a chill. "I'd appreciate it," she said. Then she hung up.

Mrs. Kelly got her jacket and went out the back door. Walking to the corner, she turned south on Adams. It was windy and the afternoon had turned cold. Leaves blew across the road. Heavy clouds were moving down from Lake Ontario and there would be rain later. Mrs. Kelly tried to keep herself from having extravagant fears. She thought of her husband's stroke and how she had found him in the backyard still holding a shovel. And she remembered Janice McNeal lying strangled in her living room and how her face had looked.

After Mrs. Kelly had gone thirty yards, she saw something in the high grass at the side of the road: an unexpected bit of color. It was a red and blue bicycle. As she got closer, she saw it was Sharon's bicycle. She poked at it with her foot. The chain had come off. Mrs. Kelly looked up the road toward the Bells' but there was no sign of Sharon. Several cars passed. Mrs. Kelly picked up the bike and moved it a few feet; the wheels moved freely. She considered taking the bike back to her house, but then set it down on the ground. She turned and walked stiffly home, moving as quickly as she could.

The fact that the chain had slipped off or had broken was one explanation why she hadn't seen Sharon from the kitchen window, but why didn't Sharon push the bike the rest of the way to the Bells', which wasn't far up the road? Perhaps a friend had stopped to give her a ride.

Reaching her house, Mrs. Kelly called the Bells again. "Is Sharon there yet?" she asked.

"No," answered Joyce, "is anything wrong?"

Mrs. Kelly thought about that. "I don't know," she said, then she hung up. She thought of the things that might be wrong. On her telephone was a decal giving the numbers of the fire department, the rescue squad, and the police. Mrs. Kelly picked up the phone and telephoned the police.

Ryan Tavich was not in the police station when Megan Kelly called. He was over at Jack Morris's Ford dealership getting the brakes fixed on his Escort. The car was up on a lift and Hark Powers had the rear left wheel off. Hark Powers used his tools roughly, slamming the pneumatic drill up against the wheel and abruptly pulling the trigger so the rapid-fire whine filled the garage. When the whine stopped, Ryan realized that his beeper was beeping. It was just three-thirty. He went into the office to call the police station.

"We got a call from Megan Kelly," said Chuck Hawley. "She thinks something's happened to Sharon Malloy, the doctor's daughter." He went on to explain about a bicycle and how Megan Kelly's living room window faced north and the kitchen window faced south, but Ryan didn't understand. Through the window of the office, he saw his Escort being lowered to the floor.

"I'll drive over and take a look," he said.

An hour later, having made sure that Sharon was not at the Bells', had not returned home, and was not visiting one of half a dozen other friends, Ryan Tavich called the state police. He still felt that Sharon would turn up but he wanted extra help. It was a precaution, no more. When the dispatcher in Potterville radioed the alert to the troopers on duty, it was picked up by private scanners around the county, including the scanner of the office of the Aurelius *Independent*. Franklin Moore was not in the office. He had to cover a city council meeting that evening and he had taken the afternoon off. Frieda Kraus, the combined receptionist, office manager, and copy editor, called Franklin at home.

Because of Sadie's dislike of her father's involvement with Paula, Franklin and Paula often met at Franklin's house when Sadie was at school. That particular Monday afternoon, Sadie wasn't supposed to be home until five-thirty—she said she was visiting a girlfriend. Paula had come over at two-thirty.

Franklin and Paula were in bed.

Shortly after four-thirty the phone rang. Franklin tried to ignore it. The phone was on a nightstand next to the pillow.

Paula pulled away and sat up. "You'd better answer it."

Even before Franklin answered the phone, he knew it was Frieda Kraus. She was the only one who would let the phone ring twenty times. And she probably knew he was in bed with Paula. She probably even had a joke to make about it.

Frieda's voice was serious. "The police think something's happened to Sharon Malloy. I thought you'd want to know."

At that moment the bedroom door opened and Sadie stood in the doorway. She held a volleyball and wore jeans and an oversized gray Hamilton sweatshirt. She stared at her father and Paula. "She had eyes like saucers," Franklin told me. Paula pulled the sheet over her bare breasts.

"I'll get on it right away," Franklin told Frieda. Then he hung up.

Franklin looked at his daughter, who was staring at the clothes scattered on the floor. "I thought you weren't going to be home till five-thirty," said Franklin, trying to keep his voice relaxed.

Sadie's face was pale. Her long hair was in a single braid down her back. "Aaron was supposed to meet me after school," she said, "but he never showed up." Then her face wrinkled in anger. With both hands she raised the volleyball and threw it at her father. It hit the wall behind his head and bounced away.

Part Two

Part Two

Fifteen

Just as we are only aware of the surface parts of one another's minds, so are we only aware of the surface parts of one another's behavior. We see the polite part, the public part, and we can only speculate on what exists underneath. But usually if the surface part is conventional and well-mannered, we assume the rest to be also. Although what does that mean? How can we assume that a person's secret self is equally conventional and well-mannered? If the inoffensiveness of one's public self is created by fear, then it would seem possible that one's private self could be anything at all.

Not long ago a student showed me an article in *Rolling Stone* magazine and I happened to notice the classified ads in the back, where there were two pages of telephone numbers with 900 prefixes. These numbers were listed under the heading of "Phone Entertainment" and offered every sexual combination one could hope for. That the magazine advertised such numbers did not impress me so much as that over two hundred were available. "Eat Boots! Man on Man!" read one, "Experience the leatherline." "Bisexual Housewives," offered another. "Sweet Sorority Girls Live," promised a third. It indicated that many people derived great pleasure from calling these 900 numbers. I myself have never called one—I wouldn't have the nerve. But neither have any of my acquaintances confessed to having called them, though I should think some must have.

I assume that many people who call these numbers conceal their partiality from their neighbors. Such conduct is an example of the hidden behavior to which I referred. I wouldn't call it immoral but it suggests a variety of unfulfilled desires within the society. Glancing at other magazines in addition to *Rolling Stone,* one finds many more numbers. How many people call them? Thousands? Over a million?

We tend to think of unfulfilled passions as pointing toward the abyss, and we fear that if we gave in to them they would demand increasingly horrible satisfactions. I am not sure that is true. But even I, who live a reclusive life, feel that if I were to submit to temptation it would be the beginning of a long slide to perdition.

Between my house and Franklin's is the white Victorian house belonging to Pete Daniels and his wife, Molly. We sometimes speak but we are not friends. But neither are we unfriendly. I keep an eye on their house when they go out of town and they do the same for me. That's simply small-town cordiality. They see me as a single, middle-aged biology teacher, somewhat fussy in his habits, who occasionally complains that their terrier leaves messes in his flower beds.

Pete Daniels is a successful electrician but I have never hired him. I don't want him inside my house for the main reason that he already knows too much about me, though he knows very little. Molly works at the Fays Drugs at our strip mall. As a result, if I needed to buy anything the least bit embarrassing—even sleeping pills or the occasional laxative—I didn't go to Fays but to Malloy's Pharmacy downtown. Donald Malloy was congenial and the fact that his brother is a doctor always made me think he knew a little more.

Pete and Molly have three children. The two older, Dennis and Jenny, are in their late twenties. Dennis is married and works with his father. Jenny married a piano tuner and settled in Oneonta. When the two children were nine and eleven, Molly had little Rosa, who was born blind. This was a great trial, but Rosa was bright and the one blessing about being born blind instead of going blind is that one accommodates to one's condition more successfully. And Pete and Molly wanted to do the right thing, so Rosa spent several years at the Perkins School for the Blind in Boston. Watertown, actually.

I had talked to Rosa. She was eighteen and meant to go to college next fall. Often she wore dark glasses because her blank eyes had a restless movement; her face wasn't fully under her control. She grimaced when she smiled, clenching her teeth, and she held her mouth open when she should close it. But she couldn't see herself; she had never had the benefit of a mirror.

I mention this because I have an admission that embarrasses me. Rosa's bedroom window on the second floor of her house was less than twenty feet from my own, or rather, what had been my bedroom window. In any case, I had often watched her undress and do other things as well. She would come back from taking her shower in the evening wearing an old brown robe and nothing else. She liked to sit down in an armchair facing the window. She would lean back, open the robe, and begin to touch herself. Perhaps I didn't watch her often, perhaps only a dozen times. Certainly it has been better since I moved my bedroom. Rosa's shades were usually open and she didn't expect that someone might be watching. After all, she shut her bedroom door.

Her behavior didn't excite me exactly. At first I found it repulsive and I had to make myself stay and watch, however odd that admission may seem. One might think I would turn away or even tell her mother that she should pull the shades. But I did neither, though, as I said, after some months I moved my bedroom. Of course I felt guilty to be watching but I overcame that guilt till watching became something of a narcotic and I would wait at my bedroom window for her to come upstairs. If I had found her actions sexually exciting, perhaps I would have been more disturbed, but it seemed it wasn't sexuality that I was watching; rather I was seeing into her deepest nature.

And then I thought: what if our positions were reversed? What if I were the one being observed? I, too, touch myself upon occasion, far more frequently when I was Rosa's age. And, though I am very private and it happens rarely, I have had sexual partners visit my house. What contortions are visible on my own face? Is my face, or my inner face, if I may call it that, any less expressive?

Often after watching Rosa at night, I would notice her the next day. Sometimes I saw her in the yard and spoke to her. I would search her face for the expressions of ecstasy she had exhibited the night before. But of course there was no trace. As for her thoughts, they were probably thoughts I have had as well. Rosa was a normal young woman. It was only the accident of her blindness that made her actions observable. In our daily activities we see the surface parts of one another's behavior and perhaps we speculate on what exists beneath. Don't we do this because we ask to what actions we might also be driven by our passions? If I could be assured of absolute secrecy, might I not, sometime, call a 900 number? But these aren't only sexual actions. All our emotions—love, hate, envy, greed, pride—have acceptable public levels, then other levels, private levels where they may move to excess. Haven't I felt envy? Haven't I taken excessive pride in my abilities? And when I am at a restaurant with friends and the waitress brings our meals, don't I look to see whose portion is larger?

Still, I have a sense of limit. At some point I tell myself I have had enough or I curb my appetite. I say no. Perdition, the abyss, loss of self-control—consider a person without a sense of limit. Isn't that what it is to be a monster, a creature whose pleasures and excesses have no restriction? We submit to what seems a small thing and soon it becomes huge, soon it owns us. Imagine such a person living among us leading an apparently conventional life. Who is anyone on the other side of a locked door, whether man or woman? Who is a person after the curtains have been drawn? What actions might occur there? Then imagine that we begin to see the person's footsteps, the effects of appetite, the scraps and bare bones of the terrible meal. How will this affect us? Couldn't it create a sense of permission that has its own consequences? As with Rosa Daniels, the more I watched the more fascinated I became, while being disgusted by my own fascination. Her pleasure became my pleasure. Even though I remained the observer, I craved to know every nuance of her conduct. Swiftly my sense of limit altered.

And in Aurelius as well, certain actions occurred that altered our sense of limit. Something awful happened and awful things were needed to stop it. That was the moral voice speaking, the superego. But wasn't there some pleasure that awful things were now permitted? I don't mean that normal people would naturally be led to wicked actions but perhaps the wickedness that they observed or imagined was taking place increased their own sense of permission, their sense of license. They could justify their actions by calling them reactions. They could do something terrible and call it punishment or revenge or retribution, but it was still terrible. Their inner temptations were transformed into overt behavior and they, too, came to share the characteristics of the monster. At least that was how it happened in my town.

Sixteen

Sharon Malloy had vanished, but for twenty-four hours after her disappearance people still expected she would turn up or telephone. Even that her abductor, if there was one, would call. But there was nothing. And with the passing days people's hope diminished.

Of course, by the next morning her picture and description had been sent all over the country. The picture showed her standing in front of a white garage door holding a baseball glove. Her chin was tilted up and she was grinning. She had a pert, oval face with braces on her teeth and they shone faintly behind her smile. She wore the blue sweater she had been wearing when she disappeared. Sharon's blond hair hung loose past her shoulders. Her knees were slightly bent and her feet apart. Her face was extremely pretty, with a look of expectation and eagerness that suggested she was not simply waiting for someone to toss her a ball but waiting for life itself. This gave her an expression of great innocence, as if she were passionately looking forward to whatever lay ahead. And what was ahead? No one knew, but that only made it worse.

Within a week Sharon's picture was seen everywhere: in store windows, post offices, banks, tacked to telephone poles, at the toll booths on the turnpike, taped to the back windows of cars. Many times a day one saw Sharon's pretty face with her expression of eagerness and expectation, and always there was the dichotomy between what she had expected and what she may have received. And didn't this lead people, myself included, to think about the unexpected turnings in our own lives? Sharon came to represent the betrayed promise—the promise that all of us had once felt—of what life seemed to offer and what it gave.

From the start the investigation proceeded on two levels: one in the world and one in Aurelius. Police departments all over the East began looking for Sharon. The state police, the FBI—each trooper and each agent carried her picture. NBC Nightly News ran a story and CNN gave ten minutes to it. Reporters and news teams arrived from hundreds of miles away. Sharon's family was in a state of shock and at first refused to talk to reporters, but Megan Kelly was interviewed fifty times. Joyce Bell spoke of her fear when Sharon didn't arrive at their house that afternoon. Sharon's teachers and friends were talked to, even Sadie. Many people developed little set speeches, though I am sure they didn't think of them as such, in which they said what a wonderful girl Sharon had been. Junior over at Junior's luncheonette, who barely knew her, said as much. In fact, many who professed friendship with Sharon had probably spoken to her only once or twice before her disappearance.

It is hard to discuss this without a touch of cynicism. Sharon's disappearance brought the chance of benign publicity to many people. Harry Martini, the principal of Knox Consolidated, appeared on Syracuse and Utica TV stations talking about the dangers of children's walking to and from school by themselves. And he described how Sharon was one of the bright stars of the ninth grade. Harry puffed himself up, looked forlorn, and wiped his eyes. I am sure he thought himself sincere, but I'm also sure that he barely recalled who Sharon was. She was a good student with a B average, but she had also been shy and didn't call attention to herself. Given the publicity and how people spoke about her, one would have thought she was the brightest and most popular student in the school.

That is not to say people were lying. They thought they were being truthful, but it was as if by linking themselves to her, by talking about her to the press or to the authorities, they were appropriating some of her importance: the importance of her disappearance. If I had spoken to Harry Martini about this, he would have been outraged. And when I questioned Ruth Henley—Sharon's English teacher—in the faculty lounge about how well she had actually known Sharon, she grew a trifle suspicious and said, rather unfairly, that I clearly regretted that Sharon hadn't been a student of mine as well.

I did not, in fact, regret that Sharon was never my student, though her older brothers, Frank and Allen Junior, had taken biology with me. But what struck me as unfortunate was the spotlight: that people hurried to announce a connection with her. Looking from my classroom window, I would see TV crews taking footage of the outside of the school. Or they would be in the halls or talking to students or teachers or administrators. Because of their lights and machinery, they were immediately noticeable. Even Herkimer Potter, a special-education student who has attended Knox Consolidated almost forever, got excused from class to tell a TV reporter from Albany that he once gave Sharon a stick of gum and she had thanked him.

I came to see it as a malignancy that so many people wanted the attention directed at them as well. It represented one of their secret passions. But when I spoke of this to Franklin, he shrugged it off.

"It makes a reporter's job easy. Ninety-nine percent of people are eager to talk."

"They want to appear important," I said.

"They want their lives acknowledged."

"Harry Martini is looking for more than acknowledgment."

"Acknowledged and authenticated," said Franklin. "It proves they're alive."

But I couldn't help thinking how people were showing aspects of themselves that were disagreeable.

The second level of the investigation, the local level, didn't attract as much attention. Although the town police were involved, espe-

cially Ryan Tavich, the inquiry was directed by the state police. The
captain in charge was Raymond Percy. I didn't know him at the time,
though Franklin and my cousin Chuck Hawley spoke well of him.
Percy had a professionalism from which every trace of personality
seemed removed. He lived in Norwich and had been promoted to
captain only recently. He had served eight years in the army, mostly
as a sergeant in the military police. He was tall, very fit, and dark-
haired with a bit of gray. His long and very narrow nose reminded me
of the blade of a hatchet. He wore dark suits and subdued neckties.
Probably he was in his early forties. He showed no defects of character and was diligent, but he also displayed no emotion. I'm not sure
what I would have preferred, though I would have liked an occasional
curse or a smile. Really, I must seem inconsistent, complaining about
some people's secret vices and that other people appear to have none.

To all appearances Raymond Percy wanted to be a machine—
perhaps that was secret vice enough. His interior life was hidden,
which only made me eager for evidence of interior life. Perhaps that
was my own weakness: the desire to see what lay below the surface,
the belief that Raymond Percy was a different man at four o'clock in
the morning when he woke up and stared at the ceiling.

Ryan Tavich was often with him.

"But what's he like?" asked Franklin.

"Thorough."

"Meaning what?"

"He generates a lot of paper, talks to a lot of people, requires a lot
of reports."

Franklin and Ryan were sitting at Franklin's kitchen table. It was
early evening during the first week of the investigation and they both
had a beer. They thought Sadie was up in her room doing her homework but she was perched on the stairs listening.

"Does he ever talk about football?" asked Franklin.

"He never talks about anything not connected with the case."

"Ever see any food spots on his shirt?"

"Come on, what are you saying?"

"I want to know what he's like. How can I write about the guy if he's a block of wood?"

I once drove past his house. Norwich is a town of beautiful Victorian houses but Captain Percy lived in a new split-level on a corner lot, white with black plastic shutters. A fenced-in yard, no basketball hoop in the driveway, no bikes or toys lying in the grass, all the drapery closed. It was hard not to think of Captain Percy's house as resembling Captain Percy himself; and why shouldn't it have? I knew he had a wife and two teenage sons, but from the outside there was no evidence of them.

Ryan Tavich took a statement from Megan Kelly an hour after she had called the police. Captain Percy talked to her the next morning in City Hall. Mrs. Kelly's story about seeing Sharon through the front window, then not seeing her from the back was gone over repeatedly. Three to five minutes had passed between those two events. Mrs. Kelly readily admitted that a number of cars had driven by during that time, even though Adams Street was not heavily traveled, but the only car she remembered specifically was Houari Chihani's red Citroën.

Later that morning, Tuesday, September 19, Ryan and Captain Percy drove to Aurelius College to talk to Chihani. He was teaching his class in nineteenth-century European history and Captain Percy had him called from class. Ryan said later that he himself wouldn't have done this, that it seemed pointless to have Chihani gossiped about. Percy had a sergeant with him, as well as a driver. There was nothing discreet about their visit. Megan Kelly had already talked to people about having seen Chihani's Citroën and some expressed surprise that Chihani wasn't in jail already, that he hadn't been arrested the previous day.

The uniformed sergeant and a college secretary escorted Chihani from class. Ryan and Captain Percy saw him in an empty office in the administration building. Ryan said they could hear him quickly limping down the hall, the soft step, then the louder one. Chihani wore a black turtleneck under a gray sport coat and he wore his beret. He also carried a cane. He was not happy.

"I meet the students of that class twenty-six times in the semester. You have just disrupted one of those times. Now I will have to schedule another class."

"Sit down," said Captain Percy.

"I do not choose to sit down."

"I'm asking you to sit down."

"By what authority?"

Captain Percy explained who he was.

"None of that," said Chihani, "can persuade me to sit down if I do not choose to sit down."

And so Chihani stood, holding his cane flat against his right leg.

Captain Percy stood as well. In fact, all four men stood even though there were enough chairs. Chihani and Percy were both the same height, a little over six feet. Both were trim, but while Percy was muscular, Chihani was wiry and angular.

"You were seen yesterday," said Percy, "driving out Adams shortly after three o'clock. Can you say where you were going?"

"Why is this necessary?"

"It is part of a current investigation."

Chihani stared at the floor, seemingly unwilling to answer. Then he spoke: "I was driving to Henderson's Orchard, where I meant to buy apples, cider, and a jar of honey." He had a contemptuous expression as if scornful that the police should be interested in his apple buying.

"As you left town did you see a girl riding a bicycle?"

"I saw no one."

"You must have passed her," said Ryan.

"I still saw no one."

"You meant to buy apples," said Percy. "Did you buy them?"

"On my way I discovered that I had not brought sufficient money and so I came home. I mean to go back this afternoon."

"Did you come back to Aurelius on Adams?"

"I turned on Drake in order to go to the bank."

"Did you get to the orchard, then turn around?" asked Ryan.

"I turned before I got there. Why is this important?"

"The girl was wearing a blue sweater and had a red book bag," said Percy. "Her bike was blue and red."

"I didn't see her."

"Where is your car now?"

"It's parked in the faculty lot."

"I'm afraid I'll have to take you downtown," said Percy.

For the first time Chihani looked surprised. "Why should you do that?"

"The girl has disappeared."

"Then I would like to call my lawyer," said Chihani.

Percy had Chihani's Citroën towed to the state police barracks in Potterville. He had already obtained search warrants for both the car and Chihani's house.

At City' Hall Chihani said nothing that he hadn't said at the college. He had not seen the girl. He had turned around before getting to the orchard. His lawyer was a woman, Agnes Whitehead. She made it clear that her client had to be charged or released. While Chihani was in police headquarters his house was being searched by a state police lab crew. After delaying as long as possible, Percy released Chihani late in the afternoon. No sign of Sharon was found in his house. The state police kept his car for another day but they found nothing to indicate that Sharon Malloy had ever ridden in it.

"The trouble is," Ryan told Franklin, "it's unlikely that Chihani could have removed all trace of her. There were traces of other people, even women, but not Sharon."

"What women?" asked Franklin.

"IIR members. Harriet Malcomb, for instance, and Joany Rustoff." They were again sitting at Franklin's kitchen table. From the other room came the sound of Sadie practicing scales on the piano.

"So Chihani presumably didn't clean up his car."

"Right. Besides, it's impossible to clean selectively, to erase one person's traces and not another's."

"Is there any evidence that Chihani ever talked to Sharon?"

"None."

Franklin called in Sadie and asked if Sharon had ever talked about Houari Chihani.

"Who?" said Sadie. Practicing the piano was something that her father made her do and Sadie didn't mind being interrupted.

"He teaches at the college and drives a red Citroën."

"That little red car? I've seen it but I didn't know who it belonged to. What kind of name does he have?"

"Algerian."

"Was he born there?"

"I guess so," said her father.

"That's a long way from Aurelius," said Sadie.

Although Chihani had been released, he remained a potential suspect. State troopers and sheriff's deputies talked to people along Adams and Fletcher to learn if they had noticed him. Many remembered the red Citroën but they were not sure if they had seen it on that particular Monday afternoon.

Soon it became generally known that Chihani had been taken to City Hall and that his car had been towed to Potterville. I would be willing to wager that each person who thought about Chihani also thought about Oscar's being arrested for placing those bombs. And people thought about the IIR in general. Indeed, some began to wonder if the group hadn't been involved with the vandalism in Homeland Cemetery, which the police continued to investigate. No proof existed that the vandalism and the bombs were linked, but Aurelius was a small town and the number of people willing to break the law was limited. So people thought there might also be a connection between the IIR and Sharon's disappearance. It was not lost on Franklin that Aaron was supposed to have met Sadie on Monday afternoon and hadn't shown up. Where had he been? Of course Franklin passed this information on to Ryan Tavich.

Ryan must have felt unhappy with himself. Though he knew that the IIR was responsible for the vandalism, he had decided not to say anything about it. He didn't see it as one more instance of his protecting the son of his dead lover or even Harriet Malcomb. He was simply avoiding trouble for a bunch of rather harmless students. Given the unpopularity of Chihani and the suspicions about the IIR, the fact that its members had been tipping over the gravestones of some of Aurelius's most respected dead would be blown out of proportion. So he had kept silent.

Seventeen

Ryan had in fact tried to find Aaron the Monday of Sharon's disappearance. He went to Aaron's apartment four times. He stopped by Harriet's apartment twice. They had become very cool to each other since August. It irritated Ryan that he couldn't look at her without desire and it irritated him that in their five weeks together he had never known what she felt about him. Ryan also visited the other members of Inquiries into the Right, including Barry, who said later, "He looked angry. I thought he wanted to hit me."

Ryan couldn't help thinking about Aaron's violence toward Hark and Sheila Murphy. He also thought how Aaron had been hanging around Sadie. Perhaps Ryan was even jealous. When he took Sadie fishing he may have seen himself as offsetting Aaron's influence. But no matter how much Ryan disapproved of Aaron, he couldn't help the fact that whenever he saw him, he saw Aaron's mother's face staring out at him, those slightly upward-tilted eyes.

Ryan should have told Percy the moment he learned that Aaron was missing, but he didn't. Monday night and Tuesday morning he searched for Aaron, waking up the members of the IIR and going twice to Paula McNeal to see if she had heard from her half brother. But nobody had heard from him.

Paula had left Franklin's house around five o'clock, soon after Sadie had found Franklin and her in bed together. She was sorry that Sadie was upset but she was also angry at Franklin for acting as if he had betrayed his daughter. It was Paula's habit when something bothered her, however, to be silent, to swallow it, so it was easy for others to think that nothing was wrong. The news of Sharon's disappearance overwhelmed her resentment but didn't make it go away. So she went home, and Franklin spent an hour or two with Ryan Tavich before going to the city council meeting. He left Sadie at my house because Mrs. Kelly was still occupied with the police.

I was struck that Franklin brought her over personally instead of letting her walk. After all, I lived two houses away. It was my first intimation of the changes that would occur because of Sharon's disappearance.

Sadie was upset about Sharon but the news hadn't quite sunk in. She was more concerned about finding Paula with her father.

"Why does he like her?" she kept asking. "Can't he see that she's only tricking him?"

"Why would she trick him?" I asked.

"Because she's dishonest." Sadie glared at me from under her bangs. Then she grinned at her own seriousness.

"But what do you think she wants from him?" I asked.

"Maybe his money, maybe our house. Maybe she hates me and is trying to hurt me."

"Maybe she loves him."

"He doesn't need that kind of love," said Sadie.

I kept a few boxes of macaroni and cheese on hand for her visits and we shared one that evening. Sadie did her homework and then watched TV while I worked on lab reports. The eleven o'clock news ran a brief story about Sharon's disappearance and showed the photograph of Sharon standing in front of the garage.

"That's my sweater," said Sadie. "That's the sweater that Paula gave me."

Ryan Tavich finally found Aaron at around eight o'clock Tuesday morning. Or rather, Ryan was parked in front of Aaron's apartment building when he looked in his rearview mirror and saw Aaron walking up the sidewalk. It was a cool morning but Aaron was in his shirtsleeves. Ryan got out of the car.

"I've been looking for you," said Ryan.

Aaron didn't say anything. His hair was loose and hung down past his shoulders. There were circles under his eyes.

"Where have you been?"

"Out," said Aaron.

"Where?"

"Just out."

"Why didn't you meet Sadie after school yesterday?"

"I was busy."

"Do you know anything about Sharon Malloy?"

"I saw something on the news last night. Did they find her?" Aaron took an elastic out of his back pocket and began putting his hair in a ponytail.

"Where were you yesterday afternoon around three o'clock?"

"I was busy."

"Be more specific."

Aaron thought a moment. "That's as specific as I'll get."

So Ryan took Aaron to City Hall and turned him over to Percy. He also told Percy about Aaron's history and the IIR and let on that he suspected the group of the vandalism in the cemetery. Chuck Hawley, who happened to be looking into the vandalism, overheard their conversation.

"Why the hell didn't you tell me that earlier?" asked Percy, more in surprise than anger.

Ryan started to speak, then shrugged. Chuck told me afterward that Ryan became rather red in the face.

Percy called the police in Troy and asked them to detain Oscar. He also had the other IIR members brought to City Hall. Then he and Ryan visited the college, where they talked to Chihani before

driving him to the police station as well. All this was noticed. By
noon most of the town knew that the members of IIR had been arrested. And it was all over the high school, though in a rather garbled
version. It was said that Jesse and Shannon had tried to resist and
were beaten up. Leon Stahl had suffered a kind of stroke. Jason Irving
had tried to climb out his back window but had been caught. Harriet
was found hiding in her closet. Joany Rustoff and Bob Jenks had
been caught naked together and were taken downtown in their underwear. Barry had wept. None of this was true, though perhaps
there was a germ of truth in each story. For instance, Barry told
me that he'd been upset but he swore he hadn't cried. It hardly mattered. These were the stories that circulated. It didn't seem far-fetched
that this Marxist group from the college had abducted Sharon.
Hadn't they already tried to blow up the high school?

Few people were convinced the IIR was completely guilty but few
believed its members completely innocent. They had clearly done
something wrong—after all, they had been arrested. Then, later that
day, we heard that vandalism charges had been brought against all
the members of the IIR except for Leon Stahl, and people recalled the
overturned tombstones in Homeland Cemetery. And those who had
never suspected the IIR of the vandalism were surprised at themselves, or so they said, because didn't it make perfect sense that the
group had done it?

Fear and ardent speculation make an unhealthy mixture. By the
end of the school day, students were talking about satanism and
witchcraft. I even heard Mrs. Hicks, the English teacher, speculating
that Sharon might be the victim of human sacrifice. By then Sharon
had been missing twenty-four hours. Many people still thought she
would turn up, but the presence of reporters, police, and various
strangers led to much conjecture. And there was this business of the
IIR members' being arrested. The fact that none of them had been
charged with anything to do with Sharon didn't matter. People had a

vague idea of their history, a vague idea of events, and out of these vaguenesses they formed a narrative.

In the faculty lounge Sandra Petoski, usually a sensible woman, speculated about Barry Sanders, saying she had always wondered if he wasn't emotionally disturbed. Others jumped in with stories about Barry, and Aaron as well, till it seemed that Sharon's disappearance had been bound to happen. And the school was only a microcosm of the town itself, because the same sort of speculation went on everywhere. Inquiries into the Right must be involved, it was argued, and the mastermind behind the group's behavior was Chihani. And as for why Chihani would want the tombstones in the cemetery tipped over—well, wasn't he a Moslem, wasn't he a Communist? Even the fact that he drove that red car was held against him. I felt the police should have acted with more discretion, but they too were naive and in situations such as these they had only a rudimentary sense of cause and effect. They couldn't foretell the effect of these events on our town.

Tuesday afternoon the members of the IIR were taken to the courthouse in Potterville. They were pressured to admit their connection with Sharon's disappearance, and the vandalism charges were a tool to make them talk. In the meantime, search warrants were obtained and their apartments were searched by the police.

Barry was escorted into an office and made to wait. Soon two plainclothesmen entered and told him that he faced five years in jail because of the vandalism. Had narcotics been involved? Barry couldn't remember any. He could think only of what his mother would say and how angry she'd be. Though he knew that Sharon was missing, he had no idea that his arrest was connected with that. One of the plainclothesmen told Barry that perhaps the vandalism charges would be dropped if he told what he knew about Sharon. Barry had known one of Sharon's brothers, but he wasn't sure he had ever seen Sharon, at least not recently.

"What does the number 666 mean to you?" Barry was asked.

Barry thought hard. Was it like 911 or had it been the number on his locker at school? "I don't know," he said. He sat very still and blinked his eyes.

The plainclothesmen asked Barry how he'd spent the previous twenty-four hours and where he had been at three o'clock Monday afternoon. Barry had been at school and in the evening he had visited his mother. He had thought he might see Aaron in the evening but Aaron hadn't been at home.

"How do you know he wasn't home?" asked the plainclothesman.

"I called and there was no answer."

"And where do you think he was?"

"I've no idea."

"And when did you last see Mr. Chihani?"

"At the meeting on Friday night." The two men alternated in asking their questions and it made Barry quite dizzy.

"And what was discussed?"

"Desai's *Marxian Economics*. Mr. Chihani talked about it and we discussed it." Barry hoped they wouldn't ask him what it was about because he had only the vaguest idea.

"Did anyone mention Sharon Malloy?"

"Not that I recall. I'm sure no one did."

"Do you think she's pretty?"

"I can't remember what she looks like."

"Do you like little girls?"

"I guess so," said Barry, who didn't like little girls but was afraid of saying the wrong thing. "They're all right, but I haven't seen many since, well, since I was a little boy."

Ryan managed to separate Harriet from the others and talked to her in a small office. "I thought you weren't going to tell anybody about Homeland," she said. She had taken out her contacts and wore glasses with clear frames. Her black hair hung on either side of her face. She wore a Colgate sweatshirt that hid her figure. Ryan could see no trace of the breasts that had once amazed him. She looked about twelve and had a pimple on her chin. Ryan felt shocked that he had ever had sex with her.

"It was bound to come out," he said.

"I'm going to tell them all that you fucked me."

Ryan found that he couldn't look at her. "Do what you want," he said.

"You think I liked it, don't you? I only did it because Aaron told me to do it. You're a short old man."

"Aaron?" said Ryan, hardly registering her insult. "Why?"

"Ask him if you want to know."

"I guess I'll have to," said Ryan, not looking at Harriet's eyes but focusing on the pimple on her chin. And he wondered if he ever had sex with any woman except as an attempt to get Janice McNeal out of his head.

None of the IIR members had anything to say about Sharon. Several, like Leon Stahl and Joany Rustoff, claimed not to know she was missing. Aaron said he had a vague memory of her, as did Barry, but the others said they didn't know who she was. As to where they had been during the past twenty-four hours, most of their movements could be verified. They had had classes, they had gone downtown. They had stopped by Bud's Tavern for a beer. Some had done one thing, some another, but each had a period of time for which he or she had no alibi.

Leon was released and Ryan drove him back to Aurelius.

"Boy, am I glad I stayed home that night," Leon kept saying. "They wanted me to come to the cemetery, they kept asking me. This is the first time being fat has done me any good."

The others were charged with vandalism; all but Aaron were released on their own recognizance. Aaron was kept in jail with bail set at $25,000. He called his half sister and she contacted her father's lawyer, Henry Swazey, who would try to get Aaron released on Wednesday. The state police in Troy had investigated Oscar Herbst and said he couldn't have abducted Sharon. He'd had a dentist appointment late Monday afternoon.

Wednesday afternoon Franklin visited Aurelius College to talk to Houari Chihani, hoping to get something to put into the *Independent* for the following day. He found Chihani in his third-story office in Douglas Hall. There was no new information about Sharon, though the police had lots of leads. Most seemed bogus: people who thought they had seen Sharon in places as far away as Chicago. But the IIR was being talked about and people couldn't get past the fact that Mrs. Kelly had seen Chihani's red Citroën.

Because Chihani had been questioned by the police and knew the IIR was under suspicion, he must have been wary of Franklin, but he didn't show it.

Franklin sat down on the other side of Chihani's desk and took out his notepad. "Do you have any ideas about what might have happened to Sharon Malloy?"

"None." Chihani had thin lips that reminded Franklin of a flattened letter *M* set above a flattened letter *W.* They made Franklin think that Chihani was smiling slightly, but he wasn't sure if that was true.

"You can't imagine why she might have been abducted?" asked Franklin, writing in his pad.

"I can imagine dozens of reasons but they are no more than possibilities. We don't even know she was abducted. She might have gone with the person willingly. Or perhaps there was no other person. Perhaps she went off by herself. At this moment she could be anywhere in the world."

"So you don't think there was any wrongdoing?"

"I am saying that as far as I know there is no automatic reason for assuming wrongdoing. She has been missing for two days. Of course wrongdoing is a strong possibility."

"She apparently disappeared from Adams Street near the town limits around three o'clock Monday afternoon. You were seen in the vicinity at that time. Is it possible you could have driven past Sharon without noticing her?"

"It is possible. Many things were in my environment: trees, birds, houses, other cars, dogs. I remember none specifically."

Franklin wrote this down. "Let's say she was abducted—what reasons can you give for that?"

"Surely your question is too hypothetical."

"Then let me ask you, hypothetically, about rape. In some places it happens a lot; in some very little. Do you have any explanations for that?"

Chihani put his elbows on the desk. "The rapist often feels a victim of societal emasculation. His victim is a pretext; she, or he, represents society. The rapist, feebly, is trying to show that he is not emasculated or he is striking a blow against his own victimization, for certainly he, too, is a victim. Sex rarely comes into it. The emasculated are seeking power, the weak and commodified are expressing their discontent. These are general reasons. There is also the rapist's specific psychology to consider and we cannot know that unless we know the rapist."

"Do you think Sharon Malloy might have been raped?"

"I have no idea."

"Do you believe that the rapist is as much a victim as the person he rapes?"

"He is surely a victim, but that isn't to say he shouldn't be punished. There are crimes which occur because a society is corrupt, crimes which are a reaction to that corruption. This is true of most crimes. The society can change itself to decrease those crimes or it can punish those whom it calls criminals. The rapist is as much a victim as the person he rapes, but in this society he is also breaking the law and so he will be punished."

"You think he shouldn't be punished?"

"I think the reasons why he rapes are more important than the rape itself. To put the rapist in jail doesn't solve the problem of rape. It merely, temporarily, removes one rapist."

"What changes would decrease the incidence of rape?"

"A society in which each member truly believed himself or herself the equal of every other member would have a much lower incidence of rape."

"But rape wouldn't be eradicated completely?"

"There may be causes for rape that are not political, but if rape has to do with power and powerlessness, then those are the illnesses that must be treated. One of the problems with this society is that it tries to deal with the causes by punishing the effects, by making the potential perpetrators afraid. There is no attempt to remove the causes themselves."

"Why?"

"Because the system depends on power and powerlessness. We cannot cleanse crime until changes are made within the society."

Not all of this appeared in the *Independent*. Franklin edited it and moved sentences around. He felt he was being faithful to the original interview, but he also tried not to get Chihani in unnecessary trouble. For instance, he didn't mention that Chihani had been in the vicinity when Sharon had vanished. But people knew this and one reason they read the interview was to see what Chihani would say about it.

Franklin also left out Chihani's theoretical explanations, feeling they would muddy the water. It might have been better not to have interviewed Chihani at all, but Franklin was afraid to have the paper appear timid.

To the question about the abduction, Franklin had Chihani reply:

"We don't even know she was abducted. Perhaps she went with the person willingly. Perhaps she went off by herself. At this moment she could be anywhere in the world. There is no automatic reason for assuming any wrongdoing."

About rape Franklin had Chihani say, "Sex rarely comes into it. It's a matter of power. But I think the reason why the man rapes is more important than the rape itself. The rapist is also a victim, but in this society he is breaking the law and will be punished. A society in which each member truly believed himself or herself the equal of every other member would have a much lower incidence of rape."

Aaron was released on bail Wednesday afternoon. The charge was vandalism stemming from the Homeland Cemetery incident. He still wouldn't say anything, however, about his whereabouts on Monday afternoon and night. My cousin said that the police came close to charging Aaron with Sharon's abduction, but that wasn't true. There was no solid evidence that Sharon had been abducted and there was nothing to link Aaron to the incident. What Chuck meant was that the police *wanted* to charge Aaron. He had refused to answer their questions. He had refused to talk. The police wanted him to be guilty because they wanted to punish him. I am not saying this was true of Captain Percy and it wasn't true of Ryan Tavich, but Aaron had made himself no friends.

Where he had been on Monday continued to be a mystery, but Aaron's impulses led him to exaggerate this mystery. He liked the fact that the police disliked him. Why else hadn't he told the police where he had been? It struck me that even if Aaron had been off doing something perfectly innocent, he still might refuse to answer. Just as a joke, just because he was like that. What's more, he had plenty of reasons to hurt us. His mother had been murdered and he had been mocked for being her son.

Eighteen

Up until now one group of people has been absent from this discussion: Sharon Malloy's family. No matter how upset we were by Sharon's disappearance, our feelings were a faint echo of those experienced by the Malloys. Indeed, it is hard to calculate another's grief, which is an emotion without limit. I think of the grief I experienced after my mother's death or after friends of mine died, some quite young and from AIDS. I try to extend that to imagine how Sharon's family felt and I realize that I can only imagine a fraction of their grief.

The Malloys moved to Aurelius from Rochester when Sharon was three. Dr. Allen Malloy's sister, Martha, was married to a local accountant, Paul Leimbach, a highly admired man who probably did the tax returns for half the town. Dr. Malloy wanted to get out of the city. His house in Rochester had been broken into several times and he felt it would be better for his family to live in a safer environment. He chose Aurelius to be near his sister and brother-in-law. He bought a large white house and set himself up as a family practitioner. He and his wife, Catherine, had three children at that point: Sharon; Francis, or Frank, who was six; and Allen Junior, who was eight. The whole family attended Saint Mary's Church. Two years after coming here, Catherine had another child, little Millie, five years younger than Sharon.

Martha Leimbach also had four children, and the two families were quite close. Three years after the Malloys came to Aurelius, Dr. Malloy's brother, Donald, the pharmacist, moved here from Buffalo.

Donald Malloy was divorced. He worked for a while at Fays, then bought a small drugstore downtown, which he expanded to sell magazines, newspapers, and soft drinks out of a cooler, the usual odds and ends. I can't believe he made much money, but having a brother who was a doctor certainly helped.

The Malloys and Leimbachs spent a lot of time together. Though they had other friends—Roberta Fletcher, who was Dr. Malloy's nurse, as well as Dr. Richards, who had an office in the same building over by the hospital—they seemed happiest with family. The Leimbachs' children were constantly with Dr. Malloy's children and the families had dinner together each Sunday after mass.

When Ryan Tavich went over to see Mrs. Kelly on Monday afternoon, one of the first things he did was to have officers contact Sharon's parents, as well as her aunt, Paul Leimbach, and Donald Malloy, to check if they had seen her. And clearly her siblings and cousins had to be found and asked the same question. Within an hour most had been located and none claimed to have seen Sharon. This was when Ryan called the state police. The family's grief can be dated from that point.

By six o'clock they had joined in the Malloys' home—five children and five adults—to await the news. The oldest boys, John Leimbach and Allen Junior, were away at college and wouldn't be called until the next day. My cousin, Chuck Hawley, was also with them, as well as Roberta Fletcher. Several neighbors sent over trays of sandwiches and potato salad, though no one ate much. But it surprised me how quickly people knew about the missing girl and how quickly they responded by seeing what they could do to help, even if it was no more than making a bowl of potato salad.

The Malloys' living room was a mixture of modern and colonial—overstuffed chairs and sofas, fabrics and drapes showing settlers' tools, end tables made to resemble butter churns. Almost the only noise was the ticking of the grandfather clock. People spoke in whispers. Now and then the phone rang, usually neighbors calling with worried questions or to express concern. Roberta Fletcher took the calls. She was a large no-nonsense woman who spoke to the callers as briefly as possible. She couldn't see why people should keep bothering the Malloys in their time of trouble.

A tall man, Dr. Malloy was sandy-haired and going a little bald, with a full red moustache that he liked to stroke from the middle with his thumb and index finger. He wore dark suits and looked every inch a doctor. He had light-blue eyes. His hands were large and pink, nearly hairless, with freckles on the backs. He always smelled of soap. I went to his office several times for flu shots but spoke to him only briefly. I suppose I have always felt somewhat uncomfortable with doctors. Some are so doctorlike that they appear to have no other personality. One wonders if people choose these professions in order to assume the profession's stereotypical personality. In this way, Allen Malloy resembled Captain Percy.

Dr. Malloy sat on the couch with his elbows on his knees, his chin in his hands, and waited. He didn't cry, he didn't speak. Now and then his wife blew her nose. The children looked frightened. Paul Leimbach kept blowing his nose. Donald Malloy sat in the rocker chewing on his thumbnail. Occasionally he would shake his head.

One must infer their thoughts. Without doubt, each was speculating on what could have happened to Sharon. She was a young lady who was always on time, always let her parents know where she was going and generally behaved like a responsible adult. Now the ugly possibilities were probably being weighed against the benign ones. As more time passed, the benign possibilities grew less likely. Clearly, Dr. Malloy was thinking awful things and with each such thought he would say to himself, But that's impossible. Then he would realize it wasn't impossible. Then he would tell himself, But maybe nothing happened to Sharon. Then he would see that something had obviously happened. At home he often called his daughter Little Pigeon and he could hardly think of that name without tears coming to his eyes.

Sharon's disappearance made terrible things plausible. Perhaps she had been kidnapped and the kidnappers would call. Perhaps she had been beaten. Perhaps she had been raped or murdered. And the irony that the Malloys had moved to Aurelius to get away from the dangers of the city was lost on no one.

Even Dr. Malloy realized that had they stayed in Rochester Sharon would be safe. He would imagine a nameless hand reaching for her, grabbing her, tearing her clothes: his slim fourteen-year-old girl whom he had seen at breakfast that morning. The dog had been jumping around. Millie had burned her toast. Frank couldn't find his biology book. And then Dr. Malloy had gone: a Monday morning in mid-September with just a hint of frost. He had driven to his office. He had seen patients and made the rounds at the hospital. He had eaten lunch with his colleague Dr. Richards. He had seen more patients. Around four o'clock the police had arrived. Did he know the whereabouts of his daughter? And then it turned out that she had disappeared.

The family spent the evening waiting together and each time the phone or doorbell rang their hearts leapt. But it was never news about Sharon. At some point after midnight the children were sent to bed. Then Dr. Malloy gave his wife a sedative. Donald Malloy embraced his brother and went home. The Leimbachs left. Around three in the morning Roberta Fletcher went home. My cousin Chuck fell asleep in a chair. Now and then he woke and changed his position. Each time, he saw Dr. Malloy sitting on the couch with his head in his hands. Chuck said he would have spoken but he didn't know what to say.

Tuesday came and went and there was no news. The Malloy and Leimbach children stayed home from school. Dr. Malloy canceled his appointments or turned them over to Dr. Richards. He went to City Hall and then to Potterville. He saw Houari Chihani brought in and then released. Of course he knew that Chihani's Citroën had been seen on Adams Street. Several TV newspeople tried to talk to him, but Chief Schmidt gave him a room in City Hall where he wouldn't be bothered. Through the window he saw Aaron being brought in, then Jesse and Shannon Levine, Harriet Malcomb, and the others, even Barry Sanders. Some he knew. He had treated Barry for colds and a variety of minor ailments, because Barry had quite a bit of his mother's hypochondria. And then Dr. Malloy saw them taken over to Potterville. Constantly, he asked if there was any news, but there never was.

At least a hundred men and women, volunteers and state police, scoured the fields around Adams Street. Dogs were brought in and given articles of Sharon's clothing for her scent. They found nothing. And this increased the speculation that Sharon had been taken away in an automobile. Neighbors who had already been asked if they had seen anything were interviewed again. TV and radio announcements called for information relating to Sharon Malloy. Several people responded who had spotted Sharon on her bike, but nobody had actually seen anything happen.

Dr. Malloy helped search the fields and his brother, Donald, went with him. Donald was weeping. Dr. Malloy's face was stiff and drawn. They walked side by side through the brush. Donald had a stick that he used to push aside branches and to poke under things. When it got dark both returned to City Hall. They found out that the members of the IIR had been charged with vandalism and released on their own recognizance. They learned that Aaron was in jail in Potterville but hadn't been charged in connection with anything related to Sharon. At some point Percy interviewed the entire Malloy and Leimbach families. Around eight o'clock Dr. Malloy and his brother went back to the doctor's house. The two boys who had been off at college came home and there was another evening of wait-ing. Again Chuck Hawley slept in the armchair. Dr. Malloy spent the night on the couch.

"He didn't seem to sleep at all," Chuck said. "At least he was awake every time I looked."

On Wednesday came news of various sightings. Sharon was seen in New York City. She was seen in Albany and Rochester and Buffalo and Syracuse. She was seen walking down a country road near Platts-burg. Each report caused a burst of optimism that disappeared when the sighting turned out to be false. Each disappointment felt worse than the one before. And the news of each sighting was met with less and less hope.

Aaron was released from jail in Potterville and returned to Aure-lius. Chihani was brought down to City Hall a second time and again released. By Wednesday afternoon so much news was coming in about Sharon—all of it incorrect—that volunteers began to man the telephones. Her photograph was pinned up everywhere.

That evening Dr. Malloy went home and again the Malloys, the Leimbachs, and Donald waited in the living room for news. Neigh-bors sent food. Once more Chuck Hawley slept in the armchair. Dr. Malloy remained on the couch by the phone but this night, accord-ing to Chuck, he slept a little.

On Thursday the *Independent* appeared with Houari Chihani's comments. "Perhaps she went off willingly," he was quoted as saying. "The rapist is a victim as much as the person he rapes. . . . The reason why he rapes is more important than the rape itself."

Dr. Malloy read it and shook his head uncomprehendingly.

On the front page was a picture of Sharon, the one showing her standing by the garage door holding a baseball glove. She had been playing catch with her brother Frank. Dr. Malloy had taken the pic-ture. There were interviews with Sharon's classmates. "She's the most wonderful friend I ever had," said Joyce Bell. "She never got angry, she was always laughing," said Meg Shiller. "I wouldn't say she was my best student," said Lou Hendricks, who had Sharon in social studies, "but she was one of the best and she was certainly a pleasure to have in class."

Members of Sharon's family were quoted. "We have no idea what could have happened," said her brother Frank. "When I saw her on Monday morning, everything was fine."

"If somebody hurt her," said her uncle Donald, "then, I don't know, I'd like to kill that person. She's a saint, a wonderful little girl."

Little Millie was quoted as saying, "I want my sister back."

Franklin had also talked to Captain Percy. "At this moment we have hundreds of officers working on the case. Thousands of people are looking for her. We still hope she'll turn up."

There was a lot of open country around Aurelius and hundreds of people searched it: troops of Boy Scouts, members of the National Guard, volunteers. One saw groups of schoolchildren exploring the woods in Lincoln Park or the surrounding fields. Both sides of the Loomis River were searched from Hamilton to Norwich. People explored Henderson State Park, the nearby lakes, and the quarry. Students missed school in order to help but there was no thought of penalizing them. There was the idea, a fantasy surely, that if everyone worked together, Sharon would be found alive and well. And if every square inch of the county was searched, then certainly she would be discovered. Even the phrase "every square inch" kept being repeated, as if not to say it violated a principle of magic. The fact that Sharon had disappeared so completely, into thin air, as Ryan had said, made magic seem possible. Before the whole business was over, psychics were consulted and people with reputed healing powers. I believe at one point even a dowser was brought in, although not by the family or the authorities.

There was another effect of Sharon's disappearance: starting on Wednesday there was a minor traffic jam at the beginning and end of school. Many children walk or ride their bikes; now most were being driven. Something had happened to Sharon Malloy. Who was to say it couldn't happen to someone else? Chief Schmidt hired two more policemen and one saw state troopers driving around everywhere.

The same issue of the *Independent* that carried the unfortunate remarks of Houari Chihani also had a story about the members of the IIR being charged with the vandalism in Homeland Cemetery in August. This didn't improve their popularity. Jason Irving withdrew from school and moved back to his parents' house in Kingston. Of course he had to receive police permission to do this. The others didn't quite disappear but they tried not to attract attention to themselves. The exceptions were Houari Chihani, whose red car was still to be seen around town, and Aaron McNeal, who didn't change his habits in any way.

The police were still trying to find out where Aaron had been that Monday afternoon and evening. There was talk of a legal hearing so that if Aaron still refused to disclose his whereabouts he could be charged with contempt. I know for a fact that the county prosecutor was working on this.

Saturday afternoon Sadie helped me rake leaves in my front yard. I was keeping an eye on her because Franklin was working.

"Aaron didn't have anything to do with Sharon's going away," she told me. She wore a red jacket and her hair was loose.

"Why do you think so?"

"Because he didn't know her and even if he had he wouldn't have taken her. He's not like that."

"Like what?" I had stopped raking by this point.

"Like the sort of person who would steal a child."

"And what's that sort of person like?" I wasn't baiting Sadie; I wanted to know what she would say.

"Mean. Aaron's not mean."

"What do you think happened to Sharon?"

"You know how people steal dogs to sell to laboratories? Maybe something like that happened to Sharon. Maybe she was taken for some kind of experiment. But you know what?"

"What?"

"I keep thinking it'd be better if she was dead, because if she's not then she's probably being tortured."

"Maybe she'll turn up safe and sound," I suggested.

Sadie looked at me sternly. "You don't believe that."

Nineteen

Franklin Moore's energetic nature was severely put to the test by Sharon's disappearance. Where he had worked fifty hours a week, he now worked seventy. In addition to his duties for the *Independent*, he was also stringing for papers in Kingston, Rome, Binghamton, and Albany, writing articles for them on the missing girl. When out-of-town reporters and TV crews visited Aurelius, Franklin was someone they talked to and counted on for information and introductions to the right people. I don't know if his being so busy was hard on Sadie, but she spent more time with Mrs. Kelly and at my house. I pretended to grumble but I enjoyed it. I let Sadie plan the menu and we ate a lot of macaroni and cheese. She spent so much time with my pickled animals that their jars found a permanent place on the kitchen table. Each morning I was greeted by the doleful stare of the cow eyes.

Apart from the official investigation run by Captain Percy, there were other groups involved—church groups, Boy Scouts, and the VFW. The Pentecostals were especially active. But during the second week a larger group, calling itself the Friends of Sharon Malloy, was formed and took the place of and, in some cases, absorbed the smaller groups. It distributed posters and raised money for information as to Sharon's whereabouts and even more money for her safe return (at first the amounts were $10,000 and $20,000, though eventually they got much higher).

The group also fielded calls from people who believed they had useful information. Most were perfectly sincere. They had seen a girl who resembled Sharon or a man behaving suspiciously (usually some-one in a van) and they thought it worth calling, though one wonders how many had an eye on the $10,000. There were also crank calls, even malicious calls—people calling about witchcraft or accusing Sharon of moral pollution, of being a filthy little girl who deserved what she got. But these made up a tiny fraction.

The Friends of Sharon Malloy worked closely with the police and helped with the searches, while the phone calls they answered saved the police a lot of time. They became part of a network of groups around the country sending out and receiving information about dis-appearances. Soon posters with the faces of other missing children began to appear around Aurelius. Some had been missing for years and many were from the West Coast.

Sandra Petoski, who taught social studies, was co-chairman of the Friends of Sharon Malloy along with Rolf Porter, who ran the Cen-tury 21 real estate office. Porter had been married to Mildred Porter, who worked in Donald Malloy's pharmacy, but they had been di-vorced for some years. The Friends of Sharon Malloy had hoped to enlist Sharon's parents, feeling that the doctor's presence would be a great boost, but neither Allen Malloy nor his wife wanted the con-stant attention, even though they gave their support. Paul Leimbach joined, though, and he brought his brother-in-law Donald, who was a great help because he could add the Malloy name to the group's at-tempts to raise reward money. Donald contributed a few hours a day to the group, helping with the phones and talking with people.

Donald was about five years younger than the doctor and he shared the doctor's florid Irishness, though he was heavier, rather stout in fact. And he had more hair than his brother, that same sandy red color. He had immaculate hands: thin, considering his size, with long, delicate fingers. Donald suffered terribly over his niece's disap-pearance, brooding and erupting in anger. Having come from large cities, both brothers felt especially betrayed to find the dangers that they had fled turn up in a small town like Aurelius. Their sister's husband, Paul Leimbach, who had been born in Aurelius, didn't share their anger, though he loved his niece and was extremely upset.

Franklin talked to Donald regularly and he took out-of-town reporters to see him as well. His anger made good copy and he often applauded Governor Pataki's reinstatement of the death penalty in New York State. Indeed, it seemed that a jail sentence, even a long one, was too light a punishment for an abductor of children. Donald posted a huge blowup of his niece's picture, at least eight feet by five feet—the same picture of Sharon standing before the garage door with a baseball glove—on the front window of his pharmacy, and though the pharmacy was certainly not the headquarters of the Friends of Sharon Malloy, the huge picture made it a focal point and one sometimes saw people taking photographs of it. Harry Martini, our principal, said the huge picture didn't do Donald Malloy's business any harm either, but his remark was dismissed as cynical. Paul Leimbach's CPA firm also had an office downtown. It, too, had a picture of Sharon in the window, though one of the regular nine-by-twelve posters.

In talking to Franklin, Donald would vent his disbelief at the psychology of someone who would abduct a child.

"Why should anyone do that?" he asked. "There's no punishment too great for such a person."

Donald often made these remarks from behind the prescription counter of his drugstore, which was slightly raised, making him taller than anyone else in the store. As always, he had on the white jacket with his name stitched in red over his heart, and beneath it the word *Pharmacist*. His glasses had colorless frames, and whenever he made an important point, he would remove them, hold them in one hand, and tap them against the palm of the other.

Donald was able to supply Franklin with many anecdotes about Sharon: a squirrel with a broken leg that she nursed back to health, the fact that she had sold more cookies than any other girl in her Girl Scout troop; that her mother had taught her to cook and that Sharon had been responsible for dinner every Wednesday evening, usually a chicken casserole or pork chops Florentine. The effect of this information was to make Sharon much more than a face on a poster, bringing increased support and pledges of money to the Friends of Sharon Malloy. Sharon was a typical fourteen-year-old and the articles in the *Independent* about her many kindnesses and what she was like around the house led people to think of her as being like a relative of theirs. Pam Larkin, a teller at Fleet Bank, let me know several times that Sharon was exactly like her sister Betsy, who had moved to California ten years ago and now lived in Bakersfield. Sharon's idealization, if I may call it that, brought her into many families and increased the level of pain and incomprehension. It seemed that everyone remembered a fourteen-year-old like Sharon who had been important to them, and so the blow of her disappearance affected them all.

In printing these stories, Franklin saw himself as doing his duty as a journalist. His job was to give information but what his readers actually got was a diminishment, a distortion of what had taken place. I may be on shaky ground, but by idealizing Sharon and by describing her disappearance in such black-and-white terms, Franklin's articles made people think in those terms too. In the faculty lounge, I heard Frank Phelan, a history teacher, say that when ninth-century Britons caught a marauding Dane, they would skin him and nail his skin to the church door. The same, he argued, should be done to whoever abducted Sharon. That the person might be sick, mad, or crippled in some way meant nothing.

But it was more than duty: Franklin was totally engaged by his profession. He wasn't just the fellow who lived next door with his doubts, griefs, and ambitions. He became his job. I have felt this as a biology teacher, that I can be so engaged by work that my fallible side, my uncertain side, slides away and I become the role I have chosen. It is wrong to say that Franklin was less human, but events in our town increasingly allowed him to change himself into his definition of a journalist. Perhaps this is what I saw in Captain Percy and Dr. Malloy: they had been absorbed by their professions. It freed them from a burden of personal obligation—their professions made their choices.

I found it queer that Franklin left Sadie alone when a girl had just disappeared, but it wasn't him, it was his profession. And by becoming his profession, he was dealing with his fears. Even in appearance— his old sheepskin coat and Irish hat, his constant rush and clutched notebook, his untidy hair and loosened tie—even in his air of knowing the facts behind the facts, he reflected the characteristics of a small-town journalist. At such times one's vulnerabilities and fears can seem to disappear.

By early October everyone in the county knew that Chihani and the IIR members had been questioned about Sharon's disappearance. This created unpleasantness and, as I have said, Jason Irving's parents thought it best to withdraw him from college and take him back to Kingston. Franklin, of course, bore some responsibility for the increased attention. But the *Syracuse Post Standard* had also done a story on Chihani and the IIR, and several papers had written about the vandalism at the cemetery as well as the two bombs deposited by Oscar Herbst. Newspapers have a need to establish patterns of causality and so they argued, or perhaps suggested, that these acts were premeditated and were part of a general conspiracy by the IIR. And they were able to find city officials and even police officers who felt the same way, though Ryan Tavich and Captain Percy never publicly discussed the group.

People dislike unattached pieces of information and so they linked

these bits into a conspiracy theory that began with the arrival of Chihani at the end of the previous year. The mildest proponents pointed
to the IIR as a Marxist reading group that espoused Marxist theories.
The more radical saw the IIR as fomenting rebellion and committing
anarchist acts. They saw a clear line from Chihani's arrival to Sharon's disappearance. Indeed, the Friends of Sharon Malloy obtained
photographs of Chihani, Aaron, Oscar, and the rest and sent them to
other parts of the country where there had been abductions. They
even sent a picture of the red Citroën. One fellow at Spencer's Texaco
noted a link between the color of Chihani's Citroën and the fact that
the devil wore a red suit. It was on the tip of my tongue to suggest
that the same could be said of Santa Claus, but I thought it wiser
not to speak. These were precarious times, and if I were seen as mocking a popular theory, then I, too, might come under suspicion.

Paula was one of those who feared the progression of events, and
she experienced an increasing dread. She knew her brother's intransi-
gence and his need to provoke. And she may have suspected his current behavior was related to the death of his mother, as if he held the
town responsible for her murder. Given Aaron's character, Franklin's
passionate reporting, the reaction of the townspeople, and the activities of the Friends of Sharon Malloy, Paula might have foreseen where
these lines of behavior intersected, and that could have terrified her.

She also saw how people treated her because she was Aaron's sister.
She felt a certain coldness in stores and on the street and how people
who once spoke to her no longer did. She was a beautiful woman
with great charm and energy. She was friendly to people and they
tended to respond with warmth. Now this changed. Each night she
took her dog for a two-mile walk through town. She regularly crossed
paths with the same people and exchanged a few words. But people
stopped speaking to her and she felt uncomfortable. She changed her
routine, taking the dog out at different times and choosing other
streets to walk along.

Even as a guidance counselor in the dean's office, she was aware of a change. The students didn't treat her differently, but she felt a coldness or curiosity on the part of the staff and custodial people—people who were from Aurelius and for whom the town was more important than the college. Paula felt them watching her and disapproving or just pointing her out as Aaron's sister. Pam Larkin at Fleet Bank was barely civil and Lois Schmidt, a produce manager at Wegmans, walked away when Paula asked some perfectly innocuous question about the lettuce. Paula knew that if she was receiving this sort of treatment, then her brother and the other members of the IIR were getting far worse.

"This is a small town," said Franklin, when she talked to him about it. "People get excited."

It was a shortcoming in their relationship—however fond they were of each other—that he, as a reporter, tended to state the obvious while she, as a psychologist, distrusted the obvious. They were sitting on the couch in the living room of Paula's house, the house she rented from her father. The couch was rather threadbare, with a design of blue and purple flowers. It was a couch that Patrick and Janice had bought shortly after their marriage twenty-five years ago.

"It's the fact that people jump to conclusions that bothers me," Paula said. "And each day with no news of Sharon makes it worse."

"Aaron has to say where he was," said Franklin.

"He claims it has nothing to do with Sharon."

"He can say that all he wants," said Franklin, "but people won't believe him."

"Talk to him some more. I'm afraid of what could happen."

Franklin made a soothing noise. "Sharon will turn up or they'll find the person who abducted her and the whole thing will be over. People will forget about the IIR."

"That's what you want to believe," said Paula. "Did they ever find the person who murdered Janice? People are upset and as each day passes the pressure gets worse. Look at us—we hardly see each other anymore."

Franklin took her hand. "I've been a lot busier and then there's Sadie. I can't leave her by herself."

"Sadie," said Paula, as if she was going to say something else. And then she didn't.

Twenty

Franklin and Aaron sat in Aaron's living room. It was a Wednesday morning over two weeks after Sharon's disappearance, the fourth of October. Aaron wound an elastic around his ponytail. "None of this is for publication," he said.

Franklin stopped leafing through the pages of his notebook and set it on the table. "I understand that."

"You speak about cause and effect. There's not a cause that isn't also an effect."

"Going back to the big bang, I assume."

"And what caused that?" asked Aaron, half seriously. "What I'm saying is that Houari Chihani's coming to Aurelius didn't cause anything. At most he was a catalyst for a few students."

Franklin sneezed, then took a handkerchief from the side pocket of his sport coat. He had developed a cold during the past few days that included a headache and an itchy feeling in his chest. "So where were you when Sharon disappeared?"

"We agreed not to talk about that," said Aaron.

Aaron was in the armchair by the window and the sun came in over his shoulder. Franklin sat on the couch, which was lumpy and too low to the floor. On the wall across from him was the red poster of Zapata. Beneath it was a bookcase jammed with books but no novels other than *The Grapes of Wrath* and *The Jungle*.

"You're trying to understand what happened," said Aaron, "by studying the traces of what happened. That's like learning about an elephant by studying its footsteps."

"You'd have me go back to the birth of the elephant? That sounds like Chihani."

"I've learned a lot from him."

"Like what?"

"Imagine two landscapes," said Aaron. As he spoke he freed his ponytail, then bound it up again. "The first is a field in late spring: flowers, everything growing. Rabbits are running around. Butterflies flutter from blossom to blossom. And lots of birds: robins, chickadees, red-winged black birds, perhaps several pheasants. A woodchuck wanders by. The apple trees are in blossom and birds make their nests in the branches."

"It sounds like Walt Disney," said Franklin.

"Exactly right."

"So what's the other landscape?"

"Just like the first but now we add the cat, the fox, the snake, the hawk."

"What's your point?" asked Franklin. Aaron had given him a glass of orange juice and he took a sip.

"The first is the landscape people hope is there, the one they like to think they live in. The second is the landscape that exists. No Sharon Malloy disappears in the first landscape. It's a landscape in which my mother wouldn't have been murdered. The trouble is it's false. Only the second landscape is true. And there's nothing wrong with it. That's how the world is: change and violent change, creatures eating each other, nothing secure. Its radical instability is a natural instability."

"This is what Chihani has taught you to see?"

"He's taught me not to yearn for the other, not to look at the world through what I desire to see."

"What does this have to do with Marxism?" asked Franklin.

"There're always imperfections, but some can be dealt with and others can't. There's nothing I can do about aging; there's something I can do about inequality and the abuse of power."

Franklin took out his handkerchief and blew his nose. He knew that an effect of being a journalist was he asked questions not for knowledge but for information and that he wanted the information not for his own life but often for something he would write and forget. Did he care one way or another about what Aaron was saying or why Aaron wanted to see a world in which the fox and the cat and the snake and the hawk were pursuing their necessary pleasures?

"Why'd you come back to Aurelius?"

"Why do you think I came back?"

"To find out who killed your mother."

"You said it, I didn't."

"And you think Chihani can help you with that?"

"He can help me see things more clearly."

"What ideas do you have about your mother's death?"

Aaron cocked his head in a way that reminded Franklin of a bird listening for something underground. "I believe she was killed by a man who lives in Aurelius. But how does this connect to what we were saying?"

"I was wondering to what degree your ideas about the world were influenced by your mother's death. Perhaps her death is the window through which you view the world."

"So if I argue for greater equality, then it's simply because my mother was murdered?"

"That's an oversimplification."

"If someone reads philosophy and history, then comes to a conclusion as to the nature of the world, that conclusion was in fact formed by his psychology, which was formed by the events in his life and by his heredity, which was in fact formed before he did any reading. Is that what you believe?"

Franklin thought how he could use none of this in a news story and how the next day's paper still had to be finished. In his mind's eye he could see the holes on page one and on the editorial page, which he would have to fill that afternoon.

"Not necessarily."

"Well," said Aaron, "let's think about your point of view and what it says about responsibility. If events occur and how you react is fated by your psychology, then that's liberating, isn't it? It means that any particular event is not your fault."

"What sort of event?"

"Your wife's death, for example."

"She died of cancer."

"So it was fated and you couldn't do anything about it."

"I couldn't do anything about it."

"Perhaps if she had been diagnosed earlier?"

"There was no sign that anything was wrong."

"But if she'd had a checkup?"

"She'd had one a year earlier."

"What if she'd had one six months or even three months earlier?"

Franklin didn't say anything. He was surprised at his discomfort. "Let's go back to my earlier question. What ideas do you have about your mother's murder?"

Aaron again assumed the expression that reminded Franklin of a bird. It had an irony that Franklin disliked, as if Aaron felt he now knew something about Franklin that he hadn't known before.

"What kind of ideas should I have?" asked Aaron.

"Like who might have killed her."

"Did you ever have sex with her?"

Franklin was surprised. "Of course not."

"Why 'of course not'? Your friend Ryan Tavich did."

"He's single."

"Do you think my mother only had sex with single men?"

"I've no idea. Do you think a married man killed her?"

"A man killed her, a man who had been having sex with her. That's all I know right now. In your frame of reference, she was fated to die because of a promiscuity that was determined by her psychology. Wait," said Aaron as Franklin began to speak. "I know I'm exaggerating, but her promiscuity and desire for men, whom she might know nothing about, raised the odds that she would chance upon someone who might kill her. My position is that her belief in a good world blinded her to the possibility that anything might happen. If she had taught herself to see the real world, the world of the snake and the fox, then she would have been more cautious and she might still be alive."

"What about Sharon Malloy?" asked Franklin.

"I don't blame children for seeing the landscape they hope is there," said Aaron. "That's what I like about them—their sweetness. And that's why they need adults to shield them. Are you suggesting that Sharon was fated to disappear?"

Franklin didn't want to think that was true. "She rode all over town on her bike; maybe that was a mistake. It put her at greater risk and so perhaps it was fated that something would happen."

"Is that her parents' fault?"

"It's nobody's fault."

"Do you think this argument could be used to justify how little time you spend with Sadie?"

Franklin found himself staring at the L-shaped scar on Aaron's cheek. "I don't want to talk about that," he said.

"It's funny, isn't it," said Aaron, "when the journalist has to answer questions, he doesn't like it either."

On the evening of the sixth of October the members of Inquiries into the Right, except for Aaron, Jason, and Oscar, met at Houari Chihani's house. According to Barry, they told stories about things that had happened to them in town. "Some woman had started shouting at Harriet in Wegmans, calling her a whore. Jesse and Shannon had been shouted at on the street. Professor Chihani wanted to discuss the incidents. He said they provided a commentary on the capitalist system and its need for scapegoats. Only this time we were the scapegoats. The whole evening was frightening and I'm sorry I went."

Chihani saw a problem and tried to deal with it by translating it into philosophy. That evening he supplied two dozen doughnuts and a gallon of cider, which was touching because he never offered the students anything except tea and crackers. The very presence of the doughnuts was an admission that something was wrong. The students were scattered around the living room, mostly sitting on the floor. Because of Jesse and Shannon's mistreatment of Barry, he sat as far from them as possible. He sat near Leon, the person to whom he had the least objection. Leon's stomach growled and he smelled of sweat.

"What is a scapegoat?" asked Chihani.

"It's someone who gets blamed for what someone else has done," said Bob Jenks.

"It comes from the Old Testament," said Leon. He sat on the floor with three doughnuts in front of him on a square of paper towel. A quarter of one of the doughnuts was missing and Leon's mouth was full. "Leviticus," he said, "the third book of Moses."

Chihani turned to Harriet. "What are the attributes of the scapegoat?"

"He has to be different from the rest," said Harriet, "even if that difference is purely the result of chance, like Barry's being albino. He looks different and he's seen as an outsider. Because he's an outsider he becomes a suitable scapegoat."

"Very good." Chihani looked at the students. "By forming Inquiries into the Right you became different. By becoming different you attracted attention. By attracting attention you put yourself in the position to receive blame when the community needed someone to blame. In a community of true equality there'd be no need for a scapegoat. People would see themselves as being responsible for their own failings. They wouldn't need to put the blame on others."

But Barry knew that wasn't the whole story. Hadn't IIR members tipped over tombstones in the cemetery? Hadn't one of them placed phony bombs on the windowsills of two schools?

Chihani discussed responsibility and how in a capitalist system responsibility for wrongdoing is put onto the shoulders of the disenfranchised, whereas true responsibility belongs to the capitalists themselves. However, since the bourgeoisie hope for the crumbs that fall down from the upper classes, they themselves condemn the lower classes with greater ferocity since, if it weren't for the lower classes, they would be condemned themselves.

"The bourgeoisie yearn to enter the upper classes," said Chihani, "just as devout Christians yearn to enter heaven. It's the task of the upper classes to keep this yearning alive."

It was at this point, slightly after nine o'clock, that the doorbell rang.

"It's Aaron," said Harriet.

But it wasn't Aaron. It was Dr. Malloy.

Barry said he looked terrible. His face was haggard, with little trace left of his healthy Irishness. Since they had expected Aaron, they were surprised to see a stranger. Barry realized that he was the only one who recognized Dr. Malloy.

"To what do we owe—" began Chihani, rather formally.

"I'm Allen Malloy. I wanted to see what you all looked like." He stood by the door and glanced around the room.

"Why did you want to look at us?" asked Chihani.

"I wanted to see your guilty faces," said Dr. Malloy, raising his voice.

The students stared at the doctor.

"Why are we guilty?" asked Chihani.

The doctor stepped toward Chihani. His face reddened. "Don't you realize that my daughter is gone?"

Chihani nodded slowly. "As if," said Barry later, "he was thinking, 'Aha, so you're *that* Malloy.'"

"You have my profoundest sympathies—," replied Chihani.

"Somebody stole my daughter!" shouted Dr. Malloy. "How could you say that this person is more of a victim than Sharon? Only a fool would say that! Only a sadist!"

Barry didn't know what Dr. Malloy was referring to, but Chihani understood immediately. "I said many things to Mr. Moore and he chose to quote a few of them. But I don't think you want to engage in a philosophical discussion . . ."

"What I want," said Malloy in a whisper, "is to see you punished."

Chihani's face wrinkled with emotion. "Believe me when I say that no one in this room was involved with your daughter's disappearance. If there is anything that any of us can do to help find her, then please tell us."

That same Friday evening Sadie was out with Aaron until ten o'clock. When she came home, her father was waiting in the living room.

"I forbid you to have anything to do with Aaron McNeal," said Franklin. He put his hands in his pant pockets for fear of grabbing her.

"He's my friend," said Sadie. Aaron had given her a silver necklace with a silver cocker spaniel and she touched it. She wondered whether to show it to her father, then decided not.

"What do I have to do, lock you in your room? Can't you see I'm scared something might happen to you?"

"There's nothing wrong with Aaron," said Sadie.

"Neither of us know that."

"I know it."

But Sadie obeyed her father, more or less. I turned out to be the beneficiary since she spent more time with me. She came to my house after school three afternoons a week and on the weekends as well. Yet even this was to cause unfortunate talk.

Twenty-one

Ryan Tavich opened his eyes. It was six o'clock, Monday morning, October 9. Ryan didn't need to look at the clock to know it was six o'clock. He always woke at six, no matter what time he went to bed. He lay on his back and stared at the ceiling. He always slept on his back. It was what Janice McNeal had called his "coffin position." It was still dark outside but there was a faint glow in the room from the bathroom light. This was something that embarrassed him slightly, his liking to leave the light on in the bathroom. Ryan found it comforting but he felt that a man of forty-four shouldn't need such comfort.

Ryan had woken up thinking about Aaron, as if he had been thinking about him unconsciously all night. He also thought of Janice and the characteristics mother and son seemed to share. From next door he heard a motor start up as his neighbor Frank Penrose revved his old Pontiac Cutlass, priming it for the drive to Norwich, where he worked for the drug company. Ryan thought for the hundredth time that if he himself didn't wake up automatically at six, then Frank Penrose would wake him five minutes later, just as he woke half the block.

Then Ryan began thinking of Arleen Barnes, who lived next door to Paula McNeal. Arleen was about thirty-five. Her husband was a chemist in Norwich. Maybe his name was Harold. They had no children. Arleen worked part-time at the State Farm office on Main Street with Barry Sanders's mother, although she dressed, thought Ryan, as if she worked for Saks Fifth Avenue. Ryan had never been to

Saks Fifth Avenue but he insured his car with State Farm and had a
sticker on his bumper that advertised this fact. Staring at the ceiling,
Ryan could see a State Farm sticker on the back bumper of Aaron's
Toyota as well.

Ryan began thinking of Arleen's house, a bungalow with green
shingles set back from the road, so that it was behind Paula's. Aaron
probably saw it every time he visited his sister. And he remembered
that Arleen had been a friend of Janice's. After all, for a time they
had been next-door neighbors. Ryan tried to remember what Harold
Barnes looked like but he could only summon up a balding head and
a general idea of plumpness. But Arleen Barnes he could recall easily,
a trim woman who liked to wear tailored suits with colorful scarves at
the neck. Ryan liked the way she looked. She dressed like someone
whose sexual options remained open. And she had a beauty parlor
appearance, carefully waved light brown hair. As he thought about it,
Ryan could even picture Arleen coming out the front door of Make
Waves, the beauty parlor on State Street just around the corner from
Main. It was owned by Cookie Evans, a cheerful, energetic woman.
Ryan knew this because he sometimes dated her and each occasion
exhausted him. No matter how much he hurried, he was always a few
steps behind her. And she talked constantly, not directly to him but
over her shoulder.

Ryan got out of bed, put on his sweats, then went down to the
basement to work with his weights. The cat followed him.

"I got an idea, Chief," he said.

For half an hour, the weights clanked and banged like old pipes.
Then Ryan showered and prepared coffee. As he waited for his
coffee, he carefully peeled the skin from a pink grapefruit, making
sure he removed every trace of the white inner layer. He cut the
grapefruit into sixteen small sections. The cat wound back and forth
between his legs until Ryan poured it a saucer of milk. Then he ate
his grapefruit, drank his coffee, and read the *Syracuse Post Standard*.

Occasionally he would put down the paper and stare at the ceiling again.

"You're lucky you're a cat, Chief," said Ryan. "Life's easier for cats. Even romance is easier."

By seven-thirty Ryan was in his Escort on his way to the beauty parlor. He had no doubt that Cookie would be there; she always opened early. And at that hour it might be empty. Ryan felt squeamish about beauty parlors. They were like women's clubhouses—the curtains and frosted glass—the places where female confessions were exchanged, which in fact was why Ryan was paying Cookie Evans a visit. He wanted to know what and whom Arleen Barnes talked about.

There were no customers, but Cookie wasn't alone. Jaime Rose was trimming his beard in the mirror. Jaime worked for Cookie. Born and bred in Aurelius, he started life as James Rozevicz but his fortunes as a hairdresser greatly increased when he changed his name to Jaime Rose. His black hair was brushed back and added an inch or two to his height. Otherwise, he was thin, angular, and in his mid-thirties. Jaime had learned hairdressing in Albany, though he told everyone, including Cookie, that he had learned it in Los Angeles. For a while he had lived in New York City but he'd been back in Aurelius for about five years. He gave his name the Spanish pronunciation: *Hi-me*.

Later Jaime told me that Cookie took Ryan into her small office, where they remained for nearly half an hour. Jaime said he had been tempted to listen at the door but was afraid to. Policemen made him nervous. They were too nosy for his taste. Then, shortly before eight o'clock, Ryan came out of the office and left the beauty parlor without looking at Jaime. By that time Jaime was working on Mrs. McAuley's cowlick.

"What was that all about?" Jaime asked Cookie.

She had begun combing out a wig that a client wanted to pick up later that morning. Cookie was only a little over five feet tall, exactly a foot shorter than Jaime. "You'd be amazed at the scandal that goes on in this town," she said.

"Nothing in Aurelius," said Jaime, "could ever amaze me."

Ryan walked over to the State Farm office on Main Street. He didn't intend to speak to Arleen Barnes, just to look at her. Ryan told Mrs. Sanders that he had lost his State Farm atlas and would like another, if they had any to spare. Arleen was talking on the phone, laughing, then putting her hand over her mouth. She wore a dark gray dress with a scarf at her neck that had yellow and violet geometrical designs. Her brown hair rose in two waves on either side of her head, then descended to a point at her neck. She wore mascara and eye shadow but not too much, at least in Ryan's opinion.

Mrs. Sanders handed Ryan the atlas. He glanced again at Arleen, who was still laughing into the phone. Ryan didn't think she was talking to a customer. Ryan thanked Mrs. Sanders, then drove over to Aurelius College.

Ryan spent twenty minutes with Paula McNeal in the dean's office, talking to her about Aaron, before going back to City Hall. He was at his desk by nine o'clock. Patty McClosky brought him a cup of coffee, black with double sugar.

"You look pleased with yourself," she said.

Ryan was surprised. He thought of his face as a blank wall between himself and the world.

"Anything new with Sharon Malloy?" he asked. He knew there wasn't because otherwise he would have been beeped.

"Captain Percy called to say he'd be here at nine-thirty, but it didn't sound like anything urgent."

Ryan sipped his coffee. On his desk was a report from Chuck Hawley describing the weekend observing Dr. Malloy and his wife and detailing Dr. Malloy's visit to Houari Chihani on Friday evening. The doctor had stayed in the house for fifteen minutes, then driven home. Later Chuck asked Barry Sanders what Malloy had wanted. "He asked if any of us had stolen his daughter," Barry had said.

Ryan expected that the investigation would soon be turned over to two or three men whose job would be to wait for something to happen. The state police couldn't afford to keep twenty men on the case. This was what had happened with Janice's murder, a great flurry of activity that trailed off to nothing. He found himself thinking about Janice's hands. She had been vain about them, keeping her nails long and painting them, talking about her cuticles. He thought of the hand that had been cut off. The left hand. He couldn't get over the fact that at this moment the hand was someplace specific: in a ditch, in a field, on a shelf. The last possibility gave him a start.

At nine-thirty, just before Captain Percy arrived, Ryan called the State Farm office and asked to speak to Mrs. Barnes.

"Morning, Arleen, this is Ryan Tavich. You get a coffee break? I was wondering if I could talk to you for about five minutes. I'll stop by at ten-thirty. See you then."

Ryan took Arleen to Junior's, then wondered if he was doing the right thing. Arleen was overdressed for Junior's and didn't fit with the video machines. Ryan took a table near the rear.

"Would you like a doughnut as well?" he asked Arleen.

"Sure. See if they have cinnamon."

Ryan got two coffees and four cinnamon doughnuts from the counter and brought them back to the table. Arleen smiled up at him. She had put on fresh lipstick since he had gone to the counter. Ryan couldn't understand how women could wear lipstick and eat at the same time. It must make everything taste like perfume. Ryan spooned two teaspoons of sugar into his coffee. Glancing up, he saw Arleen looking at him expectantly. He felt embarrassed.

"Arleen," he began, "sometimes as a police officer I'm forced to ask things which in regular circumstances I'd never ask." He stopped and wondered if he was speaking too loudly. Electronic explosions were coming from the video games. Arleen looked at him with one finger resting on her chin. "What I mean is," said Ryan, "I don't want you to take offense at what I'm going to ask, because I'm only asking it as a policeman."

"You want to know if I've been fucking Aaron McNeal?" said Arleen. She smiled quickly, then her face grew serious again.

Ryan glanced around to see if anyone had heard. A farmer, Lou Weber, was eating a jelly doughnut about ten feet away. He wasn't paying attention to anything except his doughnut. "As a matter of fact," said Ryan, "that's just what I wanted to know."

"Well, I have," said Arleen, "or I was. I haven't heard from him for over a week."

Ryan picked up a cinnamon doughnut, then set it back on the plate. "Was he with you on the day Sharon disappeared?"

"All afternoon and night." Arleen straightened the scarf at her neck. "Harold had to stay in Norwich and he called in the early afternoon to say so. I called Aaron and he was over at my place by two o'clock. He left his car in his sister's driveway. We had a wonderful time. When Harold got back the next day around five, I had the house put back together again."

Ryan tried to imagine the extent of their activities. He guessed that if he wanted to he could probably visit Arleen himself. He blushed. "How'd you know I wanted to ask about that?"

"Because Aaron said you wanted to know where he'd been. He was afraid of Harold finding out. My feeling is that if Harold finds out, then that's because he *should* find out. It might do him some good. You know, make him value what he's got."

Ryan started to comment, then thought better of it. Instead he asked, "Did Aaron say anything else about me?"

"He said you were one of the men who had been involved with his mother. Of course, I knew that already."

"He talked about Janice?"

"Sure. Janice and I were good friends, but I certainly have no idea who killed her. Aaron wanted to know who she went out with. I gave him some names, all I could remember. Maybe ten men. Sometimes Janice and I went out together and made a foursome. You know, on the sly."

Ryan thought of Aaron and Arleen Barnes lying in bed and talking about Janice's lovers. But maybe they hadn't had sex in bed. Maybe Aaron was like his mother. For Janice the bed was just one of many options. Ryan shook his head to clear it of memories. "You want any of those doughnuts?" he asked.

"I changed my mind," said Arleen. "I need to slim down."

Ryan took some napkins and wrapped the four doughnuts in two packages. He put the packages into his side pockets, one on the left, one on the right. "I'll keep them for my lunch," he said.

Ten minutes later, as Ryan drove to Aaron's apartment, he guessed it was possible that Arleen was lying, but as he later told Franklin, he didn't see why she'd bother. He was a little excited by Arleen and thought about calling her sometime, though he knew he wouldn't. He had no feelings about her husband, but he disliked the idea of doing what he shouldn't in another man's bed, mostly because he himself had been jealous that Janice was seeing other men when she was seeing him.

The Friends of Sharon Malloy had rented a storefront on Main Street, which Ryan drove past on his way to Aaron's. It had a big picture of Sharon in the window. A number of cars were parked in front. Then the door opened and Hark Powers came out with another man. Ryan was surprised to see him, surprised that Hark would have cared about Sharon Malloy one way or another. Hark was grinning and that, too, surprised Ryan, that there should be anything in the store-front that Hark would find funny.

Ryan parked at Aaron's apartment complex, locked his car, and went inside. He knocked, then knocked again. After a moment, Aaron opened the door. He wore a robe and slippers. His naked shins were thin and almost hairless. His long hair hung down over his shoulders. He stood back to let Ryan enter.

"You've caught me in my work clothes," said Aaron.

Ryan wondered if he meant something sexual, then he remembered that Aaron worked at home.

"You were with Arleen Barnes on the eighteenth," said Ryan.

"She told you?"

"Why didn't you tell me before?"

"I didn't feel like it."

"It was police business and it got you into trouble."

"What do I care about police business?" Aaron took a pack of Pall Malls, tapped out a cigarette, and lit it. The toilet flushed. With surprise Ryan realized that someone else was there.

"A guest," said Aaron.

Ryan started to comment about the guest, then said, "By not telling us, you were obstructing a police investigation."

"Your investigation doesn't matter to me."

"Don't you care about Sharon Malloy?"

"To care about her and to care about the police are two different things. You're not going to find who did it, just like you didn't find out who killed my mother. By now Sharon's probably dead. Your job is to protect property; I don't believe in property."

Ryan glanced at the books and furniture. He wondered if Aaron would mind if someone took it all away.

"Did you go out with Arleen because she was a friend of your mother's?"

"I went out with her, as you call it, because I wanted to fuck her."

"You're more like your mother than I thought," said Ryan.

"You mean because we both like sex?"

Looking at Aaron, Ryan was again bothered that he could see Janice's face buried in her son's. It kept him from being able to think of Aaron clearly. And he thought of Harriet Malcomb and how she had said that Aaron had told her to have sex with him. Ryan wanted to ask Aaron about this, but he wasn't ready to. The subject still made him angry.

"I'm not sure what I meant," said Ryan. Then he left. He didn't want to see who was in the bathroom. Part of him wanted to know who it was, but another part didn't want to complicate his thinking. Later he told Franklin that it might have been Harriet, but it might have been somebody else entirely.

As he drove back to City Hall, Ryan thought about Janice's appetite for men. She had no sexual restrictions other than the fact that she didn't like pain—or serious pain, since even spanking pleased her. Sometimes she liked to masturbate Ryan, squeezing his penis so it hurt, holding back his orgasm so the sperm would shoot farther. Sometimes she liked to have the sperm shoot in her face. She called it an absolute turn-on. She would rub it across her cheeks or forehead or make Ryan rub it until all trace was gone. Ryan had been excited and repelled by this. But he had never been with another woman, before or since, who had a passion for such recreations.

Twenty-two

Hark Powers was the first person to maintain that the L-shaped scar on Aaron's cheek stood for Lucifer, as if Lucifer had given Aaron a special tattoo, claiming him for his own. Soon everyone was saying it. Indeed, it was the sort of assertion that people liked. It clarified the world. Of course, it was always said as a kind of joke, but for some people it was less of a joke than for others.

Bullies often have a sentimental streak. They dislike believing in meanness for its own sake. They like to put their desire to hit and control in the service of some larger cause. This is no more than pretext, but it allows the bully to enjoy his feelings of power with a diminished degree of guilt. He is able to tell himself that he is hitting his victim not because he likes to hit but because his victim deserves punishment. This is how it was with Hark Powers.

It was not surprising to me, as it had been to Ryan Tavich, that Hark became involved with the Friends of Sharon Malloy. Like many others, he believed that whoever had abducted Sharon was somebody passing through town, though he also felt certain this person was connected to Houari Chihani and Inquiries into the Right. Hark had been incensed that someone from the IIR would put bombs on the window ledges of two of Aurelius's schools and he was outraged at the desecration in Homeland Cemetery. Hark had family buried in the cemetery, so that sacrilege hit especially close to home. He kept thinking about how the tombstones had been tipped over and the image was always fresh and awful in his mind. Or at least this was how he made it sound when he talked about it at Bud's Tavern.

"Atheists" was how Hark described the members of the IIR, even though Hark had rarely seen the inside of a church himself.

Hark was not stupid but he was one of those young people common in small towns who have chosen ignorance. It was almost a philosophical position adopted against the outside world and he wore his blinders with pride and defiance. On the bumper of his pickup truck was the slogan "Buy American" and on his rear window he had a little American flag. There was also a bumper sticker that said something about having to peel his cold fingers from the butt of his smoking revolver. Needless to say, he believed in assault weapons for everyone. On the other hand, he was said to be a good mechanic and he could be kindhearted: he often helped on his father's farm, which was run by his older brother. This is not to exonerate Hark, but neither would it be fair just to dismiss him as deficient. He distrusted whatever came from the outside. He didn't only dislike Houari Chihani, he disliked the whole college. And the fact that Aaron had gone to school in Buffalo was one more point against him.

Of course, Hark hated Aaron because of what Aaron had done to his ear. But in the years since, there had been a number of new insults that kept Aaron fresh in Hark's mind. For instance, the young woman who had been using Aaron's bathroom at the time of Ryan's visit was not Harriet Malcomb but Jeanette Richards, who was an assistant manager at Ames department store. She had a somewhat plain face but a dramatic figure. The problem was that she had been dating Hark Powers all fall. Then he learned that she was also seeing Aaron. In a town like Aurelius—where there are few entertainments other than TV—romance and melodrama become exaggerated. The fact that Hark's girlfriend was observed going in and out of Aaron's apartment complex set telephones jangling. Certainly, Hark offered his services to the Friends of Sharon Malloy because he was disturbed by Sharon's disappearance, but he also joined because his girlfriend was seeing his enemy.

At the storefront rented by the Friends of Sharon Malloy, Hark answered the phone, opened mail, and licked envelopes. He also took part in a few searches. Since he had his regular job at Jack Morris's Ford dealership, his time with the Friends was limited to about ten hours a week. Sharon's uncles, Donald Malloy and Paul Leimbach, were often in the storefront and Hark attached himself to them as a one-man honor guard. His muscle was in their service. He cheerfully ran errands for them, as if his connection to them gave him special importance. Hark was a large man with a moon-shaped face. He had an ironic, joking manner that suggested he knew a little more than the people around him and couldn't be fooled. Donald Malloy and Paul Leimbach liked him. They considered him one of their best volunteers, though I am sure they had no idea what a dangerous instrument he could be.

Hark began to keep an eye on Aaron and the others. And Hark had cronies, minor bullies whose help he enlisted. Sometimes, when Chihani drove to Wegmans to do his weekly shopping, one of these men followed him. It was clear to Hark and his friends that the police were interested in Aaron, apart from the charges stemming from the vandalism at Homeland Cemetery. Consequently, they saw their actions as being in the interest of helping the police, just as their work with the Friends of Sharon Malloy was in the interest of helping the police.

Occasionally Hark followed Barry Sanders as well, though he found Barry so repulsive that even the name Little Pink was not good enough for him. Hark didn't give him a name, only a label: The Pink Turd. Hark could see that Barry was terrified of him, which made this kind of minor harassment a pleasure. And the fact that Barry was frightened indicated he had something other than Hark that he was frightened of, meaning he felt guilty.

Hark may not have known that Barry was gay, but he had gone out of his way a number of times to be unpleasant to Jaime Rose. The

population of Aurelius contained a number of gay men, but Jaime
Rose was the only one who was obviously gay, though he didn't hold
up a sign. On the other hand, he liked to say, "If you've got it, flaunt
it." I once asked him why he didn't move to a city with a clearly accepted gay community.

"I've already done that," he told me. "The queers in Aurelius are
so sweet. They like to pass for straight. It makes them desperate. A
nice boy like me can always get a date."

Hark limited his treatment of Jaime to glaring looks. A year earlier, Hark had seen Jaime in Bud's Tavern and made a number of loud
remarks about fags. But Jaime turned it around on him. He was with
three of the women from Make Waves and they all went up to where
Hark was standing with his cronies at the bar. "Listen to him talk,"
said Jaime. "I believe he wants to kiss me. Do you want to kiss me,
Hark?" And Jaime pursed his lips.

Even Hark's cronies laughed. After that Hark said nothing to
Jaime in public.

When minor events like these occur, they are talked about, then
forgotten. It is only in the light of other events that they become significant. For instance, there was Hark's encounter with Houari Chihani. What happened was that Chihani had gone into Malloy's
Pharmacy to buy a bottle of aspirin. It was unlikely he knew that the
owner of the pharmacy was Sharon's uncle, despite the huge picture
in the front window. As I have tried to indicate, flesh-and-blood re-
ality didn't mean much to Chihani. His brain was too full of conversations with the dead, intellectual arguments, and philosophical
ruminations. That particular day, Donald Malloy wasn't in the store.
Chihani was waited on by Mrs. Porter.

Chihani paid for the aspirin and thanked Mrs. Porter. He was
always polite in a rather formal way. As he left, he was blocked at the
door by Hark, who was just coming in. This was told to me by Barry
Sanders, who had been out on the sidewalk. Hark's entrance at that

moment, Barry said, was no accident. Hark had seen Chihani and timed his entrance to coincide with Chihani's exit.

Finding someone before him, Chihani stepped to the left. Hark stepped to the right. Then Chihani stepped to the right and Hark stepped to the left. This was done without Chihani's looking at Hark. Now he looked up. "I beg your pardon," said Chihani.

"And I beg yours," said Hark. He was shorter than Chihani but he was also wider and more muscular.

Chihani stepped to the left and Hark stepped to the right.

Chihani stopped again. "You're doing this on purpose."

"You're doing it on purpose," said Hark.

"Stop this foolishness," said Chihani. He stepped to the right and Hark stepped to the left.

Such events have their little escalation. Chihani raised his cane and shook the handle in Hark's face. "Let me by."

Hark reached out, plucked Chihani's beret from his head, and sailed it into the street.

"That is my hat," said Chihani. "I demand you get it."

Hark grinned. Barry ran into the street and retrieved the beret. Chihani lifted his cane again and Hark grabbed it, so that both men were tugging the cane at the same time. This is when Mrs. Porter intervened.

"Leave him alone, Hark."

Hark let go of the cane and Chihani staggered back. Barry brushed past Hark and gave Chihani his beret. Hark entered the drugstore. Once on the sidewalk, Chihani turned to look at the huge picture of Sharon Malloy in the window.

"What is the reason for that picture being so big?"

"This is her uncle's drugstore," said Barry.

"Ah," said Chihani, "that explains it." He straightened his beret, thanked Barry, and walked off toward his car.

I asked Barry, "Were you going into the drugstore as well?"

"I never go there," said Barry. "I was just walking by. I mean, I go out to Fays Drugs by Wegmans."

Barry had moved back to his mother's house because the suspicions aroused by the IIR after Sharon's disappearance and the fact of his having been charged with vandalism made him nervous about living alone, or so he claimed. He felt claustrophobic at his mother's, but he also liked the attention. At least he was the center of someone's universe, even if it was his mother's. She would look at him and say, "Oh, Barry, what are we going to do with you?" Barry would roll his eyes and sigh but he was asking himself the same question.

When he couldn't stand being at his mother's, Barry would often come visit my house. I say "my house" rather than "me" because Barry often came to see Sadie, whom he liked, especially because she was a friend of Aaron's. In this relationship Sadie was the stronger, even though she was thirteen and he was nineteen, and she would give Barry advice and order him around, though in a kindly way. Sadie was making a braided rag for a project at school, and Barry would help her. Both would sit on the floor, braiding and sewing, while I sat in my old chair reading lab reports. Sometimes I'd make a fire. Late in the evening Sadie would make cocoa. This was at the beginning of October. Often I reminded myself of the falseness of it, the illusion of comfort and familial warmth, even with such an odd family as the one Barry, Sadie, and I made. Sadie was here because her father was pursuing the person responsible for abducting Sharon and because he was afraid to leave her by herself. Barry was here because people thought he had something to do with the abduction. Our domestic pleasure existed only because a young girl had disappeared.

But on Wednesday, October 11, there was a new development. A man in Somerset, Pennsylvania, east of Pittsburgh, was arrested for trying to coax a ten-year-old boy into his van. His name was Daniel

Layman and he described himself as a part-time plumber. He was unmarried and in his late thirties. He had gotten in trouble about five years earlier for fondling a little boy at a Sunday-school picnic.

Under questioning, Layman confessed to abducting three other children and killing them. One of those children was Sharon Malloy. He said he had lured her into his van, taken her to a state park about thirty minutes away, raped her, and buried her body in the woods. He described her wavy brown hair and blue sweater. He said she kept asking for her daddy.

When the state police in Potterville were contacted about Layman's confession, Captain Percy called the Friends of Sharon Malloy to say he needed volunteers to search Henderson State Park more carefully. That was the closest park, but thirty-five miles south of Aurelius there was Hannible State Park. Percy also sent two men down to Somerset to question Layman.

By Friday morning two hundred men and women were once again searching the park. The police had dogs and a helicopter. Hark Powers was in charge of a squad of twenty volunteers. Nothing was found on Friday and they all returned on Saturday. More people joined the search, but nothing was found all weekend.

The men whom Captain Percy sent to question Daniel Layman called in on Saturday with new information: Layman described the park as having a river. Henderson State Park had no river, but the Loomis River cut through Hannible State Park. So on Sunday about three hundred searchers descended on Hannible.

The other two children whom Daniel Layman confessed to having abducted and killed were also missing, and he gave vague directions to where he had buried their bodies. So search parties were sent out in two other locations as well, one near Northampton, Massachusetts, and the other in Vermont. But neither child was found and by the beginning of the following week the police suspected that Layman was lying, that he was crazy or wanted the publicity or was just one more guilty soul in search of punishment.

By Wednesday more than seven hundred people had participated in the searches in Henderson and Hannible State Parks. Some spent half a day, some spent several days. Some drove down from Utica and even Syracuse. The effect was to unite people in a way they had not been united before. And as it became increasingly obvious that Daniel Layman was lying, they became even more indignant.

Then something happened that turned people's attention in a different direction.

Twenty-three

Monday morning, October 16, Chuck Hawley arrived for work at City Hall at five-thirty. It was still dark and he could see stars. The police department has a side entrance to the building and as Chuck approached it he saw a cardboard box—a Budweiser beer case, actually—resting on the step in front of the door. Chuck couldn't open the door without moving the box, so he picked it up. People later said this was brave of him because it might have been a bomb, but my cousin is not an imaginative man and the idea of the box's containing a bomb did not occur to him. He said the box was light. He took it inside.

Josh Riley was on duty, or rather he was snoozing at his desk with his forehead on the blotter next to several Baby Ruth candy bar wrappers. Chuck put the box on the table and opened it. Neatly folded inside was a blue sweater, a white blouse, a pair of jeans, girl's underwear, white socks, a pair of Adidas sneakers, and a red backpack. Chuck began to open the backpack and then didn't. Instead he telephoned Ryan Tavich, who, at twenty minutes to six, was still asleep.

Ryan answered on the third ring and heard Chuck's excited voice on the other end of the line. "Someone just returned Sharon Malloy's clothes to us."

Ten minutes later, Ryan entered police headquarters, beating Chief Schmidt by five minutes. Captain Percy had to drive from Potterville and arrived at five past six.

Patty McClosky, Chief Schmidt's secretary, heard about the clothes and the backpack when she got to work at eight-fifteen, though by that time the box and its contents had been sent to the state police lab in Ithaca. Just after she poured herself a first cup of coffee, she called her friend Denise Clark.

"All the clothes were washed, ironed, and folded," she said, "even the socks and underwear."

At nine o'clock Frieda Kraus called Franklin from the office as he was leaving the house.

"Chuck Hawley found a box with all of Sharon's clothes right outside City Hall this morning. Denise Clark just told me."

Franklin must have wondered how Denise Clark was privy to such information. Then he called Ryan Tavich.

"It's true," said Ryan, "but I can't say anything about it right now."

Within the hour the police received calls from the Utica, Syracuse, and Albany newspapers, as well as four TV stations. Channel 9 in Syracuse sent down a crew and they parked their white van in front of City Hall at ten o'clock. At noon Chief Schmidt announced a news conference for three that afternoon.

Because of the response, the news conference was held in the city council's chambers on the second floor of City Hall rather than in Chief Schmidt's office. There was some difficulty about protocol since Captain Percy was in charge of the case. On the other hand, the box had been left on Chief Schmidt's doorstep and so Percy suggested that Schmidt take the city council president's seat. Percy sat on his right along with one of his lieutenants, Peter Marcos, a photogenic young man who had been brought down from Albany. Next to Marcos were Ryan Tavich and Dr. Malloy. The mayor, Bernie Kowalski, was on the other side of Chief Schmidt.

More than fifty journalists were present from newspapers, TV, radio, magazines, and the wire services. The *New York Times* and the *New York Post* both had a reporter. Franklin managed to squeeze his way to the front. The floor was covered with cables from the TV crews. Franklin had expected to see the box itself but there was no sign of it. He felt glad about that. He thought of the blue sweater that Paula had given to Sadie as a peace token and how Sadie had given it to Sharon. Franklin hadn't wanted to see the sweater again.

Chief Schmidt began by making a formal statement to the effect that Sharon Malloy's clothes had been found in a box outside the door of police headquarters at five-thirty that morning by a police sergeant. They had been identified by Sharon Malloy's family and sent to the state police lab in Ithaca.

"Is there any idea who put them there?" asked a reporter.

"Not at this time."

"When were they put there?"

"Sometime between three-thirty and five-thirty this morning," said Chief Schmidt. "They were blocking the door and the last person using the door had left at three-thirty."

"Were there any bloodstains on the clothes?"

"No."

"Were there any stains of any kind?"

"The clothes had been washed, ironed, and folded. They appear to have been washed several times."

"So there might have been stains on the clothes which had been washed off."

"That's possible," said Chief Schmidt.

"Was there a note or anything of that sort?"

"Nothing," said Percy.

Dr. Malloy sat at the table looking down at its surface. It was a heavy oak table, as old as City Hall itself, and had a rich golden color. Someone lit a cigarette and Percy announced there would be no smoking. The TV lights and cameras were placed at the sides of the room. News photographers crept to the front to snap pictures of the chief of police and Dr. Malloy.

"Was there anyone in police headquarters when the clothes were left outside?"

"An officer was on duty."

"Did he hear anything?"

"No," said Chief Schmidt.

"So whoever left the box might have come on foot?"

"Quite possibly."

"Does this mean the man who left it was a local person?"

Captain Percy interrupted. "We have no evidence to suggest whether the box was left by a man or a woman."

"Then the person, man or woman, is a local person?"

Captain Percy stood up and placed his hands on the table. "We've no evidence that the person responsible for Miss Malloy's disappearance and the person who returned the box are the same."

"But isn't it likely?"

"We have no evidence to that effect."

"Do you think Sharon Malloy is still alive?"

"We hope so," said Chief Schmidt, "but we don't know one way or the other."

"What was in the backpack?"

"Sharon's schoolbooks, notebooks, and school supplies."

"Will the return of the clothes change the nature of the investigation?"

"How do you mean?" asked Chief Schmidt.

"Doesn't it raise the possibility that whoever did it is a local person?"

Captain Percy spoke again, "We have never assumed one way or the other that if Miss Malloy was abducted it was either done by a local person or by someone from out of town."

"What do you mean 'if she was abducted'?" asked a reporter.

"We have no positive evidence that she was in fact abducted. We only know she is missing."

"Are you suggesting she returned the clothes herself?"

Someone laughed in the back of the room and Captain Percy looked in that direction but his face betrayed no emotion.

"I'm saying we don't know one way or the other," said Percy.

"Has Sharon's family heard from her or from anyone else in regard to her?"

"No," answered Chief Schmidt. Percy sat back down.

"Do you think she might be dead?"

"We have no evidence one way or another."

"Why do you think the clothes were returned?" asked Franklin.

"We have no idea," said Captain Percy.

"Does it seem like a taunt?"

"I can't comment on that," said Captain Percy. "We have no evidence one way or another."

"What effect does the return of the clothes have on Daniel Layman's confession?"

Chief Schmidt glanced over at Percy. "That investigation is ongoing and I am unable to comment upon it at this time."

"Did Layman say that he had removed the girl's clothes?"

"I can't comment on that."

"Do you think someone returned the clothes," asked Franklin, "as a way of indicating that Daniel Layman had no involvement in the matter?"

"I have no idea."

"Do you have an opinion?" asked someone from Channel 9. Several other reporters laughed.

Captain Percy stood up again. "We are in the business of acquiring and trying to understand a body of information. We don't know why someone returned the clothes. We don't know if the person who did it had anything to do with the abduction or even if there was an abduction. We don't know if the return of the clothes had anything to do with Daniel Layman one way or the other. We don't know if this means it was a local crime or not."

Percy wasn't being entirely truthful. When he heard about the return of the clothes, he began shifting assignments and put ten men back on the case. All day they had been questioning people who lived in the vicinity of City Hall to learn if they had seen anything. And the fact that Aaron McNeal lived only two blocks away was not ignored. Percy had acquired a search warrant that morning and lab men from Ithaca had gone over every inch of Aaron's apartment. Aaron had not protested. He had taken a chair and laptop computer into the hall and continued his work as if the police hadn't been there.

"He looked right through us," said Chuck Hawley. "It made me want to smack him." Chuck had glanced over Aaron's shoulder at the small monitor and had seen nothing but numbers. This had also bothered him. "It wasn't even words," he said.

The activities of the members of the IIR and Houari Chihani the previous night had also been investigated. Percy wanted to get a search warrant to go through Chihani's house, but Chief Schmidt felt it would be pointless. These talks took place in Schmidt's office but they were overheard by Patty McClosky and others. By the time of the press conference, the nature of these talks, mostly in a garbled form, were known to dozens of people. The main point, not lost on anyone, was that Chihani and the IIR were still under suspicion.

"The police searched Aaron McNeal's apartment this morning," said a reporter. "Was anything found to incriminate him?"

"I'm not at liberty to say," said Chief Schmidt.

Chuck Hawley had said, "They were hoping they'd at least find some pot. Then they could use some muscle on him. But he was totally clean."

"So the members of the IIR are still suspects?"

"It is mistaken to call them suspects," said Schmidt. "At this point no one is a suspect and no one is not a suspect."

"Could Herbst have driven over from Troy with the clothes?"

"I'm not at liberty to say."

Actually no evidence existed that Oscar had left his house.

"What about the kid who went home to Kingston—could he have driven over?"

"I'm not at liberty to say."

The reporter meant Jason Irving, who also had been home all night. But the IIR members who still lived in Aurelius didn't have perfect alibis. Barry's mother swore he had been home but the police didn't take that as positive proof. As Chuck told me, "Any of those kids could have ducked out for five minutes and brought the box to City Hall. Even the fat one. I mean, who's around then? You could have done it yourself."

"Would it be possible to wash all trace of blood out of the clothes?" asked a reporter.

"I don't believe so," said Schmidt.

"No, it would not," said Percy.

"So what conclusions do you draw from this?"

"That there was no blood on the clothes," said Percy.

Someone laughed.

"What about other bodily fluids?" asked a reporter. "Could all trace of sperm be removed from the clothes?"

"There we're on shakier ground," said Schmidt.

"You mean it could be?"

"That's what I've been told."

"So you're saying that no trace of sperm was found on the clothes."

"That is correct."

"Was anything found on the clothes?"

"Just the usual wear and tear."

"Were the clothes torn in anyway?"

"No, I didn't mean that."

"So if Sharon Malloy was killed, she was killed either in a way not to draw blood or she was killed while not wearing the clothes."

This was asked by a reporter from Utica. By this point the press conference had come down to the level of Twenty Questions and no one really thought about the flesh-and-blood Sharon Malloy anymore. Dr. Malloy neither spoke nor even looked up at the reporters. He held the edge of the table with both hands and sat slightly forward in his chair, not resting against the back. His brother, Donald, was at the rear of the room. His brother-in-law, Paul Leimbach, had arrived late and stood by the door. The room was hot from the TV lights. It was nearly four o'clock.

"We have no knowledge of what happened to Sharon Malloy," said Chief Schmidt.

"So it is possible that she was raped?" asked a reporter.

This was when Dr. Malloy blew up. "Don't you realize you are talking about a child? A fourteen-year-old girl? Do you know how wonderful she is? Of course whoever stole her lives here. He lives right here in this town!"

There was a jabber of reporters asking Dr. Malloy if he knew who it was. Photographers pushed to the front to take pictures. People got to their feet. Ryan put his arm around the doctor's shoulder and tried to lead him away from the table and out the back door. Dr. Malloy had begun to weep and kept wiping his eyes brusquely with the back of his hand. His brother shoved through the crowd toward the front of the room.

"How dare you ask if she's been raped!" shouted Dr. Malloy.

Chief Schmidt motioned to Ryan. "Get him out of here."

Donald Malloy reached the council table. "Sure it was someone in town," he shouted. "Someone took her. Someone stole her! Someone's got to be punished for it!"

"Who is it?" people kept asking.

Chief Schmidt found a gavel and he banged it on the table. "Unless you return to your seats, I'll clear the room."

"We'll find the person," said Donald. "The Friends of Sharon

Malloy is now offering $50,000 for any information as to Sharon's whereabouts and $100,000 for her safe return."

This created more of a stir and more pictures were taken.

Chuck Hawley took Donald's arm and urged him to the back door. Ryan had already left with Dr. Malloy. Reporters kept shouting questions and Chief Schmidt kept hitting the table with his gavel. Franklin wrote furiously in his notebook. The only person who showed no expression, who looked like the very rock of Gibraltar, according to Chuck Hawley, was Captain Percy.

When the room quieted down, Captain Percy spoke. "You know exactly what we know, which is little. We don't know the nature of this crime. We don't know that Sharon was abducted. All we know is that sometime between three-thirty and five-thirty this morning her clothes and backpack were returned to the police. The clothes had been cleaned, ironed, and folded. Her white leather Adidas tennis shoes had been polished. We don't know who did this or if the same person had anything to do with Sharon's being missing."

Again Captain Percy was not telling the whole truth. There were two other items in Sharon's backpack, along with her school supplies. The first was a mannequin's hand: a left hand, flesh-colored, with painted nails. Sharon's parents and several of her friends, including Sadie, said they had never seen it before.

The second item was a business-size envelope containing a single sheet of paper on which was a list of words constructed from letters cut out of a newspaper. The words were "CUNT," "FILTH," "FUCK," "PUSSY," "BITCH," "DIRT," "WHORE," and half a dozen more in a single column. But the words had been changed, or perhaps edited. Black slashes had been drawn across some of the letters so that "CUNT" became "UNT," "FILTH" became "LTH." All the words had been altered and the black slashes had been drawn over and over, cutting so deep into the paper that the "D" in "DIRT," for instance, was nearly obliter-

ated. Only Captain Percy and Chief Schmidt knew about the contents
of the envelope and they kept it to themselves. As for the mannequin's
hand, it was known to everyone in the office. Even Franklin knew
about the hand, although Chief Schmidt asked him not to mention
it. This hardly mattered. Within two days the presence of the hand in
the backpack became general knowledge.

Twenty-four

Captain Percy's assertion that the return of the clothing didn't indicate that Sharon's abductor was from Aurelius or from the surrounding area convinced no one. And the fact that Percy said there was no evidence that Sharon had been abducted also had no impact. The general consensus was that the clothes had been returned by Sharon's abductor to taunt the police. People saw it as an act of bravado. And possibly the person objected to the idea of Daniel Layman in Somerset, Pennsylvania, claiming credit for something that he or she had done. I say he or she but everyone around here believed that the abductor was a man.

These were ideas the police held as well, at least according to Ryan, but that didn't mean Captain Percy could tell a roomful of journalists that he believed a local man was responsible for abducting Sharon Malloy. I'm sure the journalists had gone to the press conference expecting to learn something sensational. To a large degree they had been frustrated. The return of the clothing was sinister without being dramatic. Dr. Malloy's outburst partly made up for their disappointment.

That evening on TV thousands of people across the state, and perhaps the nation, saw Dr. Malloy jump up and shout, "Don't you realize you are talking about a child? A fourteen-year-old girl? Do you know how wonderful she is? Of course whoever stole her lives here. He lives right here in this town!"

After the press conference a number of editorials appeared in area papers asking whether the authorities were doing enough to find the abductor of Sharon Malloy. As a result, Captain Percy was instructed to put more officers on the case, giving him a total—a task force, they called themselves—of twenty-five.

The increasing belief that the criminal lived among us put more pressure on the IIR. As long as people had believed that the criminal was someone from far away, Chihani and the other members of the group had been viewed with no more than suspicion. Possibly there was a link between the criminal and the IIR but even that was only argued by people like Hark Powers. Now it didn't seem so far-fetched. And the news that Aaron's apartment had been searched by the police was seen as evidence of his involvement. Chihani and the remaining IIR members were subjected to even greater scrutiny. Barry complained that people stared at him more than ever. "As if I stole something," he said.

Nor was the group being overly sensitive about its lack of popularity. Paula McNeal heard in the dean's office that the school was consulting its lawyers to see if it could legally suspend the members of the IIR before their trial for vandalism.

Toward the end of the week the clothes were returned, Bob Jenks and Joany Rustoff dropped out of college and went back to their parents' houses in Utica. A few days later they drove to Seattle, where Bob's older brother worked for a software company. This left six members, as well as Chihani. I'm afraid that Bob and Joany's departure made people even more suspicious of the others, as if their defection indicated the guilt of the entire group. Of course Bob and Joany let Captain Percy know what they were doing and how to reach them in a hurry.

People seemed to feel that if someone in town was guilty, then it would be better for the guilty party to be a person nobody liked. Aaron already had a peculiar history among us. Barry was funny to look at. Leon was fat, itself proof of perversion. Jesse and Shannon showed their scorn for the status quo in their every gesture. Harriet had a cold beauty that led people to believe she thought herself better than everyone else. And then there was Houari Chihani and his Citroën.

What many dreaded was that the guilty party might be someone whom nobody suspected, a so-called pillar of the community. For instance, what if Dr. Malloy had abducted and killed his own daughter? Or even Paul Leimbach—didn't suspicion often fall on family members? For the crime to have been committed by someone who was respected gave the community itself an element of culpability. We hadn't seen his wickedness. He'd lived among us as a friend. One cannot remove a pillar of the community without the whole community's trembling. Far better to find an outsider whose idiosyncrasies already made him suspect.

The return of Sharon's clothing made Hark's accusations more plausible. All along Hark had argued that the IIR was involved. Now here he was standing at the bar at Bud's Tavern saying, "I told you so," louder than ever. When it became known that a mannequin's hand had been discovered in Sharon's backpack, the very oddness of it gave Hark additional credibility. The fake hand made no sense. It was awful and meaningless. Hark said it was like Oscar's false bombs or even Aaron's senseless violence. So Hark found he had more listeners and his stock went up a little. And his cronies were eager to say how Hark had been right all along, because their stock went up too. It would be wrong to call them influential in any way, but they were aware of the increased notice they received.

Who were these cronies? There were three: Jeb Hendricks, who worked at the Midas Muffler by Wegmans; Ernie Corelli, who worked at Henderson's Plumbing and Heating; and Jimmy Feldman, who had a janitorial position at Knox Consolidated. They had known Hark all their lives, though they were a few years younger than Hark.

They went hunting together in the fall and fishing in the spring. In the summer there was softball. Feldman was married but the others were single. He had married while still in high school—the girl was pregnant—and I don't believe he graduated.

All, along with Hark, were men with complaints. If a favorite football team lost a game, it was because the fix was in. If state taxes went up, it was because the money went down to the city, to welfare recipients and greedy minorities. Apart from being complainers, they were rather normal young men who looked at the world and their place in it with a mixture of confusion and resentment. They liked Hark because he had opinions and placed the blame where they liked to see it placed: elsewhere. He was stronger than they were. He was louder, could drink more, and shot a deer when the others missed. Most nights two or more of these young men were to be found at Bud's Tavern drinking beer, shooting pool, and complaining. Sometimes they were joined by two or three others rather like themselves. Added to their talk was now the subject of Sharon's disappearance.

"If Aaron McNeal's not involved in this," Hark would declare, "I'll give my other fucking ear."

In these discussions truth was not a matter of logic but came from a strength of conviction and the ability to shout down one's opponents. The more attention Hark received, the louder he became, until he himself, clearly, believed everything he said.

"Wasn't the Arab's car seen right when Sharon disappeared?" he would ask.

And his cronies would nod and others would nod as well.

"It's one thing for the cops to say they don't have clear proof they can take to court," Hark would argue. "But it's another thing not to know. I mean, know in your fucking heart!"

Although I point to Hark Powers, his claims were not unlike

those heard in other taverns and houses around Aurelius. He may have been the loudest but his ideas came to be shared by many. Indeed, I heard similar ones expressed within the teachers' lounge at Knox Consolidated.

Of all the IIR members, it was Barry whose isolation I understood best, as he visited me frequently. Since the beginning of September, he had had a boyfriend at Aurelius College, someone named Ralph who hoped to become an electrical engineer. The attention that Barry received as a member of Inquiries into the Right bothered Ralph from the start. Then, after Sharon's disappearance, when charges were brought against the group for vandalizing Homeland Cemetery, he told Barry that he didn't want to see him anymore, though he assured him they were still friends. It appears they had a scene in Ralph's dorm room, where Barry confessed that he might possibly be in love with Ralph and that he saw Ralph's decision not to see him anymore as a cruel betrayal.

The Friday after Sharon's clothes turned up, Barry came to see me. He was quite open about his bitterness. He was lonely. His heart was broken. He was destined to be lonely all his life.

"No one will like me again," he said.

"What about that man in town?" I asked.

"Who do you mean?"

"That first man you were involved with." I had, in fact, remained interested in this person, since Barry refused to divulge his name.

"I didn't like him," said Barry.

"What did you do with him?" I asked.

"Nothing nice."

"But what did you do?"

"He only wanted me to masturbate him and he wouldn't touch me at all. And he was cross."

"You mean he yelled at you?"

"Nothing like that. He insisted I wash my hands and he stood beside me to make sure I did it right."

Barry's main problem, in terms of his loneliness, was that he was either at school or at his mother's. Plainly, he wasn't going to meet other men unless he expanded his social circle. I found myself thinking about Jaime Rose, but there was nothing to suggest that Jaime would find Barry anything but silly. I knew, however, that Jaime went out. He bowled and he belonged to a garden club at the library. I'd even seen him sometimes in bars, not Bud's Tavern but the bar at Gillian's Motel. So I told Barry he needed to go out more often. This was not radical advice.

"People stare at me," said Barry.

"You're not going to meet people unless you go out."

"I don't like to drink."

"There are reading groups at the library. There's a jazz society and a travel club. You have to exert yourself."

There is an egalitarian quality to needs. We all have them. Barry's need for companionship differed from no one else's. At Aurelius College that Saturday night the ski club sponsored a dance in the cafeteria featuring a local band called Unreasonable Behavior. And in the house of one of the Spanish professors, Ricardo Diaz, the Latin League was holding a Mexican dinner—tacos, enchiladas verdes, chicken mole, and Dr Pepper.

Downtown there was a function at the Masonic Temple and the Elks were holding an auction to raise money for the Little League. The Good Fellowship Evangelical Church was having a pancake supper. Aurelius's several Italian restaurants were busy and if you stood in front of City Hall and sniffed deeply you could probably detect the smells of oregano and grease. The cocktail lounge at Gillian's Motel was offering ladies two drinks for the price of one. Bud's Tavern had free buffalo wings. The parking lot of Landry's bowling alley was full of pickup trucks. The Domino's Pizza delivery truck wove its way back and forth through the town like the needle and thread tying everything nearly together. The Strand Theater was showing something called *The Stupids* to a packed house. The teenagers who worked at the sub shop on Main Street were busy making sandwiches.

That Saturday evening Barry Sanders had decided to go out—a significant decision—and had gone to Landry's bowling alley. He went not to play but to sit at a table and drink Coke. Although this seems like an innocent occupation, Barry believed he was being quite daring. Who knew the nature of his fantasies? He wore a new blue shirt and his white hair was carefully combed. He sipped his Coke, blinked his pink eyes behind his thick glasses, and whenever there was a loud crash of pins, he probably gave a little jump. Barry, in his way, was out on the town.

Aaron had also gone out that evening. He had a drink at Gillian's with Jeanette Richards, with whom his relationship was cooling, and when she left around seven-thirty he stayed to talk to an English teacher from the high school, Ron Slavitt, who wrote poetry. Aaron contended that poetry was a dead medium; Ron Slavitt disagreed. Jaime Rose was also at Gillian's, drinking alone at the bar. He liked elaborate drinks: fresh fruit daiquiris and drinks with Kahlúa.

Franklin and Paula had taken Sadie to dinner to Angotti's Spaghetti House. Paula tried to talk to Sadie about school but Sadie was monosyllabic. She had not wanted spaghetti and was eating a hamburger and French fries. Earlier that week Sadie had seen her blue sweater on the news after it came back from the state police lab in Ithaca. She had never told Paula that she had given the sweater to Sharon Malloy, though Paula knew it and Sadie felt guilty. She also had a horror, she revealed later, that the sweater would be returned to her. A horror not because of its connection to Paula but because of its connection to Sharon. Sadie even imagined that she would find blood spots where the police had found none, which was silly. When Sadie ate, her hair swept across her plate, coming precariously near the ketchup. Both Franklin and Paula were at the edge of telling Sadie to tuck her hair back behind her ears, but they forbore.

Ryan Tavich had taken Cookie Evans to dinner at Mike's Steak House out by the strip mall. Between his usual work and the time he gave to Captain Percy, he had been putting in twelve-hour days and he felt he needed a break. But he kept thinking about the mannequin's hand in Sharon's backpack. And he thought about Janice McNeal, her quick voice and how she had touched him with her hands. He could almost feel it and the memory made his food tasteless in his mouth.

Even though Cookie Evans exhausted Ryan with her energy, he found it comfortable to go out with her because she didn't mind doing the talking. Indeed, she hardly noticed whether Ryan spoke or not. As they ate, she reviewed for Ryan all the women who had come into Make Waves during the week. There seemed an endless number. Ryan nodded, smiled, and thought about Janice McNeal. Cookie counted her customers off on her fingers. Her nails were long and dark red. Her short hair was curled and frosted. Ryan thought her head looked landscaped and he told himself to remember to tell this to Franklin, who claimed he never joked.

At one point Ryan asked, "Did any of these women talk about Sharon Malloy?"

Cookie looked at him with exasperation. "That's *all* they talked about. And their husbands, of course. It's surprising how many of them think themselves in danger."

At Bud's Tavern this was also Hark Powers's subject. Sheila Murphy was tending bar and she supplied Hark, Jeb Hendricks, Ernie

Corelli, and Jimmy Feldman with pitchers of beer, as well as pork rinds and potato skins. The room was smoky and there was the click of pool balls. Country music and sometimes an old Sinatra song played on the jukebox.

"I saw a TV show," said Hark, "where the killer put the body in the graveyard. He took dirt out of a new grave and stuck the body right on top of the coffin. I bet the state cops haven't even checked the graves. You do something like snatching a girl and it's only so long before you snatch another. It's a sickness."

And his cronies thought about this sickness and about how it could be stopped.

Dr. Malloy and his family spent their night at home with the Leimbachs. They tried to have a fairly normal Saturday evening with dinner, television, and conversation but they knew they were doing nothing more than waiting for the phone to ring. My cousin Chuck Hawley sat outside Dr. Malloy's house in a patrol car listening to talk radio. Over at the Friends of Sharon Malloy a dozen volunteers, including Donald Malloy, were mailing out posters. Captain Percy was home in his neat little ranch house in Potterville reading the reports submitted to him by the Sharon Malloy task force. There was nothing in them he didn't know.

At eight o'clock, just as I was making myself a bowl of soup, Barry was leaving Landry's bowling alley. He got in his rusty Ford Fairlane and drove to the sub shop downtown because he was hungry and had grown bored watching people bowl. He had talked to no one but it was too early to go home, where his mother would ask where he had been and if he had had a good time. Then she would look at him with a worried expression.

There were no parking spaces in front of the sub shop so he parked a block away. He disliked parallel parking and needed a lot of room, two spaces instead of one. It was a cool evening with half a moon in a clear sky. Barry paused to see if he could hear any geese.

He liked it when they flew high over the town with their distant and energetic honking. This night he heard nothing except the jukebox from Bud's Tavern. Barry didn't like country music. He preferred a group called Phish. But in general he didn't see much purpose in music.

At the sub shop he ordered a veggie and cheese and a large Coke. He thought of eating at a table but there were five teenage boys in the shop who kept looking at him and grinning. Having just come in from out of doors, Barry knew he was blinking more than usual. And when he was at the counter with his back turned to the boys, he heard one of them say, "Little Pink." Although Barry hated how he looked, he had become fairly stoical about it. He no longer considered dyeing his hair, using makeup, and wearing tinted contact lenses—fantasies he had had in the past. But he didn't wish to eat his sandwich while being gawked at.

He walked back up Main Street toward his car. He would drive over to the college campus and eat his sandwich there. If he went home, his mother would ask him why he had wasted his money at the sub shop when she could have made him a perfectly good sandwich out of the food in their icebox.

When Barry was half a block from his car, someone called to him: "Hey, Little Pink, wait up."

Hark Powers and three other men were crossing Main Street toward him. Barry had an almost overpowering wish to run but he kept still.

Hark joined him on the sidewalk, standing between him and his car, which he could see parked in front of Weaver's Bakery. Barry recognized Jeb Hendricks but he didn't know the other two.

"Where're you going, Little Pink?" asked Hark.

"Home."

"What's the hurry?"

"I just want to go home, that's all."

"Is your mother expecting you?" asked Hark. "You wouldn't want to be late." Hark and Jeb Hendricks wore jean jackets. The other two wore dark sweatshirts.

"It's not that. I just want to go home."

"Whatcha got there, Little Pink?"

Barry's Coke was in his left hand and his veggie and cheese, rolled in white paper to the size of a thin football, was in his right.

"Just a sandwich."

"Let's see." Hark plucked the sandwich from Barry's hand, unwrapped it and dropped the paper on the sidewalk. Then he took a bite. "Um, veggie and cheese. It's still warm. I like veggie and cheese. Want a bite, Jeb?"

Hark gave the sandwich to Jeb, who took a bite and gave the sandwich to Ernie Corelli. Barry watched the three men chewing.

"No meat?" asked Ernie.

"I don't eat meat," said Barry.

"Meat's bad for Little Pink," said Hark. "It makes him pink."

Barry started to ask for his sandwich back but he decided he didn't want it anymore. Hark took another bite.

"What're you drinking, Little Pink?" asked Hark, with his mouth full.

"Coke."

"Lemme see."

Barry held the cup to his chest and stepped away. "No, it's mine."

Hark reached out and knocked the cup from Barry's hand. Half the Coke spilled down Barry's new blue shirt and the rest splashed on the sidewalk.

"Looks like you spilled your Coke, Little Pink," said Hark.

Barry turned and began walking toward the sub shop. He didn't have enough money to get another sandwich but he meant to wait inside until Hark and his friends were gone. His wet shirt felt cold and sticky.

"Hey, I'm talking to you, Little Pink."

Barry kept walking. Although he was afraid of Hark, he was even more afraid of crying.

Hark grabbed his shoulder, spun him around, and slammed him up against the brick front of a building. "I said I was talking to you." Hark's face was about eight inches from his own. Barry's head had knocked against the brick and it hurt.

"Leave me alone," said Barry.

Hark lightly slapped his face. "I'm the one who gives the orders," he said pleasantly.

Barry saw someone in front of the sub shop watching them. He realized it was Aaron.

Hark slapped him a little harder. "I'm talking to you, Little Pink. Why don't you tell us about Sharon?"

"What do you mean?" asked Barry. Out of the corner of his eye, he still saw Aaron, not moving, just watching.

"You wanted to touch her, didn't you?"

"Sharon? Why should I touch her?" Barry wanted to call to Aaron. He took a handkerchief from his back pocket and wiped the front of his shirt. The Coke was cold against his skin.

"I heard you were the one who took back Sharon's clothes," said Hark.

Barry looked at him. He smelled beer on Hark's breath.

"Her clothes?"

"Did that Arab give them to you?" He pronounced it with a long A: A-rab.

Barry turned quickly to his left and began running toward the sub shop. He hadn't gone five feet before Hark leapt on his back, knocking him to the sidewalk. Barry slid on his belly and his glasses fell off. Hark turned him over and tried to punch Barry in the face.

"I didn't say you could do that!" Hark shouted.

Barry covered his face with his arms and lay on his back with Hark astride him. Hark kept slapping at his arms, hitting his elbows and wrists.

Then Hark seemed to leap backward. Barry opened his eyes. Through the blur of his vision, he saw that Aaron had grabbed Hark's long hair and was dragging him backward. Hark scrambled to his feet and tried to take a swing at Aaron, who kicked him. Then Jeb Hendricks swung at Aaron, then Ernie Corelli and Jimmy Feldman. Aaron tried to defend himself, putting his back to a parked car and swinging, but he wasn't a fighter. Barry curled himself up into a ball on the sidewalk and covered his head with his hands. He couldn't stand the sound of the men hitting Aaron, the thunk of their fists. He wished he wasn't a coward.

Aaron was knocked to the sidewalk and Hark and two of the others tried to kick him, but they got in one another's way. Barry heard footsteps running toward them. He looked between his fingers to see Ryan Tavich.

"Police!" shouted Ryan. He grabbed Hark by the collar and yanked him away. The other men stepped back from Aaron, who continued to lie on the sidewalk.

"They attacked me," said Barry. He tried standing up but his knees felt weak. "They ate my sandwich. Aaron tried to stop them." He wiped his eyes and looked around for his glasses.

Ryan held Hark Powers's arm. About a dozen other people had run over, including the teenagers who had been in the sub shop.

"Ask them about Sharon Malloy," said Hark.

Aaron got to his feet. There was blood on his face. He bent over and picked up Barry's glasses from the gutter. A police car with its flashers on pulled up on Main Street. Aaron gave the glasses to Barry.

"You should be careful, Hark," said Aaron. "You've only got one ear left."

Hark was still being held by Ryan Tavich. Aaron took a step forward and kicked out, hitting Hark hard in the crotch. Hark gasped and doubled over, breaking loose from Ryan. Immediately, one of the policemen grabbed Aaron from behind.

Twenty-five

I was four when my father was sent to Korea, which was the last I saw of him. My mother moved back to her mother's house in Aurelius. We had been living in Utica, though I remember little of it: big people, busy streets. My grandfather was dead by then, but my grandmother was quite healthy, active in her bridge group and at Saint Luke's Episcopal Church. My father's family came from Utica. I hardly knew them. Occasionally an uncle would drive through on his way to Binghamton and stop for half an hour or so. I should have been unhappy that my father was gone, but I was glad. Secretly glad, that is, because my mother missed him and when word came that he had been killed she cried for days. Naturally I felt terribly guilty to feel glad, and when he was killed I even thought—irrationally, of course—that it was my fault because I was pleased to have him out of the house.

We moved back in summer and Aurelius was green. There were flowers everywhere. I was with my mother all day long every day. She read to me and we went for walks. She would tell me stories about the people who lived in the houses we passed. I remembered my father as rough. He liked to tickle me and throw me into the air, which frightened me. It seemed more convenient with him away. If three is a crowd, then he was the one who made it a crowd. After he was killed, I rarely thought of him. Of course, I received lots of sympathy. People patted my head and said it was so sad that I didn't have a father. And this made me guilty as well. As for my grandmother, she was a slower and softer version of my mother and she, too, read to me and took me for walks. It was a happy several years.

Aurelius was a busy place in the early 1950s and there was still train service to Utica. The county fair in Potterville was a big event and every summer Aurelius had its own Fireman's Field Day with rides and games of chance. I looked forward to it and was quite smug about my ability to pop balloons with darts, though I doubt it was anything special. At the Strand there were double features every Saturday afternoon. Once a hypnotist came and did tricks. He hypnotized half the audience and I felt there was something awfully wrong with me that I couldn't be hypnotized. Those fortunate people who were easy subjects got to sit onstage and quack like ducks and cry at an imaginary sick puppy and skip rope without a rope, which was very funny.

What I am saying is that the town felt like an extension of my mother's house. There was no place I couldn't wander, though my mother told me to stay away from the train tracks and not go near the river. But on weekends I climbed on empty boxcars to my heart's content and there were few pleasures to equal throwing stones in the river or dropping them off a bridge. I had half a dozen friends, though these were not terribly close friendships because I was not good at sports. But to wander anywhere and to be assured of people's goodwill was something I took for granted. Maybe I would avoid a certain street because of a rough dog or even a bully like Hark Powers, but there was no fear. Korea and Communism were far away. And there were enough veterans around and enough talk about World War II to make one think that the wars were over for good.

I don't know if I would call my childhood ideal. I often felt lonely and different from other children, partly because I didn't have a father, partly because I wasn't good at sports, partly because I wore glasses. I was sometimes called a sissy and I didn't like that. My cousin Chuck was several years younger than I. He was the oldest of four children. I saw them often but they were too little to be taken seriously. Chuck's mother was my mother's sister, and she was one more woman who was nice to me. Indeed, their refrigerator and cupboards were always open to me. If I was on my bike and was hungry, I might just as easily go to my aunt's house for a snack as to my mother's.

My aunt is an old lady now. My mother and grandmother are dead. Chuck is the only one of my cousins who stayed in Aurelius, and though we sometimes talk, we aren't close. At Christmas I buy him a bottle of whiskey and his wife buys me a tie. But in the time of which I am writing Aurelius seemed the bare bones of the town it was forty years ago. There was no longer a sense of the town as an extension of the home.

When I first came back to Aurelius from New York City twenty years ago, I expected to find the Aurelius of the early fifties. But already the train station had become a pizza parlor and there were empty storefronts on Main Street. Still, compared to New York, it seemed ideal. People never locked their houses or their cars. Several years ago when Jack Shelbourne got an alarm for his BMW, high school students took great pleasure in setting it off to hear it wail. No one had heard a car alarm before.

It was easy to know several generations of Aurelius families. I knew Hark Powers's father. He was a farmer about ten years older than I. And I knew his grandfather as well. Hark's father made Hark play in Little League, and people said that if he played badly or struck out his father hit him. For a few years a long time ago Hark's father had a 1949 Ford coupe with the hood ornament and trunk latch removed and sanded over and the whole car painted a glossy maroon with bright speckles. The muffler had a low musical sound and on Saturday nights he would drive around and around the four blocks of downtown with his friends. Or perhaps he and a friend would double-date and take girls down to the drive-in theater in Norwich. By the age of nineteen he was married, and Hark's oldest brother was born within the year.

Hark's mother came from Morrisville. I'm sure I never laid eyes on her before she had been married for some months. Then she was pointed out because she was so pregnant. She had very soft-looking sandy hair, almost like a baby's hair, and large blue eyes. She had four boys in seven years, then a fifth, Hark, ten years later. I remember one time when we still had a Woolworth's downtown that Hark got lost in the store. When I saw him, which might have been the first time I ever saw him, he was surrounded by racks of women's underwear, bawling his eyes out. He was about three and very round. The Woolworth's had wooden floors and as soon as he began to yowl people hurried toward him and their feet on the wooden floors made hollow clomping noises. I don't know what the occasion was but Hark was wearing a blue sailor suit with blue shorts. When he yowled, he squinched his eyes tightly shut and his tears seemed to pop horizontally from between his lids. His mother hurried over, picked Hark up, and gave him a little shake, then kissed him. She glanced around, almost defiantly, to see if anyone was responsible for making him cry. I was standing a dozen feet away and she glared at me quite sharply, as if I had poked her little boy or had made a face at him. Hark's mother died when he was still in high school. I don't know if it was cancer or something else. In any case, she never saw him with only one ear.

Now on my daily constitutional I would see my neighbors and not only would I see their uncertainty but it would be exaggerated by my own, as if my uncertainty were the pane of glass through which I viewed the world. And it was hard not to recall how they had been in happier, more tranquil times.

Harry Martini, principal at Knox Consolidated, had been a chubby boy with black bangs who told everyone he met he could spell *antidisestablishmentarianism*. Not satisfied with that great skill he soon bragged that he could spell it backwards. He would go into banks by himself and display his spelling ability before the tellers. He would even stop people on the street to show off his bag of tricks. *Escutcheon* was another word he was good at, though no one, including Harry, knew what it meant. I don't claim a love of proper spelling led him to become a high school principal, but I wonder.

Phil Schmidt, our police chief, was a high school football star. People said that he nearly got a football scholarship to Syracuse but it went to a colored boy instead. And shortly after that, Jim Brown became famous playing for Syracuse and I always thought, incorrectly I'm sure, that Jim Brown had gotten Phil Schmidt's scholarship.

Our mayor, Bernie Kowalski, used to have parties at his parents' cottage on Round Lake. I went to one when I was seventeen. There was beer, and couples necked or danced to "Teen Angel." The drinking age at that time was eighteen, which seemed sensible. Bernie wouldn't let anybody touch the record player. He smoked Pall Malls from a red pack and had a girlfriend from Norwich by the name of Suzie who was said to be very experienced. I stood on the dock and skipped stones across the water. I was afraid that if I drank beer my mother would smell it on my breath. I was afraid that if I danced with a girl her perfume would get on my clothes. I had come with some other boys and couldn't leave until they did. It was June, just before school let out. Around midnight some kids were thrown into the lake, girls mostly. A football player by the name of Hercel Morgan threw me into the lake because, as he said, he didn't like the expression on my face.

Years later, when I came back from New York, Cookie Evans was a cheerleader in high school. She was tiny enough to be thrown high in the air, the sort of girl you never saw without a smile. She wore a thick blue letter sweater with a golden *A* on the front. Her voice was very high, almost squeaky. Even then she was known as a chatterbox. In her senior year she at last grew a bit taller and her voice deepened, which her mother said was too bad because otherwise she could have gotten a job in the circus.

I look at Megan Kelly today, a heavyset woman who barely supports herself by cleaning houses and doing odd jobs like taking care of Sadie Moore. When younger, Megan was quite beautiful in a large, muscular way. She had four daughters and they were all Girl Scouts. When the scouts sold cookies in the spring, my mother would buy her cookies only from Mrs. Kelly's daughters. Later these girls formed a singing group. They called themselves the Kellyettes and twirled batons as they sang "How Much Is That Doggie in the Window." People wrote letters trying to get them on *Ted Mack's Amateur Hour* but nothing ever came of it.

Sometimes I think of Janice McNeal or Franklin or Ryan Tavich as children. None of them lived here, of course. They would have heard news of Vietnam and listened to the Beatles. They had bikes. There were movie stars and sports figures about whom they had passions. They put posters on their bedroom walls. They had dogs or cats to whom they told their secrets.

Allen and Donald Malloy grew up outside of Rochester, in Spencerport, I believe. Paul Leimbach has said they had sailboats on Lake Ontario. They still like to sail and Dr. Malloy was teaching sailing to Sharon. A year or so ago Dr. Malloy had a party for his fiftieth birthday. The announcement showed a photograph of the doctor as a child. He must have been about eight years old. He wore shorts and a jacket, a white shirt, and a tie. His face was as round as a penny and his short blond hair stood up straight in a flattop. He was very somber and stood on the front stoop of a house with white clapboard. He was holding out his left hand and on his palm was a yo-yo. On the bottom step, at his feet, sat Donald, three years old and resembling a little tub. He stared up at the yo-yo in his brother's hand as if staring at a religious object, and his mouth was slightly open.

Paul Leimbach was two years behind me in school. He was a thin, very serious boy who was reputed to be a math whiz. He had stacks of baseball cards and liked to ask other children, even older children,

how many doubles Ted Williams hit in 1956 or how many bases
Jackie Robinson stole in 1955. He knew these facts without having to
look at his cards. That nobody cared didn't bother him. He had a
little blue satchel in which he carried his baseball cards. They were an
area of expertise separating him from other children. He had dark
eyes, dark hair, and thick dark eyebrows and he liked to stand as still
as a totem pole, holding his satchel of baseball cards against his leg.
One imagined endless numbers streaming through his brain. What
did he think then of his future? Now he is a CPA in a small town.
And his niece has disappeared.

I walk through Aurelius and notice these people with their complicated lives, some happy, some unhappy. Of course, I have known
the young people practically from the day they were born. Aaron as a
child was entirely different from what he became; he was open,
friendly, and good-natured. I have said how I would see him delivering papers on his bike with his dog running behind him. The fact
that his father taught with me made Aaron more conspicuous, and
long before I knew about his mother's promiscuity, I noticed Aaron
and his dog all over town. The dog had a passion for retrieving sticks.
He would even bring them to strangers and bump them against your
shin until you took notice. Eventually he was killed by a truck out on
the state highway. Aaron kept his paper route until he was fourteen.
His father, Patrick, would brag that Aaron bought his own clothes
and I felt that was rather cheap of Patrick since he made a good salary.
I didn't say anything, of course. After junior high Aaron started becoming what he is today: quiet, somewhat mysterious, a man whose
actions often seem without rational cause.

Barry Sanders was a pink and pudgy child with white hair and
thick glasses. I never saw him running or playing. As I said, his father
disappeared when he was two, and his mother was quite bossy. She
always made him wear a hat in the summer, a red straw cowboy hat.
Other children snatched it from him and Barry begged them to give

it back. Often the hat would wind up on the head of the bronze Civil
War soldier holding a musket in front of City Hall. I would drive by
and see the red straw cowboy hat on the soldier's head and imagine
Barry weeping someplace. We had a policeman in those days, Potter
Malone, who has since retired and moved to Florida. He was an affable fellow who made it his duty to return Barry's cowboy hat to
him. Indeed, this often seemed his only job, so that it was once re-
marked at a city council meeting that the city employed an officer
just to return Little Pink's hat.

When Sadie Moore visits me and sits on the couch doing her
homework or reading *Anne of Green Gables,* I see not only her present
face but also her past faces, back to the eight-year-old with chocolate
smeared around her mouth. Sometimes she sits at my kitchen table
staring at the little hairless rat, Tooslow, in its glass jar. Her elbows
are on the table and her face is about six inches from the rat's face.
"Once," she might say, "Tooslow was crossing a street when a truck
came along and you know what happened?"

"Was he hit?" I would ask.

"No. A policemen rescued him. Maybe it was Ryan." Or she looks
at the rattlesnake in its glass jar and says, "Why do people call snakes
evil? They just look sad."

And Hark's cronies, Jeb Hendricks, Ernie Corelli, Jimmy Feldman—
I remember them all. Jeb and Ernie were students of mine in eighth
grade science, rather stupid boys who couldn't pay attention. But I
can remember them even younger at the swimming pool in Lincoln
Park doing cannonballs off the diving board or turning wheelies with
their bicycles on the side streets. All the usual behavior of growing
up—that long process beginning with innocence and ending where?

When Hark Powers looks in the mirror and sees a scar where his
left ear used to be, what are his thoughts? When Barry looks at his
reflection and blinks his weak eyes, what does he see? When Aaron
shaves each morning, can he see his face without remembering his

mother's? And the person who abducted Sharon Malloy, what does he see when he studies his face? Does he feel a sliver of ice in his heart?

Five years ago Aurelius had a Christmas pageant that included a chorus of angels surrounding the manger in Bethlehem. The angels were grade school girls and they sang "O Holy Night." Sadie was one of the angels, as were Sharon Malloy, Sarah Patton, Meg Shiller, Bonnie McBride, Hillary Debois, and two or three others. The angels wore elaborate white gowns made from sheets but with strings of tinsel and chains of costume jewelry. Dozens of brooches and shiny pins were attached to the fabric. With every movement the gowns sparkled and shone. The girls had cardboard wings covered with glitter, and golden halos set in their hair shimmered in the light. Their high voices in the high school gym made my teeth rattle. It is impossible for me to think about Sharon Malloy without also seeing her as an angel singing "O Holy Night." That must be true of hundreds of people in my town.

The terror that Sharon's disappearance gave rise to was not simply the possibility of Sharon's death, though that was awful enough; it also imposed the face of death on all of these children. They became potential specimens, like those in my jars. Would Bonnie McBride live to graduate from high school? Would Hillary Debois grow to adulthood? Would Sadie reach her twentieth year? This was the shadow that crept over our town: Who else would disappear? And the suspicions and fears that this shadow gave rise to, what violence might they prompt?

Twenty-six

I don't know how it is in other towns, but in Aurelius Halloween has increasingly become an important event. When I was a child it was just a matter of putting on a mask or a homemade costume and going door to door trick-or-treating. Now costumes have become rather costly or may even be rented for the night. People's houses have elaborate decorations with flashing lights and howls. There are pumpkin trash bags and fake cobwebs, tombstones and hanging skeletons, scary music and shimmering electric candles. One sees dummies in old clothes hanging from trees or lying in front yards, sometimes with knives in their chests. It reminds me of a religious occasion lacking a deity.

The children expect more as well: full-sized candy bars, boxes of assorted treats, even money. One recent Halloween when I passed out a few small pieces of candy to each child—lollipops and jawbreakers, what I thought of as old favorites—half a dozen children looked at my little offering and said, "Is that all?" One boy even turned me down.

If there is something religious about Halloween, it is hard to say what the religion might be. Nothing nice, I expect. Years ago one was buying off visiting demons with treats. Now the householders seem in collusion with the demons. Worse, with their tombstones, stuffed cadavers, and sound effects of creaking doors, screams, and wolf howls, they try to terrify the demons who come to trick-or-treat. There is a frenzy to Halloween, as if the very Prince of Darkness were being flattered and courted.

When I was young, there were marauding bands of teenagers on

Halloween—at least that was how they saw themselves—who soaped windows and overturned trash cans. Nowadays this behavior is more pernicious. One year Helen Berger's Geo was put on its roof in her front yard. A garage was set on fire on Alfred Street, several cherry bombs were scooted up the exhaust pipes of parked cars, and Mrs. Parson's collie dog Ollie was shaved naked. Malicious mischief, the police said, but there was also the sense that this behavior was intended to summon a darker force, even to seduce that darker force. And it wasn't just teenage boys who behaved badly. Hark Powers, for instance, and his three cronies were all adults and they were eager to make trouble.

All four, as well as Aaron, had been charged with being public nuisances the previous Saturday night. Aaron was more victim than aggressor, but Ryan hadn't liked Aaron's kicking Hark when he was holding on to Hark's arm. So Aaron was charged. All five were fined $300 each. Barry's mother was telephoned from the police station and she came to pick up her son. That night Barry ate dinner at home after all, while his mother sat across from him and asked how he had managed to get in so much trouble.

Because Aaron had thrown the last punch, the issue stayed open. Hark was furious that he'd been made to look bad in front of his friends. He had been painfully kicked in the groin and was unable to respond. Hark talked about it at Bud's Tavern; he talked about it at Jack Morris Ford. And each time his sense of injury increased. To his mind Aaron deserved far worse than a fine. Jeb and Ernie inflated his sense of ill-treatment. They asked what he meant to do and how he would get revenge. Hark was obliged to do something not just because he had been unfairly struck but in order to retain control over his friends.

"Wait till Halloween," Hark said.

Other people, including Sheila Murphy, heard him say this. And they later testified to that effect in court.

Sharon's disappearance created another kind of scariness that Halloween. Few children went out by themselves. Either they went in groups or their parents drove them. A number of parents held parties at home so their children wouldn't go out at all. And it wasn't a very nice night, cold with a light rain that turned to heavy snow by early morning.

Sadie dressed up as a vampire and wore a black dress and a black wig. Her face was painted white and her lips were bright red. She went with her friends Meg Shiller and Hillary Debois. Meg went as the victim of a hit-and-run accident, swathed in bloody bandages and with her left leg in a cast. Hillary was a zombie and had a zombie wig and a mouthful of oversized teeth. And she carried a club with a nail through it. They visited me. They seemed nervous about going out and I offered to go with them. That was a mistake because they were so chagrined by my offer they forgot their fear entirely. It was strange to see these three horrors standing in my living room chewing on Tootsie Rolls, while peeking from behind the blood and makeup was their thirteen-year-old prettiness.

My own time that evening was spent sitting by the front door and passing out Baby Ruths, Milky Ways, and Snickers. I had lab reports to grade, but I doubt that I had five uninterrupted minutes between six o'clock and nine. The children who came were wet and bedraggled. They looked more like refugees than demons. Often a father or mother would be waiting out on the sidewalk. Some householders dressed up as well and met their callers with larger and scarier versions of the children's own costumes. I wore my usual blue blazer and bow tie, and while it may be a costume, it is the one that people expect me to wear.

Hark and his friends had rudimentary costumes. Hark wore a black mask with a moustache and a Mets baseball cap. Jeb Hendricks had an over-the-head ghoul mask. Ernie Corelli wore a plastic Mickey Mouse mask. Jimmy Feldman wore a green grasshopper mask. They drove around in Jeb's red Chevy Blazer with an ice chest of Budweiser in the back. The longer they drove, the more rambunctious they got.

From about seven they crisscrossed the town for a while, then drove over toward the college, where there was a Halloween dance. Jeb gunned his Blazer at kids crossing the street. Then they drove into the country to play mailbox baseball, destroying six or seven mailboxes with baseball bats. Tom Schneider heard them smash his mailbox and gave chase in his pickup, but they got away. Around eight they drove to Aaron's apartment. Aaron's lights were off. Jeb parked and they went inside and hammered on the door. Their plan was to grab Aaron, then drop him off in front of City Hall without any clothes. Maybe they would hog-tie him. Maybe they would tie him naked to the Civil War monument and cover him with yellow spray paint. Maybe they would tie a dog to him as well. Discussing these options gave them much pleasure and so it was disappointing that Aaron wasn't at home.

Jeb's Blazer had a particularly loud muffler and many people heard it. And there were other groups of young men, not unlike Hark and his friends, also intent on mischief. Somebody tied the back bumper of Randy Beevis's Ford Bronco to the front door of Weaver's Bakery, and when Randy drove away the door was ripped off and the fire alarms sounded. And someone, perhaps the same person, spread vegetable oil on the steps of the police station. Chuck Hawley took a nasty spill and hurt his coccyx.

Franklin went out with Bob Alton, his photographer. Halloween was on Tuesday that year and Franklin wanted to have a full page of photos for Thursday's paper. They found six teenage boys in coats and ties carrying a seventh, Louie Hyde, in a coffin. They carried the coffin door-to-door and soon it was half full of candy. Louie Hyde had been selected as the corpse because, though he was fourteen, he was under five feet tall. Bob Alton took twenty photos and Franklin interviewed Louie, who said it wasn't bad being dead because it meant he got to ride.

Franklin also got a picture of a dummy being hauled up the flagpole at City Hall. The Elks sponsored a party for young people with apple bobbing and a costume contest. Franklin talked to the winners—the twins Tim and Tom Miller—who were dressed as a pair of dice. Bob Alton also took pictures of kids they saw on the street: Lucy Schmidt being drawn in a cart by a St. Bernard, the six Gillespie boys and girls all dressed as Big Bird. Franklin drove by Dr. Malloy's house but there were no lights downstairs. The same was true of the Leimbachs' house. Donald Malloy's house was dark as well. Franklin was busy all evening, but because of what happened later he decided it would be in bad taste to run any of the pictures.

Ryan Tavich had a date with Cookie Evans and meant to take her to the Colgate Inn for dinner, but he broke it at the last minute. He couldn't say why. He had an unsettled feeling. He spent the evening in his car, driving around town or parked on Main Street.

Cookie was not pleased with him. "At least you could have given me a day's notice so I could have gotten another date."

Sadie, Meg Shiller, and Hillary Debois stayed on the streets in their own neighborhood. Later Sadie said that they had had no fun, that it was too cold and wet. They saw a lot of other kids, but because of their costumes and the dark, they recognized very few.

"We saw big kids," said Sadie, "like adults in costumes."

"How many?" I asked.

"Maybe twenty or so, a lot more than usual."

These may have been parents watching their children, but perhaps not.

Shortly after eight o'clock Hark and his friends drove to Barry's house. All four clumped up on the front porch and Hark rang the bell. Mrs. Sanders answered the door. She was a solid woman, quite a bit larger than Barry himself.

"Trick or treat," said Hark.

Jeb Hendricks laughed.

Mrs. Sanders started to hold out the bowl of candy, then paused. "You seem pretty big for trick-or-treating," she said.

"We're kids at heart," said Hark. He stepped forward, took the bowl of candy from Mrs. Sanders, and gave it to Ernie Corelli. Both Jeb Hendricks and Jimmy Feldman began taking handfuls of candy and sticking it in their pockets. Then Jeb threw a piece of candy at Jimmy and Jimmy threw a piece back at Jeb.

"Give that to me," said Mrs. Sanders, crossly.

Hark ignored her. "Can Barry come out and play?" he asked.

"We want Little Pink," said Ernie.

"Don't you dare call him that," said Barry's mother. She snatched the bowl of candy from Ernie. When he tried to stop her, she pushed him backward so he stumbled.

"Get off my porch!" said Mrs. Sanders.

"The old lady's pissed off," said Jeb.

Mrs. Sanders put the bowl inside the door, then turned to them again, holding a black umbrella. "Get off my front porch."

"We want Little Pink," said Hark.

Mrs. Sanders jabbed Hark in the stomach with the umbrella so he grunted.

"I know who you are, Hark Powers," she said. "Get off my porch before I call the police." She swung the umbrella again and all four stepped back.

Hark considered taking the umbrella from her. He was angry at being made to look foolish. A group of children—legitimate trick-or-treaters—approached the house.

"Let's go," said Hark. They walked back to Jeb's Blazer. Jeb dumped the candy he had taken onto the ground. When he pulled away from the curb, he squealed his tires.

Mrs. Sanders called the police anyway. "You better arrest Hark Powers," she told Chuck. "He tried to break into my house."

Three patrol cars were out that night. Chuck radioed them and suggested they keep a lookout for Hark. He didn't know about Jeb's red Blazer. He thought they were in Hark's pickup.

Hark told Jeb to drive back to Aaron's apartment. It was still dark. Hark went and hammered on the door just in case. He waited a minute and hammered again. Then he went back outside.

"Let's find some dog shit," he said.

The four men prowled around the yard and found three small piles of dog excrement, which Jimmy picked up with a plastic bag over his hand. Hark told him to put half of the excrement into Aaron's mailbox. The other half Jimmy smeared over Aaron's door. As they were giggling about this, Herman Potter, who lived across the hall, looked out. "Hey, what're you doing?"

"Fuck you," said Hark. They hurried back to Jeb's Blazer.

Next they tried to find Leon Stahl, who had a small apartment over by the college.

"We'll take him downtown and leave him naked in front of City Hall," said Hark. "The fat fuck."

Leon's apartment house had a buzzer system by the front door. Hark pushed the buzzer and after a moment Leon's voice came through the little speaker. "Who is it?"

"Friends," said Hark.

"Who?"

"Aaron McNeal."

"You don't sound like Aaron," said Leon, suspiciously.

"Sure it is, let me in," said Hark.

"What's your middle name?"

"Come on, Leon, let me in."

"What's your middle name?"

"Push the other buttons," said Jeb. "Someone will answer."

There were fifteen apartments in the building and Hark pushed the buttons for all of them. After a moment there was a buzzing sound and Hark opened the door.

They hurried up to Leon's apartment and hammered on the door. Hark put his hand over the peephole. When Leon wouldn't open, Hark stepped back and gave the door a great kick.

"I see who you are," said Leon. "I'm calling the police."

"Who am I?"

"Hark Powers."

"Shit," said Hark. They went back downstairs to Jeb's Blazer. "How the fuck can these people know me with a mask on?"

"It's probably your clothes," said Jeb.

"Or the way you walk," said Jimmy.

They didn't want to tell Hark it was because of his ear.

They drove to Harriet Malcomb's apartment but she wasn't home. They drove back to Aaron's but his lights were still off.

"Let's get those two brothers," said Hark.

They got Jesse and Shannon's address from the phone book. It was an apartment near the college on Whittier Street.

Jesse and Shannon had been out earlier that evening trick-or-treating, which they did because they had no money and wanted candy. They put bandannas over their noses and said they were outlaws. After thirty minutes of trick-or-treating, they returned home to watch television. About eight-thirty, Barry called to say that Hark had come to his house. Shortly after nine, Leon called and said that Hark and his friends had come to his apartment as well. Neither Barry nor Leon liked the two brothers but they wanted to stay in their good graces. They also called Aaron and Harriet, but neither was home.

Jesse and Shannon turned off their lights, went outside, and waited. Soon they heard Jeb's Blazer coming down the street. It parked and Hark and the others got out. The brothers lived in a large house that had been broken up into student apartments. The front door was open. Hark, Ernie, and Jimmy went inside and Jeb waited by his car. After a few minutes Hark came out again.

"They're not there either."

"Chickenshits," said Jeb.

All four got back in the Blazer. As Jeb started the car, Jesse and Shannon ran up on either side. They had cans of black spray paint and began spraying the windows. Jeb yelled and pulled away from the curb. Hark shouted to him to stop. Jesse sprayed the front windshield. Jeb slammed the Blazer up over the curb and hit the brakes. Jesse and Shannon spray-painted the back window. Jeb, Hark, and the others scrambled out of the car, but Shannon and Jesse were running toward the campus. The four men gave chase but they were too full of beer to run fast and they didn't know the area. Shannon and Jesse led them onto the college grounds and disappeared.

Hark stopped in the quad with his friends around him. They could see no movement, although they heard music coming from the student center, where the Halloween dance was being held.

"I want to get back to my car before they get back there and set it on fire," said Jeb.

"Jesus," said Hark. "Jesus!"

When they got back to the Blazer, they found the windshield smashed and a cinder block sitting on the front seat. The bits of glass on the dashboard looked like diamonds in the light of the streetlight.

Twenty-seven

What Hark Powers saw as a sense of justice was in fact a sense of retribution, with himself as the punishing force. He saw himself as a weapon set in motion by the hand of righteousness. His intention on Halloween had been to punish those who had done him wrong. And the more his intention was frustrated, the more indignant he became. The fact that Aaron wasn't at home, that Barry's mother had jabbed him with an umbrella, that Leon refused to open his door, that Jesse and Shannon had painted the Blazer's windows and broken the windshield—all this, he understood, had been done to make him mad. By ten in the evening Hark had tied himself into a fat knot of anger.

Ernie Corelli and Jimmy Feldman wanted to go back to Bud's Tavern. Jeb wanted to go home. His truck, as he called it, was busted up and he'd had enough. Hark saw his control over his cronies sliding away. But he also had a sense of widespread wickedness, which came in part from the time he had spent helping the Friends of Sharon Malloy. Something was dreadfully wrong and Hark didn't want to go home until he had done something about it.

"Let's drive by the Arab's house," he suggested.

So they drove over to Maple Street. It was past ten and the streets were deserted. It had gotten colder and the rain seemed to have some substance, falling slush. The broken front window of the Blazer was a great open space. Rain and cold air poured through it. Jeb and Hark hunched down and Jeb had the heater on full blast. All four were drinking beer and the ice chest in back was nearly empty. To warm themselves up they also had a fifth of Seagram's Seven Crown.

Chihani's house was dark but his car was in the driveway.

"I bet he didn't pass out candy," said Jeb.

"He probably sat upstairs with the lights off," said Ernie.

"Jacking off," said Jimmy.

"Park in front," said Hark.

Jeb parked and nicked off the lights but he didn't turn off the engine. Rain pattered on the dashboard.

"What're you going to do?" asked Ernie.

"You'll see," said Hark. He had pushed his mask up onto his forehead. Now he pulled it down again. He stared at Chihani's house and the red Citroën.

"You think he's awake?" asked Jimmy.

"I don't care if he's awake or asleep," said Hark. Reaching into the backseat, he took one of the bats they had used for mailbox baseball. "Don't turn off the truck," he said. He opened the door and got out.

"Hot damn," said Ernie. He grabbed the other bat and climbed out the back. His Mickey Mouse mask gave him a look of immense cheer.

Hark walked up the driveway toward the Citroën. He had had a lot to drink and he weaved a little. Several maples stood along the far side of the drive and another stood in Chihani's front yard. The neighbor's house was also dark, although lights were on in other houses. Ernie hurried after Hark. He kept chuckling to himself. He didn't walk straight either. The other two watched from the Blazer.

Reaching the Citroën, Hark waited for Ernie to catch up. The car was pointed toward the street. Hark stood by the driver's door, holding the bat loosely in his hand. He stepped back, gripped the bat with both hands, and swung it toward the front window of the Citroën. The noise of the glass shattering was dulled by the sound of the rain. Hark hit the windshield again, knocking the glass into the front seats.

"Hot damn," said Ernie. He swung his bat and smashed the right headlight. This made a louder noise, almost a clang. The rim of the headlight sprang off and rolled across the grass like a small silver hoop.

Hark swung the bat at the rear window. The window starred and Hark hit it again, knocking the glass inward, then poking at the remnants with the head of the bat. There were books on the rear shelf and they were sprinkled with beads of glass. Ernie smashed the other headlight. Hark began smashing at the side windows. He would crouch down in a hitter's stance, then swing violently. He hit the side mirror, knocking it off so that it skittered along the driveway toward the street. Ernie knocked off the mirror on the passenger's side.

In the next few minutes the two men became completely caught up in the destruction, so when Chihani appeared neither Hark nor Ernie knew if he had come out the front door or had run around from behind the house. Even with his limp he moved quickly, swinging out the leg with the oversized shoe and pushing himself forward on his cane. He wore his beret and a dark sport coat. As he approached the two men, he raised his cane.

"Stop that!" he shouted.

Hark and Ernie were sufficiently startled that they stopped and turned toward Chihani. Both swayed a little.

"This is entirely unacceptable!" shouted Chihani. His voice was high and his accent seemed thicker. He was taller than either Hark or Ernie, as well as thinner. He was also sober.

Hark began to say something rude and dismissive, but as he turned, Chihani swung his cane, striking Hark across the face.

"Yeow!" said Hark, stumbling back and holding his cheek.

Ernie smashed his bat down on the hood of the car, which made a hollow clanging noise.

"You are no better than thugs!" shouted Chihani. He swung his cane at Ernie, striking him across the back. Ernie staggered forward. Chihani struck him across his plastic Mickey Mouse mask, cracking it in half. The rain and wet leaves made the driveway slippery. Ernie lost his balance, slipped, and fell backward. His mask slid down around his neck. He sat on the wet driveway holding his shoulder. Chihani hit him again on the head and Ernie yelped.

From the Blazer, Jimmy Feldman and Jeb Hendricks watched Chihani attacking their friends. They were startled by his speed. They couldn't imagine how he moved so fast. They kept waiting for Chihani to stop but he didn't stop.

"We got to get out of here," said Jeb.

"We can't leave them." Jimmy had difficulty speaking. He slowly screwed the top back on the fifth of Seagram's Seven.

"The cops will be here any second."

"Jesus, that Arab's beating both of them." Jimmy climbed out of the backseat and ran toward the others in a zigzagging lope. Ernie still sat on the ground, holding his head. Chihani had again struck Hark across the face with his cane and Hark fell against the side of the car.

Jimmy scooped up the bat that was lying on the ground next to Ernie. He had pulled down his grasshopper mask and had trouble seeing out of the eyeholes. As he tried to focus on Chihani, he tripped over Ernie's feet and stumbled toward the Citroën. He put out his hands to catch himself and his hands slid across the wet metal of the hood. Chihani swung his cane, striking Jimmy across the back of his head so his grasshopper mask flew off.

"Hey," shouted Jimmy.

Hark rubbed his face with one hand and hung on to the baseball bat with the other. Chihani swung at him again and Hark blocked the cane with the bat. He felt dazed and he couldn't get over how fast the Arab moved. The cane came at him again, hitting his knee so that Hark stumbled sideways. Hark thought of the humiliation of one foreigner in a beret beating up the three of them. It seemed like a form of cheating. He was amazed by the world's unfairness. He swung out with the bat but didn't hit anything. His mask had slipped down, partly covering his eyes, so that it was hard to see.

Jimmy pushed himself off the hood of the Citroën and swung his bat at Chihani, hitting him in the arm. Chihani smashed his cane across Jimmy's shoulder and Jimmy fell backward, stumbling again across Ernie's legs.

Hark saw that Chihani had his back to him. He swung at Chihani, hitting him in the shoulder. Chihani was immediately on him again, swinging his cane and pushing him back against the car. Hark managed to block several of the blows but he was still struck across the face.

Jimmy got to his feet and again struck Chihani across the arm. By now Jeb had left the Blazer and ran toward them across the wet leaves. He grabbed Ernie by the collar and began pulling him to his feet. His over-the-head ghoul mask didn't look like a mask. It looked real. But Jeb also had a problem with the eyeholes. As he was pulling Ernie to his feet, he was struck across the back of the head. He stumbled forward, dropping Ernie and falling on top of him. Jimmy swung at Chihani again and missed.

Hark pulled off his mask and his baseball cap and threw them to the ground. He saw Chihani driving Jimmy Feldman backward as Jeb and Ernie struggled to get to their feet. He couldn't get over how this Arab was beating them. Hark pushed himself away from the car, got a better grip on the bat, and ran a few steps at Chihani, lifting the bat. He swung hard, aiming at Chihani's shoulders. Chihani heard him and began to turn. He lifted his cane but couldn't block the blow. He received the full force of the bat across the back of his neck. His beret popped off his head like a flipped coin. He staggered forward a few feet, then fell to the ground. His cane slid across the wet leaves.

"Fuckin' son of a bitch," said Hark. He kicked Chihani in the ribs but the man made no sound.

"Let's get the hell out of here," said Jeb. He got to his feet. Ernie was on all fours like a dog. His broken Mickey Mouse mask was twisted around onto the side of his face so that it looked as if he had two faces. Jimmy Feldman was sitting in the driveway rubbing his head. His grasshopper mask lay nearby.

Hark kicked Chihani again, kicked him hard enough to move his body.

"Come on," said Jeb. "Leave him alone." He pulled Ernie to his feet. Ernie began to stagger toward the house. Jeb grabbed his arm and turned him back toward the street. Ernie staggered about five feet and abruptly vomited. The Mickey Mouse mask fell off his head and Ernie vomited onto it.

"Jesus," said Jeb.

Jimmy Feldman stood up and swayed back and forth. He picked up the baseball bat and swung it at the car but missed. He spun around and fell down again. Hark dragged him to his feet.

Jeb took Ernie's arm and led him toward the Blazer.

"My head hurts and my stomach hurts," said Ernie.

"Let's get that fucker," said Jimmy.

"We did that already," said Jeb. "Let's go home." He pushed Ernie into the Blazer, then ran back for the others. After another minute, he had Jimmy in the backseat. Hark was standing in the yard staring at Chihani's house. He had unzipped his pants and he was peeing. The light from the streetlight glittered on the yellow arc. The rain was increasingly turning to snow. Chihani still lay on the ground. Hark finished peeing, zipped his pants, and picked up both bats so he held one in each hand.

"Let's smash up his house," said Hark.

"We've got to go," said Jeb. "The police are going to come." He pulled Hark toward the street.

Hark yanked away and swung one of the bats at him, missing. "Leave me alone."

"Jesus, you're as crazy as he is. Come on!"

Jeb led the way back to the street and Hark followed, but slowly. He kept glancing back at the house as if he wanted to do more damage. Jeb pushed him into the car. Jimmy and Ernie were in the backseat moaning and holding their heads. Hark was still staring at Chihani's house. His door was open.

"Shut the door, Hark," said Jeb.

Hark didn't move. Jeb jumped out of the car, ran around the front, slammed Hark's door, then ran around the car again. He couldn't understand why the police hadn't arrived already. He felt tremendous gratitude for that. He felt lucky.

"We going to Bud's?" asked Hark.

Jeb didn't say anything. He was going to take his friends home, then go home himself. His evening was over. Ernie had the dry heaves in the back, hacking and choking. Jeb kept seeing Chihani lying in the front yard and he tried to push the image from his mind. He'll wake up, he kept thinking. He yanked off his ghoul mask. It was all sweaty inside. Jeb was the only one who hadn't lost his mask and he felt lucky about this as well. By the time he got everybody home it was snowing hard and the streets were covered. Jeb had about five inches of snow in his lap.

Houari Chihani lay in his front yard about fifteen feet from his car. The windows were smashed, the headlights were smashed, and there were dents in the hood. Hark's black mask lay by the passenger door. Jimmy's grasshopper mask lay in front of the car. In the middle of the yard, the two halves of the Mickey Mouse mask grinned up at the trees until the snow covered them completely.

The snow covered Chihani as well. About seven inches fell that night and in the morning Chihani was no more than a white mound. His cane had disappeared and so had the masks. The front seat of his car had filled with snow.

Every morning around six Irving Powell walked his chocolate Lab up Maple Street. The Lab's name was Sidney. Because of the hour, Powell never used a leash since no one else was about. And Sidney was well-behaved, always came when he was called, though he liked the snow and liked rooting his nose through it, then shaking himself. It was dark and the streetlights were still on.

Powell saw Chihani's Citroën and saw the windows had been smashed. He knew the car and knew Chihani's history, as did everyone else in Aurelius. Sidney was sniffing at a mound covered by the snow. Powell called his dog but the dog kept fussing with whatever he had found. Powell walked toward it. Sidney had pawed away some of the snow and Powell saw that it was one of those Halloween dummies people put in their yards. Powell didn't like Halloween. The previous evening had been a nuisance from start to finish. He ran out of candy early and had turned out his lights. Then his garbage cans had disappeared.

"Come on, Sidney," he called.

The dog kept pawing and snuffling the Halloween dummy.

Irving Powell hurried up to the dog and grabbed Sidney's collar. He disliked trespassing on people's lawns and was angry with Sidney. "Bad dog," he said. He glanced at the Halloween dummy. The snow had fallen off the dummy's face. The dummy's eyes were open and he seemed to be staring at Irving Powell.

Twenty-eight

It would be a mistake to think that Houari Chihani's neighbors didn't call the police. The dull clang of a baseball bat striking the hood of an automobile will upset the peace of mind of any property owner. Mrs. Morotti across the street called the police at ten-fifteen, and her neighbor on the right, James Pejewski, called a few minutes later. Neither, however, saw Chihani fall and so their telephone calls concerned only the vandalism. When they looked again, they saw Chihani lying in the wet in his front yard but they didn't realize it was him. It was Halloween. Many houses had bodies in their front yards.

Around two in the morning, long after the police had been summoned, a patrol car drove past Chihani's house. By this time it was snowing hard. The two officers, Tommy Flanaghan and Ray Hanna, knew nothing of the earlier calls but they noted the smashed Citroën. Hanna wanted to stop but Flanaghan said to keep going. Chihani's house was dark and these problems would keep till morning. In any case, they had more pressing business on their minds than vandalism.

Presumably the calls of Chihani's neighbors had been noted in the police log. Perhaps an officer had even been told to investigate when he had time. But the calls had been forgotten in the wave of other events that had their beginning early in the evening.

Sadie, Meg Shiller, and Hillary Debois had gone trick-or-treating from six-thirty to eight, but what with the wet and the cold, they didn't have much fun after the first half hour. Sadie and Meg had umbrellas, which felt out of place on Halloween and got tangled up with the pillowcases they used to carry their candy. They saw some friends and several times they joined other kids, going together to five or six houses, then separating.

By eight o'clock they were back at Sadie's. Franklin was still out in search of Halloween stories, so the girls were alone. Mrs. Kelly had been there earlier but she had left, even though Franklin expected her to stay until ten. She was afraid that someone would steal her garbage cans unless she was home to watch them. The girls were soaked through and they stripped off their clothes, putting on bathrobes of Franklin's that Sadie found for them. They tossed their wet clothes in the dryer. Meg and Hillary telephoned their parents to say where they were. Meg lived two blocks in one direction and Hillary lived about a block in the other. As they waited for their clothes to dry, they made hot chocolate and snacked on Halloween candy. What did they talk about? Their history homework for the next day. How Shirley Potter seemed to have a crush on Bobby McBride. That Meg meant to go horseback riding on Saturday. That Hillary's cousin Anne was coming to visit from Albany that weekend. That Meg thought Frank Howard was cute but the others didn't agree. He was too stuck-up. Did they talk about Sharon Malloy and what might have happened to her? No, they didn't, which doesn't mean the question didn't occur to them. They talked quickly and kept interrupting each other and laughed a lot.

"Of course we thought about Sharon," Sadie told me later. "It's something we think about all the time. It's just too depressing to keep talking about."

By nine o'clock their clothes were dry. Meg had worn jeans, and over her jacket she wore a white shirt of her father's smeared with red paint to look like blood. As a hit-and-run victim, she hadn't needed an elaborate costume, and she didn't bother putting the cast back on her leg. In any case, made from newspapers, it was wet and falling apart. Nor did she put back the bloody bandages around her head and arms.

Hillary had dressed in one of her father's suits, and Sadie had decided a black dress that had belonged to her mother made a suitable vampire outfit. The lipstick she snitched from Paula, wiping the tip with a tissue so her lips wouldn't touch where Paula's had touched.

Because it was a school night Meg and Hillary had promised their parents they would be home by nine-thirty, or ten at the latest. They were a little giddy from the amount of candy they had eaten, but they were also tired, so shortly after nine-thirty they telephoned their parents to say they were coming home. Franklin was still out with the photographer. I was home with my lab reports, glad that no Halloween reveler had rung my doorbell for at least forty-five minutes.

Hillary's mother said she would drive over and pick up her daughter, though it was little more than a block. Meg said she didn't want to be picked up. Her parents were endlessly pokey and she could be in bed before her parents even found their car keys. It was still raining, but Meg had her umbrella, a long black umbrella of her father's. Hillary said that her mother could easily drive Meg home as well, but Meg was impatient.

So around nine-forty-five Meg said good-bye and hurried into the rain. Joan Debois's Dodge Caravan pulled into the driveway about five minutes later and honked. Sadie stood on the porch and watched Hillary run out to the car, which then backed out the driveway. Hillary waved through the window. Sadie closed and locked the door, then returned to the kitchen. She still had math problems to do so she settled down at the kitchen table with another cup of hot chocolate and her math textbook. She hoped her father would be home before she went to bed, but often he visited Paula McNeal. On some nights, if she was alone, Sadie would call me around ten-thirty to say hello. I disapproved of Franklin's leaving Sadie alone, but I was hesitant to speak to him about it. It amazes me how we keep silent when we feel we should speak up. But we don't want to offend someone by calling attention to a problem, something we feel this person should do. I felt it was unsafe for Sadie to spend so much time by herself, but instead of doing something about it and possibly irritating Franklin, I let Sadie go on being unsafe.

At ten-fifteen Meg Shiller's mother called Sadie, asking to speak to Meg. She sounded cross that her daughter had stayed out late despite assuring her that she was coming home right away.

The refrigerator abruptly turned on and Sadie jumped. "Meg left half an hour ago," she said.

Both must have immediately calculated how long it would take to walk two blocks.

"Are you sure?" said Meg's mother. "Be serious now." Helen Shiller taught second grade at Pickering Elementary School. She knew how kids could make jokes when they shouldn't.

"She left at quarter to ten," said Sadie, growing scared.

"Oh, my God," said Helen Shiller, and she hung up.

Sadie called Hillary Debois but the phone was busy. Then she called me. I said I'd be right over. I put on my raincoat and grabbed an umbrella. Sadie met me on the front porch. "She's not at Hillary's," she said. "I just talked to her."

I had a flashlight and I shone it at her. I was struck by how old Sadie looked, how frightened.

"Let's walk up to Meg's house," she said. "Maybe she's home by now."

The rain was just turning to snow. I kept my umbrella over both of us. As we hurried along the sidewalk, Sadie told me about her evening and how Meg had decided to walk home. We had only gone half a block when a station wagon pulled up to the curb. It was Helen Shiller.

"Have you seen her?" she asked.

We said no. The streets were dark and deserted. The houses on this block had large yards, sometimes stretching back to the next street. A few snowflakes had begun sticking to the ground.

Helen Shiller pulled away from the curb. The fear I saw in her face, I see it still: the eyes panicked in the dash lights. Sadie and I continued up the street toward Meg's house, jostling each other under my umbrella. I kept shining my light into the dark yards. We had gone about thirty more feet when my light picked out a thin black shape in Herb Gladstone's front yard.

"What's that?" I asked.

Sadie hurried to see. "It's Meg's umbrella," she said.

I was the one to call the police. And I am ashamed of my own foolish vanity that lets me think that, because Chuck Hawley was on duty, the police responded faster than they might otherwise have. It was the first time that I felt glad my cousin was a policeman, though I have never had any reason to regret it in the past. I told Chuck what had happened.

"Cripes," he said. "Oh no."

In less than five minutes Ryan Tavich was at Sadie's house. Two more police cars arrived within minutes after that. Hillary Debois's mother called Sadie to see if there was any news. More car doors slammed outside and there were running footsteps. Cold air blew through the open doorway.

"There's no answer at Meg's house," said Joan Debois.

Sadie told her there was no sign of Meg.

"You mean she never got home? Oh, her poor mother."

Soon off-duty policemen began to arrive. By eleven o'clock we had state police as well. Sadie's cocker spaniel, Shadow, had to be put in the basement, where it barked and barked. The rain had turned completely to snow. Captain Percy arrived at eleven-thirty. His normally inexpressive face was especially rigid, as if cut from wood. I should have gone home, but Franklin was still out and I felt reluctant to leave Sadie, who was weeping. I also felt some of the excitement and wanted to stay. Though I don't know why I should have been excited to hear Captain Percy call the barracks in Utica to ask that dogs be sent down as soon as possible. Men were clomping in and out and the phone kept ringing. More and more police cars were parked along the curb and I could see people gathering up and down the street.

After Captain Percy used the phone, Ryan made a surreptitious call to Franklin.

"You better get home right away," Ryan said into the phone.

There was a pause, then Ryan said, "Sadie's fine. It's one of her friends." He hung up.

Minutes later Franklin rushed into his house and found it full of policemen.

The police searched every inch between Sadie's house and Meg Shiller's. They woke up or interrupted everybody not only on our street but also on the blocks north and south of ours. No one had seen Meg Shiller. Earlier the streets had been full of kids. People had heard their voices, their shouts. It was Halloween. Indeed, if Meg Shiller had happened to cry out, who would have found it remarkable?

And the snow was a problem. Sadie showed Ryan the place where we had found the umbrella on Herb Gladstone's front yard. His lawn went all the way back to Tyler Street. The police roused Herb but he hadn't seen or heard anything. If someone had come through his yard and left tracks in the mud, by midnight those tracks were covered with snow. Although there was nothing to say that tracks existed.

I went home at midnight, feeling that with Franklin back I was not justified in staying.

Sadie was angry with her father. "You were with Paula, weren't you." It wasn't a question.

Franklin looked guilty. His light brown hair was messy and its disorder seemed evidence of his transgressions. One even expected to see lipstick on his cheek.

Reporters from Utica and Syracuse began to arrive around one o'clock, about the same time the dogs got here from the barracks in Utica. I was in bed trying to sleep and heard them barking. At two o'clock I got up to take a sleeping pill. There was still plenty of commotion in the street.

Meg was of the fourth generation of Shillers to live in Aurelius. Her great-grandfather had moved here shortly before World War I. He was the one who dropped the *c* from the family name—Schiller— hoping to anglicize it. His own father had been born in a small town in Bavaria in the 1870s. About fifteen years ago, a year or so before Meg was born, Ralph and Helen visited this town in Bavaria—I can't remember its name—and said it was packed with Schillers. Ralph told many people in Aurelius he felt embarrassed that his grandfather had changed the family name and he was considering changing it back to Schiller. I don't think anything came of this. But it must have been odd to discover a whole town of distant cousins and to visit a graveyard where one's family went back hundreds of years.

Helen Shiller's maiden name was also German: Kraus. But she had no knowledge of her family before her grandfather, a man whom I gather she didn't like. Both Ralph and Helen grew up in Aurelius and I have known them all their lives. As an electrician Ralph had done work on my house. His father was an electrician as well, and when I first called Ralph with a problem it was because I knew that my mother had employed Ralph's father. And as I mentioned, Helen taught second grade at Pickering Elementary School. They had three children: Bobby, who was nine; Meg, thirteen; and Henry, who was sixteen. Both Ralph and Helen had siblings in town and cousins, nieces, and nephews, so there were many Shillers in Aurelius, though perhaps not as many as in the town in Bavaria whose name I've forgotten. Foolishly perhaps, I think of Germans as blond, but the Shillers were dark and short and brown-eyed. They were a good family, serious and hardworking. One of those families who never have any scandal attached to their name.

I had Meg Shiller in general science in eighth grade, and while she wasn't an A student, she was a solid B student. She was lively and good-natured and I could see why she would be such a good friend of Sadie's. She loved horseback riding and kept her brown hair in a long ponytail, as if in solidarity with the horses. She spent most weekends working in a stable just south of town for the opportunity to ride for an hour or two. She was the sort of child—young lady, I should say— who made one feel the world was proceeding along on the right course: she was happy, successful, and contented. And now she was gone.

Ryan Tavich had no sleep that Tuesday night or Wednesday morning. There were many people to wake up and ask if they had noticed anything suspicious. Indeed, some remembered seeing Meg Shiller earlier in the evening dressed up as a hit-and-run victim. And some considered it prophetic that Meg had gone from door to door covered with blood and with her face all white and bandaged.

When people heard that Meg had disappeared, they began to telephone friends, neighbors, and relatives. A few of them got in their cars to drive slowly down Van Buren Street, past my house, and slowly along the route from Sadie's house to Meg's house. It was still snowing and the roads were slippery. Because of all the traffic, Captain Percy told Ryan to block off the streets around Meg's house, which was perhaps a mistake because even more people dragged themselves out of bed to look at the barriers. I don't know if there were actually any accidents but one kept hearing thirdhand that so-and-so had slid into a tree or smacked into the rear of someone else's car.

In the middle of all this Ralph Shiller sat like a stone at his kitchen table while his wife, Helen, wept in the bedroom. Their station wagon, parked in the driveway, was slowly getting covered with snow. A police officer at the house took all the telephone calls and the two boys, Bobby and Henry, sat together on the couch in the living room, though Bobby had fallen asleep. Ralph Shiller's younger brother, Mike, who worked for the post office, was also there. He kept asking Chuck Hawley, "Do you think she'll turn up? Of course she'll turn up. Right?" And Chuck would nod and try not to say anything.

They waited for the phone to ring or for someone to come and say their ordeal was over. All of them kept thinking of what might have happened, just as the Malloys had done, and each scenario was more awful than the one before it. And couldn't there be a more benign scenario in which Meg would suddenly run through the door, happy and safe? But that was hardly likely.

Around five-thirty in the morning Ryan drove to Aaron's apartment. He worried that he should have sent an officer to Aaron's earlier, but assigning a man to find Aaron seemed the same as calling him a suspect. He also worried that too much time had elapsed and if Aaron had something to conceal he would have successfully concealed it. But none of these worries turned out to matter because when Ryan got to the apartment he found that Aaron wasn't there. The new snow told him, moreover, that Aaron hadn't been home all night. There were brown stains on Aaron's door. Sniffing, Ryan realized they were somebody's idea of a Halloween prank. And he even thought that somebody might be Hark Powers.

Ryan knew that Aaron had several girlfriends but he didn't know whom he was seeing at the moment. He wondered if *girlfriend* was still the right term. Indeed, Ryan feared that Aaron was not with any woman but was off on some darker purpose connected to Meg Shiller.

And was this darker purpose linked to the IIR or something that Aaron was involved in by himself?

From Aaron's, Ryan drove to Harriet Malcomb's apartment. He knocked on the door but there was no answer. Next he drove to Jesse and Shannon's. It seemed they weren't home either. Because of the commotion surrounding Meg's disappearance, Ryan had only the sketchiest memory that there had been some fuss earlier in the evening concerning Hark Powers. So when he drove to Leon Stahl's apartment, he was not thinking of Hark at all. He was still trying to track down Aaron.

Leon was asleep and didn't want to open the door until Ryan ordered him to and showed his identification. Leon wore striped baby-blue pajamas so big that Ryan was reminded of a tent. With the door open, Leon filled the whole frame. Around nine o'clock the previous evening Leon had called the police to complain about Hark, but nothing had happened. First Leon was indignant that the police hadn't come hurrying over; now he was annoyed that Ryan had showed up at six in the morning.

"Couldn't this have waited until later?" he said. "I have a chemistry quiz today." There was a whine in his voice.

"I'm looking for Aaron," said Ryan. "Have you seen him?"

"Of course not."

"What about Shannon and Jesse?"

"I talked to them last night but I haven't seen them either. Is this about Hark Powers?"

"Why should it be?"

So Leon explained how Hark and his friends had come to his apartment and tried to make him open the door. And he said that they had gone to Barry's house as well.

When he left Leon's apartment, Ryan drove over to Chihani's house. It was still snowing. Though he remembered that somebody had mentioned Chihani earlier, Ryan couldn't recall the context. But he figured that if Hark had visited the other IIR members he might also have paid a visit to Chihani.

Ryan pulled up in front of Chihani's house just at the moment when Irving Powell was trying to drag his chocolate Lab away from Chihani's corpse.

Ryan got out of his car.

"Bad dog," Powell kept saying. "Bad dog."

Ryan saw the smashed Citroën. He hurried toward Powell. "What's wrong?" he asked.

"There's a man lying here in the snow," said Powell. "His eyes are open."

The chocolate Lab had a beret in its mouth and shook it back and forth. This distracted Ryan and it took him a moment to realize that the man in the snow was Houari Chihani and that he was dead.

Part Three

Twenty-nine

In any text there is both overt and covert material that accesses different cognitive levels within a reader. That is one of those statements highly regarded in the teachers' conferences that I avoid. But I use it here to suggest that my own gayness will come as no surprise. Until now it has not been part of the story in the same way that I'm not part of the story. At the beginning I saw myself as only a pair of eyes. Even a window—yes, I was the window through which my story passed. Probably more than a hundred gay men live in Aurelius, ranging from the rather flighty, like Jaime Rose, to the serious—men who bear no resemblance to the clichéd idea of what a gay man should be. There is no meeting place or organization, no discussion group or social hour, but these men tend to know one another. A few are married, some have male companions, the majority are single since small towns like Aurelius tend to be unsympathetic to the gay experience. For that reason, most of these men are circumspect. Indeed, quite a few have left Aurelius, as I did myself, though I came back. I also know two local men who have died of AIDS as well as a young hemophiliac boy. And I know several others who have tested HIV-positive since this scourge has spread itself into even the smallest of localities.

I am also familiar with men who are comfortable with their gayness and celebrate it, though that has not been my experience, perhaps because I chose to return to a small town or perhaps because of my own disinclination to call attention to myself. I never talk about my homosexuality and, in truth, I have had few partners. I find the whole business rather depressing. Not that I wish to be heterosexual—a less attractive option—but human sexual experience seems designed to lead to humiliation. Celibacy for me has always stood forth as the unattainable ideal. I have no religious calling, but at times I have envied the scholar monk in his cell.

And the alternative to celibacy? The young men I find attractive are not attracted to me, meaning that my gay life is limited to men in their late thirties, forties, or even older. I have a friend in San Francisco who mentioned in a letter that the bars where men of my age congregate are called "wrinkle rooms." One wrinkled man seeking to embrace another. Surely celibacy is better. But of course I have sexual yearnings and I feel temptation. I have never touched Barry Sanders, but there are times in the night when I have thought how pleasant it might be. Even Jaime Rose. I feel I run from degradation yet yearn to embrace it. But what is degradation? Isn't it a definition that derives from the straight world? And I envy those gay men—are they really the majority?—who seem happy with their gayness.

In my years in Aurelius I have had lovers come to my house on only three occasions and I was nervous the entire time. Perhaps I am more cautious than most, but I have preferred to meet my friends in other places. Even when I am with them and engaged in sex, part of me yearns for celibacy. And I know this is wrong. I know I should accept my sexuality, but the thought of the mocking looks of my students fills me with horror. Of course, many suspect—after all, I am a single man—but they have no proof. Sadly, it is suspicion that is my subject here.

I doubt that any of the gay men in Aurelius felt fortunate because of the existence of Inquiries into the Right, but for anyone slightly out of the ordinary, the IIR served as a buffer. People have a need to believe that bad things are done by bad people. And what is bad? Isn't this defined as anything outside the common good, which is further defined as whatever the majority see as good? Why must the villain wear a black hat? Because if he didn't, how would we know he was the villain?

It was first thought that Sharon Malloy was abducted by someone outside of Aurelius. Once this became doubted, an increasing number of people looked toward Houari Chihani and Inquiries into the Right. The IIR preached the need for disorder, and here was the height of disorder. Chihani could also be placed at the scene of the disappearance. In addition, he was a foreigner with a peculiar look about him; he wore a beret and his skin was a little darker than average. Not everyone thought he was guilty, but it was felt to be convenient if he were guilty. When Meg Shiller disappeared, however, people began to look farther afield to whatever was aberrant or idiosyncratic.

I know this because I felt it myself. My unmarried condition made people suspicious. It was also known that Sadie visited me and that I knew her friends. Meg Shiller must have walked by my house moments before she vanished. Though I talked to the police, I was never treated as a suspect. The idea was absurd. But many people looked at me differently and I was talked about at school. It excited the students that the biology teacher might be a sex murderer. But others were looked at as well: gay men, gay women, the eccentric, the reclusive, the retarded. And I looked at my neighbors differently— these people who thought I might be guilty, had I believed them my friends? And I had known them all my life.

Bob Moreno, the haberdasher on Main Street, had been little Bobby Moreno who sat in front of me from first through sixth grade. When he married, I went to his wedding. At least six of his seven children had been my students. And now he thought I might be a criminal. When I went into his shop to buy a few undershirts, he stared at me as if he had never seen me before.

It must be said that in the few days after Meg Shiller's disappearance there was general hysteria. One member of the city council,

George Rossi, wanted to pass a resolution calling upon the state police to search every house in town. Rossi said they could begin with his house right away. When other members protested, Rossi had the audacity to suggest they had something to hide. It wasn't until some months later that he apologized.

Many people were questioned by the police as to their whereabouts on Halloween, including several gay men. Jaime Rose was taken to the police station and spent an hour with a state police sergeant. Though he was released, the fact that he had been questioned became generally known. I should say that in his entire life Jaime Rose had never even received a parking ticket. People put pressure on Cookie Evans to dismiss him, and eight women said they would stop patronizing Make Waves if Jaime kept working there. Cookie refused to be intimidated or to treat Jaime any differently. A few people admired Cookie for this, but there was no doubt that she lost customers.

Among the people who were questioned were Dr. Malloy and his brother, Donald, as well as their brother-in-law, Paul Leimbach. Even Ralph Shiller and his brother Mike were asked to account for their whereabouts at the time of Sharon Malloy's disappearance the previous month. Of course, they all had satisfactory alibis.

I happened to run into my cousin at the bank and let him know that I found it excessive that the victims' fathers should be harassed by the police.

Chuck was rather dismissive. "Statistically it's almost always the family." Then he softened a little. "Yeah, I felt bad about it too."

I suppose he meant that the police couldn't afford to overlook any possibility, but it upset people that the Malloys or Shillers might be suspected.

Once again FBI agents were seen going into City Hall. Ryan said that Captain Percy especially blamed himself for Meg's disappearance: if he had done everything to find Sharon, Meg would still be safe. It was something he kept repeating. And some people suggested that the two disappearances were unrelated. Perhaps Meg had been abducted by someone else or hadn't been abducted at all. This seemed unlikely, but, as Ryan told Franklin, the possibility had to be explored.

The Friends of Sharon Malloy were revitalized by Meg's disappearance. This is not to say they were pleased that it took place, but the search for Sharon had increasingly reached a dead end. Meg's disappearance gave it new life. Within hours, at least fifty of the Friends were hunting between the houses on Van Buren, somewhat to the irritation of Captain Percy, who said that their presence interfered with the dogs that had been brought from Utica and that the Friends would confuse or obliterate the trail.

By the next morning, November 1, the storefront rented by the Friends of Sharon Malloy was crowded with volunteers. And they were more eager to pursue an investigative role. Late in the morning several members, including Donald Malloy, went to the house of Houari Chihani, meaning to talk to him. They had no idea that he was dead until they arrived and found the police. One wonders what they would have done had Chihani been alive. But possibly one can have some idea considering what happened to Harry Martini, the principal of Knox Consolidated. In mentioning this, I get ahead of myself, but it is more pertinent here than later on. I should say it was absolutely trivial and had nothing to do with the disappearances, but it gives the mood of the group and of the town as a whole.

Harry Martini had been married to his wife, Florence, for twenty-five years. It was a marriage best described as frosty, and if Harry had had the courage he would have divorced his wife. But he was nervous about the school board and the general opinion of the town, though I don't believe a divorce would have jeopardized his position. Harry and his wife had two children. The older, Sally, worked for Kodak in Rochester; the younger, Harold Junior, was a student at Alfred University. Not a very bright boy but well-meaning. Though Harry and his wife lived together, they had separate bedrooms and spent little

time in each other's company. From what I gather, most of the resentment was on Florence's side. Harry had an important position that
kept him busy, while his wife, though she had a graduate degree in
history, worked part-time at Letter Perfect, an office-supply store on
Jefferson Street. She was also active in the Friends of Sharon Malloy
and in the Presbyterian church. She was about forty-five, a tall
woman with a slight moustache and gray hair.

What happened was quite simple. Early on Halloween Harry left
the house, saying he had to go over some papers with Frank Armstrong, the assistant principal. Because of her connection with the
Friends of Sharon Malloy, Florence Martini heard about Meg's disappearance early, around eleven o'clock. She immediately called Frank's
house to speak to her husband and learned from Frank's wife that
Harry had not been there all evening. When Harry returned home
an hour later, his wife asked where he had been. He said he had been
at Frank Armstrong's, and Florence accused him of lying. I can almost see Harry's expression when she told him this, a sort of superior
pout that I have observed many times. Florence demanded to know
where Harry had been and Harry refused to tell her. The next morning at the Friends of Sharon Malloy, Florence confessed that her husband had been gone the previous evening and that he refused to say
where he had been.

This may have been disingenuous. Several people claimed that
Florence knew perfectly well where her Harry had been and that she
arranged the whole scene in order to embarrass him. In any case, she
told Paul Leimbach and Donald Malloy that her husband had been
missing the previous evening and that he had been acting strangely
ever since Sharon had disappeared.

Instead of contacting the police, Donald and two other members
of the group drove to the school to talk to Harry. I saw them arrive
around eleven but I thought nothing of it, nor did anyone else, for
that matter. They were in his office with the door shut. Apparently

Harry refused to tell them where he had been the previous evening. Then they asked him where he had been when Sharon disappeared. As I have said, Donald Malloy is a large man, quite stout, and he leaned across Harry's desk in a threatening manner. All this I heard later. As it turned out, Harry had also been absent on the day that Sharon disappeared. Supposedly he had been at a conference in Utica.

I saw Harry later that day and I must say that he looked very drawn and pale. There was to be a faculty meeting that afternoon but Harry canceled it. I believe he left early.

When I got to school Thursday morning, I felt certain that Harry wouldn't show up. But I was wrong. It was typical of him that he never did what he should do and too often did what he shouldn't. This was true of him even as a child. He quite bullied the community with his overinflated spelling abilities and his tiresome questions at the bank and the supermarket. Who cared if he could spell *pachyderm*? In any case, Harry went into his office and locked the door, telling Mrs. Miller that he didn't want to see anyone or to receive any calls. That was at eight-thirty.

At ten-thirty Peter Marcos, the young lieutenant who had been brought down as Captain Percy's assistant, arrived at the school with three other men. In Albany Marcos was often assigned to the governor and he had not yet decided whether Aurelius was a step up or a step down, so he was eager to do well. Certainly he wanted it to be a step up. Ten minutes later he took Harry away.

It was a habit of Harry's—more of a trademark—to wear a flower in his lapel, usually a carnation. During the break between classes after Harry's departure, the carnation was found in the main hall. It was kicked around for a while, then little Tommy Onetti retrieved it and tried to sell it. He couldn't find a buyer so he ended up wearing it himself for the rest of the day, a slightly bent and soiled pink carnation.

Mrs. Miller said Harry was weeping when he was taken away and

at least ten other people told me the same thing. By lunchtime everybody knew that the police had arrested Harry and that he had been
in tears, while several claimed he had been in handcuffs, which was
false, and several others said he had admitted to abducting Sharon
Malloy and Meg Shiller.

Of course, Harry had done nothing of the kind. Ryan Tavich told
Franklin what happened:

"Martini was brought in here bawling his eyes out. Marcos took
him in to Captain Percy. I went as well. Before Percy could ask him a
question, Martini began blabbing this complicated story about some
woman he'd met in Utica and how she'd driven down and was staying at Gillian's Motel. He said how she loved him, how she understood him, and how his whole life was ruined. It was hard to make
head or tail of it. I've got to say that Percy was patient. Anyway, it was
clear what Martini was doing all evening—balling some lady teacher
from Utica. I'll bet ten bucks his wife knew exactly what was going
on, knew it even when she called Armstrong on Halloween."

The news that Harry Martini had nothing to do with Meg's disappearance took longer to circulate than the news that he was a suspect. When he returned to school around two o'clock the same
afternoon, several students who encountered him in the hall panicked
and ran the other way. This response was not confined to the school.
Questions were asked at the school board meeting, the PTA, and the
city council. Were the children safe with Harry as principal? There
was talk that he might be suspended, though I think this was exaggerated. Clearly, he would have been in less trouble had he confessed
at the beginning to spending his time with a lady from Utica. Then,
the next week, when Harry's supposed involvement with the disappearances was beginning to be forgotten, his wife filed for divorce.

This incident with Harry was one of many. I know for a fact that
Paul Leimbach and two other members of the Friends of Sharon

Malloy visited Make Waves and talked with Jaime Rose. Cookie said it was perfectly friendly, but who knows? Indeed, it was more significant that they were seen going into Make Waves than what came of it. Just as it was more significant that Donald Malloy and several others were seen going into Harry's office. Once people were suspected, and there were also others, it was hard to get them unsuspected. And everyone still remembered that they had been suspects long after the whole business was over.

But it was even more complicated. As I've said, I received a certain attention as a single middle-aged man who appeared to have an interest in adolescent girls. Well, I felt glad when Harry was suspected because it drew attention away from me. To be sure, I felt guilty about this. I have never liked Harry. He is silly and officious and he struts like a rooster, but the fact that I was glad he was suffering, that people were looking in his direction and not in mine, made me feel terrible. And I'm convinced that others, secretly, felt the same way.

Two other incidents should be briefly mentioned. On Monday morning, November 6, Tom Schneider showed up at police headquarters and asked to be arrested. Schneider owned a Mobil station at the edge of town. He claimed to be a pervert and wanted to be put in jail, though he said he had nothing to do with the disappearances of Sharon and Meg. But it was clear he expected to be blamed. Schneider said he'd had sex with his two children, both in their early teens. He said that his wife knew and that he was confessing because she had threatened to report him if he didn't. He said she also suspected him of having something to do with Sharon Malloy and Meg Shiller, but he swore he'd had nothing to do with them.

Ryan talked to Schneider's wife and two children. He talked to Schneider's neighbors and family doctor, and the result was that Schneider was charged with a number of counts of incest and sexual abuse. He was in jail for several days, then released on bail. Apparently he hired someone to run the Mobil station and he himself received permission to stay in Utica or Rome—I'm not sure which—until the trial date. Even though there was no evidence, people suggested he might also have been involved with Sharon and Meg. A week after Schneider was charged, someone smashed the windows of his gas station and knocked over one of the pumps. The next day the man whom Schneider had hired to run the station put plywood over the windows and closed the station. Not long after, someone wrote "Sex Maniac" on the plywood with red spray paint. No one bothered to remove it.

The second incident concerned Billy Perkins, a local drunk who lived on a small check from the Veterans Administration. Two days after Schneider turned himself in, Perkins showed up at police headquarters. He was frightened. He had been drunk on Halloween night. Several young men told him that he had probably killed Meg Shiller but Billy had no memory one way or the other. Once he had killed a dog when he had been drunk and this still haunted him. Billy asked to be locked up. He was afraid if he went out on the streets he would be beaten, even killed, by the Friends of Sharon Malloy.

My cousin was one of two policemen assigned to discover Billy's whereabouts on Halloween. They learned that he had bought a bottle of Old Duke at the liquor store around six in the evening. They talked to the two men he shared it with, who had bought two more. His landlord, Pat O'Shay, said Billy had returned to his room around midnight. He had been singing military songs. The landlord told Chuck that Billy often did this. On Halloween night the landlord had asked Billy to shut up. Billy had been apologetic and went quickly to bed.

Pat O'Shay said, "He's a wreck but he's a nice guy."

Billy agreed to go into a treatment center in Syracuse. He had been there before, but maybe this time would be different. Actually, Ryan wanted to get Billy out of town. It was clear that Billy had nothing to do with Sharon or Meg, but in the eyes of some people he was still a potential suspect and he might be in danger. It was the suspicion again, the fact that people were frightened and were eager to find someone to blame for the disappearances. But now I have gotten too far ahead of myself.

Thirty

When Ryan came upon the snow-covered body of Houari Chihani, he could imagine what had happened. He could see that someone had used a baseball bat on the Citroën and he knew that earlier in the evening Hark and his cronies had been playing mailbox baseball out in the country. Ryan guessed the Citroën had been hit about thirty times. He felt a swelling of rage toward Hark and he wanted to smash him and his friends as they had smashed the little red car.

Irving Powell stood in the driveway. "Can I go now?" he asked. He had put the chocolate Lab on a leash and he held Chihani's beret in his left hand. Sticking from under Powell's overcoat were blue striped pajama bottoms. He was a man in his fifties who had lived in the neighborhood all his life.

"Of course not," snapped Ryan, "you're part of a murder investigation." Then he relented. "Go home, put some clothes on, then come back right away. And leave your dog at home."

John Farulli was on the desk. Ryan told him that it looked like Chihani had been murdered. Ryan knew that Chief Schmidt would be called and all the police machinery set in motion. The street would be sealed off. People would be questioned and arrest warrants prepared. And because nearly every cop in the county was searching for Meg Shiller, Ryan would be shorthanded.

Soon the police began to arrive. In the hours that followed, three Halloween masks were found: a black mask with a moustache, a broken Mickey Mouse mask, and a green grasshopper mask. A Mets baseball cap turned up, as well as Chihani's cane. The police also collected

six Budweiser bottles, two half full. The snow in the yard was crisscrossed with footprints. The neighbors across the street—Mrs. Morotti and James Pejewski—said they had called the police the previous
evening. They described how some men had smashed the Citroën
with baseball bats. They were unable to identify Jeb Hendricks's
Chevy Blazer precisely but said it was a red four-wheel-drive vehicle.

"It didn't have a windshield," said James Pejewski. "I couldn't get
over it. Those guys must have been cold."

There were about ten policemen involved in talking to neighbors
and searching Chihani's yard. Mrs. Morotti made them coffee. "Be
careful," she kept saying, "it's very hot."

Franklin Moore arrived just as two attendants were lifting Chihani's body onto a stretcher. The ambulance would take him to Potterville for the county coroner to do the autopsy. Like Ryan and the
other policemen, Franklin had been up all night but he had managed
to shave. While the policemen looked gray, with circles under their
eyes, Franklin looked fresh and eager. He wore his old sheepskin coat
and his striped scarf.

"How's Sadie?" asked Ryan.

"I just drove her to school. She's all right—a little dazed. What
happened here?"

They were standing by the ambulance sipping coffee from blue
ceramic mugs. Mrs. Morotti had said a dozen times that she wanted
all her mugs back and she even put a policeman, Henry Swender, in
charge of retrieving them.

"Hark Powers showed up here with his friends and smashed up
Chihani's Citroën," said Ryan. "Chihani probably came out to protest, and so they smashed him up as well."

"Have they been arrested?" asked Franklin. He was already taking notes.

"They're not going anywhere," said Ryan. "I'll get them soon." It
occurred to Ryan that Chihani's murder gave him even more reason

to pick up Aaron and the members of IIR. He could question them about Hark and Meg Shiller at the same time.

Just then a white panel truck from Channel 9 in Syracuse turned the corner onto Maple Street, followed by a truck from Channel 5. Both were driving fast.

"You're going to be well covered," said Franklin. "They're all here because of Meg."

Ryan was already walking toward a police car. "Schmidt can deal with it," he said over his shoulder. "I can't stand talking to those people."

Ryan felt certain he knew who had been with Hark and that the red four-wheel-drive vehicle was a Chevy Blazer belonging to Jeb Hendricks. Ryan sent two men to Midas Muffler to arrest him. Then he sent two more to Henderson's Plumbing and Heating for Ernie Corelli and two more to Knox Consolidated to arrest Jimmy Feldman. He also asked that Aaron be brought into headquarters, along with Barry, Harriet, Leon, and Jesse and Shannon Levine. He made it clear that none of the IIR members were being picked up because of Meg's disappearance, which wasn't quite true.

As for Hark, Ryan drove over to Jack Morris Ford to get him. He didn't think to take anyone along. People were busy and Ryan didn't want to make extra trouble. Anyway, he wanted to clear up this business before the state police interfered.

It had stopped snowing and the sun was out. Ryan doubted there would be snow left on the ground by evening, except maybe in a few places under the trees. Right now the snow seemed to be steaming as he drove across town. It was bright and he put on his sunglasses. As he often did, he took a detour down Hamilton Street—it was only two blocks out of his way—to drive past the house where Janice McNeal had lived: a small two-story red brick house with a white porch.

Janice had been murdered exactly two years ago. The anniversary had been two weeks earlier, October 16. Ryan had sat by himself in his living room listening to Billie Holiday and getting drunk on Jack Daniel's. He'd had a fire in the fireplace. All the next day he had cursed himself for being a sentimental idiot, but he didn't mind being sentimental.

Janice's house had stood empty for a year. Then it had been bought by an engineer from Kingston who had a wife and three young children. As Ryan drove by, he saw there was already a snow fort in the front yard and two blue plastic sleds. He glanced up at what had been Janice's bedroom window and saw orange paper pumpkins on each of the windowpanes. He and Janice had had sex in every room in the house, including the attic and the basement. They had even done it in the backyard. And that was probably true of other men as well. Ryan knew for a fact that she sometimes had two lovers in a single day. Heck, she had probably had half a dozen. He banged his fist on the steering wheel, inadvertently honking the horn. He told himself that he wouldn't drive down Hamilton Street again. It was something he had told himself before. In his rearview mirror he watched the house and the blue plastic sleds get smaller.

He thought again about who had killed her. Given Janice's appetite, it could have been anyone. The person didn't have to live in Aurelius. He could live in Potterville, Norwich, even someplace else. Ryan didn't believe she had been killed by a woman. She'd been killed by one of her lovers. Maybe he killed her out of jealousy. Ryan stopped himself. It didn't need to be jealousy. It might have been one of many other reasons. But if Ryan himself had killed her—and he had felt like it after she told him she was sick to death of him—jealousy would have been his reason. He also thought of her missing hand and how a mannequin's hand had been found in Sharon Malloy's backpack. Would Meg's clothes be returned as well? And would there be a hand?

Ryan reached Jack Morris's Ford dealership shortly after nine-thirty. He parked back by the garage and got out, leaving his Escort unlocked. Although he carried a pistol and handcuffs, he didn't think of them. Shep McDonald was sweeping the snow off the new cars in the lot. From the garage came the sound of metal hitting metal and the occasional buzz of a power tool. Ryan walked toward the open double doors, trying not to step in the slush, even though his shoes were already wet from Chihani's front yard. Several people stopped to look at him but they didn't speak. They recognized him and by the way he looked they knew he hadn't come to have his car fixed.

Hark was working on the turbocharger of Pete Roberts's blue '92 Mustang, which had conked out the week before between Aurelius and Clinton. He was leaning over the front fender, which he had covered with a green pad to protect the finish. His back was to Ryan. As Ryan walked across the garage, several men lay down their tools to watch. No one knew about Chihani but they knew that Hark had been out with his friends the previous night and there must have been trouble because when Hark had showed up in the morning, hungover and sullen, he had a black eye.

As the garage became silent, Hark realized something was wrong. He turned around. He was wearing blue coveralls with "Jack Morris Ford" written across the breast pocket. His dark blond hair hung loose, parted in the middle and covering his ears. His left cheek was swollen and discolored around the eye. He had a red bruise on his forehead.

Hark didn't say anything but his eyes got wider. He was holding a socket wrench in one hand and an orange cloth in the other. Ryan was still about twenty feet away. Hark abruptly dropped the wrench, which hit the concrete floor with a clang, and sprinted toward a door in the back.

Later, in Bud's Tavern, Jerry Golding said, "Old Ryan followed him but he didn't run. Maybe he walked a little faster. He looked like a small locomotive. Purposeful."

Hark's Ford pickup was parked in the back. When Ryan walked out the door into the lot, he saw Hark standing by the driver's door, frantically going through the pockets of his coveralls. Then he stopped. His keys were in his regular clothes in his locker. Hark glanced back at Ryan. His shoulders sagged and he leaned forward against the cab of the pickup as Ryan approached.

After a moment Hark tried to summon up some fierceness. He spun around and jabbed a thumb toward his face. "See what he did to me?" he shouted. "The fucking Arab!"

Ryan didn't say anything, just kept walking. A few men had come out of the garage. Hark's face grew uncertain. He had his fists raised and he dropped them.

"Chihani's dead," said Ryan when he was a few feet away.

"You're lying."

"You got him with the baseball bat."

Hark's expression changed from defiance to surprise to fear. He pressed his hands to his chest. His hands were greasy and left black prints on his coveralls. He closed his eyes and hunched forward. A harsh honking noise came from his throat, like a motor that wouldn't start.

Ryan looked at him. When Ryan had moved to Aurelius in 1977, Hark had been six years old. Ryan remembered how Hark's hair had been almost white at the time, not much darker than Barry Sanders's. Ryan put an arm around Hark and patted his shoulder. They stood like that as about five men watched from the garage. Then Ryan led Hark across the parking lot to where his Escort was parked. Later, when he was asked why he hadn't put handcuffs on Hark, Ryan said he had forgotten to, then he said he hadn't wanted to embarrass him.

———————

By the time Ryan got Hark back to police headquarters, Jeb Hendricks, Ernie Corelli, and Jimmy Feldman were giving their statements. They said it had been Hark's idea to drive over to the Arab's house. They themselves had wanted to return to Bud's Tavern. Jeb said he'd tried to stop Hark when he attacked Chihani with the baseball bat. Ernie said he tried to stop Hark, too, but in fact he didn't remember anything after they had gotten back from chasing Jesse and Shannon. Jimmy didn't remember much either but he also had a black eye and he explained in detail how Chihani had attacked him almost for no reason. After all, he hadn't been swinging any baseball bat. And he didn't have any grudge against the Arab either. Live and let live was his motto.

Hark gave a statement. It didn't occur to him not to. He felt so defeated that even though his memory was foggy he didn't see any point in hiding anything. He didn't know why he had decided to bust up the Arab's car. It seemed like a good idea at the time. He remembered swinging the bat and hitting the Arab; he knew he hadn't meant to kill him. He was sure of that. He kept saying he was sorry. When he heard Meg Shiller had disappeared, he kept saying, "Shit, oh shit."

Barry and Leon were questioned about the previous night. Barry's mother came with him and wouldn't let Barry speak without interrupting him and saying what Barry meant and how the other members of the IIR had taken advantage of him. She said she had known all along that Hark wasn't any good but that Aaron wasn't any good either. She said she felt awful about Meg Shiller.

Again and again Barry asked, "But what about Professor Chihani?"

His mother said, "Never mind about him."

But to Barry, Chihani's death seemed worse than Meg's disappearance. Barry saw Professor Chihani all the time, and while he felt bad about Meg Shiller, he couldn't quite remember who she was.

Leon knew nothing about Meg Shiller. All he could think about was Chihani. "They killed him?" he kept asking. "But why? What had he done?" He didn't want to talk about Meg. He didn't see the point of it. He thought of the papers that Chihani had been writing and how they would go unfinished. "What a shame," he said. "Think of the work."

Jesse and Shannon admitted to smashing the windshield of Jeb's Blazer. They had hacked around for a while afterward, they said. They had a couple of beers and got home before midnight. Yes, they heard the police knocking on their door earlier in the morning, but they wanted to sleep. They knew nothing about Meg. When they learned that Chihani had been killed, they got angry.

"What the hell he ever do to them?" said Jesse.

"The assholes," said his brother.

Then Jesse began to sob and his brother put his arm around him. Ryan found himself staring at their blond goatees and blond ponytails. Their emotion surprised him and he asked himself why it should surprise him. Later he told Franklin that he didn't know diddly-squat about anybody. "You expect a person to do one thing and he does the opposite." Around noon, Ryan sent the brothers home.

Harriet Malcomb was reluctant to say where she had been until she heard about Meg.

"But why would I have had anything to do with her?" she asked. She, too, was shocked by Chihani's death. "You can't protect anyone, can you?" she told Ryan. "You can't protect the teachers and you can't protect the children."

It turned out she had begun having an affair with a married history teacher named Sherman Carpenter, whose class on the labor-union movement she was taking. Carpenter's marital troubles were known all over town. The two of them had gone to a motel near Clinton. She had gotten home around five in the morning, having been delayed by the snow.

Ryan wanted to ask her what grade she expected to get in her labor-union class and if she had any thoughts about Carpenter's wife, who had made complaints about her husband's violence when he was drinking. But Harriet was cold and imperious and stared at Ryan as if she knew something dirty about him. She wore a tight blue turtle-neck sweater and tight Levi's. She kept touching and tossing her long dark hair as if it were the object of her anger. Ryan thought of her as a ball breaker, but to Franklin the strongest term he used about Harriet was "one tough cookie." The fact that he had been intimate with her muddled his thinking.

"You've made a mess of this whole situation," Harriet told him. "Not only am I going to report it to the mayor, but I'm going to talk to the president of the college."

"Get the hell out of here," said Ryan.

As she left the room, she whispered to Ryan, "It makes me sick to think I ever let you touch me."

That left Aaron.

He had been sitting in an office by himself for two hours and he didn't like it. Ryan entered and sat down at the desk without looking at him. Because of the people involved in the search for Meg there was a lot of noise, but this office was quiet. Aaron's hands were folded in his lap and he stared at the floor. Ryan didn't realize Aaron was angry. He looked reflective, as if considering life's troubles. Ryan thought of Harriet's remark that Aaron had told her to have sex with him. He found himself disliking the complexity caused by one's loss of social anonymity. Maybe he had lived in a small town long enough.

Ryan opened the drawer of the desk and removed a yellow legal pad. He wrote the date at the top, then he wrote his name and Aaron's name beneath it. He didn't say anything. He drew little stars at the top of the page, then he drew a picture of a mother duck followed by a line of baby ducks. He was just drawing the sixth baby duck when Aaron said, "Well?"

"I drove by your mother's house this morning," said Ryan.

"Is that supposed to soften me up?" Aaron leaned back and stretched out his legs, crossing his feet. His hands were folded across his flat belly.

"I wonder if the people who live there ever think how your mother was killed right in the living room."

"You'd have to ask them," said Aaron.

Ryan saw the dislike in Aaron's eyes. He tore off the yellow sheet with the ducks, wadded it up, and tossed it at the wastebasket. It hit the rim and bounced away. "What did you think of Chihani?"

"He was harmless. He was also a smart man. I liked him."

"I wonder if Hark would have killed him if you hadn't bitten off Hark's ear," said Ryan. He had begun doodling on the next yellow sheet. Eggs this time.

"What's that supposed to mean?"

"Just what it says." Ryan decided it had been a dumb thing to say.

"You think I'm responsible for him getting killed?"

Ryan avoided the question. "D'you think the person who killed your mother lives in Aurelius?"

Aaron didn't answer.

"What would you do if you knew who killed her?"

"What would *you* do?"

"I expect I might kill him."

"What would that solve?"

"It would let me sleep better. You haven't answered my question. What would you do?"

Aaron looked away. "I don't see it's your business."

"Do you care one way or the other?"

Aaron jerked around in his seat. "Of course I care."

"Would you want to kill him?"

"How do you know it's a man?" Aaron's tone was mocking.

"Of course it's a man."

"If she was killed by a man living in Aurelius, then why haven't you found him?"

"It's not that simple."

"That's one explanation," said Aaron. Then he asked, "Do you think the same person took Sharon and Meg?"

"It wouldn't surprise me." Ryan had drawn eight eggs in a row. He began to draw cracks in them. "Why did you tell Harriet to have sex with me?"

"Did she say that?"

"Why'd you tell her?"

"She's my soldier."

"What's that supposed to mean?"

"Ask her yourself."

Ryan finished drawing the cracks on the eggs. "Who were you with last night?"

"I don't plan to tell you."

Ryan tore off the sheet of paper, wadded it up, and threw it at the wastebasket. This time he sank it. He got up, went to the door, and called to Chuck Hawley: "Chuck, take this guy over to Potterville and lock him up."

Thirty-one

The ten days after Meg's disappearance were days of dashed hopes and turmoil. The fact that a second girl had vanished and the increasing certainty that the person responsible must live in our area brought not only national attention to Aurelius but volunteers from all over the country, including a seer—this is what she called herself—by the name of Madame Respighi, who set herself up at the Aurelius Motel and, with the aid of pieces of clothing belonging to Sharon and Meg, began a psychic quest for the girls' whereabouts. She did not charge for this service and it was the general opinion that she could do no harm, though every time I drove past the motel I thought of Madame Respighi shut up in her room and locked in combat with malevolent psychic forces. Many people held her in scorn, feeling that she was trading on our town's ill fortune. She was a portly woman who dressed in gray suits, somewhat to my chagrin since I had imagined the colorful long skirts and dangling gold earrings of a gypsy. She wore black horn-rimmed glasses and her short silver hair was all curled and frizzy.

Several people showed up with dogs that had uncommon abilities. Other people came on their own, just because they wanted to join the search. Two writers materialized because they imagined book contracts. There were psychologists, law officers from around the country who had had similar cases, and social workers trained to help people deal with grief. The most disturbing visitors, to my mind, were the parents of children who had vanished in other places. They came to give solace to the Malloys and Shillers, but also in the hope that the person responsible would be captured and give information about their own children. They were sad people with defeated faces and it was hard to look at them without feeling their grief.

By the end of the first week in November everybody who might have seen or heard anything relevant had been interviewed. Suspicious automobiles had been traced. The fields and parks around town had been searched by hundreds of people. Ponds were dragged. Meg's uncle Mike became an active participant in the Friends of Sharon Malloy and the group distributed information about Meg all over the United States. Again there were calls, possible sightings, and suspicious people to be investigated.

The photograph of Meg Shiller showed a thin thirteen-year-old with long brown hair standing by a picnic table. She was waving at the photographer and had a slightly silly smile. She wore a plaid skirt and a light-colored blouse. Her hair, parted in the middle and tucked behind her ears, hung past her shoulders. She had a straight nose, almost pointed, and her lower lip stuck out slightly in a cheerful pout. Her head was tilted, which gave her a quizzical look: a little smile, a little pout, a little question mark. Within twenty-four hours the photograph took its place next to Sharon's on store windows and telephone poles and at the toll booths on the turnpike. Many people displayed the two photographs on the rear windows of their automobiles.

The fear surrounding Meg's disappearance was greater than the fear surrounding Sharon's. In Sharon's case, we could still hope that her disappearance was an isolated incident. But in Meg's it was clear that we were probably dealing with a sequence of disappearances, and almost immediately no child was seen on the street by herself, or even himself. This was true as far away as Binghamton and Syracuse. Meg's disappearance made us expect a third kidnapping, maybe even a fourth and fifth.

These fears led to a number of false alarms. Betty Brewer on Forest Street saw a man watching her house and felt he was after her daughter, Ilene. She called the police, who arrived in four separate cars three minutes later. The man watching her house—he had been walking by—was a plainclothesman with the state police. Ten plainclothesmen were patrolling the streets of Aurelius and all were eventually reported. Niagara Mohawk meter readers and town water-meter readers were reported again and again. Men walking their dogs, even mailmen, became suspect. And then at night there were the suspicious noises: the sound of footsteps in a backyard, a window rattling, leaves blowing across a front porch. Ten times a night the police would receive these false alarms and each time they would rush out because this time, possibly, the culprit might be found.

What kind of person was this culprit? The police had profiles prepared by psychologists and, according to Ryan, it seemed that everybody in town shared some of the characteristics. But that was not true. Primarily the police were looking for a single man between the ages of twenty-five and fifty or, if not single, then a man estranged from his wife. I am sure that police records were sought for several thousand men within the county, including myself. This was the time when Harry Martini was taken out of his office for the whole school to see, when Jaime Rose was brought in for questioning. One man, Herbert Maxwell, a local plumber for twenty years, was questioned by the police and revealed to be a Vietnam deserter. He lived alone and was rather solitary. He had already been punished or pardoned—I don't know which—for his desertion from the army but he didn't want it to become public knowledge. Now it was public knowledge. As a single man living alone and private in his habits, he had been suspected. That was true of many men. It was true of Ryan Tavich; it was true of me.

On the Saturday after Halloween, my next-door neighbor, Pete Daniels, happened to speak to me as we were both raking leaves. He almost never spoke to me, so his attention was surprising. First he mentioned the nice weather, then he said it was a shame about Meg Shiller.

Then he said, "Sadie Moore spends a lot of time at your house, doesn't she?"

I felt a chill. If I said no, he would find it suspicious. If I said yes, he would find that suspicious too. Of course, it wasn't any of his business, so his very question suggested mistrust. Pete had an alert expression, like a man listening for an echo. He leaned against his rake, a thin fellow in a Syracuse University sweatshirt that proclaimed him an "Orangeman."

"I'm glad to help out Franklin whenever I can," I said. "He's been very busy."

I was a subject of discussion. I saw my neighbors looking at me with new eyes. Of course, it was easy to be paranoid about this. Could I ask Pete if he thought I might have abducted Sharon Malloy and Meg Shiller? The police knew I had been at school at the time of the first disappearance and at home or with Sadie at the time of the second. But what did my neighbors know? And once that sort of talk begins, truth or falsehood means nothing. Talk has its own momentum.

The next day, Sunday, Sadie told me that her father had been trying to find someone else to look after her. Mrs. Kelly was available only three afternoons and early evenings, and besides, she had left early more than once. Franklin wanted to get another person as well. He even said he might send Sadie to her aunt's in White Plains until "all this is cleared up." Sadie protested vigorously enough that the matter was temporarily dropped. But Franklin told Sadie that she couldn't spend as much time at my house. She responded by saying she had thought that Franklin liked me.

"It's not a matter of liking or disliking," Franklin said.

Franklin also suggested that Sadie could go to Paula's house each evening.

"I'll run away from home," Sadie told him.

Then, when Sadie returned home from school Monday afternoon, she found Barry Sanders's mother settled in the living room watching television. "Like a big, ugly plant," Sadie told me.

"Tell me if you're hungry and I'll fix you a snack," Mrs. Sanders said, returning to her show. Because she claimed to be allergic to dogs, she had shut Shadow up in the basement. Sadie rescued Shadow and went to her room. Around six Mrs. Sanders prepared macaroni and cheese and green beans. Barry appeared for dinner but he didn't talk to Sadie, because he was shy with her in his mother's presence. Mrs. Sanders urged Barry to eat his green beans. After supper Barry and Sadie wanted to come over to my house but Mrs. Sanders said that wouldn't be a good idea. They watched TV instead. Shadow whined from Sadie's room but wasn't allowed to join them.

"She wants to keep me a prisoner in my own house," Sadie told me the next morning at school.

Tuesday evening I went to see Franklin when he got home about eleven. "Do you really think I might be involved with these disappearances?"

He was not comfortable. "There's a lot of crazy talk."

"That doesn't answer my question."

"Of course I don't think you're involved, but people are upset. What can I do?"

I wanted to say, Franklin, look at me, I'm your friend. Instead I said, "Well, I hope this is settled soon."

"So do I," said Franklin. "Jesus, so do I."

Charges were brought against Hark. The county prosecutor wanted to charge him with first-degree murder but Ryan had him change it to second. I like to think that Ryan felt sympathy for Hark but perhaps he knew that a first-degree murder conviction was impossible. There were plenty of people who thought that Hark shouldn't be arrested, that he had done the right thing. It was argued that even though Chihani had nothing to do with the disappearances he still represented the sort of thinking that leads to criminal behavior. One heard the argument that laws exist to keep deviants out of the community and that to seek to change these laws radically, as Chihani tried to do, was to make the community vulnerable. Chihani's preaching and the presence of the IIR had created an atmosphere that made it possible for the disappearances to take place.

The dangers of permissiveness became a general topic and I was told that Henry Skoyles, owner of the Strand Theater on Main Street, had canceled three scheduled movies as being too violent or sexually provocative, exchanging them for what he described as "family fare." I had known Henry Skoyles in school. He had been two years behind me and had the reputation for being inventive as far as obscenities were concerned. Once he had called the principal "turdhead" and soon it seemed that everyone was using the word. Now he felt called upon to bring back the Walt Disney version of *Aladdin* and run it for the entire month.

But I'm not doing justice to the terror. Not only did we know that horrible things had happened, we were afraid that horrible things were about to happen. This made us even more suspicious, as if suspicion itself could keep us safe by keeping us alert.

With Meg's disappearance many new people joined the Friends of Sharon Malloy. More often, this group was called the Friends, since it now also included friends of Meg Shiller, though legally it was still the Friends of Sharon Malloy. The Friends decided they could help by organizing teams of volunteers to patrol Aurelius. By the weekend they had three cars with three people in each watching the streets of Aurelius twenty-four hours a day. No longer were they simply trying to find the missing girls, they were trying to keep more girls from disappearing. If I had suggested at school that they were a vigilante force, I would have been reproached. I'm sure others felt as I did, but such was the degree of fear that one had no choice but to applaud the Friends.

Sharon's uncles, Paul Leimbach and Donald Malloy, were the most active in organizing these patrols, but Meg's uncle, Mike Shiller, was also involved. There was talk that the men on these patrols should wear a special cap or armband to indicate their status as protectors, but Leimbach said it would make them too much like a police force. Donald Malloy got a number of magnetic triangles from a highway construction firm in Utica. These were bright Day-Glo orange, sixteen inches high, and the Friends displayed them on the front doors of their patrol cars. I don't know how many times a day I would look from my classroom window or from a window at home and see a vehicle with those orange triangles slowly passing by. It was both reassuring and frightening. I know that Ryan Tavich disapproved of the patrols, though Chief Schmidt felt they couldn't do any harm and was glad to have them on the streets. Captain Percy's feelings were mixed.

Paul Leimbach and Donald Malloy spent less and less time at work. Both were heard to say that the police weren't doing enough to find the culprit or to protect the citizens of Aurelius. At a city council meeting, Donald proposed a six o'clock curfew for anyone under the age of eighteen. Despite some protest his proposal was accepted with modification. Beginning immediately, anyone sixteen years or younger could not be out on the street after seven at night without an adult.

I was tempted to remind people that Sharon had vanished in the midafternoon, but we had reached a time when people, myself included, were circumspect in their speech. Everyone, it seemed, listened for a nuance of guilt, some double meaning that would point a finger. When I spoke, I felt that people listened not to my words but to what lay behind them. And of course people felt they heard some-

thing when they heard nothing of the kind. Far better to remain silent and to wear a brave smile, to praise the Friends for their sacrifice.
Briefly I even considered joining them—this was when I felt I was
being watched—but then I rebelled in my own little way and refused,
though I told no one of my refusal and it was only to myself that I
refused.

Once the curfew was in place, Henry Skoyles canceled the second
show at the Strand and even the first show was sparsely attended.
Many stores and restaurants open in the evening changed their hours.
Junior's began closing at seven and the Aurelius Grill at eight. Wegmans, which had closed at midnight for years, now closed at nine
o'clock. Night meetings were canceled. Rehearsals for the fall play at
the high school were canceled, as were rehearsals for the Christmas
pageant at Saint Mary's Church. Business fell off at local bars and
restaurants. People who never locked their doors, locked their doors.

On the other hand, pizza deliveries doubled and the video stores
did a big business. The liquor store out at the strip mall was also more
active. The town library reported more visits and church attendance
increased. And I must say that a higher percentage of my students got
their homework in on time. From what I heard in the teachers'
lounge, this was true in many classes. The Morellis, across the street
from me, obtained a large dog from the pound in Utica, a German
shepherd that barked all night long and terrorized the neighborhood
cats. Indeed, a number of people bought dogs.

Much of this was reported by Franklin, and by writing about it he
seemed to increase the level of fear among us. His articles led to more
meetings being canceled, to more stores closing early. Yet it seemed
that if Franklin were to write nothing, that would increase the terror
even more. So he wrote everything he could. But because of his connection to Paula and Aaron, because he had often interviewed Chihani, even because he was not originally from Aurelius, it was thought
he was not telling as much as he knew. It was assumed he was con-

cealing information, as if the police had suspects, like Aaron or other members of the IIR, whom Franklin knew about but about whom he was silent.

This put Franklin in an impossible situation. To write was to create fear; not to write was to create fear. And he could never write enough; he was always thought to be concealing worse things.

Thirty-two

Fat Leon Stahl continued his daily routines as if nothing were out of the ordinary. Chihani's classes were taken over by other faculty members and the course in which Leon had been enrolled—Nineteenth-Century Class Relations—was assigned to Sherman Carpenter, the professor having the affair, however brief, with Harriet Malcomb. Although upset about the death of Chihani, Leon thought little about the disappearances of Meg and Sharon. It wasn't that he was callous; rather, like most other students at the college, he lived in another world. Many students never left campus, unless it was to go to one of the pubs or lunch counters. Leon knew about the missing girls and perhaps he worried about them, but the fact that Harriet, whom he imagined he loved, was sexually involved with Professor Carpenter was of greater significance.

In Leon's ten months as a member of the IIR, he had matured somewhat. He had added a small black goatee to his small black moustache and he wore a variety of sport coats, tweeds and herringbones that he purchased at thrift shops in Utica. None were in the best condition, nor did they fit. And as the weather got colder he also took to wearing a plaid porkpie hat. While most of the students carried their books in backpacks, Leon had an old leather briefcase, also from a thrift shop. And he bought new glasses with wire frames. He saw himself as an intellectual, and perhaps he was. At least he always had his nose in a book. He was even able to read while walking and this was how I often saw him, walking downtown from the campus reading a book.

It was on such a walk that Andy Wilkins and Russ Fusco found him. These were young men who worked at the rope factory. More important, they were volunteers in the Friends and took part in the patrols, though they were off duty when they came upon Leon. They were a self-satisfied pair with exaggerated opinions about their good looks. Andy had played tackle for the Terriers and even managed to graduate from high school. Russ was from Norwich but he had moved to Aurelius after getting the job at the rope factory. Both were in their midtwenties.

Who knows what they thought? Neither was known for being a bully, nor was there much to be said in their favor. They were young men who drank beer, tended toward inarticulateness, and were shocked, excited, and indignant about recent events in our town. They wanted to ask Leon a question; this was what they claimed. And it may have been true, but the question concerned Leon's involvement with the IIR and the IIR's involvement with Sharon and Meg. Both Andy and Russ knew Hark Powers, and while they were not friends, they felt that Hark had gotten a raw deal. After all, Chihani had beaten Hark with his cane.

Leon was walking down Monroe Street toward Main. It was just past noon and he meant to have lunch at the Aurelius Grill. Every Wednesday the Grill offered a meatloaf special with mashed potatoes and gravy. It had become a ritual with Leon, especially since his favorite waitress cut him an extra-thick slice of meatloaf. The day was mild, with small white clouds drifting across a blue sky. Leon read as he walked, a book by Terry Eagleton on Marxist literary theory.

Andy was driving his green Camaro and he coasted to a stop at the curb. When Leon got even with the car, Andy called to him, "Hey, you."

Leon kept walking. Later he said he hadn't heard anyone.

Andy called to him again but Leon didn't stop. Andy put the car in reverse, backed up rapidly, hit the brake, and got out. Russ Fusco got out as well.

Andy stood in the middle of the sidewalk as Leon approached, reading his book.

"Hey," said Andy again. He couldn't imagine anyone's reading a book, much less reading while walking.

Leon kept walking. He seemed oblivious to Andy's presence.

Andy reached out and knocked the book from Leon's hands. It skittered across the sidewalk and Russ picked it up. The title made no sense to him but he recognized the name of Marx. He showed the title to Andy.

"Give me my book," said Leon, becoming aware of the two men. His tone was peremptory. He didn't see why anyone would knock a book from his hand. He was taller than Andy and Russ and weighed what the two men weighed together. Russ said later that Leon's porkpie hat sat on his head like a raisin on a cupcake and that description was repeated by many people.

"I want to ask you a question," said Andy.

"Give me my book," said Leon, a little louder.

"You'll get it when I'm ready to give it to you," said Russ.

At that point, Leon charged them. Considering the value he placed on books, this was a religious matter with him. Leon knocked Andy to the sidewalk. He tried to snatch the book from Russ's hand, but Russ jumped back. Leon charged Russ but by then Andy had gotten to his feet and he grabbed Leon from behind.

The result was that Andy beat Leon. He broke his glasses, knocked him to the ground, and kicked his porkpie hat into the street. And when Leon was huddled into a large moaning mass, Andy took the book and tore it up. This happened in the middle of the day and people saw it. Before Andy was finished, a police car with Chuck Hawley and Ray Hanna screeched to a stop and they dragged Andy away from Leon. Russ hadn't touched Leon, but neither had he done anything to stop his friend.

Though Leon wasn't seriously injured, he had been hurt. Andy was furious that a fat creature like Leon would dare to attack him. Leon was furious that they would take his book and destroy it. He pressed charges and Andy and Russ were arrested. Leon also insisted that he be taken to the hospital. X-rays showed no internal injuries and two Band-Aids made him as good as new.

Franklin wrote about the affair for Thursday's *Independent.* People learned that Andy and Russ were active in the Friends of Sharon Malloy. Leon's membership in the IIR and his connection to Chihani were emphasized. Andy claimed that he just wanted to ask Leon a simple question (he didn't say about what) when Leon attacked him. Leon said he had only tried to get his book back.

Franklin talked to Paul Leimbach about the incident, hoping to get an apology from the Friends. "People are upset," said Leimbach. "Consequently mistakes will be made." Nobody found this reassuring.

Thursday night somebody threw rocks through the windows of Leon's second-story apartment near the college, getting glass all over the rug and damaging a cassette player. Leon was at the library at the time. No one was charged, though Ryan established that Andy or Russ couldn't have been involved. On Sunday night around ten o'clock someone again threw a rock through Leon's window. Leon called the police. Chuck Hawley answered the call but found nobody in the neighborhood. "Deserted" was the word Chuck used. The streets were deserted.

On Monday morning the academic dean at the college met with Leon and asked if he would like to take a leave of absence. The tuition he had paid for the fall semester could be applied to another semester. Leon accepted. Now that the world had caught his attention, he had grown anxious. He didn't see why anyone should steal his book or break his windows.

"After all," he said, "I never even went to the cemetery."

The fact of his membership in Inquiries into the Right was not seen by him to be important.

"A discussion group," he kept saying. "Why should we want to kidnap a little girl?"

On Tuesday Leon packed his trunk and went home to Dunkirk on the shore of Lake Erie. The police had his phone number if they needed him. This left five members of the IIR: Aaron, Harriet, Barry, and the Levine brothers. They no longer held meetings. Barry and Aaron sometimes met. Sometimes Aaron saw Harriet. Jesse and Shannon went back to their skateboards, but they still called themselves Marxists. Their particular form of Marxism, however, required no study. It was simply an alternative to all that was wrong with the world, while their use of Marxist jargon gave them an edge in their arguments with other students. "Praxis," they would say. "Epistemological dialectics!" But of course we were not done with them yet.

Although the attack on Leon was censured, a few saw it as a much-needed tonic against the forces of anarchy. They even saw it as an action performed by the Friends of Sharon Malloy, though Andy and Russ had been off duty at the time. The Friends became a force within Aurelius but it never seemed they were motivated by a sense of power so much as by fear: the loss of more children. Their use of power stemmed from that fear rather than from an enjoyment of power for its own sake. There were some members who abused their power but the group itself seemed well-intentioned.

But their fear led them to overstep their authority—I felt it did. An example was their visit to me on the day Leon was beaten up. I should say that many people received visits and none felt bullied by them. At least they didn't complain.

I had finished my class preparations for the next day and had

settled down to browse through *Scientific American*. I must admit
that I rarely read more than the first few paragraphs of any story, but
the pictures are a pleasure and there is always at least one story relevant to tenth grade biology. Once a month I have one of my students
report on it for extra credit.

My doorbell rang at nine. At first I thought it was Sadie, though
she usually knocks or just opens the door. Now, like others, I was
keeping it locked. Sadie was still being cared for by Barry's mother,
The Lump, as Sadie called her. And since it was Wednesday night, I
knew that Franklin would be busy with the paper.

Through the curtain on the glass of the front door, I saw three
people standing on the porch. I turned on the light and recognized
them as Donald Malloy, Agnes Hilton, and Dave Bauer. I felt alarmed
since I knew they were all members of the Friends. On the other
hand, Agnes Hilton worked as treasurer and secretary for the Ebenezer Baptist Church while Dave Bauer was associate director of the
YMCA and also a volunteer fireman. And they looked friendly, especially when I turned on the light.

I opened the door and invited them in. There followed a minute
or so of foot stamping, coat removing, and hand shaking. It was a
cold night and all wore heavy coats. Again I was struck by their
friendliness, but even more by their desire to appear friendly.

"We wondered if we could talk to you briefly," said Donald Malloy, cordially. "It won't take much of your time."

I invited them into the living room. Agnes said something flatter-
ing about the furniture, though it was nothing special. She was a
redheaded woman in her late forties who always wore dresses. Either
her husband was dead or he had somehow vanished, because she
lived alone with a younger sister. There was a wedding ring on her
finger, however, so presumably there had been a Mr. Hilton at one
point.

I offered them tea.

"That would be very nice," said Dave Bauer.

Agnes Hilton volunteered to help, but I said I could do it. I wanted a moment alone to collect myself. I went to the kitchen and prepared a tray. In the cupboard was a tin of Danish cookies I'd been saving and I put a dozen on a plate. These situations are always foolish. Should I put the cookies on a best plate or an ordinary plate? I chose the ordinary plate, Syracuse china. I poured the water into the teapot and carried the tray into the living room. Dave Bauer and Agnes were seated on the couch. Donald was in the armchair, the chair in which I always sit.

Donald closed the *Scientific American* he had been glancing at. "Pretty fantastic this human-genome project," he said. "That Watson is a man whose hand I'd like to shake." He put the magazine on the coffee table. He had an open, affable face and his freckles made him seem younger than he actually was. He wore khakis and one of those tan rag sweaters from L. L. Bean. When he leaned forward to put the magazine on the table, he made a little *oomph* noise.

I put the tray next to the magazine.

"You must be upset about the Terriers," said Bauer.

The Friday evening football games at the high school had been canceled because of the curfew, which meant the team was no longer a contender within its league. I had to think a moment before I knew what Bauer was talking about.

"It's a shame," I said. I poured the tea into three mugs. "I'll let you add your own sugar and milk."

"I take mine plain," said Donald.

I handed him a cup, then poured one for myself and sat down in the armchair on the other side of the fireplace. Though I had laid a fire with birch logs, I was saving it for Friday night. I arranged my face into an expectant expression.

"I expect you're wondering why we're here," said Donald, and he smiled at his companions. Bauer took a cookie.

Agnes explained their connection with the Friends of Sharon Malloy and there was a certain amount of talk about the missing girls. I'm afraid I was anxious not to say the wrong thing and I was also anxious not to seem nervous. Bauer took another cookie. He was one of those wiry young men who can eat all day and never gain a pound. In the summer he was involved in coaching Little League and in the winter he directed a basketball program at the Y. I hoped he wouldn't discover my indifference to sports. Then I grew perturbed for feeling bullied by these people.

"But what has any of this to do with me?" I asked.

"I gather you saw Meg Shiller on the night she disappeared," said Donald. He looked quite comfortable in my chair. His tea sat on the coffee table, untouched. He hadn't taken a cookie.

"She came to my house with Hillary and Sadie before they went trick-or-treating. They wanted to show off their costumes."

"So you know Meg?" asked Agnes.

I was struck by her use of the present tense. "I know Sadie, and Meg's a friend of Sadie's. Of course I know them from school as well. Meg was in my general-science class last year."

"And what time did they visit you?" asked Donald.

"Around six."

"And you didn't see Meg again?"

I didn't speak for a moment. Then I said, "May I ask the reason for your interest? I've already talked to the police and it would seem these matters—if they are indeed significant—are a subject to be discussed between me and the authorities and no one else. At least I am under no obligation to answer your questions." I got quite out of breath saying all that.

The three looked at one another. Their expressions showed a friendly and mild exasperation, as if they had been afraid that my question might come up.

"We've spoken to many people," said Bauer. "We understand you've talked to the police, as have others. But we felt there'd be no harm in sifting through the material once again. Not that you're hiding anything, but possibly the police missed something."

It was on the tip of my tongue to ask what made them competent investigators, but it seemed more protests on my part could be interpreted as defiance and I had to ask myself if it was worth the risk.

"I didn't see Meg again that evening," I said.

They asked more questions and I described how Sadie had come over to my house and how we had gone out to look for Meg and how Sadie had found the umbrella.

"You were the one to call the police?" asked Agnes.

I admitted I was. I tried to answer their questions coolly, without slowing irritation. I described how I had remained in Franklin's house till midnight, then come home.

"I have another question," said Donald, "and I must say I have absolutely no wish to offend you."

I waited, expecting the worst.

Donald glanced at Mrs. Hilton, who nodded to him in return. "What we would like to know is whether you are homosexual."

Though I expected to be surprised, I was shocked nonetheless. "My personal life is none of your concern," I said.

"We understand that," said Donald. He again looked at the others for support, then he tried to smile affably. Though he looked cheerful with his large Irish face, he was not a man whom I suspected of much cheer. "You must see," he continued, "that we are not asking for ourselves but in the interest of finding the missing girls. Do you know other homosexuals in Aurelius?"

I hesitated again. "I may."

"What about Jaime Rose?" asked Agnes Hilton.

"Is he homosexual?" I responded.

"What about Aaron McNeal?" asked Donald.

"I very much doubt it. He has girlfriends all over town." His question surprised me and I wondered if it had been prompted by Aaron's friendship with Barry.

Donald began to speak quickly, leaning forward with his elbows on his knees and his big stomach resting on his thighs. "Whether you're homosexual is your own business, but we wondered if there were an organization in Aurelius of gay men. We'd like the chance to address them, just to make certain that all possible avenues have been explored."

"We've talked to other groups too," said Bauer. He described a group devoted to ballroom dancing that met at the Episcopal church and I found it incredible that he would compare an organization of gay men to a ballroom-dancing club.

"We've talked to the Masons and Kiwanis Club as well," said Agnes. They looked at me with kindly concern, as if there was something wrong with me. I looked back at them blankly, trying to hide the fact that I thought something might be wrong with *them.*

"I know of no organization of gay men in Aurelius," I said, which was true. In fact, I felt they already must know this, which meant they had come not for this sort of information but rather for the chance to look at me more closely.

"I know you're upset about the missing girls," said Donald, leaning back in the chair, "especially since you're close to Sadie. It's a terrible thing that's happened not only to the families of those girls but to the town as a whole." He gently rubbed his cheek with his right hand, as if touching a bruise. "I'm sure you're concerned with all that's happened—the bomb scare at the high school, the death of that professor, and of course the mistrust. But our normal life won't resume till we know what happened to Sharon and Meg. Their extraordinary disappearances has forced us to take extraordinary measures."

"Do you really think our lives will return to normal?" I asked. "Even if we learn what happened?"

"Perhaps not," said Donald.

"But we hope so," said Agnes Hilton. "And we certainly pray for that."

Thirty-three

Two days after Halloween, Ryan Tavich got a telephone call. He heard a low female voice speaking in a whisper.

"You can let Aaron McNeal out of jail," she said. "He was with me on Halloween night."

The fact that Aaron was in jail in Potterville had been reported in the *Independent*.

"And who're you?" asked Ryan. He'd been expecting something like this. He tried to place the voice but couldn't.

"I don't wish to say," said the woman rather primly.

Ryan made a regretful noise. "I'm afraid I can't let McNeal go free just on your word. I don't know who you are and I don't know any of the particulars of the time he spent with you."

"Surely you can guess the particulars."

Ryan wondered if that was true. "But I still don't know who you are. Why should I believe you?"

"If I gave you my name, would you promise not to reveal it?"

"I'd need to talk to you," said Ryan.

"You are talking to me."

"I'd need to talk to you in person."

"That's impossible." The woman's voice rose a little.

"Then Aaron will have to stay in jail." Ryan waited.

"But why?" asked the woman.

Ryan decided to stop fooling around. "Because I want to talk to you face-to-face. Take it or leave it."

There was a pause as Ryan listened to the woman breathe. He

heard a cash register ring somewhere behind her. Who still used an old-fashioned cash register? Captain Percy came into the office with two of his men. They walked over to a survey map tacked to the wall and Percy pointed to a spot north of town.

"It would have to be very private," said the woman.

"Anywhere you want."

"If you were convinced that Aaron was with me, would you let him out of jail right away?"

"Of course."

"Then we should meet this morning." The woman was silent for a moment. "What if we meet in the reference room at the library at nine-thirty. There's never anyone there."

Ryan agreed and they hung up. He wondered about the woman. Her voice wasn't a girl's voice but he couldn't guess her age. And he wondered about the cash register. He could see it in his mind's eye—chrome with black keys—but he couldn't think where it was. The library was three blocks away and Ryan decided to walk. Captain Percy and his men were still studying the wall map. In the past month, Percy had lost some of his military bearing. Not that he had become any warmer, he just seemed less confident. Like all of us, thought Ryan.

Grabbing his sport coat, Ryan walked out of City Hall and turned right, up Main Street. It was a cool, sunny day and a few last leaves were blowing along the gutters. There wasn't much traffic but he saw a few people he knew and he waved. Cars were parked diagonally in front of the Friends of Sharon Malloy. Sharon's picture was on the right side of the door and Meg's was on the left. Ryan passed Junior's and the Key Bank. He passed Weaver's Bakery and Malloy's Pharmacy. The huge picture of Sharon in the window at Malloy's smiled out at him. He glanced through the door but saw no one inside, or maybe he saw a movement—he couldn't be sure. Reaching Carnegie Library, he climbed the steps and entered the general reading room.

About ten people were looking through the newspapers and magazines. Ryan recognized nearly all and nodded to several. The librarian, Mrs. Wright, raised her eyebrows at Ryan.

"I got to check some stuff," he said. He hurried by her before she could offer to help and climbed the stairs to the second floor. The reference room was empty. The radiators were making clanking noises. Ryan took a volume of the *Encyclopaedia Britannica* and sat down at a table by the back wall but facing the door. He opened the volume to an article on Tibet and began to glance through it. He thought how he would never visit Tibet and, for that matter, how he would probably never visit Europe. He wondered if he felt bad about that and decided he didn't.

Someone entered the room. It was Mrs. Porter, who worked at Malloy's Pharmacy. He felt annoyed, afraid that her presence might scare away the woman he was supposed to meet. Then, to his surprise, he saw that Mrs. Porter was walking directly to his table, and, with greater surprise, he realized she was the woman he had talked to on the phone. It made him remember where he had seen the cash register; at least that was settled.

Mrs. Porter was a respectable-looking woman in her forties, plain, but in good shape, wearing a three-quarter-length blue wool jacket over a dark dress. Ryan expected her to say something like, "I'm so ashamed."

Instead she said, "Is this good enough?"

Ryan had seen her a hundred times but never outside the pharmacy. He realized he knew nothing about her. He vaguely remembered a Mr. Porter, but he had no idea what the man did. The woman had never been pretty, Ryan was sure of that, but she was well-dressed and her dark brown eyes were attractive. She was neither thin nor fat: compact, was how Ryan described her.

"Sit down," he said.

She hesitated, then sat at the table across from him. She folded her hands in front of her. "Should I get a book too?" she asked, somewhat ironically.

"If you like." She didn't move. Ryan looked down at his hands, which were square with short fingers. He looked at Mrs. Porter's hands, which were large with long fingers, probably bigger than his own hands. "What's your first name?" he asked.

"Mildred," she said.

Abruptly, Ryan remembered she had been married to Rolf Porter, who ran the Century 21 real estate office and was co-chairman of the Friends of Sharon Malloy with Sandra Petoski. He couldn't remember if they had children.

"Tell me about your relationship with Aaron," asked Ryan.

"There's no relationship. He's come to my house several times and spent the night. I'm not sure if he'll come again." Her tone was slightly defiant, as if she expected Ryan to disapprove. She looked him in the eye without blinking.

"And he was with you on Halloween?"

"He left the next morning when I went to work."

"How long have you known him?"

"I've known who he is for years. A month ago he spoke to me in the pharmacy. Then he came in a day after that and we talked some more. Two days later he came to my house in the evening. I didn't send him away." Again her voice had a defiant edge. Ryan wondered what Aaron had found attractive about her.

"What do you talk about?" asked Ryan.

She appeared unsure for a moment, as if Ryan were suggesting that a man in his twenties and a woman in her forties would have no common subjects. "All sorts of things."

"Did he talk about Houari Chihani?"

"No."

"Did he talk about Sharon Malloy?"

"A little."

"Did he talk about his mother?"

"Yes, a number of times."

"Like what?"

"He talked about her sense of humor, how she was energetic, how she always seemed interested in him. He even talked about how she had brushed her hair."

Ryan had a sudden memory of Janice sitting before her mirror brushing and brushing for up to half an hour. The memory almost disarmed him.

"Did he talk about her murder?"

"Not directly. It's a very painful subject for him."

"What about her relationship with men?"

"He said that she'd probably had sex with over two hundred men in Aurelius. He was impressed by that. I asked if he was going to match her number with women and he said he might."

"What did you like about Aaron?" asked Ryan.

"He was nice and he wanted me. Does that surprise you?"

Ryan looked away. They were still alone in the room. He closed the volume of the encyclopedia that lay before him. "Did you know his mother?" he asked.

Mrs. Porter hesitated. "She came into the pharmacy a number of times."

"To buy things?"

"Of course."

"What kind of things."

"The usual things."

"Did she buy condoms?"

"Yes."

"Did she talk to Donald?"

"Sometimes he waited on her."

"Did they seem friendly?"

"Not especially. They were rather cool to each other, actually."

"What did you think of her?"

"I don't know if I had an opinion."

"You must have."

She looked down at the table, then looked back at him. "She was your lover too, wasn't she?"

Ryan felt irritated by the question. Then he almost smiled at his prissiness. "For a while."

"Did you like her?"

"Very much."

"She must have been an amazing person to have so many men feel so strongly about her. Do you like Aaron?"

"I find him a pain, but it's hard for me not to like him. He looks like her."

"Do you still think of his mother?"

Ryan leaned back. "I'm supposed to be the one asking the questions."

Mrs. Porter clicked her tongue against her teeth, a dismissive noise. "Then ask."

"Have you ever been involved with Donald Malloy?"

"Of course not."

"Why 'of course not'?"

"He's my employer."

"Do you find him unattractive?"

"I've never thought about him in that way."

Ryan considered Mrs. Porter's feelings about men. He had thought that women who liked sex always showed it, but Mildred Porter showed nothing. Ryan guessed he had been wrong about that as he had been wrong about other things.

"Are you going to let Aaron out of jail now?" she asked.

"Right away."

An hour later Ryan released Aaron from jail. Ryan didn't speak as they walked to his car. He wanted to make Aaron curious, if that was possible. The sky had clouded over and the temperature was dropping. There would be snow by evening. Aaron looked straight ahead through the windshield and said nothing.

"Tell me," said Ryan after they had driven a few miles, "what do you see in Mildred Porter?"

"She likes sex." Aaron continued to stare straight ahead. He was angry at Ryan for putting him in jail. His anger made the L-shaped scar on his cheek seem darker.

"She must be twenty years older than you and she's plain."

"Eighteen years. I fucked her body, not her face."

Ryan was rather shocked. "You must have liked her."

"Give me a choice between a plain woman who likes sex and a beautiful one who's indifferent, I'll take the plain one. I like Mildred Porter. She's passionate and modest."

"Will you see her again?"

"I doubt it."

"Why not?"

"I've already been down that road."

"What do you know about your mother's murder?" asked Ryan.

"No more than you do."

"Are you sure?"

"That's what I said, isn't it?"

Ryan drove in silence for a moment. The fields between Potterville and Aurelius were mostly cabbage fields. At this time of year they were gray and picked over. The few heads that had been missed reminded Ryan of decomposing skulls.

"Do you think your mother's murder is connected to these missing girls?" asked Ryan.

"I have no idea."

"Are there men you suspect might have killed your mother?"

"I have no idea."

"Why did you tell Harriet to have sex with me?"

"Ask her yourself."

After Ryan dropped Aaron off downtown, he drove over to Bud's Tavern. He wanted to explore an idea that had occurred to him. It was not quite eleven-thirty and Sheila Murphy was behind the bar washing glasses. Sheila's red hair was piled up on top of her head and as she glanced up at Ryan she brushed a couple of loose strands away from her face. She was a large, buxom woman who, in her midtwenties, was beginning to get heavy. From the kitchen came the smell of cooking meat.

"Lunch isn't ready yet," said Sheila. "You want a beer?"

"I want to talk."

Sheila looked regretful. "I'm pretty busy. Could we make it later?"

Ryan tried to look affable. "I guess I could take you back to my office and we could talk there."

She was silent for a moment. "What d'you want to talk about?"

"Were you friends with Janice McNeal?"

"We knew each other," said Sheila, surprised.

"I want to know more than that." Ryan sat down on a stool.

"Like what?"

"Did you go out with men together?"

"I don't see that it's any of your business." Sheila had raised her voice. She glanced quickly toward the kitchen.

"Then let's go to my office."

"All right, dammit." Sheila bit her lower lip, leaving a trace of lipstick on her teeth. "Sometimes I'd visit her house. I liked her. We'd go out with men. Sort of blind dates. Either I would know the men or she would."

"Would you have sex with these men?"

Sheila folded her towel into squares and set it on the bar. "Sometimes. If we liked them."

"So you knew the men she'd been involved with?"

"I knew you'd been into her pants all right," she said crossly. Sheila again pushed away a strand of hair. "I didn't know all her men."

"Did Aaron ask you these questions?"

"When?"

"That night in the motel when he bit you."

"How'd you know that?"

Sheila had both her hands on the bar, leaning toward Ryan. He was turning his stool slightly to the left, then to the right. There was something almost childlike about it.

"You didn't tell him, did you? That's why he got mad."

"I told him it was none of his business. And it's none of yours either."

"Did you tell him anything?"

"We were joking. At least I was. I said his mother had been laughing about a professional man. That was what she called him, 'a professional man,' like it was a joke. He asked who it was and I wouldn't say. I realized he'd gone out with me just to ask these questions and it hurt my feelings. But also I didn't want to get anyone in trouble. We were wrestling. He said he'd give me the Hark treatment if I didn't tell. I thought he was joking. I told him to fuck off. That's when he bit me."

"Who was this professional man?"

"I don't want to say. I mean, I don't know if she was ever with him."

"Whether you want to or not, this is police business—you have to say."

Two men entered the bar and Sheila moved toward them.

"I promise you," said Ryan, "I'll take you to my office."

Sheila glared at him. "Well, the fact is, I don't really know. But I bet it was Dr. Malloy. Are you happy now? Janice said she liked fucking doctors, they always smelled clean."

Ryan watched her move down the bar, already greeting the two men. He recognized them as farmers but he didn't know their names. He thought about Janice and her appetites. Then he left the tavern and walked back to his car. He drove over to Janice's house on Hamilton Street.

In the next hour, Ryan talked to Janice's neighbors, Floyd and Lois Washburn on the left side and Mrs. Winters on the right. He had talked to them immediately after Janice's murder but now he wanted to talk to them again. His question to each was the same: Had Aaron McNeal spoken with them recently?

All three said that Aaron had visited them several times in the past few months. He had wanted to know what people they had seen entering Janice's house around the time of the murder.

"He even asked if I'd seen you," said Mrs. Winters. She was a retired teacher and her living room had the musty smell of old books and too many cats. "'Did you ever see Ryan Tavich?' That's what he asked me. But he asked about other men as well."

"Who?" asked Ryan. He stood in Mrs. Winters's hallway.

"All sorts of men. No, that's not true. He was interested in what he called 'professional men.' There were several lawyers, an accountant, a professor, an engineer."

"Was the accountant Paul Leimbach?"

"Yes, it was."

"What about the professor?"

Mrs. Winters blinked her small black eyes. "Professor Carpenter over at the college."

"And had you seen any of these men?"

"I told him that I didn't spend my days and nights looking to see who was visiting his mother."

"Did he ask about Dr. Malloy?"

"Never."

Floyd and Lois Washburn gave Ryan pretty much the same answers. They were having lunch in the kitchen and Ryan accepted a cup of coffee. Floyd repaired home appliances and wore green pants and a green shirt.

"He rattled off a bunch of names," said Floyd. "Most I didn't know but you were one of them. Of course I'd seen you with Janice but that was some time before she was killed."

"You'd think we'd kept a list," said Lois. "I mean, he seemed surprised that we hadn't."

"Tell you the truth," said Floyd, "I tried not to see who was going in there. It could be embarrassing. Like your dentist—can you imagine your dentist having an illicit affair?"

"And you know for certain," said Lois, "that he'll be touching your mouth with the exact same hands."

When Ryan left, he had learned scarcely more than he had in the weeks after Janice's murder, and what he had learned concerned Aaron rather than his mother. Yet he felt good about this. It made Aaron's behavior seem less arbitrary. Ryan drove over to the college. He wanted to talk to Sherman Carpenter in the history department, the man with whom Harriet Malcomb had gone to a motel on Halloween. Ryan had talked to him earlier in order to verify Harriet's story. Now he had another question.

Carpenter was with a student and Ryan waited in the hall. Other students passing by looked at him curiously. He could hear Carpenter laughing and telling a story about John L. Lewis and his thick white eyebrows.

When the student left, Ryan stuck his head through the door. "One question. Did Harriet ask you anything about Janice McNeal?"

Carpenter was seated at his desk, which was covered with papers. "Come in and shut the door, will you?"

Ryan stepped into the office and shut the door. Carpenter was an athletic man in his late thirties. Ryan had nothing against him except that he looked and talked like a professor: too much tweed and facial hair.

"She asked if I'd been fucking Janice."

"And had you?"

"A couple of times. To tell you the truth, she was too bossy. Do this, do that. I didn't like it."

"When was this?"

Carpenter rubbed his forehead. He looked both sheepish and ironic at the same time, as if he were embarrassed but not too embarrassed. "About a month before she was killed."

"Did Harriet ask if Janice had ever mentioned 'a professional man'?"

"Yes, but Janice never did. For all I know, I was the professional man. Janice and I didn't talk much. Mostly we just got down to work, if you know what I mean."

Ryan found himself clenching his teeth.

"Did Harriet ask if Janice had mentioned Dr. Malloy or Paul Leimbach?"

"No, she only asked about one man in particular." Carpenter again assumed his expression of ironic embarrassment.

"And who was that?"

"She asked if Janice had ever mentioned you. I told her I only remembered one time. Janice said that the women you went out with called you Old Silent. Harriet laughed at that."

The day after I was visited by the Friends of Sharon Malloy, I decided to get a haircut. This was not entirely casual on my part. I mostly went to a barbershop called Jimmy's where an elderly man by the name of Jimmy Hoblock cut my hair. Indeed, he had cut it when I was young. But I had noticed that Make Waves advertised itself as a unisex hair parlor so I decided to have Jaime Rose cut my hair. You will understand that my curiosity was getting the better of me.

I drove downtown after school and after a short wait I found myself in Jaime's chair.

"Been a while," he said.

I explained that I had had my hair cut the previous month.

"I mean since I laid eyes on you," he said. Jaime had an immaculate black beard that he must have trimmed hair by hair. It wasn't bushy but clung neatly to his cheeks. The sheet with which I was covered seemed made of black satin.

I said that I'd been busy and that in any case the awful events in our town had dissuaded me from leaving the house unless absolutely necessary. Cookie Evans was working on Brigit Daly across the room, talking constantly as she trimmed and combed.

"It's hardly worth living here anymore," said Jaime.

"Do you think you'll leave?"

"I've thought of it. I have friends other places." He gave a slight emphasis to "friends." Jaime was not especially effete, but neither did he strike one as masculine.

"I can't believe that whoever is responsible lives in Aurelius," I said.

"Oh, I wouldn't be surprised."

"Are you serious?"

Jaime looked at me in the mirror. He knew more about me than I cared to have him know, though we had never been together, nor were we interested in each other—in that way, I mean. On the other hand, he knew I would help him if he needed it, as I knew he would help me. I wouldn't have felt the same way in New York, but Aurelius was a small town.

"Believe me," he said, "I've known some doozies."

"That doesn't mean one of them might abduct a little girl."

Jaime went back to my hair. It was the first time in my life I'd had a razor cut. I wondered what it would cost me.

"Perhaps not, but if I were to tell the police about two or three of our fellow citizens, it would make quite a squawk."

"Who do you mean?" I asked, as mildly as I could.

Jaime winked at me in the mirror. "Don't be pushy."

"If you know anything about those girls," I said firmly, "you should tell the police."

"Of course I don't know anything like *that*," said Jaime, defensively. "I'm just saying that some people aren't what they pretend to be. In fact, some people are quite nasty."

I was dying to know whom he meant but I felt that I couldn't be insistent. "We all have secrets," I said.

Jaime sprayed something on my scalp. "Some are darker than others." He snipped some more. "Do you know those two brothers in that Marxist group at the college?"

"Jesse and Shannon Levine?"

"That's right."

"Do they have dark secrets?"

"Nothing like that. I happened to speak to them at the bar at Gillian's and they were abusive. I was quite surprised."

"Apparently they beat up Barry Sanders, or tried to."

"Doesn't surprise me. Really, I was only making small talk." Standing behind me, Jaime put his hands on my cheeks and turned my head a little to the left, then to the right in front of the mirror. "It could stand some thickening," he said.

"I'm afraid I'm rather past thickening."

"What a dreadful thought," said Jaime. "Perhaps I should leave here after all. What am I doing in such a silly town? Even Syracuse would be better."

"Do any of these people frighten you?" I asked. "I mean the people with secrets?"

"Of course not," he said, fluffing my hair to make it stand up a little. "I'm just making conversation."

Shortly, I was through. Really, the whole thing was just a little blip in a long day dominated by my teaching. And even this event would have remained unimportant if it weren't for what happened later. My claim that I visited Make Waves primarily to see Jaime Rose is probably untrue. The fact is my hair was thinning, and I was getting balder. From vanity and nothing more I thought Jaime could do something about it. And my hair looked much better, I'm sure of it, for at least several days.

Thirty-four

Ever since Meg Shiller's disappearance, the door to the police station and the three other doors to City Hall had been under surveillance twenty-four hours a day. Captain Percy was hopeful. If the same person was responsible for both disappearances, then surely he would return Meg's clothes, just as he had returned Sharon's.

The question raised later was how many people knew about the surveillance. Watching the doors required someone to scan four video monitors around the clock. Two of the cameras were in the stockroom of Weber's Shoes, across the street and north of City Hall. The other two were on the second floor of Bob Moreno's men's haberdashery, to the south. The monitors themselves were in the basement of City Hall. Bob Moreno knew the cameras were upstairs, as did Charlie Weber. So when the question arose as to how the person who had taken the two girls knew that the police station was being watched, the answer seemed obvious. Too many people knew about it for the secret to remain a secret.

Frieda Kraus, who in the opinion of many people kept the *Independent* afloat, got to work at seven-thirty each morning, sometimes earlier. Franklin had been lucky to hire an insomniac with the energy of a Mack truck. If she had had any writing ability, she might have taken over the paper, but fortunately for Franklin she didn't. She was perhaps fifty, had five Siamese cats, and a large garden. Two of the cats lived at the newspaper office because they didn't get along with the three at home. Frieda had many boyfriends when she was younger but none stuck. It was Franklin's opinion that she had worn them out. Now she had an ongoing relationship of convenience with a self-employed roofer who visited weekly from Norwich. Because of her energy and constant talk (mostly she described the sporting events she watched through the night on her satellite-dish TV), she was a difficult person to spend time with.

Frieda was a second cousin of Meg Shiller's mother, Helen Kraus Shiller, and so she was especially affected by Meg's disappearance. Not that anyone was unaffected. Frieda was a solid-looking woman with short black hair brushed forward like Marlon Brando's in the movie *Julius Caesar*. She wore glasses with great oversized lenses that magnified not only her eyes but her eyebrows and upper cheekbones.

As she walked the six blocks from her apartment to the office, Frieda thought how dull the day ahead would be. Since the paper had gone on sale the previous night, there would be little to keep her busy. Stores were still closed and few people were visible, though a couple of cars were parked in front of the Aurelius Grill across the street. As Frieda approached the front door of the *Independent* she saw a Miller's beer case wrapped with silver duct tape hanging from the knob. Sometimes a local stringer would leave a late story about a night basketball game or even about a traffic fatality taped to the front door. But this was the first time there had been a box.

The tape was wrapped around the doorknob and Frieda used her Swiss Army knife to cut through it. Then she unlocked the door, went inside, and put the box on her desk. Before investigating its contents, she fed her cats. Then she opened the box. When she lifted the lid, the first thing she saw was a hand, palm upward, with bloody fingernails. She quickly stepped back, knocking over a chair. It took her a moment to realize the hand was false, a rubber Halloween hand to fit over one's own. This hand, however, had been filled with plaster of Paris and was solid. It rested on a pile of folded clothes.

Frieda called Chuck Hawley at the police station and Franklin at home. Then, as she waited for the police, she took several photographs of the box with the hand, which appeared in the following Thursday's newspaper. Frieda knew that the police were watching City Hall. It didn't surprise her that the box had been left at the *Independent*.

Captain Percy was the first to arrive. He seemed angry, but more likely it was frustration.

"Why'd you open the box?" he asked Frieda.

"How was I to know what it was till I opened it?"

Franklin appeared several minutes later to find his office taken over by the police. Indeed, he had to use the back entrance while the front door was photographed and checked for fingerprints and the area around it searched.

When Franklin entered, he saw Percy take an envelope from the box and put it in his pocket. "What's that?" he asked.

"None of your business. I don't want you in here."

"Are you going to kick me out of my own office?"

"Exactly right," said Percy, and he did.

Apart from the hand, the box contained the clothes that Meg Shiller had worn on Halloween. They had been washed and folded. At first there was excitement because of the red stains on the white shirt, then it became clear they were paint stains and part of Meg's costume. Her parents identified the clothes. There was something awful about thinking of Sharon and Meg naked someplace. At least that was how it seemed now that their clothes had been returned.

The police reports that came back from the lab in Ithaca that afternoon revealed that nothing inside or outside the box or around the front door of the *Independent* gave any sign who had left it there. And no one had seen anything. Roy Hanna had completed his patrols of Main Street about five that morning and said nothing had been attached to the door when he passed at four-thirty. Members of the

Friends took it on themselves to ask people living downtown if they had seen anything suspicious. At times they appeared just as the police were leaving. And of course they asked the same questions that the police had asked.

Percy complained to Paul Leimbach about the presence of the Friends, though technically he should have complained to the co-chairmen, Sandra Petoski and Rolf Porter.

"We want to make sure that everything that can be done is in fact being done," said Leimbach, rather aggressively.

Ryan maintained that, even though Percy didn't like Leimbach and saw him as a nuisance, he was grateful for the volunteers during the searches and had a sense of their power—political power. So he was careful not to offend Leimbach.

"I assure you everything's being done," said Percy.

"The girls are still missing," said Leimbach.

"It doesn't help to have your people in the way."

"They want to make sure that nothing is overlooked."

Percy had pink cheeks—not naturally pink but as if they had been scraped with rough sandpaper. In contrast, his forehead was quite pale.

"And you think something is?" asked Percy.

"Have the girls been found?"

Franklin, who witnessed this exchange, said that Percy's voice sounded as brittle as dried sticks. He stood very straight, with his arms folded. Public confrontations between people who dislike each other but can't show it can be very painful.

"What would you do that we're not doing?" asked Percy.

"I'd search every house in town," said Leimbach. "Every house in the county."

"That would be against the law."

"Aren't the girls more important?"

When they were alone that morning Percy and Chief Schmidt opened the envelope that Percy had taken from the box. They were in Schmidt's office.

Again there was a list of words made up of letters cut from a newspaper and pasted to a sheet of paper. Certain letters had been crossed out—almost ground away with a dark pencil—so that "SLUT" became "LUT" and "WHORE" became "WHRE." Fingerprint analysis of the sheet of paper revealed nothing.

The psychologists provided by the FBI made much of the fact that Meg's clothes had turned up more quickly than Sharon's had. They also spoke of the difficulties of leaving the clothes at the newspaper and how shrewd the person had been. On the other hand, leaving the clothes was a public statement. The psychologists claimed that, even though the person responsible was trying to protect himself, part of that person wanted to be caught. At some level, the person was horrified by what he was doing. As a result, he would begin to take greater risks and act with greater frequency—not out of bravado but out of a wish to be stopped.

Ryan Tavich was present at these meetings.

"What you will see," said a psychologist from the city, "will be increased brutality and daring on the part of the criminal, which one could almost interpret as a cry for help." He was a small black-bearded man in a tweed jacket. Ryan said that he looked like a sleek rodent.

"You mean there'll be more disappearances?" asked Schmidt.

"Most certainly," said the psychologist. "At least there will be attempts. All this is consistent with classic acceleration patterns."

Ryan objected to these professionals, feeling they were taking advantage of our troubles to charge a fat fee. "All I know," he said later, "is we got a town packed with assholes."

Another incident should be mentioned at this point. Madame

Respighi, the psychic investigator, was still at the Aurelius Motel, engaged in her arcane inquiries. Two days after the box of clothes was found at the office of the *Independent,* she was given the white shirt with red paint stains to investigate or sniff or think about, however she did her work. The police were not in favor of this, but Meg's parents asked that it be done and the Friends of Sharon Malloy asked as well. In fact, they insisted. Although Captain Percy thought it was absurd to give the shirt to a psychic, he felt he couldn't refuse.

Madame Respighi received the shirt and retired to the privacy of her room while members of the Friends waited outside. Donald Malloy was there and perhaps six others, including Sandra Petoski. Sandra was one of those people who need to be involved with everything and talk about it endlessly. One wonders how much her classes suffered during this period.

After ten minutes Madame Respighi summoned the group. As I have said, she was a rather conventional-looking woman who favored gray suits and horn-rimmed glasses. Indeed, gray suits were her trademark. Though she lived in northern California, she was originally from Brooklyn and had a faint Brooklyn accent.

"Several images have manifested themselves," she told them. She sat on a chair by the table and the others stood. It was a motel room like any other, a mixture of the cozy and the impersonal. She held the white shirt with the red paint stains in her hands—her fists really. "I see a basement with a dirt floor," she said.

I won't lead you through this, which was quite protracted. Of course the Friends hung on her every word. She described a house in need of paint, a white house perhaps a hundred and fifty years old. She described a front porch. A long, narrow three-story house with a one-car garage in back. She described a bow window and black shutters. She described maple trees in the front. She described a man living alone. The house could have been one of many in Aurelius, but the more she described it, the more particular it became.

"Can you give us the name of a street?" asked Donald Malloy.

"A famous explorer," said Madame Respighi. "A ship."

"Hudson Street," said Sandra Petoski.

I should say that we also have streets named after De Soto, Cook, and Francis Drake.

More questions were asked, a street map was produced, and it was decided that Madame Respighi was talking about Irving Powell, who lived on Hudson Street and who had been the one to discover Chihani's body. By this time it was late Saturday morning.

"Do you see a dog?" asked Sandra Petoski, thinking of Powell's chocolate Lab, Sidney.

"No, I don't see a dog," said Madame Respighi.

Donald Malloy wanted to go directly to Powell's house. But Sandra decided it would be better to call the police. She called and spoke to Ryan Tavich.

After she explained to Ryan what Madame Respighi had said, Ryan told her, "We can't search Powell's house without a search warrant and we can't get a warrant on the word of some crazy psychic. Come on, Sandra, use your head."

Ryan was later criticized for his lack of tact. "From now on," Captain Percy told him, "I talk to these people."

Sandra told Malloy and the others how Ryan had responded.

"Then we'll go over there ourselves," said Donald.

Irving Powell had worked in the city clerk's office for thirty years, and the elected clerk, Martha Schroeder, claimed that he ran the place. A widower with grown children, he lived by himself with his dog. He was a mild-mannered fellow in late middle age. He belonged to the Readers' Club at the library, a garden group, and also a chess club. As far as I know, he wasn't gay, which was a blessing.

Around noon Malloy, Sandra Petoski, and several others went to Powell's house and explained their business. Powell kept them out on the porch. In any case, the dog was barking inside. It took him about ten minutes to realize what they were talking about. He was a bony man with a slight stoop who favored cardigan sweaters and always leaned forward to listen.

He said, "You certainly may not search my house."

Malloy and the others retreated to the sidewalk. If Powell was guilty, they felt he might destroy the evidence. Sandra said they needed more people, and Tom Simpson drove to the Friends' office for help. By twelve-thirty, fifty volunteers were milling around the house. When Powell looked out the window, he called the police, claiming that his house was under attack. Four police cars arrived within a few minutes and Captain Percy arrived shortly after that. He was not happy to see the Friends.

"Why didn't you call us?" asked Percy.

"We did," said Donald. "We talked to Ryan Tavich. He wasn't interested."

By now quite a crowd had gathered. Irving Powell stood on his front porch holding Sidney by the collar. It was unclear who was protecting whom. Franklin had arrived and was interviewing Sandra Petoski. "We felt we had no choice but to act," she kept saying. Someone shouted at Powell, calling him "pervert." At first this seemed a joke, but such was the tension in the crowd that it only took a moment to realize how serious people were. There was the hope that something would be found and Powell would be arrested, just to bring matters to a close. Consequently, a certain amount of gossip was circulated. Some suggested that Chihani had been alive when Powell found him and that Powell had finished him off. Many people were willing to think ill of Powell even though he had led, as far as I know, a blameless existence. But the fact that Powell seemed blameless meant nothing. Who knew what he did in the dark of the night when he was by himself?

Captain Percy went up on the porch to talk to Powell. "The best thing," he said, "would be to invite two or three of them into your house and I'll come along with Chief Schmidt. Or you can just call your lawyer."

"But this is absurd," said Powell.

"I don't want to tell you what to do," said Percy.

"If I let them in, will the rest get out of my yard?"

"If they're satisfied."

"I hate this," said Powell.

Captain Percy tried to look patient but he only grimaced. Chuck Hawley said that Powell was on the verge of hysterics, though I don't know if that was true. Think of living your whole life in a town, being a respected member of the community, and suddenly you are suspected of perversion, of murder, and over a hundred people surround your house. Even in his worst nightmares, Powell could never have anticipated this.

"Come in by all means."

Donald Malloy, Sandra Petoski, and Dave Bauer of the YMCA represented the Friends. Percy, Chief Schmidt, and Chuck Hawley represented the police. Powell led them through his house.

"Dave Bauer crawled into the backs of closets," said Chuck. "The basement didn't have a dirt floor. It was solid concrete."

After a lifetime in the same house, Powell had acquired a lot of belongings. And he had his dead wife's things. And his three grown-up children had things in the house. Shortly a TV truck pulled up outside. The fact that Madame Respighi had seemingly pointed a finger at Irving Powell was significant news.

The police and the Friends spent an hour in the house. Nothing was found.

"Of course, something could still be hidden," said Malloy.

"Get your laboratory people," said Powell almost in a panic. "Spend as much time as you want. You're welcome to do whatever."

"I don't think we need a lab crew," said Sandra Petoski.

"Then how'll we be sure?" asked Malloy. They were on the front porch. There were TV cameras and freelance photographers.

"Please," said Powell, "if it means a lab crew, call them."

So Captain Percy called the lab crew. But why draw this out? Nothing was found. But once Powell was suspected it was hard to get him unsuspected. Several of the Friends, including Donald Malloy, suggested that the lab crew could have looked harder. And that Saturday evening someone threw a rock through Irving Powell's front window. As a result, a policeman was stationed outside his house twenty-four hours a day for the next five days. Powell himself volunteered to help the Friends in any way he could. He had been frightened and it was pathetic to see him.

Madame Respighi never apologized, but then again, it wasn't necessarily his house she saw in her "images." I blamed the whole thing on Suspicion with a capital S. It was like a revolving searchlight. Sometimes it illuminated one person, sometimes another. For a short time Irving Powell lived in a state close to terror. Then attention turned elsewhere.

Among the people gathered outside Powell's house were Barry Sanders and Jaime Rose. They had been walking past. Make Waves closed at noon on Saturdays. Barry was on his way to the college from his mother's house and Jaime was accompanying him more out of idleness than anything else. It was a mild fall day and many people were getting their yards ready for winter. Barry, as was usual during the day, wore a hat—a golfing cap, actually—and dark glasses. Jaime was fond of leather and wore leather pants and a black leather jacket over a sweatshirt. Both looked rather out of place in Aurelius.

I had mentioned to Franklin my talk with Jaime some days before. And I may have exaggerated a little to make my story more in-

teresting. Franklin decided that he wanted to speak with Jaime
himself. So he strolled over through the crowd. He and Jaime knew
each other, though not well.

"Oooh," said Jaime, "a newshound."

After they had traded greetings, Franklin said, "I'd like to hear
more of your thoughts about people in Aurelius."

"I have to get over to school," said Barry, and he walked away
rather quickly. Perhaps this was from shyness, but anyone watching
might have suspected something else. And that was the trouble,
people watching: there were over a hundred people who might have
noticed the three of them together.

"I have many thoughts," said Jaime.

"Someone told me you weren't surprised about what had been
happening here," said Franklin, misquoting me a little.

"The rascal," said Jaime. Campy behavior was a total act with
Jaime, who mostly behaved like anyone else. Of course, he was aware
of having an audience. "I hate how people talk," he added.

The two men began walking slowly down the sidewalk toward
town. They were about the same height and both were slim. Franklin
wore his Irish fisherman's hat. Jaime was bareheaded. He was vain
about his hair and disliked covering it.

"Do you have any idea who might have taken the girls?" asked
Franklin.

"I never said I did," said Jaime. "I only said I knew people with a
certain nastiness about them."

"Who?"

"Don't be silly. Do you think I care to have you print their names
in the paper?"

"But if they had anything to do with Meg or Sharon?"

Jaime looked scornful. "I never said that. They just have desires
slightly out of the ordinary."

"How many people are we talking about?" asked Franklin, who had begun to imagine several dozen.

"Two or three, no more."

"Docs that include Jesse and Shannon Levine?"

"Of course not. They're boorish, that's all."

"What kind of desires do you mean?"

"That's the trouble. Just because a respected member of the community likes to be tied up and spanked is no reason to think he had anything to do with the disappearances. And what would happen if I gave you names? Look at Irving Powell. Who in the world would think that silly man guilty of anything? And now they're ransacking his house. I think we've talked long enough."

"But if one of these men—" began Franklin.

"No," said Jaime, "I shouldn't even be seen talking to you."

But by then it was too late.

Thirty-five

The idea of brutality as a cry for help was one I had trouble understanding. It made the motivations of the person responsible for the disappearances increasingly enigmatic. The return of Meg's clothes gave us further assurance—as if we needed it—that the person not only lived in Aurelius but had inside knowledge about the activities of the police. We needed such reminders because otherwise we might tell ourselves it was impossible that the person was one of us.

Sunday night I was downstairs dozing over a book when there was a sudden knocking at the front door. Startled, I dropped the book, a Daphne du Maurier thriller that I was rereading. It was close to eleven. I was going to refuse to open the door but then I forced myself out of my chair. It was Sadie.

"Someone's trying to get in our back door," she said. She wore an old-fashioned flannel nightgown and her feet were bare. She kept glancing over her shoulder and I let her in.

There is nothing so infectious as fear and I wished I had a pistol or rifle—many people had been buying them—but I only had a few dull kitchen knives.

"Where's Franklin?"

"Out."

"And Mrs. Sanders?"

"Asleep on the couch in front of the TV. I can't wake her. Shadow's locked in the basement. She keeps barking." Sadie stood by the fireplace. In her slenderness and with her small breasts, she reminded me of a plant before it blossoms. She pushed her hair back over her shoulders.

"What happened?" I asked.

"I heard the screen door in the back squeak, then someone turned the handle of the door. It was locked. Then the person yanked it hard. That's when I ran."

Though I felt her fear, I didn't want to think it was true. The night was windy; perhaps the screen door had banged in the wind. My hope that there was no one there kept me from calling the police. I had heard of many false alarms that had made the callers look foolish. Old Mrs. Sherman had locked herself in her bathroom after hearing mice in the pantry. She had refused to come out even for the police. Finally her daughter drove up from Norwich. Chuck Hawley had a good laugh about this.

"Let's go see," I said.

"By ourselves?" Sadie didn't move.

I took the poker from the fireplace set. "At least we can wake up Mrs. Sanders."

Sadie nodded and followed me. I gave her an old wool jacket from the hall closet and put on my overcoat. We moved quietly onto the porch. The street was deserted. The wind sent a few dead leaves skittering across the yards. Most of the houses were dark, but the blind girl's bedroom light was on. A fragment of moon hung over downtown and dark clouds kept crossing its face. Sadie nudged me from behind and I jumped, then I recovered myself. I have never been particularly brave. As a child I found even camp-outs too scary.

We crossed Pete Daniels's yard. The streetlight sent our shadows right up his front steps. We moved into Sadie's yard. Only the living room light was on in her house. Even the porch light was out. I held the poker along my leg so it wouldn't be obvious. I wondered how often a person endangers himself just from fear of getting laughed at.

We climbed Sadie's front steps, which creaked. She stayed right behind me. I opened the front door and we entered. Shadow was still barking in the basement, a steady yapping. The living room was to the left off the hall. The TV was on. The eleven o'clock news from Syracuse was reporting a double marriage at Saint Joseph's Hospital. There were images of happy celebration. Mrs. Sanders lay on the couch with her head on a cushion. Her shoes were off and her mouth was open. If she hadn't been snoring I would have wondered whether she'd had a stroke. She was a large, round woman with fiercely permanented silver hair. Her Scottish plaid skirt was rucked up so I saw the mottled white skin on the inner part of her thigh. I looked away. A muted chatter came from the television.

I went over to the couch and shook Mrs. Sanders's shoulder. She didn't respond. I shook her harder and her head slid off the cushion. She opened her eyes, then sat up quickly.

"What are you doing here?" she asked.

"Sadie couldn't wake you. She was worried."

"I'm a good sleeper," said Mrs. Sanders.

Sadie stood behind me. I began to leave the living room.

"Where're you going?" asked Mrs. Sanders. She was looking at the poker and I realized she was nervous about me. I looked down at the poker as well.

"Can't be too careful," I said. I proceeded down the hall to the kitchen.

Behind me I could hear Mrs. Sanders saying, "I don't like him being here."

I didn't hear Sadie's reply. I went to the back door, which was locked. I turned on the back-porch light and unlocked the door. A garbage can was on the back porch with its lid off. Sometimes we have trouble with raccoons and I wondered if that was what Sadie and the dog had heard. I replaced the lid. Nothing on the porch indicated that somebody had been trying to break in, but I didn't know what those signs would be. Something broken, probably. Sadie had let Shadow out of the basement and the dog pushed through the screen door behind me, jumped up on my legs, then scampered down the steps. Immediately, she started barking.

I looked across the yard. Someone was walking toward me between the trees. Instinctively, I raised the poker.

"Are you really going to attack me?" came a voice. It was Aaron. I recognized his ponytail before I saw his face.

"What are you doing back there?" I asked.

"Short cut. Is Sadie still up?" Shadow stopped barking and ran up to him. Aaron bent over to scratch the dog's ears.

"Were you here earlier?"

"What are you talking about?"

"Sadie thought she heard something."

By this time Sadie had joined me on the back porch.

"Aaron," she said.

Aaron stopped at the bottom of the steps and looked up at us. His ponytail was pulled tight so it pulled at the corners of his eyes, giving him a somewhat Asian appearance. "I got news for you," he said, speaking to Sadie. "Your father's going to marry my sister. They're going to do it this week."

I thought it was rather good news, but looking at Sadie and Aaron, I could see that my feelings were not shared.

"What's going on out there?" called Mrs. Sanders.

"A wedding party," said Aaron. Then he laughed.

After my visit to Jaime, I began to notice the Levine brothers' hostility to him. Of course, Jaime had told me about the encounter at Gillian's bar, though he didn't say specifically what he had said to them. Possibly Jaime had addressed them and they didn't like his tone. But that was not the case. What they objected to was Jaime's friendship with Barry Sanders.

Then on Monday morning, as they were walking by Make Waves, they stopped to look in the door. There was Jaime putting curlers in Mrs. Adams's hair. Her husband was on the city council. Jesse and Shannon stood in the doorway, pointed at Jaime and laughed. It was not a real laugh but a cartoon laugh, a Woody Woodpecker laugh. Cookie chased them out. At first it seemed they would refuse to leave but then she sprayed them with some sort of sweet-smelling scent, which quite offended them.

On Tuesday Jesse and Shannon went into the Aurelius Grill when Jaime and Barry were having lunch together. I think that Jaime and Barry were no more than friends, or incipient friends, but the Levines found their friendship objectionable. In their minds they seemed to have confused Marxism with a kind of puritanism. And perhaps they felt that Barry was letting down the IIR.

Barry and Jaime were sitting at a table and Jesse and Shannon joined them. Their identical blond goatees made them look slightly goofy.

"Nobody asked you to sit down," said Jaime.

"Little Pink did," said Jesse.

"He winked at us," said Shannon.

"I never did," said Barry.

"What's for lunch?" asked Jesse.

"Leave us alone," said Jaime.

"Don't we have a right to eat?" asked Shannon.

"He wants to keep us from eating," said Jesse.

Jaime signaled to Ralph Stangos, who owns the Aurelius Grill. Ralph is also a volunteer fireman and athletic. Whatever he felt about Jaime, he knew that Jaime was a steady customer. Stangos wiped his hands on a towel and began to come over.

"Looks like you're eating soup," said Shannon, pointing toward Jaime's tomato soup.

"I'd like a little soup myself," said Jesse.

"Let me give you some," said Shannon. He reached out, put his finger under the lip of the bowl, and flipped it into Jaime's lap. Jaime shoved back his chair. "Ooops," said Shannon.

"You did that on purpose," said Barry.

At that moment Ralph Stangos grabbed Shannon by the back of the neck. "Out," he said. "Both of you."

That was perhaps the most significant episode. But there were others, and I may have forgotten some. Twice they hooted at Jaime on the street. This went on for several days and I know Jaime considered getting an injunction against them.

Barry came by my house that evening and told me about the business at the Aurelius Grill.

"Jaime had to go home and change," he said. "There was tomato soup all over his pants."

We sat in armchairs on either side of the fireplace and drank tea.

"Why are they bothering him?" I asked.

Barry's eyes behind his thick glasses were a pinkish blur. "Shannon says homosexuality's reactionary. But I guess Jaime spoke to them at Gillian's and they didn't like what he said."

Barry sipped his tea and blinked. We discussed Franklin's marriage to Paula, which was to occur the next day at the courthouse in Potterville.

"Sadie's very upset about it," I told Barry.

Franklin felt that Sadie would have to accept their relationship if he and Paula got married, which they had been talking about for some months. He also felt bad about leaving Sadie by herself and thought it would be better if Paula was in the house. Paula was kind and intelligent. Franklin could see no rational reason why Sadie would continue to dislike her. Of course, Sadie needed no rational reason.

I also thought of what Jaime had said about the secrets of some of the men in Aurelius. It made me wonder about the man with whom Barry had been briefly involved while he was in high school.

I asked Barry if he was sexually involved with Jaime.

"No, nothing like that. We're just friends."

"Do you ever see that man you used to be involved with?"

"What man?" Barry was on the defensive immediately.

"When you were in high school."

"I don't want to talk about him."

"Is he still in town?"

Barry repeated that he didn't want to talk about him.

"Does Jaime know this man?"

"I don't know."

Barry stood up and said he had to leave. I apologized and tried to calm him.

"Have some more tea," I said.

"I really have to go."

There was no keeping him. His mother had told him to come over to Sadie's at eight and it was shortly after. I was annoyed with Barry. We had known each other a long time and I felt he should trust me.

Meanwhile the Friends continued their patrols. They talked to people; they were in contact with other groups around the country. Even though it seemed obvious that Irving Powell wasn't involved with the disappearances, they talked to his neighbors. And they had their own police scanners, so that when someone thought he heard a strange noise or saw something out of the ordinary and called the police in a panic, the Friends would respond as well. Sometimes they even arrived before the police. Captain Percy made various protests to the city council but the council members didn't interfere. In the midst of this fear a few more people left Aurelius and several others sent their daughters to stay with relatives in towns where they thought the girls would be safe, though the whole idea of safety was increasingly problematic. There were empty seats in my classes. When I reported them, I was told that so-and-so had transferred temporarily to a school in Rome or Baldwinsville. And the word *temporarily* would hang in the air and no one would question it.

As suspicion grew, people's gossip and allegations became increasingly nasty, often verging on slander. I know for a fact that I was talked about, but it was at a level of such ignorance that it was more provoking than frightening. For instance, one day I entered my fifth-period classroom after lunch to find someone had written "Ferry" on the blackboard. Some years earlier we had had a history teacher by the name of Margaret Ferry and I thought at first it was a reference to her. One look at the grinning faces of my eighth graders, however, proved that the word was a misspelling. The hearty cheer of their attentive faces was repugnant. I was tempted to say something but instead I erased the word and began class. We had a surprise quiz that hour in which no one did well. The message was not lost on them.

But suspicion was felt throughout the school. The teachers' lounge became increasingly silent. Usually it was a place of criticism, backbiting, and gossip. But now people were uncertain as to the identity of whomever they were speaking to. Was the Sandra Petoski I had seen every day for years the same Sandra Petoski who was co-chairman of the Friends? And what if there was a third Sandra Petoski, someone more sinister?

I tend to use the term *dark side* almost as a comic term. Mrs. Hicks's passion for chocolate was her dark side, as was Harry Martini's affair with the lady teacher from Utica. But now we had evidence of something truly dark. It increased our sense of how dark such a darkness might be. Someone among us had stolen two little girls. And what had this person done with them? That was the question we didn't ask. So in the silence of the teachers' lounge, I never had the sense that my colleagues had nothing to talk about; rather, they were afraid of what there was to say.

On Wednesday afternoon Franklin and Paula were married by the town clerk in Potterville. Ryan went with them and acted as witness.

All three had taken off work for an hour. Ryan skipped lunch. The clerk, Mitchell Friedman, kept making jokes about tying the knot and making an honest woman out of Paula, but Ryan said she and Franklin were as serious as if they'd been at a funeral. When it was over, Franklin kissed the bride and Ryan shook their hands. They drove back to Aurelius. When Sadie got home from school shortly after three o'clock, she found she had a new mother. She wasn't happy about it. Franklin and Paula spent about an hour bringing over some of Paula's things from her father's house, which would be put up for sale. Franklin didn't have much time, because the paper had to be at the printer's by five o'clock. There was a problem with Paula's dog, Fletcher, who didn't get along with Shadow. Some friends in the country took Fletcher until Franklin and Paula could decide what to do.

Franklin wrote a short article about their marriage. In fact, he must have written it before they were married. It only gave the basic details, although it identified Franklin as editor of the *Independent* (as if he needed identifying) and Paula as a psychological counselor in the dean's office at Aurelius College. People read the article and shook their heads. Many felt they already knew too much about the Mc-Neal family. People wished Franklin well, of course, but I don't believe there were any celebrations.

Thirty-six

The Malloys and Shillers never really became friends but during this time they were quite close. The very sadness, however, that brought them together also kept them apart. After all, each grieved for a different girl. But they were in constant contact with one another, each inquiring if the other had heard anything new. Ralph and Helen Shiller were not directly involved with the Friends but Ralph's brother Mike was there every day. Mike took a leave of absence from his job at the post office. A second brother, Albert, also gave some of his time to the Friends. And Helen Shiller had two brothers and a cousin who participated in the patrols.

Ralph and Helen Shiller tried to continue their lives but they lived in a state of near paralysis. They would move forward for a few minutes, then once more realize that their daughter was gone and be knocked down again. Luckily, Ralph had men who worked for him in his shop. The awful thing was not knowing anything, nor could they stop themselves from imagining the dreadful things that might have been done to their child. The oddity of the returned clothes and the fake hand made even the most gruesome scenario possible. Ralph began driving around town in his van, not going on calls or errands, just looking. One would see the van slowly pass by—a blue Ford with "Ralph Shiller, Electrician" printed on the side in white—and see Ralph's dark, sad face peering over the wheel.

As for Helen, she rarely left the house. Meg's brother Henry was in my biology class and he was often absent. There was no way I could grade him down for this. He had always been a happy boy, but now his face was immobile and he seemed incapable of paying attention. Other students spoke to him in whispers, but many preferred to leave him alone. The younger brother, Bobby, was in fourth grade and I know nothing about him, which doesn't keep me from wondering.

The Malloys were similarly afflicted. Dr. Malloy stopped going to the office entirely. He sat at home by himself or went down to the police station. Like Henry Shiller, his son Frank, a junior, missed a lot of school. Little Millie was in third grade. The doctor drove her to school and picked her up every day. He drove her to her friends' houses and waited outside while she played. He was obsessed by the fear that something might happen to her.

His wife, Catherine, would only go out to see the Leimbachs or the Shillers. They were all aware of being watched, of people's sympathy. They were glad for the kindness, but every time they saw someone looking at them sadly they were reminded of the reason for their grief and the disappearance rose up fresh before them. Dr. Malloy drove a maroon Chevrolet pickup. One day I noticed a gun rack across its rear window. The next time I saw it, several days later, there was a rifle. This was New York State in November. Hunting was popular. But I didn't think Dr. Malloy had the rifle because of deer hunting. He, too, would drive around town, slowly turning the corners, looking at different houses.

Often it was Paul Leimbach who directed the car patrols in Aurelius. Altogether there were twenty cars, no more than five were on the road at once. The precision that made Leimbach excel as an accountant was applied to the patrols. Each car had a sector. Each drove according to a certain pattern, then would abruptly change to another, as if that quick shift might surprise a prowler, someone with a diabolic interest in young girls.

I've known Paul Leimbach all my life, though not well. With his passion for baseball cards as a child and his passion for numbers as an adult, he seemed to wish to transform the world into data to be measured and weighed. He was without physical chaff, muscular and sinewy. Someone told me that he slept no more than four hours a night. He had a dark, attentive face and seemed to study his surroundings, poised motionless like a hawk in a dead tree. One could never imagine him being taken by surprise, yet his niece's disappearance took him by surprise. It was data that could be digested by none of his machinery.

Leimbach's own daughter, Jenny, was twelve and he had a terror that she was in danger. His wife, Martha, wanted to send Jenny out of town, but Leimbach refused. He felt it would be unfair to Dr. Malloy. Not that he saw himself as risking his daughter because Sharon had disappeared, but he felt—God knows how he verbalized this—that it would be unfair to have Jenny be too safe. On the other hand, he made sure that she was never alone. If he or Martha was not with her, then fifteen-year-old Mark, or Scott, a senior in high school, would be.

I expect Donald Malloy gave over forty hours a week to the Friends. Increasingly, Mildred Porter ran the pharmacy, though Donald would come in once or twice a day to fill prescriptions. He lived by himself on Dodge Street, though I gather he had a cat; his three-story house, though quite narrow, was on a large lot. For some years there had been some thought he would marry, but he never did. Having been divorced, perhaps he didn't want to try again. He had no children. For a while after moving to Aurelius he had dated several women. He had been thinner then and moved faster. He was the sort of man who looked as if he had played football in school and slowly the muscle had turned to fat. Not that he was grossly fat at the present time, but he was heavy. Perhaps he still dated occasionally, but I didn't know of it.

With Agnes Hilton and Dave Bauer, he visited many houses just as they had visited mine. They always tried to be friendly but there was no hiding the fact that whoever they were visiting was suspected in some way, if only in a tiny way. Donald held meetings at his house to develop possible scenarios as to what might have happened to the girls, and these meetings led to further visits. Of course, not all the visits were friendly, so some people came to fear Donald and worked to stay in his good graces.

Franklin had again tried to interview him for the paper during this time but with no success; or rather, Donald said he would be glad to answer any questions but he didn't want to be the special subject of an interview.

"I'm just a tool," he kept saying. "My only purpose is to find those girls. I have no other work."

"But you have a whole life to talk about."

"Perhaps later, when this is over," said Donald.

His passion to find the girls might have been remarkable had it not been just like his brother's passion or Leimbach's passion or Ralph or Mike Shiller's passion. I had known these people for years. Leimbach helped prepare my taxes. Dr. Malloy was my doctor when I needed one. Ralph Shiller had done electrical work on my house. I bought stamps from Mike Shiller and prescription drugs from Donald. They were some of the most obliging and friendly faces in Aurelius. Their children were my students and the students of my colleagues. Now the group of them had been set apart, as if a terrible mark had been put on their faces. In a way they had been moved outside our community to form their own dreadful community. The rest of us would see that mark and pray that it wouldn't fall on us.

"I'm just a tool," Donald said. Who could blame him for wishing to shed his human side, the part that suffered? So what if he pushed his way into people's houses to ask questions? We felt sorry for him. And his very stoutness, the weight that he carried under his dark suits or his white pharmacist's jacket, seemed to be the physical shape of his grief, as if without his grief he would be quite thin.

Dr. Allen Malloy was often with Captain Percy and visited him at his house in Norwich. In their sense of duty and their wish to be considered dependable and honest, the two men resembled each other. Both had a rather stoical attitude. Both were florid with a calm exterior, their very redness seeming to testify to the violent activity within. And they had children more or less the same ages, so certainly Captain Percy could empathize with Dr. Malloy's loss.

According to Ryan, Percy's growing friendship with Dr. Malloy only exacerbated his guilt at not having found the person responsible for the disappearances. Percy would make long lists of possibilities, then discuss and investigate them. In this he resembled the Friends of Sharon Malloy, making a minuscule search of the possibilities, then exploring each. He even began to confide in Ryan, whom he had formerly disregarded, preferring instead his own colleagues.

But Percy felt uncomfortable with the Friends, or rather he disliked their attempts at police work. Though he was friendly with Dr. Malloy, he wasn't friendly with Leimbach and Donald. Percy disliked the patrols and he objected to Donald's questioning Aurelius residents. This wasn't professional rivalry. Percy believed that without the patrols whoever was responsible for the disappearances might be more willing to expose himself. And he felt that Donald's interviews merely put people on their guard.

For Captain Percy, everyone in Aurelius was a suspect, even Ryan, even Dr. Malloy. He disliked the hares running with the hounds. He recalled how Ryan had been removed from the inquiry into Janice's murder, and the fact that hands were continuing as a bloody motif wasn't lost on him. One thinks of any community as being crowded with secrets. Percy saw his job as peeling away the skin protecting those secrets, till at last he discovered the secret of the missing girls. In his computer files he had data on everyone in Aurelius—perhaps not the very old or very young, but I'm sure their names were listed. When Harry Martini was brought into the station confessing about his affair with a lady teacher in Utica, Captain Percy already knew about it. And I am sure he knew about my unfortunate period in New York City. He knew about the dark habits of all of us, or almost all of us.

It is dreadful not to be allowed to have secrets. Years ago I happened to uncover a nest of baby moles in the backyard and I watched them writhe miserably in the sunlight. We were like that. A private life is the buffer between the interior self and society. Percy wanted to strip the shell from everyone. One imagined him prying into bathrooms and into people's bedrooms at night. I knew nothing of Percy's political persuasion, but in his heart he was a totalitarian. He saw freedom as people's ability to hide and he wanted to eradicate that power. And of course he felt that information would be safe in his hands or in his computer files. Wasn't that a kind of ignorance? Because what is safety and where is it to be found?

For Captain Percy there existed not only the issue of the missing girls—certainly terrible in itself—but also the issue of someone's trying to hide from him. It would be wrong to say that the second, in Percy's mind, was worse than the first, but it was huge. Someone in Aurelius had taken the girls, someone whom Percy probably saw often. This person was taunting Percy by the return of the clothes. Indeed, it was hard for Percy not to reduce the matter to a struggle between himself and this unknown person whose purpose, seemingly, was to ridicule him. Percy had his superiors in the state police and they must have asked why the investigation was taking so long. No matter how much they trusted him, it was possible that he might need to be replaced. Percy knew that if he failed to find who had taken the girls, his career would be damaged. He took this personally. He felt that the person responsible for the disappearances was out to hurt him as well. He felt he was being played with.

Ryan had told Captain Percy about his conversation with Sheila Murphy and what she had said about Janice's "professional man."

And he had told him about Professor Carpenter, whose alibi for the time of the murder was being investigated.

"How'd you hit upon her?" Percy had asked. They were in an office in City Hall being used by his task force.

"All along I'd thought that Aaron had no reason for biting Sheila, that he'd done it out of perversity or because he was drunk. But what if he had a reason? Not a good reason but a reason. And once I realized that Aaron was trying to find who killed his mother, then it seemed his attack on Sheila was linked to Janice. She was always looking for ways to meet men. Sheila's friendship opened up a whole new bunch of guys to her."

"But they wouldn't be professional men."

"I'm sure Janice was using the term somewhat ironically. Was it how somebody referred to himself? Was it someone like a doctor or lawyer, or someone who lifted weights, or someone who really wasn't masculine but only seemed masculine?"

"What does that mean?"

"I don't know. Janice's irony always had something mocking about it. For instance, it could be someone who appears to like women but really doesn't."

Percy decided that Ryan should go back to Mrs. Porter. Ryan met her again in the reference room of Carnegie Library. She had refused to come till Ryan told her that in that case he would be forced to visit the pharmacy.

"I don't like this," she said as she sat down across the table. "I feel you're taking advantage of a confidence."

"This isn't about Aaron," said Ryan, wondering if that was true. "I think you knew Janice better than you indicated. You were friends, weren't you?"

"Is this necessary?"

"I think it is."

She looked into Ryan's face, then looked away. "I visited her house a few times, but I don't think I could say we were friends." Around her neck Mrs. Porter wore a white silk scarf fastened with a cameo showing a woman's face in profile. She kept touching the cameo with her fingers as she spoke. "I was still married at that time. She knew about my relationship with Rolf. That it wasn't . . . satisfactory." She paused.

"Did you meet men at her house?"

Mrs. Porter nodded. She looked back into Ryan's eyes, almost angrily.

"And did Aaron ask you about these men and if you knew any of the other men who went out with his mother?"

"I gave him five names. He seemed satisfied with that."

"Were any of them what you might call professional men?"

Mrs. Porter raised her eyebrows. "There's you, of course. Janice had just broken up with you. And Henry Swazey, the lawyer. She liked him for a while."

"She saw him after she saw me?"

"During, I think."

Ryan thought he heard a touch of malice in her voice. He decided to change the subject. "I'm curious about your relationship with Donald Malloy."

Mrs. Porter looked at him sharply. "I assure you it's entirely professional."

"Do you know anything about his life outside the pharmacy?"

"Nothing. Of course, I know his brother and how upset Donald's been about his niece. . . ."

"What about before Sharon's disappearance?"

"I know nothing about his private life."

"Do you know if he dates women in town?"

"He's never mentioned anyone. He doesn't talk much and I expect he values me partly because I don't talk either."

"Do you like him?"

"We have an entirely satisfactory professional relationship."

"Is that what he calls it, 'a professional relationship'?"

"Of course not—that's what it is."

"Do you know if Donald ever was with Janice McNeal?"

"I know nothing of the kind."

"But he talked to her."

"He waited on her a number of times. I said that before."

"Did he sell her condoms?"

"Perhaps."

"Does Donald have friends?"

"He's close to his brother's family and Paul Leimbach's."

"Did you ever see him at Janice's house?"

"Never. What are you suggesting?"

Ryan said later he couldn't stop thinking about Mrs. Porter and Aaron. It should be repeated there was noticing sexual about her. Though well-dressed and in good physical condition, she gave not the slightest hint of the provocative. Yet Ryan imagined Aaron and Mrs. Porter rolling naked in her bed. He felt embarrassed during the entire conversation. He was terrified that he would blush and consequently he blushed.

Captain Percy's new interest in professional men included a dentist, the lawyer Henry Swazey, Paul Leimbach and Dr. Malloy, and a local architect, as well as Donald. All were interviewed. Soon Percy learned that Donald had dated three women some years before and that he had had sex with one of them, Joan Thompson, a nurse at the hospital. She was forty and single, though she said she had a steady boyfriend.

"I hardly remember Donald Malloy," she told Ryan. "That was years ago."

"Was there anything in any way remarkable about him?" asked

Ryan. They spoke in the hospital cafeteria. Joan Thompson wore a white nurse's uniform with a little cap.

"Nothing. Maybe that's remarkable by itself. He was quite dull. We'd go out to dinner and he'd hardly speak."

"How did you happen to meet him?"

"Through his brother, the poor man. Then Donald called me. Or perhaps I called him, I don't remember."

"What was he like in bed?" Ryan hated questions like this.

"Forgettable." Joan Thompson laughed. "Or at least I've forgotten. It only happened once or twice. He didn't seem very interested. But he was very clean, I remember that, and he had beautiful hands."

Ryan also visited Leimbach. They spoke in a back room at the Friends of Sharon Malloy. In the front room phones kept ringing. Twenty people were at work. Ryan felt something was wrong. Then he realized that he heard no laughter.

Leimbach sat at a desk. He tended to bite off his words, giving his speech a rapid-fire quality. He wore a dark suit and a blue striped tie that was perfectly knotted.

"I don't see that my relationship with my wife is anybody's business," Leimbach was saying.

"It's not your relationship with your wife but your relationship with other women."

Leimbach unwillingly confessed to having seen a woman in Syracuse two or three times.

"But all of it was a long time ago," he said. He sat with his hands flat on the desk in front of him.

"Do you see yourself as a professional man?" Even as Ryan asked the question, he knew that he had phrased it clumsily.

"What do you mean by that? You think I dig ditches? I'm an accountant."

"Tell me about your friendship with Janice McNeal."

"What friendship?"

"You know perfectly well."

"I don't know what you're talking about."

Ryan leaned forward across the desk. "You forget. I was involved with her myself." He didn't care to say that neighbors had seen Leimbach entering Janice's house.

"She told you?" asked Leimbach, sitting perfectly still.

"Just tell me about it," said Ryan.

"She was crazy, completely crazy. I was only with her twice. She hurt me."

"How did she hurt you?"

"She . . . you know. She left scratches on my penis with her nails. Jesus, was that a mistake. She really told you?"

"I wonder who else she told?" said Ryan, unable to help himself.

Leimbach gripped the edge of the desk. "These things never go away, do they?"

After Ryan left Leimbach, he drove over to Dr. Malloy's office. The nurse led him into a consultation room. At first Ryan was going to sit on the examination table, then he chose a chair. Growing bored after five minutes, he took off his loafers and weighed himself: one hundred and fifty-three pounds. He was still standing on the scale when Dr. Malloy entered.

"I was under the impression that this was a police visit," said Malloy, looking at Ryan's shoes.

Ryan colored slightly. "I was just passing the time." He slipped his feet back into his loafers. "I have to ask you a personal question. Were you ever involved with Janice McNeal?"

"Of course not." Dr. Malloy wore a blue three-piece suit. A stethoscope was tucked in his side pocket. "I mean, she called me several times for no reason I could figure out and once came to the office pretending to have a stomach pain."

"How do you know she was pretending?"

"I couldn't find anything wrong with her. Let's say that for what she wanted I wasn't the right person."

"Have you had affairs with other women?"

"That's none of your business."

It occurred to Ryan that it would have been better to talk to Dr. Malloy in the police station rather than on the doctor's turf. "What about Paul Leimbach or your brother—were they ever involved with Janice?"

"You'd have to ask them." Dr. Malloy stood with his hand on the doorknob.

"Did Janice specifically say that she wanted to have sex with you?"

"It was more a matter of looks and innuendos which I was able to ignore."

"When was this?"

"Just before she was killed. Maybe a week or so."

"Do you ever call yourself a professional man?" Ryan winced to himself as he asked the question.

Dr. Malloy looked at Ryan for a moment, then blinked. "I call myself a doctor," he said.

Ryan managed to catch up with Donald Malloy just after the pharmacist had come back from one of the patrols. They stood on the sidewalk outside the Friends' storefront. It was midafternoon and the sun was already low. Donald seemed in a hurry and was impatient with Ryan's questions.

"Tell me who she was again?"

Ryan looked into Donald's eyes, which were light blue and very still. "You don't remember?"

"Was she Aaron McNeal's mother, the one who was killed?"

"Did you ever go out with her?"

"Obviously not."

"Why do you say it like that?"

"Her reputation. I couldn't afford being seen with her. Also I didn't find her attractive."

"I thought you didn't remember who she was." Ryan tried to stand so he wasn't looking directly into the photographs of Sharon and Meg.

"It's coming back." Donald was staring at Ryan as if he thought him an absolute fool. "Don't you realize the only thing I think about now is my niece?"

"Janice came into your pharmacy."

"Yes, I remember that."

"What did she buy?"

"I can't recall."

"Did she buy condoms?"

Donald appeared shocked. "You can't expect me to tell you what a customer bought. I don't think even a court of law could force me to do that."

The fourth professional man Ryan talked to that day was Harry Martini. Ryan went over to Knox Consolidated just before school let out. Martini denied ever having been involved with Janice. He said he disliked seeing women who lived in Aurelius. "I was tempted," he said, "but you've got to stay away from your home ground." Considering the affairs that he admitted to, Ryan believed him. Later he would turn his information about all four men over to Percy.

As Ryan was leaving Martini's office, he saw Sadie taking a coat from her locker. He offered her a ride home and she accepted.

"It would be more exciting to ride in a police car," she said as she got into Ryan's Ford Escort.

"Maybe next time."

She talked about school and people she knew.

"How are you getting along with Paula?" asked Ryan.

"She tries too hard." Sadie wore a red coat and a long gray ski cap with a tassel that hung down her back.

"Maybe you're jealous."

"So? Why couldn't she have found some other man?"

"They love each other."

"What about my mother?"

"She's not here anymore," said Ryan. He had begun to say "dead," then stopped himself.

"The only good thing about Paula's being in the house is that Aaron can come over without my dad's getting upset."

"Does he hang around a lot?" said Ryan.

"He doesn't hang around. He visits."

Ryan parked in front of the house and went in to say hello to Paula. She was in the kitchen and wore an apron over her jeans. Her glasses were steamy from the heat of the dishwasher and she wiped them on her sweatshirt. She had made cookies. When she saw Ryan, she laughed. Sadie had gone to her room.

"It's difficult trying to be nice," she said. "I thought I was nice already. I haven't made cookies since Aaron was small."

"So how'd you get off work to go home and bake?" asked Ryan.

"I go in at eight and leave at two. I skip lunch. By the time I get here I'm famished."

"The happily wedded woman," said Ryan. He considered saying something about Sadie, then didn't.

"I am happy," said Paula. "I love Franklin more than I could possibly say."

Thirty-seven

When Cookie Evans got to Make Waves around seven-thirty Friday morning, she found the front door ajar. She assumed that Jaime had gotten there before her, though he mostly didn't arrive until eight. Pushing the door open, she saw the mess. That was the first word to come to her, "mess." The next was "wreckage." Chairs were overturned, the mirror was broken, a table smashed. Magazines were scattered everywhere. Noticing them, Cookie saw they were spotted with blood. Then she saw blood on the fragments of the mirror. The wallpaper showed a variety of poodles engaged in tonsorial activities: perfuming, combing, trimming, fluffing, beribboning. It, too, was flecked with blood. A display rack of shampoos and conditioners had been tipped over. The room had a sweet smell from the broken bottles of scent. Cookie took this in all at once, then began to look more closely. She said later, "I thought I'd come to the wrong place." A black Italian loafer with a little tassel lay in the middle of the floor. She recognized it as one of Jaime's shoes.

"Jaime?" she called. There was no answer.

She should have shut the door and called the police but a mixture of indignation and curiosity pushed her forward. Tiny as she was, Cookie had never felt herself in danger from anything. Besides, Louise Talbot had an eight o'clock appointment and Cookie would have to call and change it. The radio was on, a light-rock station from Utica, but there was static and the music faded in and out.

"Jaime?" Cookie called again. She entered the shop, leaving the door open behind her. Sunlight from the doorway slanted in a triangle across the floor, glistening on the spilled shampoo.

Beyond the salon were a stockroom and a smaller, so-called consultation room, which Cookie reserved for clients who wanted privacy. There was also a bathroom. Cookie looked into the stockroom first. It hadn't been touched. The consultation room, however, was wrecked: overturned chairs, broken bottles, the computer smashed on the floor. Cookie noticed her startled face staring up from pieces of the mirror. She went toward the bathroom. It had no windows and the light was out. She flicked the light switch. It was then she found Jaime Rose.

He was bent over the sink with his head wedged against the faucets. He wore nothing but a black T-shirt and a pair of white socks. Three feet of a yellow broom handle protruded from his rectum. The broken-off broom head lay between Jaime's feet, its black bristles pointing upward. A long line of blood curved snakelike down the broom handle onto the floor, where it formed a dark puddle. Jaime's hands were tied behind him with an extension cord and his head was twisted so he faced Cookie. His mouth was gagged with bloody gauze wound around his head. His eyes were rolled up. His T-shirt was torn and Cookie could see cuts and blood on his skin. Two dried streams of blood emerged from his nose and disappeared into his black moustache and beard.

Cookie heard herself make a noise, a low wail with her teeth clenched shut. The telephone was ripped from the wall. She ran out to the street, meaning to call the police from the insurance office next door. Driving down State Street was one of the Friends patrol cars with its orange triangle. Cookie waved to it. "Hey," she shouted.

The car, a cream-colored Mazda sedan, pulled to the curb and the driver rolled down the window. It was Paul Leimbach. With him were two other men, Russ Fusco and Bud Shiller, a cousin of Ralph and Mike's, who worked for Aurelius Oil driving a truck. Leimbach smiled at Cookie. "Hey, yourself," he said.

"Someone's killed Jaime. You've got to get the police."

Leimbach quickly scrambled out of the car, leaving it jammed diagonally against the curb. The others jumped out after him.

"Where is he?"

"He's already dead. He's in the bathroom. Somebody . . ." Cookie couldn't bring herself to describe the broom handle.

"Call the police on the radio," Leimbach told Shiller. Then he and Russ Fusco ran toward the beauty salon.

"Wait," said Cookie, "you probably shouldn't go in there." But by then they were inside.

Cookie ran in after them. The floor of the salon was slippery with spilled shampoo. By the time she reached the bathroom, Fusco was crouched down vomiting on the floor. Leimbach was staring at Jaime.

"The police are on their way," said Bud Shiller, hurrying across the salon. He looked into the bathroom. "Jesus Christ!"

Captain Percy entered the salon several minutes later with two troopers. More police cars arrived and soon Chuck Hawley began roping off the area with yellow tape. Ryan Tavich was over in Potterville, appearing in court in a case involving half a dozen break-ins, a case that had dragged on for several months.

Percy was furious at Leimbach. "You had no right to go in there! You're not policemen! You're nobodies! God knows how much stuff you destroyed."

"We thought we could help," said Leimbach.

"By puking on the evidence?" shouted Percy.

They were outside and a crowd was gathering. Paul Leimbach was held in such esteem because of his work with the Friends that people were shocked by Percy's tone. Chief Schmidt intervened and led Percy away. More police cars arrived. It was one of those fall days that are intermittently sunny and cloudy. A few drops of rain fell.

Chief Schmidt went over to talk to Paul Leimbach. "You really need to be more careful," he said.

Leimbach couldn't see he had done anything wrong, though Russ Fusco was ashamed he had thrown up and hoped people wouldn't talk about it. Eventually the lab crews arrived. An hour later Jaime's body was removed from the beauty salon on a stretcher. The broom handle was still stuck inside him for the coroner to deal with. With the handle sticking out, yet covered with a red sheet, Jaime seemed about four feet wide.

Peter Marcos, the state police lieutenant, took two men over to Jaime's apartment in the Belvedere complex, near City Hall. It was the same complex where Aaron lived, though a different building. Jaime's apartment was on the first floor. The door was locked and Marcos got the manager to open it. Inside, a large collection of compact discs was strewn around the rug. A plaster replica of Michelangelo's *David* had been knocked to the floor and its head had come off. One of the troopers accidentally stepped on the head, crushing it. Marcos checked the bedroom and kitchen, but only the living room had been disturbed.

Marcos sent his men to talk to neighbors. A woman upstairs, Clara Schloss, who worked the afternoon shift at the rope factory, said she'd had to stamp on the floor around two in the morning because the music was so loud. She called it foreign music. Jaime, or somebody, then turned it down. Several other neighbors said they had heard the music, even people in other buildings. It was salsa, and the same CD had played over and over. Marcos checked the disc player and found a CD by Juan Luis Guerra. Nobody had heard any shouting or other noises, possibly because of the music.

Everyone was talking about Jesse and Shannon Levine and their antagonism toward Jaime. At ten o'clock Percy sent two police cars to pick up the brothers. The cars drove fast, blaring their sirens at intersections. The brothers' apartment was on the second floor and ran the length of the building, meaning they could look out their windows and see the police arriving. Six policemen under Marcos raced up the stairs and hammered on the door. There was no answer. The police kicked the door open. There was food on the table—bowls of cornflakes and freshly poured milk. The back door was open. The police ran down the back stairs and into the yard in time to see Jesse and Shannon climbing over a fence.

For some weeks afterward people living in the area told how the state police had rushed through their backyards. Since the Friends of Sharon Malloy listened to the police calls, in a short time about twenty members of the Friends were also searching for Jesse and Shannon. And because some policemen were in plainclothes and a number of the Friends knew only that they were looking for two young men, there was a certain confusion as to who was who. Dogs barked. A gun was fired, though the police denied it was them. A young trooper was wrestled to the ground by Russ Fusco and Bud Shiller. A few people, seeing strangers running through their backyards, called the police.

Jesse was at last found in a tree house belonging to Bobby Hicks, whose mother taught English at the high school. One of the Friends happened to see a basketball shoe sticking through a hole in the wall of the tree house. Of course, he didn't know it was Jesse's. The Friend, Don Evans, who worked at Aurelius Lumber, climbed up the ladder. When he got to the entrance the person inside kicked him and he fell backward. Don grabbed a branch and hung on but he was still twenty feet off the ground. The tree was an old maple. Three policemen ran into the yard, saw Don hanging from the branch, and assumed he was either Jesse or Shannon. Don was about their age. They ordered him to drop to the ground. Don refused to and told the police that

Jesse (or perhaps Shannon) was in the tree house. The police didn't believe him. Don managed to swing his legs up so that he hung from the branch somewhat like a sloth. He yelled at the police and they yelled at him. His change and keys and pocket comb fell from his pockets, pelting the police. More people ran into the yard, including some Friends, and Don was identified. Several of the Friends hurried off to get a ladder.

Jesse was still in the tree house out of sight. The police shouted to him but he didn't answer. Four troopers climbed the ladder—actually two-by-fours nailed to the tree. When the trooper in the lead got to the top, Jesse kicked him in the head. Luckily, he held on, but he slipped and the trooper behind him nearly fell. There followed a stand-off as the police shouted commands to Jesse—still unidentified—and he refused to respond. More policemen entered the yard, as well as other Friends, people who lived nearby, and Franklin. A cold frame was broken and a black dog was running around.

Marcos arrived to take charge and ordered his men to rush the tree house. Eight men climbed the ladder. The first two were knocked off by Jesse, though only one fell all the way to the ground. A third trooper was accidentally knocked off by one of his fellows. Once the police had managed to get up the ladder and were wrestling with Jesse, it became obvious that the tree house could not support the weight of so many men. It began to break apart. Franklin, who had his camera, took several pictures of state troopers clinging to branches, though he was prevailed upon not to use them in the paper. Boards from the tree house fell to the ground and there was a lot of shouting and cries to watch out.

Jesse had scrambled onto a branch. By this time the fire department had arrived with ladders, which they carried across the yards. The ladders were put up against the tree and the troopers marooned on branches were rescued. Jesse then climbed to the top of the tree and shouted insults at the police. "Capitalist running dog" was one. His blond goatee waggled. A trooper followed him and managed to hook a handcuff around Jesse's ankle. Jesse was then offered the choice of climbing down or being yanked out of the tree. He climbed down, assisted (none too gently) by several troopers. He was then bundled into a police car and taken to City Hall.

When Ryan returned to Aurelius from Potterville at one o'clock, Jesse was in jail, though he refused to talk. Shannon hadn't been found yet. The preliminary report from the coroner said that Jaime Rose had been strangled and stabbed. The broom handle had been pushed up through his rectum after he was already dead. Police talked to dozens of people but no one had seen Jaime either taken from his apartment or going into Make Waves. He had left work at six and gone to the Aurelius Grill, where he had had dinner by himself. That's all anyone knew.

It took Ryan an hour to get the details sorted out. He talked to Cookie and then to Franklin. He looked at Jesse sitting gloomily in the holding cell. He thought of how Jesse—or had it been Shannon?— had dumped the bowl of tomato soup in Jaime's lap at the Aurelius Grill.

For the remainder of the afternoon, Ryan helped direct the search for Shannon. Roadblocks were set up as far away as the turnpike. Jesse and Shannon's apartment was searched for clues that might link the brothers to Jaime's murder or to the missing girls. By four o'clock it was dark. Police dogs were brought from Utica, but so many people were trying to help search for Shannon that the dogs got overexcited and weren't much use. The Friends were elated to be doing something constructive. I don't know to what degree people thought Shannon might be to blame for the missing girls but there seemed no doubt in their minds that the brothers had killed Jaime. There was, however, no proof, except that the brothers had been plaguing Jaime for several weeks. What existed was a great desire that Jesse and Shannon be guilty.

At seven o'clock Ryan went home, parking in his driveway. His house was dark. He had eaten nothing since morning and he was famished. He unlocked his front door, turned on the hall light, went down the hall to the kitchen, and stopped. A loaf of bread was on the counter. The mayonnaise was open. A small pile of sliced ham was on a plate along with a hunk of cheese. The ham had a slightly sour smell. Then he noticed that the window in the back door was broken.

Ryan heard a voice behind him and he spun around.

"I'm sorry I broke the window. I'll pay for it. And I'll pay for the food too. I was starving."

It was Shannon. He was sitting in the half dark on the living room couch, where he had been sleeping. In his lap was Ryan's cat, who was purring loudly.

"What're you doing here?" asked Ryan. He thought how Chief rarely purred when he held him.

"I'm turning myself in."

"For what?"

"Beats me. For what all those cops were chasing us for."

Ryan turned on the lamp. Shannon wore jeans and a gray sweatshirt. There was mud on his clothes and mud on the couch. His muddy sneakers were on the floor.

"Someone murdered Jaime Rose," said Ryan.

"You're shitting me." The cat jumped onto the floor.

"Did you do it?"

"No way."

"Why'd you run?"

"You'd run too if a million cops came screaming after you. What were we supposed to do, stand still? How was he killed?"

Ryan decided not to answer that. "I'm going to have to take you downtown."

When Ryan brought Shannon into City Hall without handcuffs, Captain Percy was still directing the search. Ryan realized he should have called, but he had been afraid that a bunch of troopers would come tearing over to his house. A dozen men were in the office, including my cousin, and they stared at Shannon as if he were pink and had feathers. Ryan took him to a holding cell, then locked him inside. Jesse was in the next cell. The brothers looked at each other but didn't speak.

Ryan turned back to Percy. "Those kids didn't kill anyone."

"That's not for you to decide," said Percy.

Later that evening Ryan went searching for Barry. He wasn't home and his mother wasn't home either. She was baby-sitting for Sadie. Ryan went over to the college, looked through the library, and at last decided to go by Aaron's.

It was nine-thirty. Aaron opened his front door. Glancing over Aaron's shoulder, Ryan saw Barry sitting on the couch with a glass of milk in one hand and a sandwich in the other. A spot of peanut butter was on his cheek.

Barry was frightened. "Someone's looking for me," he told Ryan. "Someone's been calling my house. When I pick up the phone, no one's there."

Neither Barry nor Aaron had heard about Jaime. When Ryan told them, Barry threw himself onto the couch. He lay there for a moment, then his shoulders began to heave.

"Who did it?" asked Aaron. He seemed watchful and he looked at Ryan suspiciously.

"We don't know yet," said Ryan. He understood that Aaron suspected that he had killed Janice, but it surprised him that Aaron should suspect him of involvement with Jaime's death. He wanted to tell Aaron that he had loved Janice and would never have hurt her, but the idea of a connection between the murders of Janice and Jaime began to fill his mind.

"Do you have any idea who might have done it, Barry?" asked Ryan.

"Why should I?" Barry kept his face pressed into the cushions.

"Because maybe the same person is looking for you."

Thirty-eight

All week there was the sense that the person responsible for the missing girls was growing more reckless, though whether from a desire to save himself or harm himself there was no way to know. But it made me think about Sadie's fear that someone had tried to break into her house on Sunday night. I was tempted to put it down to nerves because I just didn't want it to be true. I told myself it was impossible, that no one would try to break into her house. But then it happened a second time and this time it was more frightening.

Imagine being alone in a house at night and hearing a noise, a floorboard creaking or a window sliding up. The mind at once interprets what it might be: something benign like wind or the house resettling or something wicked. You wait for another sound. You hear the furnace click on, the humming of a light, a clock ticking. Lists of alternatives roll through your mind. If you feel guilty or scared, maybe you fear the worst. If you feel content and live in a place you think safe (but what is safe?), you might return to your book. Then comes another noise.

Saturday night Franklin and Paula went out to dinner in celebration of their three-day-old marriage. Ryan was supposed to join them with Cookie Evans, then he had to work. Cookie excused herself as well. She was so disturbed by Jaime's death that she had closed the beauty parlor for the rest of November. And she would have left town if the police hadn't asked her to stay.

Franklin and Paula drove to the Colgate Inn in Hamilton. Franklin said they would be back by nine-thirty. Mrs. Sanders came over and made dinner for Sadie. There was some question as to how late she could remain but it was agreed that if she had to leave early Sadie would come to my house.

As usual, Mrs. Sanders spent the evening watching TV. Shadow was shut up in the basement because of Mrs. Sanders's allergies. Sadie took a shower, then read in her room, which was across the hall from the living room. At times, she could hear Mrs. Sanders's laughter rising over the laughter of the TV audience. Then at nine-thirty the telephone rang.

Sadie thought it was her father calling to say he would be late, but then she heard Mrs. Sanders say, "Who is this?" And then: "What do you mean he's been hurt?" Sadie went out into the hall just as Mrs. Sanders hung up the phone.

"Something's happened to Barry," she said. "I've got to get home right away."

Sadie was wearing her pajamas. "Should I get dressed and come with you?"

Mrs. Sanders looked at her watch. "Your father should be home any minute. You'll have to go to that man's house." She meant me.

Mrs. Sanders began pulling on her coat. "We have to hurry."

Sadie put a coat over her pajamas and followed Mrs. Sanders onto the front porch. Her car was parked in the driveway. "You scoot now," she said. "I'll watch from the car 'till you get there."

Sadie was halfway across the Danielses' front yard as Mrs. Sanders backed out of the driveway. It was then that Sadie heard her dog barking. Shadow was still in the basement. Mrs. Sanders backed onto Van Buren and stopped. By then Sadie was between my house and the Danielses' and she waved to Mrs. Sanders to go on and Mrs. Sanders pulled away. But Sadie, instead of continuing to my house, stopped and turned back toward her own. Shadow was upset at being left alone and Sadie knew that I wouldn't mind if she brought the dog with her.

Sadie ran back across her yard and up the front steps. It is probably fortunate that she made no noise. Her dog kept barking and for
the first time it occurred to Sadie that Shadow was frightened. The
barking had a frenzied quality. Sadie ran down the hallway. Then, as
she was about to open the basement door and the dog fell silent, Sadie
heard the back door rattling.

She thought it was the wind, but looking through the darkened
kitchen she saw the silhouette of a man against the glass. At first she
thought the person might be Aaron, but he was too big to be Aaron.
Shadow started barking again and Sadie saw the man pause and raise
his head. The man's gloved hands were pressed against the glass with
the fingers wide apart. His face was a round dark blur between them.
He turned his head slowly as he stared into the dark kitchen.

Sadie was afraid to go back down the hall to the front door since
the living room lights were on and she would cross the person's line of
sight. She was afraid that if the man saw her, he would grow even
more desperate, that he would rush around to the front. Sadie's bedroom had an extension phone. She would call the police. First, however, she opened the door to the basement. Shadow jumped up on
her, then dashed into the kitchen barking. The dog's paws slid and
clicked on the kitchen tiles.

Sadie hurried into her bedroom, picked up the phone, and found
it was dead. The dog was barking and leaping at the back door.
Quickly, Sadie opened the bedroom window, which looked out on
the side yard toward my house. I expect we should be grateful that
Franklin's many activities had kept him from putting up the storms.
Sadie swung her legs over the sill and hopped to the ground. At that
moment Shadow jumped up, putting her paws on the sill. Sadie lifted
her through the window. Suddenly she heard glass shatter as the window in the back door broke inward onto the kitchen floor.

Sadie dropped Shadow onto the ground. Instead of staying with
her, the dog dashed around toward the back of the house, barking

again. Sadie was too frightened to call the dog and draw attention to herself. She aimed and ran to my house.

By nine-thirty I was thinking about going upstairs. I like to read in bed till I feel sleepy. Since I had not heard from Sadie, I assumed that Franklin had gotten home. Maybe it would be truer to say that I had forgotten about them. I was still reading Daphne du Maurier's *Jamaica Inn,* and its desolation and stormy weather filled my mind.

However, when I heard Sadie's footsteps on my front porch, I quickly rose from my chair. The porch light was on and I saw her through the glass. She kept knocking rapidly, though she must have seen me coming. She wore an oversized jacket and kept looking back over her shoulder. I sensed her terror even before I opened the door. It gave me a chill.

"He's back!" she cried. "I saw him!"

I looked out across the dark yard. I could see no one.

"Who?" I asked.

"I don't know," she said almost angrily. "Whoever was trying to get in the house."

I led her into the living room and asked her to explain. She was quite frantic and wouldn't sit down. Her jacket was a red plaid mackinaw belonging to Franklin and Sadie was almost lost in it. On her feet were an old pair of sheepskin slippers.

During the week I had thought of buying a gun like many of my neighbors were doing, but even the idea of a gun frightened me and so I hadn't done anything. The only time I shot a gun was at the state fair as a child but I suppose it wasn't a real gun, and anyway, I missed. But I had a flashlight and I went out onto the porch and shone it around the yard. I heard no noise. The dog had stopped barking. I meant to call the police, but as I stood on the porch I saw a car driving down the street. Then I noticed the orange triangle on the door. I signaled with my flashlight and the car, a cream-colored Mazda sedan, pulled to the curb. I recognized the car even before the driver got out. It was Leimbach and he was alone.

The oddness of his being there by himself didn't occur to me at first. I felt glad to see him and I hurried across the yard.

"What's the matter?" asked Leimbach. He wore a heavy overcoat and a scarf.

I explained that Sadie had said someone was trying to break into her house through the back door. Immediately, Leimbach got out of the car and hurried toward the house. I ran after him, mostly because I didn't want to be left alone. Sadie came with me. I still had my flashlight, and as the beam slanted across Leimbach, I saw he was carrying a pistol in his right hand, what is called an automatic. I should have been comforted by this but I wasn't. As he ran, the tails of his overcoat flapped around his knees. Sadie whistled for Shadow but there was no response.

We entered the house. It was very quiet. Leimbach hurried down the hall, turning on the lights as he went. Our feet seemed to make a lot of noise. The window in the back door was broken. Leimbach tried to step around the glass but some of it cracked beneath his feet. He opened the door. The screen door was ajar. The screen had been cut and the hook lifted.

"I'll call the police," said Leimbach. He was businesslike and excited at the same time. He held the pistol down along his leg. With his overcoat, he looked like a larger person and I thought of the silhouette Sadie had seen. Leimbach picked up the kitchen phone. "It's dead."

Leimbach had a phone in his car and we went back outside. The wind had gotten stronger and it was cold.

Sadie kept whistling for her dog. "Where's Shadow?" she said. "She won't come."

After Leimbach called the police, he hurried to see where the phone line from the street entered the house. We went with him even though the good fortune that had led him to appear so promptly had begun to worry me. On the other hand, Leimbach spent hours every day driving up and down the streets. The fact that he had arrived so fortuitously wasn't enough reason to suspect him. I stayed with him and shone my light for him. The phone line came into the northern corner of the house and went down the wall by the porch. It had been cut. The copper wire shone in the light. When she saw it, Sadie moved closer to me.

We went back around the house and I climbed the front steps; Leimbach and Sadie were a few feet behind me. I shone my light into the dark corners. I found myself thinking that if anything happened, I'd be too frightened to scream. Franklin's porch extended across the front of the house and at one end a glider hung from the ceiling. It was swaying slightly. Something lay on the seat. I took a few steps toward it.

I must have made a noise, because Leimbach hurried up to my side. "What is it?"

I was afraid I might drop the light. "A hand," I said.

It lay on the seat of the glider: a woman's pink, slender hand. At first I thought it was real until I saw how the wrist was finished off with a sort of attachment: a mannequin's hand.

Leimbach stood beside me. "Oh God," he said.

"That wasn't there before," said Sadie. She held on to my arm. I shone the light around the yard but I saw nothing. The glider swayed and the hand rocked back and forth, almost as if it had some life to it. I could feel Sadie shivering.

"Where's Shadow?" she said. "Why doesn't she come?"

I had no answer for that.

The police and Franklin and Paula arrived at the same time a minute or so later. There were two police cars and my cousin was one of the four policemen in them. Leimbach said someone had tried to break through the back door and the window was smashed. Chuck and two others immediately ran around the side of the house. They had flashlights and the lights swung across the dark backyards. I tried to tell Franklin and Paula what had happened.

Sadie gripped her father's hand. The bulky mackinaw made her look like a slightly smaller version of Franklin. She was no longer concerned for herself but was worried about her dog. "Shadow," she called. "Come on, girl." Then she would listen.

After a few minutes Chuck came running back. He told the other policemen to call the station and get Ryan and Captain Percy. Then he turned to Franklin, trying to speak softly so Sadie wouldn't hear. "There's a dead dog back there, a cocker spaniel. Its neck is broken."

Sadie ran toward the backyard, followed by her father. The dog lay by a tree about twenty feet from the porch, a dark patch on the ground. Sadie threw herself on the dog, hugging its body and calling Shadow's name. Blood ran from the dog's mouth and nose and it got on Sadie's coat and on her face. Franklin gently pulled her away from Shadow, picked her up, and carried her to the house. Sadie had her face buried in his neck. I followed him into the living room.

"Where's Mrs. Sanders?" asked Franklin.

"She had to leave," I said.

I had never seen Franklin so stricken. He sat by Sadie and kept touching her hair. Getting a wet washcloth, he washed the dog's blood from her face. Sadie lay curled on the living room couch, weeping. After a while, she fell asleep. Paula covered her with a blanket and sat beside her. I thought of myself in Franklin's place: almost to lose your daughter because you had been slow. Maybe Franklin and Paula had stayed for dessert or a second coffee or a brandy. Maybe they had sat in the car kissing before driving back to Aurelius, and because of this Sadie had almost been killed.

Within the next hour there was a lot of confusion as police arrived and explanations were made. Nothing was found of whoever had been trying to get into the house, though fingerprints were taken. The dog was sent to the lab as well, since Shadow might have bitten or scratched whoever had killed her. Percy spoke particularly sharply with Paul Leimbach, asking how he happened to be in the area and why he was alone when the Friends usually patrolled in twos or threes. Leimbach said that he often went out by himself and that he went down Van Buren Street four times each night. Percy also told Leimbach to show him the permit for his pistol. Leimbach was cool but helpful. Whatever dislike Percy had for Leimbach was clearly reciprocated. Percy's suggestion—never explicitly stated—was that Leimbach himself might have been the man at the back door. Ryan didn't interfere but watched carefully, as if prying into Leimbach's brain with his eyes.

Aaron arrived around eleven. He had heard a garbled report downtown and he came to make sure Sadie was safe. The question came up why Mrs. Sanders had left early. Sadie had said that something had happened to Barry. Ryan repeated this to Aaron.

"Nothing happened to Barry," said Aaron. "He was with me the entire time."

Percy sent two troopers to Mrs. Sanders's house to ask about the phone call. Our naïveté was remarkable. It amazed us to think that the person who called Mrs. Sanders might be the same person who tried to break into Franklin's house. It amazed us that he would know about Barry and his mother, that he seemed to know us so well. Even though the evidence indicated this person was one of us, we were astonished all over again each time the possibility was raised. How could it be one of us? Who? A policeman? A neighbor?

The next day, Sunday, it snowed. I woke in the morning to the quiet that a foot of snow on the ground will cause. I heard my furnace go on. I could see big flakes drift past my bedroom window. Something about watching them led me to think of other winters, going back to my earliest memories. Though we had had wet snow on

Halloween and flurries a few times since, this was the first real snow of the season. And although I was approaching fifty, I found it exciting. Had it been Monday instead of Sunday, school would have been canceled, and I felt a moment of regret that it wasn't Monday after all. When I was a child, I used to sled on the hill in Lincoln Park, near the hospital. I had a sled with runners, a Flexible Flyer. Nowadays children have plastic sleds, though one still sees a toboggan or two. It was eight o'clock and I made breakfast. Looking from a window, I saw a police car parked in front of Franklin's house. Because of the snow on its roof, I assumed it had been there all night. A little cloud of exhaust indicated that its motor was running.

The quiet in the streets was like fear. Everything was shrouded in it. I've said that people were buying guns. Owing to the time required to get a pistol permit, many bought rifles. George Fontini had a sporting goods shop on Main Street and he completely sold out his supply of hunting rifles, even the expensive models. And he sold a number of pistols. He even said, making a joke of it, that he had sold his crossbows and soon expected to sell out his darts.

Jesse and Shannon remained in jail over the weekend. They denied any involvement in Jaime's death, though they had no alibi. The coroner said that Jaime had died between midnight and four in the morning, which was not a time when many people have good alibis. On the other hand, the lab reports showed that neither Shannon's nor Jesse's fingerprints had been found in Jaime's apartment or in Make Waves. Nor had the two been charged with the murder. At the moment, Jesse was charged with assaulting a police officer and Shannon with breaking into Ryan's house.

The question that people asked was, If Jesse and Shannon were not responsible, then who killed Jaime and why? It was hard for me not to think of what Jaime had said about people with secrets. He'd probably said it to others as well. It seemed obvious he had been killed by somebody with whom he had been sexually involved who did not want that involvement known. The additional question was whether this person had anything to do with the disappearances. Was it the same person or was it another person using the disappearances as a smoke screen?

The police talked to everyone they could find who knew Jaime. They talked to me as well. A state police detective came to my house, a plainclothesman by the name of Mitchell.

"I know nothing about him," I said. "He cut my hair not long ago. Normally I get it cut at Jimmy's but Jimmy had closed his shop for a week to go hunting."

"Who were Jaime's friends?"

"I have no idea. Perhaps Cookie Evans would know."

We stood in the hall. I wouldn't even let Mitchell into my living room and I could see he was irritated with me. I was entirely unhelpful, but I found it objectionable that certain assumptions were being made about my life.

Barry was also questioned. He said he knew Jaime a little bit but that was all. He said he felt someone was looking for him, too, though he gave no sensible reason why this should be so. Because Barry was nervous and stuttered, the police assumed he was a hysteric or was lying to make himself appear important. Barry said nothing about his own experiences with men in Aurelius and instead suggested that someone was after him because of his involvement with Inquiries into the Right. He explained how some members had been forced to leave town. It was just his own bad luck, said Barry, that he had no place to go. The police felt Barry was being overanxious. He seemed so inconsequential that it was hard to imagine he might know something.

Among the police there was the sense that they were drawing their circle smaller. Percy had mostly kept his suspicions under wraps, but now he began to move more aggressively, especially after Ryan talked to Sheila Murphy. He felt certain that whoever had murdered Janice was responsible for the disappearances and had also killed

Jaime. And he brooded about what Sheila had said about Janice's "professional man." Twice he had had Sheila brought to City Hall and had questioned her personally. And he questioned Dr. Malloy, who swore he had never been involved with Janice. He even brought in Donald Malloy, who was extremely indignant.

"How dare you suggest I was involved with such a woman," he said. "She was no better than a tart!"

Saturday night, after someone tried to break into Franklin's house, Percy quickly brought in men to search the area. A number of houses were vacant. Not many, perhaps twenty in the whole town, but they were the houses of people who had left because of their fear. Some were retired people who had gone south for the winter but some were families with teenage daughters. More would leave soon. As Percy saw it, the empty houses could offer protection to whoever might be prowling at night.

In fact, the house directly behind Franklin's, belonging to Maggie Murray, a retired schoolteacher, stood empty. Every New Year's Day she went down to her sister's in Fort Lauderdale for the remainder of the winter. This year she had left shortly after the first of November. According to Percy, someone could have parked in Maggie's driveway, then cut across the backyards to Franklin's house. That was one reason he had been suspicious of Leimbach, whose car had appeared so opportunely.

And on Sunday he received further reason to be suspicious of Leimbach. A large envelope with Captain Percy's name on the outside was dropped off at the police station. Afterward no one could determine where it came from, if it had been slipped in with Saturday's mail—though there was no stamp on it—or if it had been left outside the front door and brought in. Dozens of people went in and out all the time and someone might have picked it up and tossed it on the desk as a way of being helpful.

By the time the envelope was passed on to Percy, it had been knocking around for a few hours. Percy opened it as he stood by the front desk. Ryan was nearby and he saw Percy give a little start. Inside was a piece of paper with the name "Leimbach" printed on it in big letters. The letters were written with crayon and it was clear that they had been traced over and over with many different colored crayons, as if someone had first written "Leimbach" about ten times with black crayon and then had done the same with green and red and blue and brown and yellow, until the letters were an inch wide and greasy with the thick, almost violent application of waxy color.

Thirty-nine

After Meg Shiller's disappearance, Captain Percy initiated a number of strategies that he hoped would lead to the apprehension of the person responsible. For instance, ten girls who bore a resemblance to Sharon and Meg—all were tall and slender, with long hair—were being surreptitiously watched. License plate numbers of passing cars were fed into computers at half a dozen locations to see if a pattern could be determined or if the numbers could be matched with the license plates of about a hundred people who were known to be in their cars at the time of the disappearances. And there were other projects I knew nothing about. Though they were expensive, it was decided in the upper echelons of the state police that it would be better to pay the price than to lose another girl. Sadly, the expense didn't help)—not in that way, at least.

One of Percy's efforts entailed using a decoy. He brought in Becky DeMarino, a thirty-five-year-old state police officer from Corning who was quite small. When she was youthfully dressed, one might think she was in her early teens. The plan was for her to walk along the side streets and for troopers to be hidden along the way. It was more complicated than this and I'm giving only the briefest idea of his plan. For example, I know Percy had a van with the name of a lighting firm painted on the side, while inside was a man with a radio and two troopers.

Becky DeMarino carried a pistol and a transmitter so that if anyone spoke to her, the conversation would be heard in the van. She came to Aurelius on Wednesday, November 15. Lieutenant Marcos was in charge of the operation, if it can be called that. It was supposed to start on Friday, then Jaime's body was found. Consequently, it didn't start until Sunday.

On her walks, Becky DeMarino wore a pink parka and pulled a red plastic sled. With a ski cap and a scarf wrapped around her neck, she looked about twelve. I am told they had her practice walking like a child—meaning she had to meander and appear purposeless. Ryan said she had been instructed to skip occasionally. One may infer from this the degree of desperation felt by the police. Despite the feeling of dread in the town, there was a certain amount of sledding in Lincoln Park that Sunday and Becky was to patrol the streets in the general area, pulling her sled behind her. A young girl out on the street in the dusky afternoon: perhaps our abductor would be tempted.

But again the problem was that quite a few people were aware of the plan. The police knew, of course. Then, when Becky was walking down Walnut Street with her sled, one of the Friends' patrol cars drew up beside her. The driver—I believe it was Henry Polaski—meant to tell her to go home and was ready to drive her. Another man was in the car with Polaski. Of course, they saw that Becky wasn't a child and after a brief chat they went on their way. Did they understand she was with the police? Did they tell others about a woman pulling a sled who looked about twelve but was really in her midthirties?

At that time of year, it was dark in Aurelius by four o'clock, especially on a snowy afternoon. Becky walked along the edge of the park near the hill where kids had been sledding since morning. Although there were trees, they were scattered and children sledded between them. The sidewalk was about fifty yards from the hill and only the fastest sleds could coast that far after their speedy descent. The children had come either with their parents or in a group. The fear of something happening was so prevalent that no child came alone, and many were not allowed to come at all. I remember times when there were over a hundred children sledding at the park, but on that particular Sunday the most was about twenty. Still, there was shouting and dogs were running around. But after three o'clock everyone started going home.

It was about quarter to four when Becky walked down Johnson Street, which bordered the park. The streetlights had come on though it was still light enough for Becky to see about six kids sledding, their bright-colored parkas muted in the gloom.

As she reached the sliding path, she saw a green sled on the sidewalk, an inexpensive plastic sled with an orange piece of cord attached to the front. She paused, and at that moment heard someone calling.

"Karla! Karla!"

Becky turned and saw a woman running down the hill toward her, though she was still nearly a hundred yards away. The woman fell, then got to her feet again.

"Karla, where have you been?"

Becky waited as the woman ran, then walked a little, then ran again. She seemed both angry and frightened. She was a youngish woman wearing a three-quarter-length green down jacket and a blue and red ski cap.

"Karla, I told you to come right back up the hill!"

Then, when she was still twenty yards away: "You're not Karla. Where is she?"

The woman began running again.

"That's her sled," she said. Then she stopped and put her hands to her face. She began to scream.

In the sound truck, the technician wearing the headphones yanked them off his head. The driver nicked on his lights and pulled forward, his tires spinning in the snow.

The woman kept screaming. That was the first anyone knew that a third girl had disappeared.

The woman's name was Louise Golondrini. She was a thirty-year-old single mother who worked at the rope factory. She had a boy-friend but he was doing construction in Florida right now. She lived with another single woman, Pam O'Brien, who had an eight-year-old boy named Harry. Pam also worked at the rope factory but on a different shift. Louise was from Utica and had moved to Aurelius two years earlier when she had gotten her job.

Her daughter, Karla, had been in my eighth grade general-science class the previous year. She suffered from what they call an attention deficit disorder, that is, she stared dreamily from the window or drew horses in her notebook. I could have flunked her but out of kindness I gave her a D. She was pretty in a pale way, thin with long dark hair. All these girls, these thirteen- and fourteen-year-olds, are so clearly in transition that they are almost nothing at the moment. That's not quite right, but one tends to focus more on what they are becoming than on what they are. Now Karla Golondrini would become nothing at all.

Becky DeMarino's pink parka was almost the same color as Karla's, according to her mother. That was why she had at first mistaken Becky for her daughter. They had been sledding since two o'clock and Louise Golondrini wanted to go home; she was cold and her feet were wet. Her car was parked in the lot at the top of the hill. Karla wanted to go down one more time. Her mother finally agreed but said she would wait at the top. Karla slid down the hill and her mother lost track of her in the increasing dark. She waited. Five minutes passed. A dog was jumping around and she was distracted. Then she called for her daughter. Standing on the hill, hearing no answer, she began to think that something awful might have happened. That was when she came running down through the snow. When she had seen Becky DeMarino in her pink parka, she felt great relief. It hadn't lasted long.

Karla had been gone less than ten minutes when her mother began to scream. Because of the radio van, the police were alerted right away. A dozen troopers fanned out across the hill looking for Karla. Police visited nearby houses as volunteers searched the neighborhood. By four-thirty, roadblocks were erected on all the roads leaving Aurelius. More were set up at the turnpike and on Route 20. But as Chuck Hawley said, "We all knew the girl was still someplace in Aurelius."

Louise Golondrini wanted to stay in Lincoln Park but at last she was prevailed upon to come to the police station. "My baby," she kept crying. Roberta Fletcher, the nurse who worked for Dr. Malloy, was called. Dr. Malloy came, too, as did his wife. Dr. Malloy tried to give Louise a sedative but she didn't want one. They took over Chief Schmidt's office. Really, there was no place else to wait. Soon the Shillers came. It must have been awful for Louise to realize she was now part of their company.

By five o'clock over a hundred people were looking for the missing girl. It had been snowing lightly all day, sometimes no more than flurries, but with evening it began to snow harder. TV trucks arrived from Syracuse and Utica, even Binghamton, and their bright lights made the fresh snow sparkle. Lincoln Park was not far from where I lived. Sadie and I walked over to watch. She was the one to tell me that Karla had disappeared. I had been home reading the Sunday paper. Someone had called Franklin and he dashed out of the house. Paula hadn't wanted Sadie to go out, but then she came as well. Sadie walked on one side of me and Paula on the other, as if I were a fence between them. Paula was a few inches taller than I, while Sadie was a few inches shorter. The snow was quite deep and I was glad that I had worn boots.

The news of a third girl's disappearing touched us like a sickness. It was as if the disappearance were caused by no human agent, as if our town were under one of those afflictions you read about in the Old Testament. People spoke to one another in hushed voices. Their faces were drawn; some were weeping. They looked hunched. The flashing blue lights of the police cars provided the only color, creating blue faces, blue weeping. In the surrounding houses, I saw more faces pressed to the windows.

"I knew who she was," said Sadie, "but I don't think I ever talked to her."

"Her poor mother," Paula kept saying.

There was an ominous quality to the silence. Because of their heavy coats and hats and scarves, the people on the hillside seemed more like human shapes than human beings. They walked stiffly and I was reminded of how the dead walked in that movie *The Night of the Living Dead.* The police were very busy. Excited staticky voices came over the speakers of the police radios. They seemed to be speaking numbers mostly. At six o'clock we walked back to my house and I made tea.

Captain Percy had a list of fifty people whose whereabouts he wanted to know as exactly as possible. The list included some people I've never mentioned as well as Harry Martini, Sherman Carpenter, and Henry Swazey. It even included me. One man visited by the police was Greg Dorough, a lawyer in town who happened to be gay and who lived with a man who was a technician at the pharmaceutical company in Norwich. One wouldn't have thought they were gay if one hadn't known. In any case, the unpleasant part was that Greg was visited—I am sure of this—*only* because he was gay. The visit was very brief: the police wanted to know where Greg had been during the afternoon. Still, a visit is a visit. I was with Sadie when the police came, and I felt relieved that Paula was with us too. Otherwise I might have heard more remarks about my interest in young girls.

The police also looked for Paul Leimbach, Donald Malloy, Mike Shiller, and others closely related to the missing girls' families. Aaron they found in his apartment with Harriet. He said Harriet and he had been working all afternoon preparing a memorial service for

Houari Chihani. Mike Shiller claimed to have been ice fishing at the lake. Donald Malloy at first couldn't be found, then Percy realized that he was among the volunteers scouring the park for evidence of Karla and had been one of the first to respond.

Percy learned that Paul Leimbach had been alone in his car, ostensibly patrolling his assigned section of Aurelius, when the disappearance occurred. People later said that Percy overreacted but it seemed he couldn't do otherwise, especially since he had received the piece of paper with Leimbach's name printed on it in such an obsessive way. In any case, he brought Leimbach into the police station and turned his car over to the lab crew. Chihani was dead, Jaime Rose was dead, Oscar Herbst was still in Troy, other IIR members had left town, Hark Powers was in jail, and so were the Levine brothers—now that the supposedly worst among us had been accounted for, it was necessary to turn to the others, including the best.

Leimbach wasn't accused of anything but he was asked to account for his movements. Everybody was very polite, or tried to be. They were in a corner of the police station, since Louise Golondrini was still in Chief Schmidt's office. Chuck Hawley was there. He said that Leimbach wore dark pants, a dark turtleneck, and a dark jacket. Almost like a commando, my cousin said. Leimbach claimed to have been driving around Aurelius for about three hours. During the first hour Jamie Fendrick had ridden with him, but then Jamie had to go to work bagging groceries at Wegmans. So from two-thirty to four-thirty, when the police picked him up, Leimbach had been alone.

Had he known Karla Golondrini?

No, he had never met her.

He was shown her picture. Did he recognize her?

He couldn't recall having seen her before.

Karla's mother was brought in to see if she recognized Leimbach. She didn't recognize him. Then she asked, "Is that the man who took my baby?" She started shouting and a policewoman had to get her out of the office.

"Why am I here?" asked Leimbach. "It's absurd."

Ryan brought out the piece of paper with Leimbach's name written on it in a dozen colors. Earlier in the day Ryan had tried doing the same thing—tracing a name over and over. "Janice" was the name he traced. He realized that whoever had written Leimbach's name had spent at least an hour doing it.

"You dragged me in here because of this?" asked Leimbach.

"You weren't dragged," said Ryan.

Lieutenant Marcos said, "You must see that we have to investigate all the possibilities."

Ryan knew everything depended on Leimbach's car. If any trace of Karla was found, then Leimbach would be arrested. If his car was clean, he would be released, although that wouldn't necessarily mean he was innocent. Already people who lived in the area that Leimbach claimed to have been patrolling were being asked if they had seen him. And some had noticed a car with an orange triangle on the front doors but hadn't noticed the make or seen who had been driving.

At some point a lab technician came into the office and spoke to Marcos in a whisper.

"Did you spill something in the car?" asked Marcos.

"I got a Coke and a hamburger from McDonald's and I spilled part of the Coke," said Leimbach.

"And you cleaned it off with water?"

"I stopped at a gas station and got some water, yes."

"And it was only the spilled Coke that you cleaned off?"

"Of course."

At six o'clock Leimbach was sent home.

Around the same time a red wool scarf was found in the snow in the northwest corner of Lincoln Park. It was brought to the police station and identified by Louise Golondrini as belonging to Karla.

Police roped off that area of the park and searched it inch by inch, even sifting the snow through a screen. After two hours, they found a pen, a silver Cross fountain pen, about ten feet from where the scarf had been found.

"They were excited it might belong to the guy who snatched Karla," said Ryan. "Although on the other hand, maybe it didn't."

The only place in town that sold Cross pens was the office-supply store where Florence Martini worked, Letter Perfect, on Jefferson Street. It was suggested that the pen might belong to her husband—soon to be her ex-husband. He had told the police that he'd been home most of the afternoon but had driven over to Wegmans to do some shopping around three.

Lieutenant Marcos drove to Martini's house with the pen. Martini said it wasn't his. Though he had a Cross pen, it was a chestnut color with gold trim. Marcos asked if he could see it. Martini searched through his desk. He had an office in the downstairs den. His wife stood in the doorway.

"I can't find it," said Martini. "It's probably at school."

"Didn't I give you a silver one as well?" asked his wife.

"No," said Martini, "you never did."

Marcos visited the owner of Letter Perfect, Noah Frankenmuth, around nine. Frankenmuth lived on Butler Street. He was painting an upstairs bedroom and was annoyed at being disturbed. He had a toy dachshund named Fritz that kept dashing around Marcos's ankles. Marcos was afraid he might step on it.

"I have a computer list of people who bought Cross pens back at the store. Can't this wait until tomorrow?"

"No," said Marcos.

They drove to the store. Frankenmuth checked his computer files, then printed out a list of twenty-five people who had bought Cross pens in the past two years. Five of the pens were plain silver. One of the people on the list was Paul Leimbach's wife, Martha, who had bought the pen the previous February. "She said it was a birthday present," said Frankenmuth.

Marcos drove over to Leimbach's house. He drove quickly, sliding on the corners.

The Leimbachs lived in one of the newer houses on Myrtle Street, a Cape Cod with a large picture window facing the front yard. They were watching television.

"Looks like mine," said Leimbach. "At least I had a silver one. I lost it sometime this summer. It was a present and I felt bad about losing it. Where'd you find it?"

"I'm not at liberty to say," explained Marcos.

Later Marcos said he had been tempted to arrest Leimbach then and there, but he restrained himself. He still hadn't told Captain Percy what he had learned, so he drove back to the police station.

Percy was not pleased. "Now he's been tipped off," he said. He assigned a man to investigate the other four people who had bought silver Cross pens. It seemed clear, however, that the pen belonged to Leimbach, which didn't prove he had been the one to drop it in the snow. Two troopers were sent to talk to people in Leimbach's office to see if he had mentioned losing a pen.

It snowed more that night. The police gave up their search of the park about eleven-thirty. By then there wasn't a square inch of snow that had not been trampled. And Donald Malloy had been quite thorough, leading twenty members of the Friends across a hundred backyards. All through Aurelius the snow had been tromped on, turned into slush, made muddy. But that night another six inches fell. Yards, sidewalks, and the city park were all covered with fresh snow. On Monday morning there was no sign that a search had taken place.

Forty

It was hard to think that Thanksgiving was a week away. We had so little to feel thankful for. The previous Thanksgiving I had made a small turkey and invited Franklin and Sadie. This year I had no plans. School would be closed, of course. I thought of driving to Utica and having Thanksgiving dinner in a restaurant by myself, but that would have felt like a betrayal of my friends in Aurelius, as if I were having fun in secret.

Jaime Rose was buried on Tuesday. At first I was going to go to the funeral, then I didn't. I didn't want to be looked at. Half a dozen times at night my phone would ring; when I answered no one was there. This disturbed me and I had my number changed. Later I found out that others were getting calls, too, but at the time I thought I was the only one.

The funeral was a small affair. Cookie Evans went and some friends of Jaime's drove up from New York. And his mother came from Clinton. Barry went, though his mother told him not to. Aaron and Harriet went with him. And there were a few total strangers, who went because Jaime had been killed in such an awful way. A plain-clothesman made a list of the mourners. Ryan said there was the chance that Jaime's murderer might show up.

Also on Tuesday Shannon and Jesse were released on bail. They were never charged with anything in connection with Jaime, just the attack on a policeman and the break-in, though Ryan felt these charges would be dropped. The police were divided over whether Jaime was the victim of a homosexual love affair that had gone wrong or if there was a connection to the missing girls. This put even more pressure on the gay population of Aurelius. Gay men as far away as Norwich were questioned. But I recalled how Franklin had talked to Jaime on that day when Irving Powell's house was surrounded by members of the Friends of Sharon Malloy. Many people had seen Jaime and Franklin together and someone might have been afraid of what Jaime would say. And Barry had been with them as well.

Captain Percy made much of the call to Mrs. Sanders on Saturday night. She said that a man's voice told her that Barry had fallen down the front steps and had broken his leg. And so she rushed home. Some people thought the call had been a prank but Percy felt certain that the person responsible for the disappearances had made the call. And he stressed to Ryan that it indicated that someone had known that Franklin wasn't at home and where Mrs. Sanders was to be found.

Percy also brought Aaron to City Hall and questioned him with Ryan. Percy sat on one side of the desk and Aaron sat on the other, while Ryan stood by the door. Aaron kept glancing at him and each time Ryan thought how much Aaron disliked him.

Percy began by saying that he knew that Aaron had returned to Aurelius to discover who had killed his mother. He also knew that Aaron had questioned Janice's neighbors and that the assault on Sheila had been because she had refused to tell him something about Janice. Then he stared at Aaron as if expecting him to disagree.

"You're a clever guy," said Aaron.

"Don't be cute," said Percy. "Did you talk to your mother before she was killed?"

"We talked on the phone about twice a week."

"Did she say anything about the men she was involved with?"

"She might say that she had met a man she liked but she'd never mention any names."

"Do you have any idea who this professional man might be?"

Aaron stretched his legs out in front of him and crossed his arms on his chest. "Maybe Tavich, maybe you."

"Could it have been Dr. Malloy?"

"Possibly."

"But your suspicions are more precise than that."

"Possibly."

"Aren't you friends with Sadie Moore? She was almost abducted the other night. By not telling us what you know, you're risking her life."

Aaron looked away and didn't say anything. Percy asked him a few more questions, to which Aaron replied uncommunicatively. Then he sent Aaron home.

"He thinks he can find this person by himself," said Percy.

The interview had depressed Ryan. "Either that or he doesn't trust us. Did you ever know Janice?"

"Do you mean was I involved with her? Of course not."

"She had that same kind of stubbornness."

For a few days it seemed that someone was stalking Barry, then it stopped or perhaps Barry was mistaken. He claimed to have heard his back door rattling or the front doorbell ringing when his mother hadn't been home. And there was something about a car driving by slowly but Barry couldn't remember the make. It had been blue or cream-colored—he wasn't sure. And there were phone calls, someone on the other end of the line who refused to speak. But surely he could have been called by someone other than his potential murderer. Many people were receiving anonymous calls. Later we learned that members of the Friends of Sharon Malloy were making phone calls to harass people they imagined to be suspects. This turned out to be Donald Malloy's stratagem. He claimed that if pressure was put on a number of potential suspects the guilty one might crack. What wasn't clear, however, was whether the Friends were making *all* the calls.

Aaron felt that the phone calls to Barry were important and he made it his business to find out what Barry was hiding. With whom had Barry been involved in high school and what had the man done to frighten him? The police didn't know anything about this, nor did Franklin. But Aaron knew and I knew, though we had no names. Aaron took Barry back to his apartment after Jaime's funeral and scared him. Barry said that Aaron even slapped him. Barry was extremely upset and talked to me about it soon after.

"But what did you say to him?" I asked.

"Nothing. I refused to tell. I only said what I'd told you before, that he was 'a professional man.' I never thought Aaron would hurt me. He completely lost it."

At the time I didn't realize the significance of that term for Aaron, but he became quite ferocious and as a result Barry gave Aaron the man's name.

On Monday ten girls were withdrawn from Knox Consolidated by their parents. The oldest was sixteen, the youngest was twelve. All went to stay with relatives in other towns. About fifteen girls had already been withdrawn and their absence made visible holes in our classes. Karla Golondrini had few friends but many acquaintances. There was more weeping on Monday and this was made worse by the presence of TV reporters. There was even the suggestion that the school should be closed till the matter was over. But Harry Martini argued that the children had to have a place to go. If they were in school, at least they were safe, whereas if they weren't in school, who knew where they would be? Lou Hendricks said, loud enough to be heard by many people, that since Harry Martini had been visited twice on Sunday by the police, perhaps he had his own perverse reason for wanting the girls to be kept in school. I thought this quite unfair, as did many others. But some, I realized, didn't.

Nobody blamed the families who took their children out of school or left town completely. I'm sure others would have done the same had they been able. At school there was less shouting in the halls and less conversation in the teachers' lounge. The silence spread to other places as well. At Wegmans one saw fewer people talking to one another. The restaurants were nearly empty, the movie theater deserted. The various reading groups, sewing groups, garden groups, and travel groups all stopped having meetings. Only the video stores did well, and the pizza parlors, at least those that delivered.

On Wednesday there was a service for Karla at the Good Fellowship Evangelical Church. It was called a Service of Hope. Many people attended and the building was packed. Louise Golondrini spoke about her daughter, how she liked dogs and collected Barbie dolls and wanted to be a nurse. How she would never harm anything and fed stray cats and put crumbs out for the birds. How she loved Aurelius and how important her friends were to her. And how everyone was praying for her safe return. I was glad I hadn't gone; I wouldn't have been able to bear it.

Karla's picture took its place on the telephone poles and store windows. Someone noticed that all three girls had long hair and many girls suddenly cut their hair short, as if that would protect them.

The police were very discouraged. Searches were made, experts were asked their advice. Captain Percy had lost a lot of his self-confidence. "If you have any ideas, any suggestions, you only have to tell us," he said on more than one occasion. It was proposed that lie detector tests be given to a number of people. Percy was not keen on this, saying they weren't completely reliable, but he didn't close the door on the possibility.

The owners of the other four silver pens were traced. Two lived out of state. One lived in Aurelius but was in Florida for the winter. The fourth lived in Norwich and worked for the drug company. In any case, all four had their pens. It was at this point that Percy arranged to have Leimbach watched twenty-four hours a day. This was a closely guarded secret, but again, secrets were hard to keep. Once more Captain Percy was urged to permit lie detector tests. Leimbach would receive one, other people also. "Hell," said my cousin, "they were ready to test the whole town."

Among the Friends there was much complaint. Donald Malloy said that Percy should be thrown out of town and somebody else brought in who could do the job right. He was vehement about this. Dr. Malloy still had faith in Percy, or at least he didn't criticize him in public. His brother, however, complained to the mayor, Bernie Kowalski, urging him to take charge. And Donald talked to Will Fowler, the city manager, who carried out the daily business of running Aurelius.

"Where's your sense of responsibility?" he asked Fowler.

Fowler, however, supported Percy. Percy was a professional, which was how Fowler saw himself. It was amateurs like Donald who made trouble. Not that Fowler said this, but he said we were going through a hard time and patience was required of everybody.

Whatever spirit we had as a town was gone. Our general contentment was like a tissue torn away to reveal what had always existed: uncertainty and fear. The men and women who were supposed to lead us quarreled with each other. The best among us were suspected along with the worst. And winter was fast approaching. Every day we had a minute or two less sunlight and every night the streets were empty except for policemen and the patrol cars of the Friends.

At the time, I thought that the person responsible for the disappearances must have felt invincible. We were his toys and could do nothing. But beneath his sense of omnipotence, what were his fears? Three girls had disappeared and he had nearly taken Sadie. Didn't he ask himself where his craving would stop? And when he took risks, was it to taunt the police or to offer them opportunities for his capture?

On Wednesday afternoon Chuck Hawley knocked a paper bag off Ryan's desk onto the floor. Picking it up, he glanced inside to see if anything had been disturbed. The police station was full of people coming and going. A press conference had been held in the morning. Afterward Chief Schmidt had tried to coordinate efforts with the Friends. They were complaining of harassment, while the police said the Friends were being too aggressive with their questioning.

In the paper bag was a pink parka, neatly folded clothes, and a mannequin's hand on top.

"Shit!" shouted Chuck.

The commotion that followed was a mixture of embarrassment and disbelief. At least twenty people crowded around my cousin.

Percy emptied the contents of the bag onto a desk: jeans, panties, blouse, green sweater, socks, parka, hand. There was fifty-seven cents in change, two sticks of Juicy Fruit gum, a red cloth-covered elastic called a scrunchy, an empty gum wrapper, a gold chain and heart engraved with the words *Friends Forever,* a ring depicting two clasped hands, and two blue plastic barrettes. At the bottom of the bag was a pair of red snow boots and a pair of red mittens. There was also a white envelope that Percy slipped into his pocket.

"He was right here in the room," said Chuck.

Ryan thought: Along with two hundred other people.

Captain Percy, Lieutenant Marcos, and Chief Schmidt discussed whether the delivery of the clothes was meant as a message. Ryan listened but didn't contribute. Whatever side was right, he felt that the person responsible was set upon a course of action that would lead him to reveal himself. Maybe he was horrified by his actions, maybe he was losing his sanity, maybe he was swollen by conceit and a sense of power. Ryan didn't care why he was revealing himself; he only wanted him revealed.

The envelope again contained a sheet of paper with a list of mutilated words, "CUNT" became "NT," "FUCK" became "CK," "FILTH" became "LTH." The mutilated letters had been ground away with a crayon. Percy set the paper on a desk next to the sheet of paper with Paul Leimbach's name written on it.

"The same guy must have done it," said Ryan. "Look how crazy it is."

"Does this mean that Leimbach's innocent?" asked Marcos.

"He could be accusing himself," said Percy. "It's happened before."

The return of the clothing led Percy to make up his mind about the polygraph testing. "I'll test the whole county if I have to," he said. He called Albany and made plans to start as soon as possible.

The Friends, too, stepped up their activities, openly ignoring Percy's request not to act without informing the police of their plans. In the wake of Karla's disappearance, the fact that someone had tried to break into Franklin's house and that a mannequin's hand was found on the porch was of particular concern. Though the police were already keeping a twenty-four-hour guard on Franklin's house, the Friends felt more should be done. Donald Malloy announced that the Friends would keep two men outside Franklin's house. Even better, Donald suggested that Franklin should let them come inside. Franklin refused. He appreciated their help, but he didn't want his house full of people. Donald responded by accusing Franklin of risking his daughter's life. Donald and four of the Friends visited the office of the *Independent* to talk to him.

Franklin denied he was endangering Sadie. Donald said that he was using her as bait to catch the person responsible so he could scoop the other papers and the TV reporters. Franklin and Donald traded rather harsh words before Frieda Kraus told them they were behaving like children. At that moment, Mike Shiller rushed into the office to announce that Karla's clothes had been returned and that Captain Percy meant to administer a lie detector test to everyone in Aurelius. That caused quite a sensation. In any case, by that night a Friends' car was parked in front of Franklin's house on Van Buren Street, along with a police car.

One thinks of the application of pressure. A person acts because something forces him to act. But is it one thing or the accumulation of many things? A few people were upset at the thought they would have to undergo a lie detector test. Harry Martini said he would resign before taking such a test. He even contacted the ACLU. Like me, most people had only the vaguest idea about a polygraph test and some imagined it to be like a truth serum that would force them to blurt out their sins going back to farthest childhood. And the threat of a test must have put extra pressure on the person responsible for the abductions. He must have wondered if he could avoid such a test; or, if he had to take it, whether he would fail.

It was during this period when our blindness was most profound that Aaron moved his private inquiry decisively forward. This was partly because of what he had learned from Barry but also because he felt that Sadie was in danger. Soon after Karla's clothes were discovered on Wednesday, Aaron obtained the hands of half a dozen mannequins from the JC Penney in Utica. He put each hand in a shoe box on a cushion of red cloth. In the palms he placed photographs of his mother and on the backs he wrote, "With love, Janice." On top of the hands he laid a sheet of pink tissue paper. Then he wrapped the shoe boxes with red paper and tied them with red ribbon. He got Harriet and Barry to deliver them. It seemed fitting that the job be done by the remnants of Inquiries into the Right. One box was delivered to Paul Leimbach's office, the second to Malloy's Pharmacy, the third to Dr. Malloy's office, the fourth to Ryan Tavich at the police station, the fifth to Sherman Carpenter at the college, and the sixth to Henry Swazey, who had been Patrick McNeal's lawyer and one of Janice's lovers. Ryan was the only one to receive the shoe box in person.

"What is this?" he asked Barry.

"I don't know," said Barry, blushing. He started to leave.

"Wait," said Ryan, "you don't go till I know what it is."

He opened the box and lifted out the layer of pink paper, revealing Janice's photograph and the hand.

"Jesus," he said.

"Can I go now?" asked Barry.

"Who told you to deliver this?"

"I'm not at liberty to say."

Ryan called to Chuck Hawley. "Lock this kid up. A week in jail will help his head."

Barry told. "It was Aaron," he said. "Aaron made me do it."

Ryan was so surprised that he let Barry go without learning if other people had received boxes.

"That's why he told her to fuck me," he said out loud.

Chuck Hawley thought he had misheard. "Huh?" he said.

Ryan didn't answer. He thought how Harriet had gone out with him simply to ask about Janice. "His soldier," said Ryan.

Leaving the police station, Barry dropped off the second box at Dr. Malloy's office. The doctor was not in and Barry was glad not to have to give it to him in person. The third box he left with the history department secretary at the college.

Leimbach's accounting office was being run by his partner, Frank Kanter, while Leimbach took a leave of absence. He told Harriet that he'd call Leimbach and say that he had a package.

"A gift, right?" said Frank.

"Sort of," said Harriet.

She delivered Henry Swazey's box to his office on Main Street, giving it to his secretary. She had dated him, just as she had dated Sherman Carpenter and Ryan, so she was happy not to see him in person.

Mildred Porter was in the pharmacy when Harriet dropped off the last package. Mrs. Porter said that Donald would be in around six to fill prescriptions.

The next day Mrs. Porter told Franklin what happened.

"I gave him the package when he came in and I told him who had delivered it. He was in a hurry, but he took it back behind the counter. He asked me if it was important. I said I knew nothing about it. His back was to me. When he opened the box, his whole body stiffened. Then he shut the box and ran out of the pharmacy, taking the box with him."

At seven o'clock Roy Hanna, who was on duty in the police station, received a call from a man who refused to identify himself. "Paul Leimbach killed those girls," said the caller. Then he hung up. Aurelius had no 911 system and there was no way to trace the call. Roy immediately notified Chief Schmidt. Similar calls were received at the sheriff's department in Potterville and at the state police barracks. Captain Percy was with Dr. Malloy at Mallow's house. When the phone rang, Sharon's older brother Frank answered it. "What?" he said. "What?"

He put his hand over the mouthpiece. "Someone says Uncle Paul killed Sharon and the other girls," he told his father.

Captain Percy took the phone but the line was dead. "Was it a man or a woman?"

"A man."

"Did you recognize the voice?"

"It was muffled. It didn't sound like anyone."

A similar call was received by the Friends of Sharon Malloy. Leimbach wasn't in the office. Sandra Petoski reported the call to the police. She also called her co-chairman, Rolf Porter, at his real estate

office and he said he would be right over. A little later, when Donald
Malloy came into the office, he told Sandra to call in more of the
volunteers. He asked about Leimbach's whereabouts. Sandra didn't
know.

"We've got to find him," said Donald. The phone was ringing and
more people kept coming into the storefront. It was cold with the
door open and people tracked in slush from the sidewalk. Cars were
honking on the street.

Donald's overcoat was open and Mrs. Petoski saw that he had a
pistol stuck in his belt.

"Something's going on," said Donald. "Sadie Moore might be in
danger."

Mike Shiller came into the office with several other men.

Donald gave Shiller the cardboard box with the hand. "Look
what one of those Marxist kids dropped off for me."

Shiller opened the box. "Jesus," he said.

"Go find out what they're up to."

"What the hell," said Shiller. He called out to two other men.
"Let's go," he said.

Franklin was at the *Independent.* Around eight o'clock Sandra
Petoski called him from the Friends' office to tell him about the calls
concerning Leimbach. "People are terribly upset and Donald was saying something about Sadie."

Franklin left the office immediately.

About this same time three men came to Barry's house. Mrs.
Sanders recognized them as members of the Friends. She told them
that Barry wasn't there. The men—one of them was Mike Shiller—
ignored her, entered the house, and searched for Barry. Mrs. Sanders
said, "I hope you realize that you're breaking the law."

"That's what you think," said Shiller. Mrs. Sanders called the police station but the line was busy. Once Shiller was satisfied that
Barry wasn't in the house, he and the others left.

Harriet's neighbors said three men came looking for Harriet as well. Perhaps they were the same ones. Harriet wasn't home. The three men knocked, and one put his shoulder against the door.

The student who lived next door said, "I think he would have busted it if I hadn't come out into the hall. They asked who I was and took my name."

Forty-one

Sadie was at home with Paula. Because of Sadie's dislike for her new stepmother, she was spending an increasing amount of time in her bedroom. She had a small stereo and was listening to a group called the Indigo Girls. Too loud, Paula thought, but she chose not to complain. Paula was in the living room trying to read. Shortly before eight o'clock, there was a hammering on the door. Paula went to the door and opened it a crack. It was Donald Malloy. He wore a heavy overcoat and tweed cap.

"Sadie may be in danger," he said. "I need to come in."

"You can't come in," said Paula. She saw other men out in the street, perhaps six of them. The police car was still parked at the curb but it appeared to be empty. An hour earlier, Aaron had called her and told her about delivering the six hands. As a result, she was suspicious of Donald, even scared.

"Is she in the house?" asked Donald.

Paula began to shut the door but Donald pushed against it from the other side, shoving Paula back into the hall. Two men followed Donald into the house.

"Get out," said Paula. "You can't come in here."

"This is for her own good," said one of the other men.

"Have you seen Paul Leimbach?" asked Donald.

"I haven't seen anyone. Now get out." She tried to block their way, standing between them and the living room. They had left the door open and she could hear shouting out on the street.

"Where's Sadie?" asked Donald.

"She's in her room."

"See if she's there."

"Of course she's there. Get out of this house!" By now Paula was frightened.

"I want to see," said Donald.

Paula walked quickly to Sadie's room and knocked. There was no answer. The music was still playing. She turned the handle. It was locked. Donald pushed past her. Paula saw a pistol in his hand.

"Leave her alone!" said Paula. "She's angry at me, that's why she won't open the door."

"What did she do with the hand that was found on the porch?"

Paula said later that Donald's eyes looked oversized, with a line of white beneath the iris. "The police took it."

"You're lying."

"What in the world's wrong with you?"

"Sadie's in danger. I must see her."

Donald tried the handle, rattling it. Then he stepped back and hit the door hard with his shoulder. The door slammed open with a crash. Donald ran into Sadie's bedroom. The window was open and Sadie was gone.

It was at this point that Franklin ran into his house to find his daughter missing.

Two pairs of footprints led from the window through the snow in the backyard. The small pair must have been Sadie's. The other pair was at least size ten and plainly a man's: a pair of Timberland boots. About twenty feet from the house, Sadie's footsteps stopped, as if the man had picked her up and carried her. At the sidewalk, the prints merged with others and became lost, although there was enough to show that they led west away from downtown. The policeman from the cruiser came hurrying down the block with a coffee mug and told Donald and the others to get away from the prints.

Within a few minutes three more police cars arrived at Franklin's house with their sirens going full blast. From my front porch I watched the men jump from their cars and run through the snow. Ryan was among them. I quickly got my coat from the hall closet.

Donald Malloy kept asking Paula, "Who could have taken her?"

She stood at the curb and stared up the street. She was frantic and refused to go inside, even though she didn't have a jacket. "I heard nothing," she kept saying. "Nothing at all."

Franklin wanted to be pointed in a direction and given the chance to hunt for his daughter. He turned to Paula, then walked into the street and looked around him. He kept taking off his hat and pushing one hand through his hair. He looked as if he'd been betrayed, as if some awful mischief had occurred of which he had no comprehension. More people came running up to the house. Ryan Tavich was talking to the state police on the radio. Sirens could be heard in the distance. It was incredible that two girls had disappeared in three days. I got a coat from my house and gave it to Paula. The thought that something awful had happened to Sadie filled me with horror.

Donald Malloy was equally frantic. He kept running back and forth from the house to the sidewalk. He had gotten a flat attaché case from his car and he carried it with him. With his overcoat and hat, he seemed late for a business appointment.

"It's not right that she's gone," he repeated.

People were saying all sorts of things, so there seemed nothing unusual about his words. Police cars kept arriving and driving away. The night was getting colder and the wind blew snow across the yards.

Abruptly Franklin screamed out, "Where is she?" Paula ran to him and the two of them stood in his snowy yard, holding each other. No one approached them.

At that moment, a maroon Chevrolet pickup pulled up to the curb. It was Dr. Malloy. He had picked up the police calls on his scanner. Without turning off the engine, he jumped from the cab. He looked around, then ran to his brother. He seemed to have only the slightest interest in what was happening and whatever might be wrong with Franklin.

The doctor grabbed the lapel of Donald's overcoat with one hand. They stood on the sidewalk. "Why do you keep accusing Paul?" the doctor shouted. "What do you know?"

I was about ten feet away. Of course, I had no idea what he was talking about but I was struck by his face, its mixture of incomprehension and anger. Donald's back was to me and his shoulders seemed to get smaller. He was still holding the attaché case. He wore a pair of yellow rubber boots that shone against the snow.

"I'm not doing anything," said Donald. Other people had stopped to watch. Ryan took a step toward them, then paused.

"You're making people think that Paul took Sharon!" shouted the doctor.

Donald pushed his brother away. "How d'you know he didn't?"

The doctor slipped and regained his balance. "He's your friend! You know he's innocent!"

Donald leaned forward and hissed something at the doctor. I'm sure very few people heard it. "He's a fool," he said.

At that moment a policeman jumped from his car and came running toward Ryan. "There's a report of a man carrying a girl up the hill at Lincoln Park."

"Let's go!" someone shouted.

Dr. Malloy looked around him. Surely he had noticed us before, but the fact that something was terribly wrong seemed suddenly to strike him. "What's going on?" he demanded.

"Franklin's daughter is missing," someone told him.

Donald ran out into the street. "The park!" he shouted. He climbed into a car driven by one of the Friends.

"No, wait!" shouted Ryan. He stood on the sidewalk holding up his arms. Most people didn't pay attention. The Friends, especially, hurried to their cars. Franklin was running up the street. Malloy stood on the sidewalk and stared at his brother. A patrol car spun its tires on the ice, making a high whine.

Donald shouted from the open window of the car. "It's Leimbach! Leimbach's got the girl!"

"No!" shouted Dr. Malloy. He began running toward his pickup truck. Many people were yelling and the sound of all the car engines was like anger or frenzy. Headlights swung across the fronts of the houses and the leafless trees. I stood with Paula as people ran around us in the semidark.

"Wait," shouted Ryan again. Then he, too, ran toward a car. Soon there was no one left in Franklin's yard. In a few windows I could see faces. The wind blew across the trampled snow.

"Take me there," Paula said. We hurried toward my car.

At the edge of town, Lincoln Park bordered on about sixty acres of a wooded preserve through which had been cut cross-country ski trails. The police search of the area on Sunday had been done very methodically, with sections cordoned off and combed inch by inch. This Wednesday evening there was no plan. By the time Ryan got to the park dozens of people were running through the snow. Only a few had flashlights. The fact, or supposed fact, that someone had been seen carrying Sadie was enough for them to lose their heads. There had been three calls to the police station, by a woman and two men, each reporting a man carrying a girl. It seemed clear that the man was Paul Leimbach, though I am not sure if people asked themselves why they thought this. They had a passion for wanting to think it was someone specific and Leimbach's name had been given to them. But it was more than that. The name had been given to them by Donald Malloy. And wasn't he in a position to know?

It was said later that over two hundred people, mostly men, searched through the park and adjoining woods. Because of the lack of coordination, because of the shouting and darkness and sense of

imminent closure, there were many false alarms, many sightings that
were only sightings of one another. Ryan managed to control most of
the police and he had lights brought from the highway department.
He also sent men to surround the general area, though it was so
large—over three hundred acres—that the men were spread ridicu-
lously thin. But he also called for more police and sheriffs deputies.
These calls were picked up by people with police scanners, and soon
people were driving toward the park from all over town, or at least
that was how it seemed. And of course the television stations received
word as well. I drove to the park with Paula and parked on Johnson
Street. We saw dozens of people on the hillside among the trees.
Lights bobbed in the darkness. I kept the car running and the heat
on. Paula sat hugging her knees with her feet drawn up on the front
seat. She still wore the heavy coat that I had brought for her, a dark
overcoat that my father had worn fifty years before. She stared from
the window and didn't speak. At times she shivered.

Ryan was doing his best to coordinate efforts and had set up a
command post at a corner of the park at Johnson and Walnut. He
was skeptical about the sightings of a man carrying a girl up the hill
and he was skeptical about the footprints leading from Sadie's window. Why would she have walked? Why hadn't she cried out? But for
now there was no way to pursue those questions. The search had been
taken out of his hands. He did, however, send a policeman to Aaron's
apartment.

It seemed to Ryan that he heard shouts coming from fifty directions. And there were bouncing lights and vague shapes. Then,
shockingly, he heard a pistol shot. He sent several policemen to investigate, then called the rescue squad for an ambulance. The fact that
ten hours of darkness stretched ahead was frightening, and Ryan ordered two men—not police officers—to build a fire so that people
could warm themselves. When he heard two more shots, he began
sprinting up the hill.

Franklin had run to the park on his own. It was four blocks from his house. He had a flashlight and he scrambled up the hill, sliding in the snow, falling, then getting to his feet again. Because of the shouting, he thought Sadie had been found and he ran toward wherever he heard noise. In this way, he found himself moving deeper into the park. There was noise ahead of him and noise behind. People ran past but no one knew anything or they would say something like, "She was seen over there!" Two men told him that Leimbach had been spotted. Franklin was wearing low hiking boots and snow got inside them. At some point his Irish fisherman's hat was snatched away by a branch. His British scarf caught on things. He kept slipping and tumbling in the snow, which in places was over a foot deep. If he couldn't find Sadie, then he wanted to run until he passed out. And when he fell and hurt himself, even the pain felt good to him, as if it was proof of something: the purity of his wishes, the intensity of his effort. Far better to push himself, to run as fast as he could, to fill his brain with physical exertion, than to have thoughts that led to no place except regret.

Franklin was past the top of the hill and had entered the wooded area where there was more shouting. The branches kept cutting his face. He called his daughter's name but there was no answer. The snow wasn't as deep between the trees but there were branches and fallen logs. He kept an arm up to protect his face. At one point he yanked off his scarf and threw it away. He could see nothing but the beam of his light bouncing along in front of him. When his foot caught between two fallen branches and he was thrown forward it felt as if someone had grabbed his right ankle. He fell over a log and toppled heavily into the snow, dropping his light. Snow got under his shirt and down his back. The pain in his ankle was like a bright glare. He lay in the snow breathing hard and feeling nauseated. Then he retrieved his light and tried getting to his feet. Right away he fell again—his ankle wouldn't take his weight. It felt as it had when he'd sprained it in a basketball game a few years before. He was sick in his stomach and there were lights before his eyes. He lay in the snow and slowly straightened his leg. Getting to his feet again, Franklin pulled himself up by a branch and stood on his left leg. He was angry at everything—the snow, his boots, himself. The pain in his ankle was like pain he deserved. He tried to put weight on the ankle but it hurt too much and wouldn't support him. He hung on to the tree and tried not to drop the flashlight.

Other than being in the woods, Franklin had no idea where he was. He hopped forward, moving from tree to tree. "Hey!" he shouted. He tried to break off branches to use as a crutch and at last found a dead one. He trimmed the twigs from it and hit it against a tree trunk to shorten it. The branch was about four feet long, with a bend at the top. He trusted his weight to it and began to hobble forward.

After ten minutes Franklin came to a cross-country ski trail. He had skied these woods with Sadie in other winters and he knew there were lean-tos where skiers could rest. Franklin turned left and began to make his way along the trail, though he had no idea if he was following the trail out of the woods or going deeper into them. He couldn't put any weight on his ankle and he was afraid to put too much weight on the broken branch. Twice he fell. He felt frantic that his pain should distract him from his daughter. Then he heard a gunshot somewhere behind him. He stopped and tried to see between the trees. It seemed that his light was getting dimmer.

Franklin found a lean-to about three hundred yards up the trail, though it took ten minutes to reach it. In the meantime he heard two more gunshots. Franklin's shirt was soaked with sweat; his socks were wet from the snow. He ducked inside and collapsed on the long bench that ran the length of the back wall. He set the broken branch beside him. At least he was out of the wind. Franklin saw a small potbellied stove but he didn't have any matches. He turned off his light, then sat up on the bench, leaned forward, and began to massage his ankle.

After several minutes Franklin saw a light on the trail. Its beam swung across the trees. "Hey!" he called. Franklin tried to get to his feet and fell back again.

Someone appeared at the entrance of the lean-to and flashed his light across him.

"Who are you?" demanded a voice.

"Franklin Moore," said Franklin, blinking.

"The newspaper guy, right? It's your kid they're looking for."

"That's right. Who are you?"

"Martin Farmer. What're you doing in here?"

Franklin didn't recognize the name and he could see nothing behind the man's light. "I twisted my ankle," said Franklin.

"And you can't walk? Hey, too bad."

"Will you help me?"

"Sure, I'll tell them you're here." The man began to leave.

"Wait!" said Franklin. He turned on his light. Farmer's face was a blur. Franklin saw a dark-red hunting cap and red wool jacket.

"I can't carry you myself," said Farmer. "I got a bad back. I'll get a bunch of guys. Funny running into you." The man disappeared.

Franklin leaned back against the wall and put his foot up on the bench. Even the slightest movement hurt him. By his watch he saw it was ten o'clock. He turned off his light. The air felt damp, as if it would snow again. The wind in the trees made a sighing sound.

Someone was running down the path. Franklin called out. "Hey, give me a hand!"

The person kept running. Had he been mistaken? Was it the wind?

Maybe five minutes later Franklin heard someone else, the heavy sound of running feet. He started to call out, then he heard his own name being called.

"Franklin, Franklin." It was a high, reedy voice.

"Here!" cried Franklin.

A figure appeared in the doorway. Franklin shone his light in that direction. The light had gotten so dim he could barely make out the person's dark legs and yellow boots.

"There you are," said the voice. It was Donald Malloy.

"I sprained my ankle," said Franklin. He felt tremendously glad to see him. He began to relax.

"So I heard," said Donald. He sat down heavily on the bench and Franklin felt it sag. Donald had a flashlight and shone it briefly in Franklin's face so that he blinked and looked away. Then Donald turned it off, becoming a large indistinct shape in the glow of Franklin's light.

"They're out there," said Donald. "They're all running around."

"What about Sadie?" asked Franklin.

"Another little girl," said Donald with a sigh.

"Jesus. She's my daughter."

Donald leaned back against the wall. His breathing made a hoarse sound like the sawing of wood. "I never had any children," he said.

Franklin tried to make him out in the darkness. He thought that Donald must be exhausted from all the running.

"Is there any trace of her?" said Franklin. "I've got to get out of here."

"There must be a trace someplace," said Donald. "But there's nothing here. Everything's coming to an end."

"What do you mean."

"It will be over soon. Maybe tonight, maybe tomorrow."

"What were those shots?" asked Franklin.

"That was me," said Donald. He took out his pistol, showed it, and set it on the bench beside him. "They were signal shots."

"Who were you signaling?"

Donald didn't answer. He was still breathing heavily. Franklin's light reflected off the barrel of the pistol.

After a moment, Donald said, "Why didn't you interview me?"

Franklin felt he must have misunderstood. "For the paper?"

"I could have told you many things."

"You said you didn't want to be interviewed."

"I wasn't ready then."

"I was going to try again."

Donald sat up and hissed at him, "You should have done it sooner." His tweed cap had slid down his forehead as he leaned back against the wall. Franklin saw that Donald still carried the attaché case. He couldn't imagine carrying an attaché case through the woods. He realized something was wrong.

Donald reached over and picked up the branch that Franklin had been using as a crutch. Abruptly, he threw it into the dark. Franklin heard it hit against a tree on the other side of the path. He started to speak, then remained silent. The wind in the trees made the branches rattle and click together.

"You won't be needing that," Donald said.

Forty-two

Paul Leimbach had been at the state police barracks in Potterville studying the mug shots of child molesters when the call came over the radio that Sadie Moore had disappeared. Of course, he had gotten permission from Captain Percy to look at the pictures and Percy knew he was there. Leimbach left the office and ran for his car. By the time he was driving out of town he heard on his radio that a man had been seen carrying a girl up the hill in Lincoln Park. He called his wife on his car phone.

"People have been telephoning," she said. "They've even come to the house looking for you."

Leimbach thought she meant people from the Friends. The road was mostly cleared of snow but some of the curves had patches of ice. Though he drove fast, six state police cruisers passed him on the way to Aurelius with their lights flashing.

He called Sandra Petoski at the Friends' headquarters.

"Something's wrong," she said. "People are saying things. I think you should go to the police station."

Leimbach's pistol was in his desk at his office, so he drove there first. On his desk was a shoe box wrapped in red paper with his name on it. He grabbed the shoe box as well as his pistol and hurried back to his car. On the way to Lincoln Park, he opened the shoe box and found the hand and the photograph of Janice McNeal. It was too dark to read what was written on the back, but the hand gave him a chill. He didn't understand why he had gotten it. He realized that his name had been mentioned in connection with the disappearances and that the police knew he had been briefly involved with Janice, but none of it made sense to him. He parked on Johnson Street, along the edge of the park, and got out. Up at the corner by Walnut, he saw a bonfire with some men standing around it. Eight or nine police cars were parked with their blue lights flashing. There were moving lights on the hillside. Men were shouting. He could see their dark shapes running between the trees. Wind blew snow across the ground. Leimbach stood under the streetlight and buttoned his overcoat. He put his pistol in his coat pocket. Then he drew on his gloves.

Before he had gone ten feet into the park, he heard his name being called loudly. Two men ran toward him. Then more men joined them. Looking toward the hill, he saw other men stop and begin to move in his direction. Ten, fifteen men. Their response startled him. At first he felt almost a sense of pride, as if his leadership skills were being acknowledged. Then he was struck by how fast the men ran and by the anger in their voices.

Leimbach recognized Mike Shiller in front of the others. He took a step toward him. "Mike—" he began. He grew aware of the contortion of the other man's face, the violent mask.

"Bastard!" said Shiller.

Leimbach put up his hand but Shiller didn't stop. He leapt forward, tackling Leimbach at chest level and knocking him back so they fell into the snow. More men came running up. Leimbach raised an arm to defend himself but Shiller hit him in the face. Two men grabbed the collar of Leimbach's coat and began dragging him toward the street. Leimbach tried to get his pistol from his pocket but because of his gloves he couldn't feel the trigger. Then someone kicked him and the pistol discharged, its explosion like a slap above the shouting. The men dragging Leimbach let go and jumped back. Leimbach rolled over into the snow, twisting and grabbing at himself.

Half a dozen flashlights pointed at him and in their gleam the snow turned red. People grew quiet.

Others were running toward the group around Leimbach. Ryan was one of them. He heard someone crying out but he didn't realize it was Leimbach till he shoved through the crowd of men.

"Who shot him?" demanded Ryan. He pushed Mike Shiller aside. He was out of breath and furious with everybody.

"He shot himself," said Shiller.

"It was an accident," said another man.

"He was trying to commit suicide," said someone else.

"I hope he dies," said Shiller.

Ryan tore away part of the fabric of Leimbach's trousers above his left knee. "Get that ambulance over here," he said.

The rescue squad ambulance was parked about a hundred yards away, at the corner. Several men began shouting at it and the ambulance began to move toward them.

Shiller held the light as Ryan fashioned a tourniquet from a handkerchief. The ambulance bumped over the curb, its red revolving light coloring the faces of the men.

"He's the one who took those girls," said Shiller.

Ryan had remained crouched down by Leimbach, who seemed barely conscious. "You've no proof."

"Then we'll get proof," said Shiller. "It's in his house."

"If it's there," said Ryan, "then the police will find it."

"You fuckers take too long," said Shiller.

At that moment one of the men shouted from beside Leimbach's Mazda. "Look what he had on his front seat!"

Half a dozen lights focused on the man, who was holding up a mannequin's hand with brightly painted red nails. Nobody spoke for a moment.

"Come on!" shouted Shiller.

"Let's look in Leimbach's house," shouted another.

Shiller and two other men began moving toward the road. One man broke away from the group around Leimbach to join him, then a second and a third.

"Wait!" said Ryan. But the men were already running toward their cars. Ryan started to follow, then there was a whining noise as the wheels of the ambulance began to spin in the snow. Leimbach groaned. "Get a stretcher over here now!" shouted Ryan.

The Leimbachs' house on Myrtle Street was dark except for a light above the front door and one in back by the garage, where there was a basketball hoop. Martha and the children had gone to Dr. Malloy's. Mike Shiller and the others drew up in front of the house in three cars. There were eight of them. Later, Fritz Mossbacher, a mailman who worked with Shiller, told Captain Percy what happened.

"There was no one home and Mike went around to the back. All the doors were locked. Mike just picked up a rock, smashed the window in the side door, and let us in. Like he knew just what he wanted to do."

Mike Shiller believed there was evidence to be found in Leimbach's house. Maybe there was some kind of weapon. Maybe there was chloroform. Maybe there was Meg's pillowcase of Halloween candy, which had never turned up.

"Donald had told us that Leimbach was always fooling around with Sharon," Mossbacher explained, "tickling and teasing her. He said Leimbach couldn't keep his hands off her. Mike had no doubt that Leimbach was guilty. And there'd been that fountain pen and those phone calls. Then that hand in his car. So we ripped everything apart. We searched the basement and the other rooms. We weren't too careful about what we broke."

But they found nothing. There was some excitement at finding girl's clothes but they belonged to Leimbach's daughter. The house was extremely neat. Dishes had been put away; clothes were on hangers or in bureaus; newspapers were in a pile in the blue recycling container. Instead of quitting their search, the men grew angry.

"Mike kept saying that the fact that we didn't find anything didn't mean shit," said Mossbacher.

So the men proceeded to wreck the house. I'm sure there was more involved here than the certainty that Leimbach was guilty. There was also the weeks of frustration and knowing nothing, weeks of accumulated anger. The men were upset and wound tight. They were ready to vent their feelings on anything and it was almost chance that let that thing be Leimbach's house.

"They started throwing dishes around," said Mossbacher. "I guess I did too. One guy smashed the microwave, another guy started pulling everything out of the cupboards—food, you name it. Mike and Charlie Potter pushed the refrigerator down the basement stairs. Jesus, what a noise it made. They had a waterbed and one of the guys kept stabbing it and water came through the ceiling, a real waterfall. They put a kid's bed through a window. Guys were laughing. Some of them really got off on it. I mean, why bust the TV? It got perverse."

Mossbacher was asked if Shiller had told them to do this.

"We all did it. Nobody needed to tell us."

Luckily a neighbor called the police and luckily there was someone at the police station to take the call. Chuck Hawley responded with two other officers and forced Shiller and the rest to get out of the house.

"You should be on our side, not his!" shouted Shiller. "Don't you have kids?"

Chuck was holding on to Shiller's arm and Shiller pulled himself free. About twenty people stood along the curb. On either side of Leimbach's front walk was a border of white stones poking out of the snow. Shiller bent over, grabbed a stone, and threw it at the picture window.

"The window completely shattered," said Mossbacher, "almost exploded. There's a hedge in front of the house and it got covered with glass. The curtains were blowing. It was a real mess. Chuck Hawley was fit to be tied. He put the cuffs on Mike. And he wasn't too gentle about tossing him into the back of the cruiser either."

Later, when all was known, it was seen as ironic that at the same time Mike Shiller and the others were destroying Leimbach's house, Dr. Malloy had gone to his brother's house. He was by himself and he had to break in through a back window. The next day the doctor said he hadn't understood why Donald had begun to accuse Paul Leimbach, that the men had always been friends. He couldn't see why his brother was acting the way he was, and he hoped that he could find some reason for his behavior. And perhaps he had other suspicions, almost unarticulated suspicions, though he later denied this. But who knew if those denials were one hundred percent true? Of course, Dr. Malloy had often been in his brother's house but he had rarely been upstairs and he had never seen the attic.

Franklin held his notepad on his knee because Donald Malloy wanted it where he could see it. The beam of Franklin's light had grown dim. He couldn't see to write and his pen clogged in cold weather. But he wrote down what words he could. He didn't want to make Donald angry. In the dark he could barely discern the other man's shape beside him. Donald made Franklin write down basic facts about his life: when he had been born in Rochester, the years he had worked in Buffalo, the years of his failed marriage.

"Somebody did something to upset me," said Donald. His voice was tight, as if he could barely keep from shouting.

"What happened?"

"Somebody sent me a hand, a hand in a shoe box. There was a picture of Janice with it. And on the back of the picture Janice had written, 'With love.' That Marxist girl sent it."

"Harriet Malcomb?" Franklin wondered if he could believe Donald about anything.

"Do you remember Janice's eyes? I hated her eyes."

"Was it a joke?"

"It upset me," said Donald. "It wasn't a real hand, just a mannequin's hand. The box had a ribbon around it."

"Did you give it to the police?"

"Why'd she send it?" said Donald, more to himself than to Franklin. He stirred on the bench and it shook slightly. "It must have been the hand they found at your house, the hand that was meant for Sadie. It couldn't have been a joke." He paused, then spoke angrily. "Why aren't you writing this down?"

"I am," said Franklin, writing Harriet's name in the dark.

"Don't lie to me!" said Donald.

They sat quietly except for Donald's heavy breathing. Donald's pistol lay in his lap.

"Whoever sent me the hand knows that I've been protecting someone. It's my duty to protect him—even my mother said that. It's lucky she's dead now, that she'll never know. Do you have any idea how terrible this has been?"

Franklin moved his legs and a pain shot through his ankle. "Who is it, who are you protecting?"

"Can't you see who's guilty?" said Donald, raising his voice. "Don't be so stupid!"

"Who is it? Leimbach?"

"Leimbach's a fool!" Donald's voice was almost a squeal.

"Is it your brother? Allen?"

"He makes me ashamed!"

"Allen abducted his daughter?" Franklin was afraid of the man sitting next to him.

"People think he's so good. Doctor this and doctor that. My mother protected him and I protected him too. But he's an animal. He's like rotten fruit."

"Nobody knew," said Franklin. He wished he could see Donald's face, but he turned off his light. Better to save it for later, when he might need it badly.

"How can you write if the light's off?" said Donald.

"The batteries are almost gone."

"Here, use mine." Donald turned on his light and set it on the bench. Its strong beam cut across the path and into the leafless trees. Franklin could see that Donald was smiling, a vague, fatuous smile.

"My brother's clever," said Donald. "Of course, I knew about it. I've always known about his bad habits."

"The lie detector test will expose him," said Franklin, trying to keep his voice as flat as possible.

"Allen wants to hurt me," said Donald. "He'll make the test say that I did everything."

"But you've been protecting him."

"I've always been the good brother," said Donald. "I tried very hard. Again and again I covered up for him. Why'd she send *me* the hand? Didn't she see it was Allen?"

"Was your brother involved with Janice McNeal?"

"Of course he was," said Donald, raising his voice. "Can't you understand anything?"

"Tell me about it."

"It's not a nice story . . ." Donald stopped.

Franklin waited for Donald to speak. From far away he could hear shouting. The bright light made Donald's yellow boots shine. "Can you help me get down the hill?" asked Franklin.

"Wait a minute," said Donald. "You're trying to rush me. Why aren't you writing this down?"

"I am, I am," said Franklin, writing some words on his pad. "Was it a man's hand or a woman's hand in the box?"

Donald grabbed his pistol and turned violently. "You're messing with me!" He swung the pistol, hitting Franklin on the side of his head. Franklin slid off the bench and tried to protect his head with his hands.

"Don't you know I could kill you?" shouted Donald.

Franklin rubbed his face. It was numb with cold and he could feel nothing. He knelt on the ground.

Donald kicked at him. "Get up here and do what you're supposed to!"

Franklin dragged himself back up onto the bench. With Donald's light he hunted around for the notepad and pen. Every move hurt his ankle. Locating the pen and pad, he sat up again.

"I don't like you," said Donald. "I've never liked you. I was glad when your wife died."

Franklin wiped the mud from his pen. He tried to speak calmly, without showing his anger. "Okay," he said. "Tell me about your brother and Janice."

"That woman hurt him," said Donald after another pause.

"What did she do?"

"Shhh," whispered Donald. "She hurt him with her hand. She grabbed him and hurt him."

"I thought he liked it," prodded Franklin.

"He never did. That's a lie to say he did."

"Your brother?"

"Allen. She would reach into Allen's pants and pull out his little boy. Then she would yank it and squeeze it. She said she liked to see it shoot. He hated it."

"Then why'd he let it happen?"

"Because part of him was sick. I already told you that."

"But he kept seeing her."

Donald was still whispering. "That was his sickness."

"Did he kill Janice?" Franklin realized that his face was bleeding. He wiped his cheek on the sleeve of his coat.

"When she grabbed him again, Allen took her throat. He squeezed her just like she squeezed him, but he squeezed her until she didn't make any noise."

"What about her hand?"

"Hands follow their appetites. One hand's dirty and one's clean. He took the dirty hand."

"Does he still have it?"

"Of course. They're all together."

Franklin shivered. Donald was hunched forward and his voice was hushed. Franklin could see the pistol next to Donald's leg but he was afraid to reach for it.

"What about Sharon?" asked Franklin. "Was she dirty too?"

"She had dirty thoughts," said Donald.

"Did you touch her?"

"I never touched her!" Then, more quietly, "Allen touched all the girls."

"Did Allen stop Sharon on the road?"

"Her bike was broken and he stopped. He had touched her before and he was afraid. He asked if she was going to tell. She wouldn't answer him. He hadn't wanted to touch her but she made him. She wanted to show him her fur. He was afraid she was going to tell. She was friends with Sadie Moore. She might tell Sadie; she might even tell Aaron. Aaron had been asking questions about his mother. So Allen told her to promise not to tell but she wouldn't answer. Then he covered her mouth. She tried to scream and he wouldn't let her. He held on to her mouth. When Sharon was little she was nice but she wasn't nice anymore. She was getting too big to be nice. She made him touch her, then when he touched her, she pretended it was his fault. And her fur smelled on his fingers. It made his hand dirty. She would grow up and grab men like Janice did. My brother wanted to save her from that. He wanted to make her into a church."

In the distance someone was blowing a whistle.

"You're not writing," said Donald angrily.

"I am," said Franklin. "These are shorthand notes. I can put it all back together later. What about Sharon's hand?"

"Don't you see." Donald lowered his voice. "It's the hand's fault. It likes to grab and squeeze. It eats. Hands eat. It's covered with piss and shit, even worse things. It likes touching them, rubbing itself in them."

"What did he do?"

Donald laughed very quietly. "You know what he did."

"He cut off the hand?"

"It's how you get rid of the filth. The left hand's the bad hand. He needed to clean them, clean all the girls."

"And Meg's hand?" asked Franklin.

"All the hands are together."

There was a hollow thumping noise and with horror Franklin saw that Donald was patting the side of his attaché case.

"Are they there?" whispered Franklin.

Donald made a soft clucking noise with his tongue. "Shall I show them to you?"

Franklin tried to keep from thinking about the attaché case but his mind would go no place else.

"Why Meg and Karla?" insisted Franklin.

"They weren't any better," said Donald. "They came into the pharmacy. My brother saw what they were like. They had dirty thoughts. They stuck out their little chests, their little titties. I could see them. They laughed and flirted. They showed their bare legs. They also wanted to grab little boys. And besides, Sharon was lonely. Allen had to get her company, girls who were as bad as she was. Girls with fur. But he didn't want to hurt them, he wanted to make them better."

"How did he get them?"

"In his car. He pulled up beside them and squeezed them and put them in the back."

"Why didn't they run?"

"Why should they? The car had orange triangles on the doors. He was a Friend."

"And Sadie as well?" Franklin could hardly say her name. Its hugeness filled him with sorrow.

"She's bad. She came into the pharmacy. She hurt herself and I had to touch her leg. Aaron was with her and they asked questions. But she only pretended to hurt herself. She wanted me to touch her leg. She wore a ring with a dove. Aaron must have made her bad. He wanted to make her like Janice."

"Allen didn't take her?"

"He tried. I don't want to talk about it."

It wasn't quite hope that Franklin began to feel; more of an open space that was taking shape before him, and Sadie stood in that space. "So he didn't get Sadie?"

Donald raised his voice. "I said I didn't want to talk about it!" He paused, and when he spoke again, he spoke quietly.

"The girls love each other and they love their filth. Have you seen the way they smile? You don't think those are real smiles, do you? Allen thought no one would find out. He thought only my mother knew. But he's bad. Didn't he have a bad daughter? And she got it from him. Now my brother's built a church with three girls. You might think they're dead but they're not. They move and they shine. They sparkle in the light. All the filthy words have been made clean. You know how there are good numbers and bad numbers? All the good numbers protect them. My brother prays there. He wants to be made better, but the badness goes right to the bottom of him. Not even knives could scrape him clean. I should tell the police about him. But he's my brother. I'm supposed to love him."

"What about Jaime Rose?" asked Franklin, writing Jaime's name on his pad.

"He was like Janice. These people, their faces are masks. They smile and look happy. They pretend to like you. D'you know how ugly the skull is when you take the skin away? That's when you see the teeth. Their real faces are like that. My brother settled him, all right. Jaime reached into Allen's pants. He squeezed Allen's little boy and he was going to tell about it. Allen couldn't let that happen; he took him back to the beauty shop. That name, it's almost funny. A filth shop, a cunt shop!"

"And Barry?"

"Oh, he'll die soon. He told after I explained to him that he couldn't, that it would be wrong to tell. He has to be taught how to be silent. My brother will fix it. He's a good fixer."

"But Allen's dangerous."

Donald chuckled. "Oh yes, he's very dangerous."

"He should be stopped."

"Oh, I agree. He's made himself dirty, very dirty." Donald paused. "It's cold, but not too cold, don't you think? Once Allen is gone and the others are gone, then things will be better. We don't have much time. Isn't it awful, this rushing around? We must make it quiet again. People are afraid of death, but they're wrong. Death is very quiet. The girls sit so quietly. Sometimes I think they're praying."

"You should talk to the police."

Donald laughed. "They'll never believe it was him. You see, he always seemed like the good one. He did so well in school. But I've seen him when he was sleeping, when he grinds his teeth. I've watched him when he didn't know I was watching."

"You should talk to Ryan Tavich."

"You're trying to trick me," said Donald.

"No," said Franklin. "I'm your friend."

"You pretend to be writing but you're not writing anything." Donald snatched the pad from Franklin's knee and shone his light on it. There were scratches on the paper, half letters only.

"You're trying to make a joke of me!" shouted Donald, throwing the pad onto the snow.

"It's in my head," said Franklin. "I'll write it later."

Donald made a hissing sound. "I could make you believe me."

"I believe you." Franklin felt desperate. "I've got it all." He heard a click, then another as the clasps of the attaché case sprang up.

"Here, look!" said Donald.

Franklin twisted away, pushing his good leg against the ground. Donald held the light in one hand and something awful in the other. Franklin jerked away. Then he sprang forward out of the lean-to, grabbing the side and pushing forward again on his good leg across the path. He stumbled against a tree and fell onto his stomach. He began crawling through the snow. The beam of Donald's light cut through the air above him. Franklin crawled between the trees. He crawled over a log and collapsed.

"I'm glad we've had this talk," said Donald. The light kept swinging back and forth over Franklin but didn't settle on him.

"Sadie's a pretty name," said Donald. "I'm sure we'll find her."

Forty-three

Donald came out of the woods by the parking lot. A Salvation Army wagon had arrived from Utica and a woman in a dark uniform was handing out cups of coffee. To the others, Donald must have looked like one more person hunting through the woods. He didn't pause but cut across the parking lot toward the sledding hill. It was the shortest way toward town.

Ryan saw him coming down the hillside. Or rather, he saw a man carrying an attaché case and he saw the yellow boots. He knew it was Donald. There was a way that Donald ran, bent over and never straightening his legs, that reminded Ryan of an animal. A wedge of light from Donald's flashlight cut across the snow in front of him. Ryan was with Chuck Hawley and they were making their way across the hill toward Aaron, who apparently had just arrived. Ryan believed that Aaron might know something about Sadie. Then Ryan stopped and turned toward Donald.

"That's Donald Malloy," said Chuck.

"Hey!" Ryan shouted. He began jogging toward Donald. He wanted to ask him about what Dr. Malloy had said and he was curious about the attaché case. He meant to look inside it.

Donald stopped on the hillside. Flicking off his light, he stuck it in the pocket of his coat. He stood facing Ryan, holding the attaché case in front of his belly with both hands. His cap was tilted back on his head. Standing higher up on the hill, he looked huge. As Ryan got closer, he saw Donald was grinning. Ryan pointed his flashlight at him in time to see him move his right hand from behind the attaché case. When Ryan saw Donald's pistol, he at first thought he was mistaken. It led him to delay a moment. Then he jumped just as Donald fired. His body jerked and he felt as if he had been kicked. His flashlight flew through the air. There was a second gunshot. Ryan hit the snow and rolled. He tried reaching for his pistol but none of his muscles would do what they were supposed to.

Aaron was halfway up the hill when he heard the gunshot. He saw someone fall but he didn't know it was Ryan. Then there was a second shot. He began to run up the hill. Ahead of him, Chuck Hawley, intent on Donald, was tugging his pistol from its holster.

"Donald!" shouted Chuck. Then he fired: one, two, three times.

Donald Malloy turned and ran back up the hill. There were trees and Donald ran behind them. He paused and fired back down the hill. Aaron could see men by the bonfire stop and fling themselves to the ground. It never occurred to him that he might get shot. He saw Chuck running toward the man lying on his back in the snow. Aaron ran after him. The man's flashlight was still on and it stuck straight out of the snow like a torch. The triangular wedge of its beam seemed to brush the low-hanging clouds. It was only when Aaron reached the flashlight and looked over toward Chuck that he realized the other man was Ryan Tavich.

"Oh shit," Chuck kept saying. "Oh shit." He was crouched down in the snow beside Ryan, who was twisting on the ground.

Aaron grabbed the flashlight, then ran up the hill after Donald, who was just cresting the top. There was shouting up ahead. Aaron slipped, then regained his balance. When he reached the parking lot, he saw men running toward him. Maybe there were twenty men. He didn't see Donald.

"Is it Leimbach?" someone shouted.

"Where's Donald Malloy?" said Aaron. He could see the Salvation Army wagon and the woman inside staring at him. Several troopers had their weapons drawn. People were moving in all different directions.

A man grabbed his arm, someone he had never seen before. "Who's dead?" the man shouted.

Aaron gestured down the hill, then he pulled himself free. He ran toward the woods. A small sign showed a glyph of a cross-country skier and a pointing arrow. Aaron's light swung across it. He thought of Donald Malloy running down the path ahead of him. He knew that Donald had been mixed up with Barry Sanders. He knew now that Donald had killed his mother. A professional man—that's how he described himself. Aaron wanted to hurt him so much that it made an iron taste in his mouth. He ran so fast that he kept slipping and once he fell.

Aaron ran down the path, swinging the light to either side to make sure he wasn't missing any footprints cutting off into the woods. There were the parallel tracks of cross-country skis and heavy footprints imprinted across them. He began to fear that Donald wasn't in front of him, that he had missed him. Aaron stopped to listen. Up ahead he heard someone calling.

"Hey! Somebody!"

Aaron didn't recognize the voice but he began to hurry forward, not quite running. He wondered if it was a trick but could think of no reason for a trick. He imagined Donald's getting away from him and how awful that would be. It had begun to snow, and fat flakes drifted across the beam of Aaron's light.

"Hey! Help me!"

Even before Aaron noticed the dim figure standing in the path, he recognized the voice as Franklin's. It occurred to him that Franklin was his brother-in-law and it made him wince, not from dislike but from something like embarrassment.

"Help!" called Franklin. He could see Aaron's light approaching him.

Aaron kept the light on Franklin's face, so that Franklin was forced to turn away. He was standing on one foot. Like a duck, Aaron thought.

"Franklin," he said.

Franklin held up a hand to shield his eyes from the light. With his other hand he was leaning against a tree. "Aaron? I've sprained my ankle. I can't walk."

Aaron approached. "Donald Malloy shot Ryan," he said.

"Jesus, did he kill him?" Franklin stumbled and had to grip the tree with both hands.

"I don't think so. Malloy ran into the woods."

"He's looking for Sadie. We've got to find him," Franklin said in a panic.

"He won't find her." Aaron moved the light away from Franklin's face. "I've got her."

Aaron had taken Sadie to the Aurelius Motel. Harriet was with her. He had done it to protect Sadie. He had hoped that the delivery of the hands would force the killer to show himself, but first he wanted to make sure that Sadie was safe. And then he had thought of making her disappearance look like another abduction. Wouldn't that also provoke whoever was guilty to think that someone else was trespassing on his crime? After Aaron had learned about Barry's brief relationship with Donald and how Donald had scared him, Aaron had been almost certain that Donald had killed his mother and abducted the girls. But he wasn't entirely positive. He wanted to make the person act, to reveal himself publicly so there'd be no doubt about his guilt.

"But somebody saw her being carried into the park. They called the police. Is she really safe?"

"That's what I just said." Aaron felt angry with his brother-in-law.

"You've got to help me down the hill."

"I have to find Malloy."

Franklin grabbed Aaron's arm and nearly lost his balance. "Aaron, I'll die up here. I'm freezing."

"He's the one who killed my mother." Aaron's voice was flat, as if he were reporting the weather.

Franklin was silent. Then he said, "I know."

"Son of a bitch," said Aaron, pulling away.

Franklin fell onto the path and groaned. Aaron stood without moving, his light focused on Franklin. Neither of them spoke. Franklin tried to sit up. His sheepskin coat was covered with snow and there was snow in his hair.

Aaron thought of leaving him. He thought of Franklin freezing into a block of ice so that when he broke he would break into thousands of pieces.

Aaron reached forward and grabbed Franklin's wrist. "Pull," he said. Franklin pulled himself up onto his left leg and Aaron grabbed him around the waist. "Put your arm over my shoulder."

Franklin hung on to Aaron's shoulder and hopped forward. It was slow but they kept moving.

"Once I was going to kill Ryan myself," said Aaron, "but I wasn't sure."

It took ten minutes to get out of the woods. They didn't see anyone, but when they reached the edge of the park they found two state troopers. The Salvation Army wagon had gone. The troopers helped Franklin down the hill. Aaron watched him go, their lights bobbing. He thought of how he had let Donald get away and tried to tell himself it had been for the best. He thought of Donald's standing trial. It wasn't punishment enough.

Donald Malloy only ran through a corner of the woods and soon he was out on the street again. It must have amused him to think of the police searching the woods when he was running down the alley between Juniper Street and Spruce. He carried his pistol in one hand

and his attaché case in the other. He wore a dark-brown overcoat that reached just past his knees. He'd lost the cap he'd been wearing. There were cars on the street but the alley was empty. In the past month he had gotten to know all the alleys and backyards of Aurelius.

Donald entered Barry Sanders's yard from the back, then he waited by the corner of the house to make sure no one was around. It was snowing again. He waited a couple of minutes for the street to clear. He must have known that the police were looking for him, that his name was on all the radios. He climbed over the railing and walked heavily across the front porch. He hammered on the door.

When Mrs. Sanders opened it a crack, Donald heaved his shoulder against it, knocking her aside and entering the hall.

"Where's your son?" he demanded. There was snow in his thin sandy hair.

"Get out of here," said Mrs. Sanders. "Get out of my house."

Donald hit her hard across the side of her face with his pistol so she fell back again. "Where's Barry? Where is he?" His shout was very high, almost a squeal.

"He's not here." Mrs. Sanders knelt and touched her bleeding face.

"You're lying. Don't you know how bad he is?"

"He's not here," Mrs. Sanders repeated. She tried getting to her feet.

Donald hit her again with the pistol and she fell to her knees. "Don't you know it's bad to lie? You can be punished. Don't you know I'm in charge of punishment? Look!" He knelt down beside her. Taking a small key from his pocket, he unlocked the attaché case. The two shiny latches clicked upward.

Mrs. Sanders began to scream.

Donald closed the attaché case and ran into the living room. "Barry!" he called. "I'm coming."

Barry was upstairs. He hurried and locked himself in the bathroom. Donald must have heard him because he ran up the stairs. Mrs. Sanders continued to scream. Barry thought she had been hurt and he wanted to help her but he was too frightened. He hid inside the shower with the curtain drawn. He squeezed his eyes shut and wished he could disappear.

"Barry, you're a bad boy!" shouted Donald. Doors slammed as he ran into different rooms. "I'm going to make you clean! I'm going to make you a church!"

Barry jumped out of the shower and ran to the window. Donald tried opening the bathroom door and found it locked.

"Barry, I don't want to hurt you. You have to be healed and made better."

Barry tried to open the bathroom window but it was stuck. The window led onto the roof of the side porch.

"Open the door, Barry, and I'll only hurt you a little bit." Donald threw his weight against the door; the panels of wood cracked. He grunted, then kicked the door, breaking the lower panel, so that Barry could see his large yellow boot.

There was a stool in the bathroom where his mother sometimes sat and brushed her hair by the mirror. Barry picked it up and smashed the glass out of the bathroom window.

"Barry!" screamed Donald. "I'm going to have to hurt you terribly!" He again threw his weight against the door, but it held. He threw his weight against it a third time. Then he shot through the door. The bullets ricocheted off the sink. "Barry, you are very wicked!"

But Barry was already out on the porch roof. He crawled to the edge and looked down. It was a drop of about fifteen feet. Barry sat on the edge with his feet dangling over the side. The wind blew against him and he was cold. He tried to make himself jump but he couldn't do it. Just then he heard the bathroom door smash open as Donald hit it again. Glancing over his shoulder, he saw Donald's huge shape staggering across the bathroom. Barry jumped. He hit the ground with his knees bent. He rolled to his side, hurting all over, but managed to stand.

"Barry!" shouted Donald. He was halfway out the window. The snow flicked around his face.

Barry ran.

Donald didn't jump. He hurried back downstairs and out the front door. Mrs. Sanders was hiding in the kitchen and she heard the door slam. Donald ran across the yard toward town. He was still following Barry's tracks but he lost them at the street. By that time Barry had reached the next block and was cutting across a back lawn toward the alley.

Donald ran across the front yards toward downtown. His footprints in the snow showed a straight line. It wasn't clear where he was going. Later some people suggested he was going to the police station. Others said he was going to the Friends' storefront, where his car was parked. Several people saw him run through their front yards. They said he was hunched over as if following a trail. They said how big he looked with his coat open and blowing around him. They mentioned the attaché case and how it banged against his leg.

Sheila Murphy was standing in the entrance to Bud's Tavern. She had no customers except for drunk Tommy Shepherd and she'd gone out to the doorway to look at the snow. She was wondering where everybody was. Then she saw a man running down the center of the street, half bent over, "as if he was sniffing something," she said. She realized it was Donald. The street was covered with slush but fresh snow was falling hard.

Then Sheila saw a pickup truck coming down the street behind Donald. She squinted her eyes at its high beams. The lights swung across Donald and the driver braked abruptly, causing the truck to slide sideways until its rear wheels hit the curb.

The driver opened the door and got out. Slowly he lifted a rifle from the rack above the back of the seat. All his actions were unhurried. He left the truck's door open and its lights on. The snowflakes in the high beams looked immense. Sheila couldn't see the man's face; the snow was too thick. She called back into the bar. "Hey, Bud, there's a guy with a rifle. Call the police!" Then Sheila hurried into the street, rubbing her arms with her hands against the cold.

Donald Malloy ran across Main Street toward City Hall and the Civil War monument, where the bronze soldier stood at attention with his musket and bayonet. On the obelisk were the names of men from Aurelius who had fought in the war. Bronze stars marked the names of those who had died. The snow seemed to spiral around the monument.

Donald paused by the monument to catch his breath. That was when the man from the pickup truck raised the rifle to his shoulder. The rifle shot, muffled by the snow, made a dull crack. Donald staggered, started to fall, then caught himself against the leg of the bronze soldier. He turned toward the man who had shot him. He took a step forward and started to speak. The man with the rifle kept it against his shoulder, as if preparing to shoot again. Donald stopped and stood motionless. Then he shook his head, more to clear it than in disagreement.

He stood by the monument with the snow swirling around him. His head seemed to sink into his shoulders, making him thick and rectangular in his big overcoat. "Coffin-shaped," said Sheila. Then he turned away and began to walk down the sidewalk. He didn't walk straight. The man with the rifle at his shoulder sighted down the barrel. He could have blown Donald's head off, but he didn't fire. Instead, he lowered the rifle slowly and began walking after him down the street. Sheila followed behind.

Donald stumbled a few feet and then fell to his knees. He threw away his pistol and it skittered through the snow. He leaned forward on his knees with his forehead in the snow. He stayed that way for a moment. Then, without haste, he felt through his pockets and withdrew a key. He fit it into the attaché case. The latches popped up with a little shiver of light. Opening the case, he took out what first looked to Sheila to be a square piece of metal. Light glittered on its surface. Sheila saw it was a cleaver. Donald raised the cleaver over his shoulder. His left hand and forearm were flat on the snowy sidewalk. He held the cleaver high over his head. Four cars came to a halt by the monument, including a police car. Abruptly, Donald brought the cleaver down hard on his wrist. His whole body arched and his head bent back so he stared straight upward. His yellow boots kicked up. Blood spilled across the snow. Slowly, he raised the cleaver again and swung it down on his wrist. Then he brought it down a third time. Sheila screamed. Donald's hand tumbled away into the snow. A high arc of blood spewed from his wrist, turning the snow red. Donald staggered to his feet, dropping the cleaver.

"Malloy!" someone shouted.

Donald didn't seem to hear him. Gently, he picked up the severed hand, wiped the snow from it against his overcoat and set the hand in the attaché case. He closed the lid. Sheila could hear the latch click. Blood kept gushing from his wrist into the snow. Donald straightened up and took a step away from the men who were now getting out of their cars. His arm with the missing hand swung at his side, spraying blood. The men began to move toward him. Donald took another step. Then he stopped, swayed slightly, looked up at the white flakes cutting across the streetlight, and fell forward onto his face as red drops scattered in half a circle, making an arc in the fresh snow.

The men in the street hurried forward but Dr. Malloy was first. He approached the attaché case and flipped open the lid with the barrel of the rifle. Four hands lay on a cushion fastened down by elastic. A fifth hand, Donald's hand, lay across them. Except for Donald's hand, they hardly looked human. Their fingers were curled as if trying to clutch something, a ball or a breath of air. The oldest hand was dark brown and skeletal, its skin like leather. Its fingernails were painted a dull red. The most recent hand still had some flesh color. It seemed like a child's hand. The other two were gnarled and dry: monkey hands. The skin at the wrists was scalloped and puckered. Donald's hand was bright pink and looked absurdly healthy in comparison. It lay across the others like a soft tuber. Blood oozed from its stump onto the red velvet.

Allen Malloy stared down at the hands as the other men joined him.

"What is it?" said Sheila Murphy. "What is it?" She pushed forward so she could see.

"Dr. Malloy," said someone coming through the men. It was Captain Percy.

The doctor turned, wiping the snow from his face. He seemed surprised to see other people. He handed Percy the rifle.

Forty-four

This is how they looked: three dead girls propped up in three straight chairs. The fourteen-year-old sat in the middle. She was taller than the others by half a head. The two thirteen-year-olds sat on either side of her. Across the chest of each girl was an X of rope leading over her shoulders, down around her waist, and fastened in the back. All three girls were barefoot and their ankles were tied to the legs of their chairs.

Donald Malloy had sealed off the attic, removing the door and molding and fitting a piece of sheetrock over the opening. Then he had wallpapered the wall so no one could tell from the second-floor hall that a door had been there. The wallpaper was light blue with small bouquets of dark-blue flowers. Around the bouquets were chains of yellow buttercups making a diagonal pattern like chicken wire.

It was Dr. Malloy who found the trapdoor in the closet when he had come earlier in the evening, and he was the first one into the attic. Then he kicked out the sheetrock so the police could climb the stairs, kicked it hard in his anger so the pieces flew into the hall. After that he had gone looking for Donald.

Chuck Hawley took the photographs of the attic for the police department. He says he doesn't have to see the pictures again to know what they show. He says he sees it all the time anyway: three dead girls propped up in three straight chairs.

In Lincoln Park a monument was put up to the girls. It was dedicated in the spring. A square piece of obsidian, ten feet high and three feet thick, with the girls' names and dates printed on each of the four sides. When it was dedicated, half the town went and I went as well. Bernie Kowalski made a speech. Father Murphy of Saint Mary's Church spoke, too, quite a long speech that people had trouble following. Nothing the two of them said made anything better. They spoke of the horror we had gone through but they didn't make anything better. The parents of the dead girls were given the chance to speak, though they chose not to. Ralph Shiller said he was glad it was all over, but he didn't want to speak in front of a crowd. Paul Leimbach was there, walking with a cane. Mike Shiller was there with some of his friends from the post office, the same group who had smashed up Leimbach's house. You would think that they might have acted guilty, but they didn't. To my mind they still looked angry, as if their anger was something that was now part of them and couldn't go away. Karla's father was some fellow in California who had never even seen his daughter. Even so, he came all that distance. My colleague Lou Hendricks said he was the luckiest of the parents, but many thought that was too cynical.

Aaron McNeal wasn't there. He had left town by that time. Franklin came with Sadie and Paula, with Franklin standing in the middle, surreptitiously holding the hand of each. He looked very handsome in a dark tweed suit. Paula wore a dark dress and her black hair shone. It was April but quite warm, and there were daffodils. Ryan Tavich was there with Franklin but he, too, would be leaving shortly. Eventually he settled someplace out West.

For some people there were too many memories, too many things they wanted to forget. It made it difficult to stay in Aurelius. Dr. Malloy and his family would move back to Rochester. The fact that Allen had shot his brother was, for our town, too big a piece of information: to shoot your own brother in the back with a rifle. And Franklin had told people how Donald had accused Allen, as if Dr. Malloy, and not Donald, had killed the girls. For some people the whole thing was still a mystery. They looked at Dr. Malloy with mistrust. How could he be a doctor under those conditions? Even Paul Leimbach was talked about. And the fact that Mike Shiller had wrecked Leimbach's house—some people defended it. They said that Mike had done the right thing at the time. There were many arguments about this, even harsh words. The suspicion didn't just go away. It just slipped back to wherever it hid. I had the feeling it would stay with us always, as if we would never be able to look at one another again except through its filter, a colored lens of suspicion. That is why Bernie Kowalski's words about putting it all behind us were such a lie. And that big black stone, as if it were pushing down upon the suspicion, keeping it underground—but it didn't work like that.

Consider Ryan's leaving town. I think of Ryan as trying to cut a thread, trying to forget Janice, trying to forget the dead girls. He had been shot in the shoulder. Now when he moves that shoulder, he'll always remember us. He can't put Aurelius behind him. It's inside him wherever he goes. And Aaron too. His mother's grave is here and his sister is here. Whenever he sits and glances from a window and lets his mind wander, won't he soon be thinking of Aurelius? Even if he hates it? All these people who are trying to make their lives go forward, won't these memories tug at them? And Franklin, when he wakes in the night, won't he hear Donald's reedy voice in the dark telling him once again about filth? I am sure it has happened. I am sure he turns to Paula in the night and holds on.

For me, at least, work is a better remedy. It's something I can trust: a daily schedule, repeated actions that I imagine benefit the common good. I teach more. I have my hobbies. I spend more time with my students. At times it seems that I think of them as sexual creatures more often than I did in the past. Not that I would touch them. But I consider Donald talking to Franklin in the woods. If you could look to the bottom of a human being, what desires would you find? And what desires are concealed beneath my white shirt and bow tie, my civilized veneer?

Donald Malloy had lived with his desires a long time. Who knew how he struggled? He must have seen them in his face every time he looked in a mirror. Later we learned that when he lived in Buffalo he had touched a girl in his pharmacy. He had taken the girl's hand and rubbed it against his genitals. She told her parents and they confronted him. He begged them not to make it public. He promised the girl's parents he would see a doctor. He said he would leave the area. He begged them not to ruin his career. Nobody knew about it, not even Donald's brother. The girl's parents kept quiet until the news of his death appeared in the papers. How many other girls had he touched? What awful sweetness did he discover in these experiences? And when he killed Janice McNeal, what sort of sweetness did he find there?

How that sweetness must have sung to him and how insistent it must have grown as it led him to take more chances. Is it possible that voice exists in all of us but in most it is quiet? When I help a tenth grader with his biology assignment and I feel the heat of his body beside mine, the heat of his cheek, don't I hear a sweetness calling to me? Of course, I do nothing. I move away or send the boy back to his desk, but sometimes I have fantasies. In my dreams I do things that I shouldn't. But I am a good man. I have a respected position. I would never do anything wicked. But isn't my fear one of the reasons I live alone? What do you do with your fear? And do you dream?

I think of my neighbors. I see men looking at young girls on the street. Or I see how the young high school athletes are observed by both men and women. What desires do these people push down inside them? Is it good to pretend we don't have such feelings?

And the place where Donald worshipped cleanliness. Surely I am not the only one to think of him up in his attic—his church. Don't others wonder what it felt like to give in to desires like his?

The three girls were buried at the beginning of Thanksgiving week. Their families had decided to join together to hold a single observance at Saint Mary's Church. Identical coffins stood at the front of the church, and of course the church was packed. TV and newspaper people came from all over. Franklin said it was a zoo. And a mob of people went to Homeland Cemetery as well. There were no speeches and the funeral was kept as simple as possible. The mountain of flowers at the church was later taken to the hospital and to a home for the elderly. I'm sure many were stuffed in garbage bags and thrown away.

Houari Chihani had his service too. There were many such tributes at the end. They existed for the living, of course, for what could the dead care about such things? Aaron and Harriet arranged for Chihani's service in early December. They held it in the Unitarian Church, thinking, I expect, that that church would have been the least objectionable to Chihani. Indeed, the room was scarcely more than a social hall. All the members of Inquiries into the Right attended. The students paid for a plaque to be put up in the corridor in the history department at Aurelius College. It gave Chihani's name and dates and the word *Teacher*. That was all. After a while, I am sure that people had no idea of its significance.

Donald Malloy was buried in Homeland Cemetery. His stone was hardly a foot across and very low to the ground. It had his name— D. Malloy—and his dates. Some people didn't want him buried in Homeland, as if the presence of his body might corrupt their own well-loved dead. I know there were questions raised in the city council meeting. But by then Donald had been buried and to dig up the body and put it elsewhere would have caused unwelcome publicity.

Dr. Malloy, Ryan Tavich, and Captain Percy went to Donald's funeral. They were the only ones. Of course, Dr. Malloy kept it as secret as possible. Ryan arranged it with Ralph Belmont, the funeral director, with whom he played basketball on Thursday evenings, or used to play. The vast majority of people didn't know about the funeral until it was over. And Dr. Malloy had delayed it until December, until after the three girls had been buried, a rainy day with sleet in the afternoon. Nobody wanted the television trucks to reappear. We had had enough of being famous. Not that there wasn't a little mystery about the funeral. A little puzzle. Malloy's body had been kept at Belmont's Funeral Home. Everybody knew it was there. The body had been prepared and Donald's severed hand lay at his side. The closed coffin was in a cooler, though that probably isn't the right name. But it had a big chrome door like a refrigerator that you might find in a large restaurant.

During the first week of December when it came time for Donald's funeral, Ralph Belmont opened the coffin and saw that the hand was gone. At first he thought he might have made a mistake and he looked through the coffin, but the hand wasn't there. Then he realized somebody had stolen it. He told Ryan—after all, they were friends—but he didn't tell Dr. Malloy and hoped that he wouldn't wish to see his brother's body. But Allen had no desire to see his brother's face again. And he probably only went to the funeral out of a sense of duty. But that's not true. He wanted to see Donald put in the ground and covered with six feet of dirt, in a corner of Homeland far from the three girls. He wanted to see his brother covered up and forgotten.

Ryan tried to find out what had happened to the hand but he was circumspect. He was afraid to have it generally known that the hand had been stolen. He knew there would be some people who would say that the hand had not been stolen. They would say it had escaped, crept away, using its fingers as little feet. People believe all sorts of foolish things. So Ryan asked a few questions, and when he still couldn't learn the whereabouts of the hand, he decided to keep silent. Oddly enough, Madame Respighi, before leaving Aurelius, claimed that Donald had been buried without his hand, though no one believed her. She claimed to see Donald's hand floating in a jar next to other jars. People laughed at her. But she had faith in her visions, or whatever they were. She ignored her critics, shrugged her shoulders, and took the bus to Utica or maybe Syracuse.

Certainly it was no trouble for someone to steal the hand. The back of the funeral home wasn't locked, nor was the cooler. Ralph Belmont was always with Franklin and Ryan on Thursday evenings, although they didn't play basketball again until Ryan's shoulder got better. The lid of Donald's coffin hadn't been screwed in place. Belmont's wife was far on the other side of the house, and what would a person steal from a funeral home anyway?

Donald's face in death was as expressionless as a fat knee. His fine hair was stuck in place. He didn't appear to be sleeping. He didn't appear to be waiting. His body was simply a husk, a shell. All the bad thoughts were gone. His church of dead girls had been erased from his brain. I had only to lift the coffin lid, take the hand, put it into a plastic bag, then lower the lid again. Of course, I had a flashlight.

My collection of biological specimens is now above my desk: my pickled punks. The frogs, the rat, the snake, the eyeballs of cows, the fetal pig, the human fetus with its eyes closed. I don't show them to my classes anymore. They keep me company in a gloomy way. I wonder what the cow eyeballs ever saw and what the history of the human fetus might have been. Donald Malloy's left hand is now among them, turning slightly darker in its jar of formaldehyde. It's in the center, in the place of honor between the fetal pig and the human fetus. For me it's a reminder of what is always there, of the longings that lie within people, the longings we hide within ourselves. I look up at Donald's hand swimming in its liquid. I think of it as my private teacher. My own academy. It instructs me. By now the right hand and Donald's body have rotted away, but the left hand is safe. Though the wrist is ragged, the veins and arteries, the tendons and muscles are all visible, and the bone, of course. Sometimes I'm sorry I can't show it to my classes; it makes everything so clear. I try to think what those fingers felt and I scare myself: the necks of the three girls, their tenderness.

Donald Malloy was very particular about his hands. I recall their pinkness when he waited on me at his pharmacy, the neatly pared cuticles, the buffed nails. At times he even wore clear nail polish. Now the fingers point downward, the wrist points up toward the top of the jar. Not many hairs on the back; a few dozen short red ones. The fingers are curled, the knuckles are thick and swollen in the liquid. The thumb extends outward as if planning its own departure. The wrist bone shines. And the nails, how carefully they had been trimmed.

About the Author

Stephen Dobyns is the author of more than thirty novels and poetry collections, including *The Church of Dead Girls*, *Cold Dog Soup*, *Cemetery Nights*, and *The Burn Palace*. Among his many honors are a Melville Cane Award, Pushcart Prizes, a 1983 National Poetry Series prize, and three National Endowment for the Arts fellowships. His novels have been translated into twenty languages, and his poetry has appeared in the *Best American Poetry* anthology. Dobyns teaches creative writing at Warren Wilson College and has taught at the University of Iowa, Sarah Lawrence College, and Syracuse University.

ALSO BY STEPHEN DOBYNS

"Stephen Dobyns is one of the most imaginative and fanciful authors of our time." —*San Francisco Chronicle*